THE DONKEY SHOW

COMMONPLACE v.3

Michael Patrick Welch

Equator Books
Los Angeles
www.equatorbooks.com

Published by Equator Books

Copyright © 2003 Michael Patrick Welch

All rights reserved. No part of this book may be reproduced or transmitted in any form or by any means, electronic or mechanical, including photocopying, recording, or by any information storage and retrieval system, without the written permission of the Publisher, except where permitted by law.

Published in the United States of America
Printed in Canada

Book Design by Michael Patrick Welch
Additional technical assistance by Thomas Norton

Visit the Equator Books Website at: http://www.equatorbooks.com

Cataloging-in-Publication Data

Welch, Michael Patrick.
 The donkey show / Michael Patrick Welch
 p. cm.
 LCCN 2003106738
 ISBN 0-9669188-1-9

 1. Carnival—Louisiana—New Orleans—Fiction.
2. Man-woman relationships—Fiction. 3. Drugs and sex—
Fiction. 4. New Orleans (La.)—Fiction. I. Title.

PS3623.E464D66 2003   813'.6
                              QBI33-1496

10 9 8 7 6 5 4 3 2 1

AUTHOR'S NOTES

RANDOM
- SPEELCHECK street names
- falls off bike ("dumbass!")
- obits: anyone under 25 = gunshot wound (mention lazer-printed Tshirts of dead homies "1985 – 2002"
- CHANGE NAMES! _____ = Shee-La. _____ = Stedman. _____, _____ and _____)
- more body language ("slouched triumphantly" — Fante)
- She describes Fried Green Tomato poboy to him
- Without a car, and working where I do, I spend too much time in the cheesy touristy places, not the 9th. ward
- POLICY: The way Managers will throw a four-pound mistake-steak into the garbage can in front of their employees, rather than let their employees eat it…
- Jude is not a YES MAN, and I've never heard of a YEAH man – YES can be a hollow lie, while at least in our context here, YEAH always represents an affirmative push forward.

THE KIDS
- Pat's grammar theories ("I be" is "O.K.")
- straighten out days Pat teaches: Monday, Tuesday, Thursday.
- ANTHONY-the-quiet: Wears glasses…The only kid who doesn't march…only thing he ever wrote: 'our last teacher quit because…'
- With no 'baby' or sweet concern (in there twice?)
- The scene w/Devon and HEADPHONES (how Pat cowers to Black kids)
- The kids are constantly saying, 'I don't want to work, I'm tired I'm…"
- THEY DIDN'T HAVE A SUB WHEN HE TOOK OFF?: "You guys were in here by yourselves?" "Yeah." "With the computers?"
- WHAT DOES "catch you out there" mean?

MIZZY
- Describe her bike: =VH=
- Add that she is 24, from Washington D.C.
- She and Pat discuss N.O. MUSIC, both think its tired "We are the birt place of jazz, so now we're famous for jazz, when we could have been famous for being a BIRTH PLACE, a place where things are born, not just jazz, but new shit all the time, people would say, 'I'm gonna travel to New Orleans to get fucked up AND check out The Newwest Shit,' instead of continually forever celebrating this thing they invented hundreds of years ago…'"
- Mizzy's Thorns: shower washed them out, so I wouldn't be picking at them the rest of the day.
- "She has no innate desire to belittle, the way the rest of us humans have."

INCONSISTENCY:
- Jude's talk of his costume comes way before he meets Brad and gets his car back — maybe he ditched original costume to be Brad for the day?.

LUNDI GRAS
- my fridge can't even chill a jug of water, his pukes ice out its door.

FUCKING PARADES
- (Night Off) Staying at Mizzy's, I am a closer bike ride to Magnolia High
- Management sends him home because of mismatched socks
- Pat walks out over dispute over apron while he's trying to prepare 25 glasses of water for a 25-to

OVER
- Morning – hated still wanting sex – how could I still want sex? - sighing…
- "The cook's house is haunted now, filled with the ghosts of our sex; if he knew what went on his house, he'd have to move out"
- 'This is what Jude was talking about when he said I'D DEFINITELY see him'
- OPP cleanup crew?
- Brad offers read his cards when they get home

AUTHOR'S FURTHER NOTES

For Morgana and Jude, and also Brad, who better pay Mark back or he's out of the club.

My parents — who have always provided me with food and clothes, guitars and good educations — are not the parents in this book...

A small bit of thanks to David Drake, a healthy portion of thanks to Rosalie Siegel, and a disgusting amount to Phil, who has gone way above and beyond my expectations in every regard. And oh shit, *definitely* Claire Harth.

And a special apology to Jude's family: I told Jude again and again, "I will be stuffing your character full of lies. Let me change the name." But he would not let me.

TABLE OF CONTENTS

Act One: HIS STORY

ch 1 - animals everywhere .... (newness) 3
ch 2 - warring .... (worry) 19
ch 3 - he wanted out .... (experience) 31

Act Two: THE STORY (PROPER)

ch 4 - schooled .... (damn) 47
ch 5 - the donkey show .... (relief) 57
ch 6 - mardi gras .... (damn) 71
ch 7 - coming true, coming true .... (racist) 83
ch 7.5 - city of coincidence ....
ch 8 - white bitch .... (following) 105
ch 9 - i don't like you .... (falling/hurting) 119
ch 10 - last night/first parade .... (behind glass) 133

Act Three: LOVE STORY

ch 11 - another parade .... (behind glass) 171
ch 12 - parade practice .... (wet) 185
ch 13 - our parade .... (behind fence) 207
ch 14 - fucking parades .... (cheating) 217
ch 15 - lundi gras .... (vulnerable) 231
ch 16 - the war seems over .... (beauty/sadness) 251

"The landscape and city, institutions and people,
telephones and door handles, laws and phrases–
his curiosity had tried to swallow all of these things,
it had devoured and appropriated them.
And still he stands outside of them. A mere observer."

- Drago Jancar, *Mocking Desire*

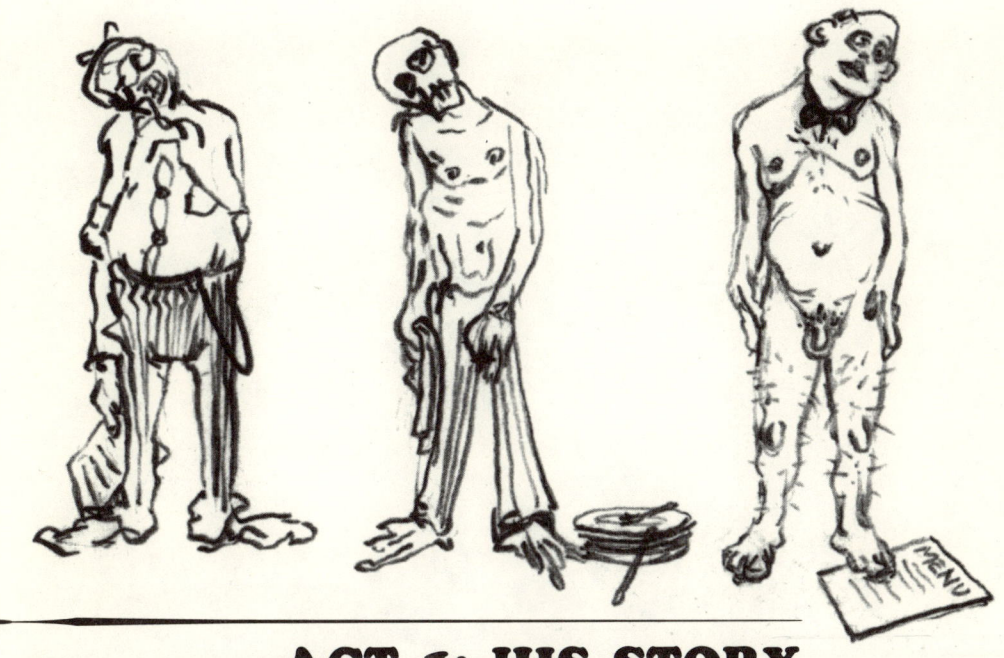

ACT 1: HIS STORY

ch 1: animals everywhere

*T*hree months ago I sold my truck, quit The Paper in Tampa and escaped to Costa Rica to get stoned, swim in the ocean, eat fish, chase gorgeous Latin prostitutes and write for six hours a day: my ideal life, the one I've dreamt of — animals everywhere. But now I'm off that dream and down into a reality of scraping half-eaten seafood off tourists' dirty plates. There are just as many animals now but...

Now I wait tables on world-famous Bourbon Street. Truckless, I pump a used bicycle to-and-from my new job and everywhere else in NO through a heat heavier than FLA's, arguably thicker than Costa Rica's. *Bike-ridden* is a refreshing lifestyle change; FLA's evilly expansive geography keeps you trapped inside your motor vehicle, always, forever, or until an Officer asks you to step out. But now I sweat more than I ever have, and for the first time in my life I worry over dying. Even pedaling home from work at 1 a/m, the dark air is barely cooler and no less wet than daytime's white sun, and under the weight of these morning hours — half-asleep over handlebars after a challenging night choked in a bowtie and vest — I am ripe-as-hell for the kill. My rusted chain sings falsetto to the silent, broken streets, announcing the new $80 throbbing in my sock, and I'm almost too exhausted to fear for my life, almost.

At some point during each of my 30-NO-days here so far, someone has infected me with at least one new ill crime story. Tonight's was told after work, in a bar (as usual), by some young white guy named Jaime with a purple, swollen cheek and pinky. I overheard Jaime recounting to the bartender how *just now* he'd been riding the wrong way up Toulouse, not noticing that old black man wobbling on crutches on the sidewalk ahead — until as Jaime pedaled past, the old man whipped around, swinging a crutch. Jaime's hand covered his face. That's what broke his pinky. No money was exchanged. I'm told there often isn't. Often it's just anger. Or displaced creativity, *I* think; the old man ran off, crutches under his arm.

Most of the other stories passed on to me by strangers have been way iller than Jaime's, and so no fun to retell, or even remember. But all these anecdotes, both the clever *and* the nauseating, always share the same moral: *It's only a matter of time before you are knocked off your $89 Men's Comfort Cruiser.*

Not that this surprised me; I'd never visited before arriving here the day after Mardi Gras, but I'd already learned much about the city via The Radio. During my past lifetime trapped traversing FLA's flat aimlessness, The Radio fed me miles of NO Bounce Music: electronic hi-hats stuttering like Lawn Sprinklers behind men proclaiming pride in their city and its crimes. It wasn't White Guilt that drew me to the sound, the way true White Guilt Sufferers will swear. The Lawn Sprinklers were just, for better of worse, the freshest, most *interesting* thing on The Radio. My truck lacked a tape deck, and I was as sick of guitars as I was of driving. So, long before I'd ever considered selling my truck and escaping somewhere, *anywhere*, The Radio had taught me to sing the mispronounced names of every scary NO street and housing project.

I now continue this education nightly on Bourbon Street, under the tutelage of the ubiquitous Radio in The Dish Pit. And directly following these 7-hour lessons, I'm forced to study what I've learned, biking home in the dark. When my $80 and I roll directly under, say, a moonlit Calliope street sign (pronounced *Kal-ee-ope*), all the macabre Murder Music I've memorized floods back through me, forcing my legs and heart to pump faster, pursuing the imaginary 133bpm high-hats. In an attempt to block the threatening Lawn Sprinklers — which were much more *interesting* safety-sealed inside my truck — I fill my head with my own song, a tiny, defenseless, saccharine pop tune featuring imaginary guitars that jangle and shimmer over my own feminine voice singing…

*I - can't
find - my
way
a - rrrrrouuuuuuuuund.*

Quietly though. Under my breath. *Don't attract attention…* My brain alone sings it vehemently, whenever I'm forced to pedal faster than I want to, simply because I *need* to. I hate nothing more than when my Needs overcome my Wants — that's really why I moved here. So sometimes I need this Fight Mumble…

*Despite all
the North - Stars
and sun - sets
and shit,
I – can't – find – my - way – around.
Despite all
the free – ways
with clear - ly
marked ex – its,
I – can't – find – my - way – around.*

…because geographic ineptitude is my permanent genetic disorder, and because one whole month navigating NO's broken streets hasn't taught me how to avoid neighborhoods where people who don't know me, who've never met me, are already angry enough at me to knock me off my bike. So I pump like hell and strike up my own song, imagining it played by that terrible high school marching band that practices down the street from my mansion: I imagine their bright, huffing brass chasing behind me down the street toward Esplanade, toward home, their tall fur hats slanted back as they run, unable to keep up with my bike and my song …

Despite all
gas sta - tion
at – ten - dents
God bless - them,
I - can't - find - my - way – around.
Despite all
the ghe - ttos
where I've been
taught less – ons,
I - can't - find - my - way – around...

And then my fucking chain jumps off.

"*Fuuuuuck*!" I howl up at that Calliope sign, immediately wishing I hadn't howled. My eyes go everywhere: *No one heard me, no one around?* If humans haunt the nighttime sidewalks around where my chain fails me, I don't even stop; I continue pedaling, freewheeling fake — *Everything's okay, I'm NOT a wounded animal, ready to be eaten* — until I can coast far enough past them, hide behind some dumpster, hurry fix it and, as the South says, "Get the fuck."

If the streets seem clear though, I don't waste time with *It's only a matter of time*. I immediately bail off sidesaddle onto my trembling knees, and my sweaty fingers and eyes struggle with tiny, rusted gears in a neighborhood where one person is killed every day…

At these Moments I paddle against almost as much fearful anxiety as last Friday afternoon, pounding The Quarter in search of this Bourbon Street job I did not want: my chain unchained every three hot blocks so that I showed up to interviews, dripping shirt feebly tucked in, hands black like I'd sailed down a water slide then performed a brake-job on a VW bus…

Still somehow I'd managed employment, and spent my first night's tips the next afternoon on a new chain that slips only every twelve blocks. Plus, with enough practice hooking it back on, I'm now so fast and efficient that somehow my hands remain clean. I don't understand how this is possible, grabbing a bike chain directly without soiling my hands. It's like a religious miracle, voodoo, and I acknowledge it as such, before hopping back on again, and bolting off in the wrong direction.

- 2 -

"You know what? I hate you, you little son-of-a-bitch. You're the worst disappointment of my life," my Mom spit into my hair as I stood in her kitchen in FLA, on her clean phone, trying to talk to John. Back from my two-month Costa Rican hiatus, I figured I could take refuge inside my parents' cold condo until I figured out where to go next. But nowhere compelled me like the place I'd just returned from, so I was unable to feel confident in any North American steps forward. My soul wouldn't move, and it held my body back.

John is an extremely tall white guy I befriended and got into much good trouble with in Costa Rica. He continued sleeping on the beach there for a week after I'd left. You can just sleep and build fires on *any* beach in that whole country. In FLA, I've been kicked off the beach *during a sunset*… But now John was back at his apartment in New Orleans, and he sounded happy: "Whoa! What did she just say to you?" he laughed, assuming my Mom *had* to be on *some level* joking; his heart is too sweet…He laughed again when her scratchy throat screamed My Dad's name up the condo's teal-carpeted stairs, before she ran up to retrieve Dad manually.

"She doesn't mean it," I lied to John, who'd been good enough to call me on his nickel since he knew my tight circumstance. "They're just simple people with bad tempers and sloppy mouths." That part's true.

When John asked me where I'd go next, I wanted to hang up and go lay down. But then he offered, "Move here. New Orleans is great, super unpretentious, friendly…"

I didn't reply, distracted by my mother's angry cigarette breath screaming back down the stairs and landing again on my neck. Through the kitchen ceiling I listened to my father's feet fall from his bed onto the floor. But my attention clamped a hold of John's voice when he added, "It's cheap to live here too. Super cheap. I barely have to *work* when I don't want to. Cheap and wild…"

It took nothing more. But there was more: John's promise to procure me a great apartment before I arrived, combined with the wind of my Mom's screams, finally blew me out the condo door, hugging only two backpacks gorged with warm-weather clothes. I caught a local FLA bus for the first time ever, to the Greyhound station for the first time ever, where I left for NO, for the first time, ever.

- 3 -

The next day I was heaving those backpacks through the wet hell of downtown NO, in search of a public bus going to somewhere called *Mid City?* NO was deader than I've seen it since, with everyone sleeping off Mardi Gras pains. I'd avoided Carnival altogether, arriving the day after, figuring that running from sterile FLA to a city with no littering laws would be shock enough without trying to do it in the midst of the party. Just *moving* was *my* celebration. Despite the heat and struggle, my lungs shuddered icy with the glee of breaking off! Going forth! *Somewhere new! Alone! Common Street? What's that! Hey!* I was definitely ready for my first New Orleans Moment, which came immediately…

The fifth time the boiling air forced me to pause dragging my bags, a black high school boy climbing into the car at my elbow asked me for a dollar. Slumped on his parking meter (20-minutes left on the dial) I laughed at him. A positive laugh though, a real one. I felt good.

"What, bruh?" His brow furrowed under a red tennis headband. "You can't spare a dollar?"

"I'm as poor as anyone, man," I smiled, glowing, perspiring. This was amazing: *Communication so soon after arriving? In Florida, no one EVER talks to each other!*

"You ain't givin me a dollar cause I'm black, ad it?"

I laughed again, my heart as warm as my new home's air. He was testing me, testing whether I was a good white person or a bad one. I always do well on this test, so I don't mind taking it. But still, smiling, "Oh Jesus, of course that's not it," I vocally assured him. "I just moved here, just stepped off the bus to live here man! I *need* my money right now."

The boy then reached into his shiny, red jersey shorts and brought forth a neat knot of bills: "You take this then, bruh?" His bejeweled fingers offered me a $100.

"Oh whatever!" blasted out of me without permission, along with a high-pitched laugh, a false one upon realizing this was actually some vague racial confrontation...

"Take it, bruh," he insisted, brow still furrowed, money still there.

"No man, it's cool," I promised, glum-faced, lifting my bags and dragging them away.

His hand and the cash followed my chest another foot until: "Ah'ight, suit y'self, bruh. Welcome to New Orleans."

Gallons of sweat and screaming muscles later, I met and hugged John outside the Fine Dining restaurant where he's a *sous-chef*. John carried half my bags onto another city bus (*What a great public transportation system here!* I thought then) which eventually dropped us at the biggest single house I've ever seen — the fucking whitest, frilliest, sky-high wedding cake of a mansion stretched out across the flattest green lawn. At our backs, a long, silver tour bus slowed. Behind its impossible tint, flashbulbs detonated-then-died. Caught between the bus' shadow and the mansion's, John admitted, "Well man, this is where you live…"

Now, today, I'm writing my second $325-check to my 90-year-old landlord, who creeps around in the mansion's main basilican structure. I myself lord over five rooms in back, in what locals call

The Slave Quarters — though I've felt less of a slave since moving in, having sold less than 40-total-hours of my life to Bourbon Street this entire month, to retain the privilege of this castle, plus the freedom to wash every day's restaurant meals down with many big gory drinks.

- 4 -

The Kitchen hosts a small oven where we busboys bake, for twenty seconds, garlic bread, to bring out as appetizers for our esteemed patrons. Co-operating the oven with me is a twenty-four-year-old black kid named Dwaine, who punctuates every sentence with, "Y'dig?" He's a sweet kid, but talks too much, and then because his talk is sweet, it's a conflict. Dwaine recently began believing in God and reading the Bible, so as I heat up garlic bread for tourists who have no qualms paying $6.75 for a bottle of Coors Light and throwing away an uneaten redfish filet, Dwaine tells me about God. My first night on the job he trained me between retelling me the story of Noah's Ark as if he'd just heard it. He explained every tedious detail, and his sweetness wouldn't allow me to demand he stop. I just listened, thinking, "And you're *how* old?" Though he did teach me that after the Ark was full, the doors were so big that only God could shut them, so He came down Himself to close the doors for Noah. I like that image: the huge fucking Hands-of-God slamming shut the giant doors...

But Dwaine's scared of Hell like it's a real place, and for 8-hours he details to me all the things he's doing and avoiding so that he doesn't end up there. Around the third hour tonight, as he talked and talked while pulling some garlic bread from the oven, he burned himself, "Ouch!" then turned to me and said, "Man, if this is hot, imagine *Hell*. Y'dig?"

The rest of the staff is mostly black guys, which I like because FLA was so segregated. I held at least five restaurant jobs during my Tampa life, but never served alongside one black guy. They stayed in the kitchen and The Dish Pit. The staff at this new job offers a fair illustration of NO Race Relations as I've experienced it: half the black waiters are nicer and much more fun to work with than the stiff, white jerks at The Paper, but the other half either ignore me like I'm dead, eye me like they wish I was dead, or bully me like they might eventually help me be dead. Still, a good ratio though, I think.

Then there's Bourbon Street. I'd thought it dried up in the summer, but every night past our window staggers a wet wave of white people with pink, drunken heads and limp hands barely gripping plastic cups. I'd assumed this behavior was limited to Mardi Gras, that The Fools descend from the North after the weather here cooled. But no. Every night white men purchase *45-cents-a-dozen* beads from Bourbon's million Indian-owned Bead Stores, then walk around pretending it's Mardi Gras, baiting and begging women to lift their shirts. Meanwhile, the staff inside the restaurant fights to manufacture some illusion of elegance. But when the sun sets, hope is lost; the crowd outside doubles, becoming one massive, onward-writhing, puking-and-pissing blur, with little interest in Fine Dining. The sky ceases to change, business and time itself slow to halftime. The simple autonomy of chewing a breath mint makes you wonder *Well, the mint is gone; how long did that take? How much time did I burn eating that thing? How many do I have to eat before they'll let me go home?* And usually not too many mints into it, I find myself no longer able to confidently pour water and serve bread and clean-and-set tables with *that distracting flock of retards migrating never-endlessly past this window churning me seasick...* They are awesome. I am transfixed.

- 5 -

I owe this all to John, though I can't repay him because immediately after saving my life, he followed his girlfriend to Germany, leaving me 100% friendless. But solitude hasn't attacked me yet, not with its teeth at least, not in these days and days of invaluable free time, spent much as they were in Costa Rica, though without the ocean and the prostitutes. I'm at relative peace here. I'll save up for a new bike. Everything is fine.

Then my parents started calling.

They left no apologies on my answering service, just a dozen happy messages offering to rent a van to bring me all the things I'd left behind. But I didn't want my possessions if my parents came with them. Not yet. So, when they called I didn't call back, hoping they'd take the hint. They kept on though, until one unanswered message finally threatened not to bring me my stuff, though really, I didn't mind sleeping on the bare floor of my furniture-less apartment.... I didn't hate them. I just wanted none of their mad influence. They raised me to throw tantrums, and I grew up to yell at and torture my girlfriends. Of course most of them were as screwed up and mean as my parents and me, but maybe I could have calmed them instead of making them worse.

But since those girlfriends, my infantile temper has pretty much worn away — until I get around my parents and find myself screaming again. So, wanting it *all* to wear off completely and forever here in NO, I haven't spoken with them since I left FLA. Until today...

The atmosphere was gorgeous, a relatively cool afternoon. I sat outside the peaceful little Coffeehouse across the street from My Mansion, pecking my laptop when I heard my name in the rare air: "Patrick! Patrick!" *Huh? Damn, how'd they know where I live...* But something inside of me allowed me to be happy to see them. They stood in awe of My Mansion, almost proud-seeming. That felt good. And of course my eyes welled up seeing all my stuff again: my clothes, my books, my guitars, my drum machines and samplers, my giant xylophone, the paintings of drunks slouched in corners my friend Marcus gave to me before he moved back to Sweden. The sun danced prettily in my parents' gray hair as we dragged my entire life out of their rented van and into The Slave Quarters — except for the futon, which Mom decided would serve as perfect cushion to haul some furniture she'd be more than happy to buy for me, "Since we're here." I didn't want them buying me anything; that is an invisible trap, I know. But earlier in the week I'd spent tips on a bed at a Magazine Street furniture store and hadn't been able to transport it home, so we climbed into the van, all smiling.

Traffic freaks my Dad out; years ago, my parents participated in a big car-wreck, and it changed them. He now operates a car sort of how I do my bike: with the idea of *death around every corner*, flinching on the brakes whenever anything on the road even moves. So, of course the Third World driving style of The Quarter and all the drunk pedestrians would put him ill at ease — but he was already biting the inside of his cheek, winding himself up on straight-and-simple Esplanade, before we'd even reached Claiborne. To make it worse, he was counting on me to direct him...The only help I could give was when he began mumbling the F-Word, which is very unlike him, I became scared that he'd scare himself into a wreck, and so I said, "Dad, easy."

His head exploded out his mouth: "Don't you fucking tell me how to fuck! Fuck! FUCK! Fucker fucker! You, you son of a bitch fuck! FUCK!"

I said nothing. He finally quieted, but didn't calm. Then he began again: "Fuck you! Telling me what I can't say and fuck!" Then he stopped. Then he started. "Don't you fucking tell me!" Then stopped. When he started again, I didn't get mad. I simply opened the van door and stepped out onto Rampart. Flip-flops impede fast walking, so I slipped mine off to walk faster — remembering that they were the flip-flops I bought in Costa Rica made me sadder than anything else... From two blocks away, my Mom called to me out the van's window, but I just waved them on, thinking of past fights with past girlfriends, and how my family has always taken their anger and frustration out on those we love. *No more. No more ever.*

I walked and sweated and stopped in a bar. Since it's not cool to ask for change unless you buy something, I bought a beer To-Go, and got change for the bus. Standing at the bus stop sipping beer, slipping my flip-flops back on I realized the asphalt had burned my bare feet. Their bottoms were padded with water-filled blisters.

When the bus finally dropped me back at My Mansion, I spotted my parents waiting for me at the Coffeehouse across the street. I tried sneaking into my Slave Quarters, but they saw me and followed me over. I made it in first though, and shut them out. They knocked and knocked, but I sat on my living room floor, calmly returning e-mails, ignoring their knocks in every way, remaining still and calm, cold, not even thinking. *I will not participate. They want a fight. I don't. I want peace, forever*.

After a half-hour, the knocking and shouting of my name ceased. They drove thirteen hours back to Florida, and I returned to my peace.

- 6 -

Attempting to rescind the further fear he'd just donated, Lani added, "But they only attack *me* cause a my gray hair; they see me ridin in the dark with these thick fuckin bah-focals on, and they assume I'm feeble." He ended with a drawling chuckle, for all the pitiable fools who've *ever* assumed him feeble.

Lani had just admitted to being mugged *five times* on our street alone, Esplanade (pronounced *Es-pluh-nayd*), though not in our safe neighborhood: farther down, just outside The Quarter, under that overpass where that Nightclub is constantly surrounded by cars booming bass and flashing wide silver rims, if not red-and-blue lights. Lani rides a bike too, because even behind his giant glasses his eyes barely work. But thankfully he was able to see me from his window, tugging on my futon — before skidding off in defeat, my parents had rolled it out of the rent-a-van and into the spice garden outside my door. And since this April air is like wearing a hooded jacket made from the hot moist towels they give you in Japanese restaurants, Lani stepped outside to introduce himself and offer me his neighborly help.

Before even bending over though, he told me everything: in his 25-years here, he's mostly read tarot cards for a living, not seeming to notice that he mispronounces the name of his profession, leaning into the second syllable: *tuh-ROH*. Still, he claims a higher *tuh-ROH* pedigree because unless there's a festival in The Quarter, he mostly works from home, by appointment, rarely hustling his mysticism on Jackson Square with the lesser of his ilk. But knowing his profession helped me more efficiently process his fantastic mugging stats; *If he makes his living at any kind of card table, then I'm sure he's prone to inflating his figures, especially to widen strangers' eyes...*

Then after tightening his white ponytail, Lani finally did bend down and wheeze, wrenching the futon onto his thick shoulder like he would carry it by himself. But he quick-dropped it onto his open-toed foot, when another long tour bus rolled up outside our black iron gate; Lani didn't want these "potential clients" witnessing him struggle, red-faced and panting. His rent is even cheaper up in the front of The Mansion, where these busses rattle his bedroom window all day. His wife hates it, but Lani considers it free advertising, and so stands erect, straightening his jewelry for their photos. I've never had my picture taken as much I have in this month living here: coming out into the morning light just for a moment for coffee's sake, hungover sick-looking in a busload of tourists' lenses. Usually, I scratch my genitals for these photos, but since Lani was there helping me, and tourism is his livelihood...

When the cameras were gone, we hefted the dead weight together and Lani continued, "So yeah, as I was sayin: that's five times *just this year* I been mugged." Silver-and-turquoise necklaces bounced off his chuckling chest, but they and he calmed when he realized I wasn't laughing along. "This has been an especially bad year though," he revised, holding his wrists up and shaking their silver nests of bracelets: "Them stupid kids mistake all this old Native American junk for...what's that new metal those little bastards are all into now? Platinum?"

"Yeah," I answered, surprised. *He must listen to The Radio...*

On my living room floor, amid my boxed past, we dropped the futon and Lani rallied, "So, since you don't wear no jewelry, and you got red hair instead a gray, you should be fine on Esplanade. They won't be so quick to mess with a redhead. Besides, muggers are the least thing a biker's gotta watch out for..."

Seems a man who makes his living delving into strangers' souls would wield tact mightily, but... "First of all," Lani persisted, "everyone on the road's fuckin drunk. You seen them Speed Limit signs plowed over on the medians? Bent all backwards like Limbo Dancers? How y'think that happened? Who y'think done that? I think his initials are D.W.I.!" Lani's laughter shook a clear sweat-drop from the tip of his nose onto my futon, where I would sleep tonight. "You especially gotta watch out for the *parked* cars: someone's always opening a fuckin door on you... Then there's the potholes! *Street craters*, man! And most of em been around so long, they're protected by the Historical Society, same as our mansion, so no one's allowed to even patch em up! I'll tell you, at night in the dark, them damn potholes'll bite onto your tire an throw you down an bust you open quicker than any little 14-year-old black kid..."

Then Lani stopped talking, closed my front door behind him, and soothed us both by lighting a joint without asking my permission. His psychic powers must have told him that I am an addict. "I don't really smoke too much," he qualified. "One of my clients just gave me this one *jernt* here as a tip." Exhaling the inaugural cloud, his bejeweled finger held it out to me...

I took it, passed it back, took it, passed it, took it, and when our heartbeats and brainwaves were good-and-slow he added, "You know what though man: even if my eyes weren't half-fucked, I still wouldn't want no damn car; there's freedom in going without."

I'd have shouted 'Hell yes!' if I hadn't been holding in smoke. Instead I just nodded vigorously, affirming my first ever NO friend.

- 7 -

An hour later I rode to my job. It was hot and yes, the chain fell off. Upon arrival, I ran upstairs to the bathroom to paper-towel away the sweat and change into my Monkey Suit: black pants, white tuxedo shirt, black vest, maroon bow tie and stiff black wingtips. As I tied and buttoned and fastened, the bathroom's dry-cracked speakers blasted tepid jazz, distorting it into insane, manic beauty. Its rhythmic static echoed off the bathroom tiles, and I turned myself into a waiter. At that Moment, after such a day, it was the perfect music...

Then, bending down to tie my shoes, I came eye-level with another, identical pair of wingtips under the bathroom stall — another employee, taking a dump. The smell of shit wafted out and hit me in the face, and as I gagged and rushed my task, a voice behind the door asked me, "It's like a tradition, huh?" It was Dwaine. And what he meant was: It's too hot to wear our Monkey Suits on the way *to* the restaurant, so all the employees, when they arrive, show up in plain sweaty clothes and change in the bathroom with the overdriven jazz. But with that smell hitting me in the face, his question seemed to say, 'Shit in my face, everything shitty, everything smelling like shit and being shit: it's like a tradition, huh?'

But regardless of Dwaine's intended meaning, I chuckled, "Yes," looking at myself in the mirror; I looked good all dressed up. Clean. Being at work didn't seem as bad right then — especially since I've finally determined a permanent safe route home, through The Quarter, an experience I look forward to: despite the still-looming threats, I relish surges of insane happiness, balancing a cup of beer in one hand while steering with the other, before locking up at this Nightclub, bringing my beer in with me, watching the band for 15-minutes, for free, before unlocking and pedaling on, to the next club, with my same beer, different band, still free... The music is almost always the same tepid, overly-traditional jazz or blues or funk: amazing players without ideas of their own, impressive dexterity lacking the kind of true creativity possessed by the long-dead originators of the forms. But it's still always fun seeing so many humans flying across their instruments on any given night, while I'm alone, on this bike, spending less than $20 total for all the small buzzes I've captured. Freedom.

I exited the bathroom and spent the next 8-hours on my blistered feet, surprisingly happy, listening to Dwaine prattle-on about Hell.

ch 2: warring

*I - can't
find - my*
*way
a - rrrrrouuuuuuuuund.*

    I sang it today pedaling to The Quarter to job-hunt during this Depression. I think it's a Depression, but maybe I'm too young to recognize one. Plus, The Media's kaleidoscope hurts my eyes now after 3-years at The Paper. So though My Mansion's rent includes free cable TV, I just can't pay attention anymore, to their rendering of This War Shit.
    And this same self-imposed ignorance made possible my pedaling onward > > > under Esplanade's tangles of oaks keeping sun off my pre-cancerous freckles > > > past the usually *bumpin* Nightclub under the Claiborne overpass > > > breezing past mansions that normally chatter at each other like crazy senior citizens in mismatched polyester, but that now stand silent, sober > > > past plantations that shared nothing visual in common until this new sameness of flags > > > through the red light at the barren intersection of Rampart and into The Quarter, worrying about nothing but potholes...

19

Before This War Shit, NO's cheap rent had me hallucinating ownership of myself, tricking me to believe I'm allowed to drop-and-let-shatter any less-than-ideal employment situation. I'd work for a month, take a month off, work a month to buy a new bike — finally a new bike — then take a month off to just pedal around... My last job, at a café on Royal, met its denouement at lunchtime on the soup line. Looking forward to my small break before I'd work another dinner shift, I whistled into the soup-steam (*Despite all - the North–Stars - and sun–sets - and shit...*), pouring a last cup of gumbo for our final lunchtime customers. But as I daydreamed of Freedom, or of just sitting-the-fuck-down, Management crept behind me muttering, "No whistling in the restaurant."

No...what? Management was serious, too. So, mid-pour and mid-whistle, I dropped-and-let-shatter the ceramic soup bowl. Oysters slid down the apron I untied and let drift to the tile like panties in a love scene. Stomping through The Dining Room kicking away shrimp and sausage from my shoes, I shed my vest and tossed my bowtie behind me before spinning out the revolving door. Outside in just a white shirt and black slacks, I looked like any other businessperson; I'd never felt so relieved to look like a businessperson, and so pleased at my gall that anger never found an opening. I whistled my song loudly down Royal to a Bead Store where I bought a pack of mint gum and a dollar draft To-Go. Down the over-populated sidewalk, I gulped the beer in two blocks, then stopped to pitch the cup into a trashcan outside of a seafood restaurant (a ritual of civility seldom practiced here), before unwrapping a piece of gum and sidestepping into said restaurant, which gave me a new job — within fifteen minutes of my last.

Days later though, swooning with safe arrogance, I decided I deserved a break from *all* of civilization's burdens, including the telephone, which I did not use to call my new employers and tell them not to expect me on my first day. Another bridge burned. But there were so many bridges then...

A diminutive savings sustained my unemployed mansion lifestyle until last Sunday; after a glorious month had been mine alone, I was relaxing at The Coffeehouse across the street and accidentally picked up *The Times-Picayune's 'Back-to-School' Job Listings* section: enough newspaper to wrap a sea of mullet, and all of it restaurant want-ads. Guilt reached into my book bag and took out a pen. I was very picky about which ads I conceded to circle before stuffing the paper into my bag for a projected Monday attack.

Monday came. I got a lot of sleep that day.

Tuesday, the planes hit the buildings and this War Shit commenced.

Still, today with *Picayune* and ballpoint in my backpack, I steered my new wide black beach cruiser onto Royal, trying not to sweat through my job-hunting clothes. I pedaled faster than I wanted to past the giant pink sugar-cube café where I'd dropped that gumbo. Its lacy doors were shut tight and silent. I continued at a Need rather than a Want pace, past the beautiful, green slat-board shack where I never showed up for work: like every building on Royal, it stood coldly closed.

So I cut right, down a skinny alley with pastel stucco walls, then left onto a wider street I didn't recognize. Hundreds of dead shops and bars stood shoulder to shoulder, seeming familiar, but I was sure I hadn't ridden here before — then I recognized my first NO jobsite, where I'd worked with Dwaine, and a street-sign outside its closed doors reading, 'Bourbon.' It all just looked so different now…

As Lani says, "I only go down to Bourbon if I need to feel better about myself," and I too have felt better lamping on Bourbon's corners, observing a million drunk humans who thought they were wild and free, when really they were following The Instructions, consuming the canned version. And it's because of them that it was true: I never had biked on Bourbon. But in today's rare, windless 80-degrees, the street was like an abandoned soundstage where the actors, directors, and the guy who makes it hot outside had all walked off The Job. Without tourism cheapening the atmosphere, there was space to appreciate how every wall in The Quarter is of a different age, texture, color and material than every other decaying wall. Architectural pathos vibrated in an emptiness matched only by the silent day I moved here, when they'd just finished sweeping away Fat Yesterday. Only on Ash Wednesday and during Wars is The Quarter free to be the famous pink, yellow, pale-green, dark-blue, white and orange quilt of sweating wood, iron, brick, stucco, lace, colored glass and alcohol that used-to stir the souls of real artists. Its cracks, chips and fades unobscured by white flesh, The Quarter is living proof that, left the fuck alone, things falls into their own perfect composition.

But after facing locked doors at two of the *want*-address I'd circled, and scoffs at two others, The Quarter's *de*-composition seemed to say, *We've seen this before, knew it would happen again… Why you think we never wasted money fixing or painting things?* Still, I climbed wide stone steps into a restaurant on Tchapatoulus. The building's sheath was smooth, City Hall gray, its cool innards coated in fresh velvet, black and red. Stepping through The Dining Room to the bar, my image reflected off empty, black-marble dining tables. Behind the bar, a young white guy leaned against liquor bottles, gazing up at a TV as blandly as watching baseball, but I heard explosions and a News Voice up there and so — I looked down the bar, to the only other human: an older bald man with a small brown beard, sitting on a stool, his back against velvet. He chewed rocks from a tumbler and stabbed at his folded newspaper with a red ballpoint. He was dirty. Not sleeping-on-the-ground-dirty; more like he worked hard, perhaps on a shrimp boat … *At least he has a fucking job*, I thought, but still asked him, "You circling the want-ads?"

Head down, his drunken English accent replied, "No mate. Just The Crossword."

"That's good, cause the want ads," I held up my folded *Picayune*, "are worth nothing."

"You're telling me!" he cockneyed. Still looking down at his paper he announced, "I had to let go of all but *one* of my waiters, and today I gave even *him* the day off. That hotel across the street that's always at 90% capacity even during the worst bloody heat is now down to 10% because all the conventions have been cancelled. Next week we were supposed to have 80,000 people in town, but that was for an aviation conference, so of *course* they're bloody well not coming now!" His laugh decayed sadly. He glanced up finally from The Crossword to ask me, "Last night I should have seated at least 150 folks in this place, but you know how many I sat?"

Now, seeing his face for the first time, I recognized him, but didn't remember his name: months ago, that night I went to Liuzza's with Eve — the only date I've been on since moving here — he'd insinuated himself after overhearing us laughing about the X-Rated Circus we were at that Moment preparing for by getting drunk. His eyes swam, but his accent was charming and he bought us Bloody Marys and made us laugh harder. If we came down to his restaurant on Tchapatoulus, he said, where the walls are all velvet, he would make us a big meal for free. Within a half-hour, he'd even offered me a server job, which I declined because the Bloody Marys seemed to be making us friends, and I don't like letting friends down...

But more than my friendship he wanted Eve, who barely found me attractive, so I didn't fear losing her to a red-nosed 60-year-old. I simply laughed along as he addressed me while staring into her face, or at the hem of her skirt when she rose to go use the rest room. I didn't cease laughing until he offered us a ride to The Circus; I didn't want him chaperoning the only date I'd managed in forever. But without even silently consulting my eyes, Eve accepted his offer; she didn't have her car with her and she hates bicycles, which now makes me wonder why I ever bothered with her.

Anyway, from the backseat of the drunken Limey's car I had stared at the shaved nape of Eve's professional haircut, knowing that he wouldn't just drop us off. And he did follow us into The Circus, to stand between our shoulders. He stopped buying our drinks, but continued drowning his own charm, drinking until he was punching me too hard whenever something particularly dirty happened on stage, and hugging Eve hard and often, whenever.

But peeking around his big belly's vertical horizon, I always found Eve's eyes burning holes into The Circus. She was rapt, I assumed, and aroused by the pornography, I hoped. But during the finale — a girl hand-standing on stage spinning a ceramic plate on the tip of a dildo protruding from her vagina — I noticed Eve was gone. The Brit caught me staring into the empty space she'd left and he spit in my ear, "I saw her! She just went to the bathroom! Over there!" He thumbed in the direction of the EXIT and slobbered, "She'll be back. She's a good kid. You two are good kids. You're a lucky boy. And really, if you *ever* need a job, you have one with me. I PROMISE."

But today, months later, two days into This War Shit, he didn't recognize me as he answered his own question: "Four. I sat only four people today. And I sat them myself cause I can't even afford to pay the hostess six-an-hour."

Another of his laughs decayed. He looked back down, stabbed his newspaper. I walked out without reminding him.

- 2 -

When I can't for some reason find a new job immediately, I usually abort French Quarter hunts to drink cold beer with the rest of the world. But today there was no rest of the world, no bad examples to follow. So I pedaled on until I'd X'd out every *Picayune* ad except one, for a Fine Dining place on Canal. In my arrogant pre-War days I avoided Fine Dining because I never wanted to concentrate so hard at a job where I'd still wear a nametag. But entering this place on Canal, I really wanted to work there, would've worked hard, never walked out…

The *Hours of Operation* etched in gold in the glass front doors promised the place was open, but inside was like a deserted castle in a Marquez novel: celestial miles of empty, glass-and-gold tables, and a twisted gold staircase blooming from the middle, up into a second floor Dining Room. But no waiters loafed about in unwarranted cummerbunds. Expecting any second to find the decaying king face-down-dead in his soup, I yelled into the emptiness, "Hello?" like a naked teen in a bad horror movie.

Moving past the bar, I surveyed all I could steal: real silver silverware, small oil paintings, oversized bottles of wine. I walked to the back and knocked on the side of a computer just outside the kitchen's mouth…

"Hello?"

I didn't feel right penetrating a strange kitchen, so I walked back and sat at the bar. The palace was silent except for the Margarita machine whirring lime-green slush, and my small, malevolent mental voice suggesting, *Steal something... depression... serious... desperate times...* I tried blocking the voice by dwelling on my past arrogance: *I deserve no options... deserve a depression sitting on my chest...* Waiting for Management to emerge and hire me, I sanded my teeth together, reprimanding myself for using that last bowl of gumbo as a tool of my caprice: *Soon I'll be hungry and wish I had that gumbo... I'll be like that starving grasshopper, some over-obvious allegory...*

"Hello?"

But the voice persisted — *take what you can, while you can* — until finally I counted a slow ten before leaning far over the bar, snatching a To-Go cup and milking the Margarita machine. When my cup ranneth over I ran it to the front of the restaurant and ducked into the empty Waiting Area to sit on a miniature sofa beside the vacant Hostess' Stand. Not wanting to be caught, I gulped as much Margarita as my mouth could hold. Cold pain rabbit-punched me in the temples. When the tears flooded in I worried I might not be able to see if Management came out of the back, so delirious I slugged another mouthful to get it over with. My throat seared. Halfway to blackout, I opened wide and breathed, hoping NO's humidity would thaw my insides. But I sucked in only conditioned air.

Finally the icepick subsided, and I was left with a thin but relaxing tequila buzz. Wiping my eyes I saw that I was still alone. I set the empty cup on the hostess' podium, next to the blank reservation book and another cup, full of tea and fat ice-cubes — further sign of inhabitants. My buzz stood me up and walked me back past the bar, past the computer and into the uninhabited kitchen. Everything was silver: silver cookware hung from silver hooks, silver cupboards and drawers, ceiling, floor, and everything perfectly clean, lacking even the lingering heat of recently prepared meals. The Margarita carried me through the kitchen into a white hallway leading to a half-open office door. Inside the office a Latin lady counted piles of money on her desk. *I wonder if it's her life savings she's pooling in the face of The Depression...* When I knocked on her open door she flinched like a wingless bird, then froze, silent, vulnerable, profitable...

"There's no one outside watching the restaurant," I deadpanned. "I've been out there a long time trying to figure out what to steal."

She didn't laugh. She rose and stepped around the desk, placing her body between her money and me. I closed my mouth tight so she wouldn't smell tequila. Holding my arm she walked me out and back down the hallway.

In the silver kitchen she quit holding her breath, released my arm and slowed our walk. Facing my liquor-mouth away I admitted, "I realize it's ridiculous at this point, but I'm here in response to your ad in the paper."

Into The Dining Room our reflections in every mirror gave the restaurant an illusion of occupancy. We stopped finally at the bar where she explained, "I'm subbing for everyone today: all the waiters, Managers, hostesses, it's just me..." She recited the same bleak hotel and convention statistics I'd already learned, until she noticed me looking guiltily past her to the Margarita machine and, "Do you want a drink?" she giggled. "We could all use a drink right now... And it's the least I can do since you came all the way out here. Again, I'm really sorry. But if Mardi Gras isn't cancelled this year, come back and see me after The New Year and I'll hire you, I PROMISE."

- 3 -

With all *The Picayune's* obsolete options X'd out, I abandoned my reconnaissance, but continued sightseeing through The Quarter's gallons of cool, empty air. Rolling slowly past Jackson Square, I sipped that second Margarita feeling like things might still turn out OK. *Wars are supposed to be GOOD for the Economy; maybe that just takes a few days to kick in...* Especially when dead, The Square is epic: The Cathedral's long spike goring the gray clouds that seem to always hang above regardless of weather elsewhere in the city. No matter how many postcards, or T-shirts, or times I'm forced to ride through it before and after bad jobs, The Square's shadows provide solace. I was also heartened to spot another lonely bike-rider there, a Hemingway-but-skinny white man, a less virile, clean-cut version of my neighbor, Lani. His clothes were stained with paint, and a bungee cord held a tall stack of canvases to his back fender. Silently, inwardly, I exalted my fellow artist, who eats this Depression to fuel his creation. I held my flat hand perpendicular to my forehead, saluting him in passing…

"Wait!" he squeaked.

I skidded to a stop, rolled back.

"Would you like to see my paintings?" he asked.

"Yeah, definitely, I could use some beauty right now."

In silence he began unhooking the bungee chord. Wanting him to know I'm local, I killed the silence: "Though actually there's plenty of beauty out here today, eh? The Quarter's perfect when it's empty like this. Isn't it? Without all the tourists?"

Silence.

"It's so nice out that it almost doesn't bother me that I can't find a job."

I noticed the artist's pause, and just then realized that he might be expecting me to actually buy something, so I added, "Oh, yeah, I'm broke by the way. Sorry. But I'd still really like to see your art."

He began wrapping his paintings back up.

"No, seriously, I'd like to see them. I went to school for painting so I'm sure I'd appreciate them more than all the tourists you normally have to…"

He rode off.

In his absence I noticed, in the distance, my *actual* neighbor Lani sitting at his card table beside a sign reading: *47 years experience*. On two separate occasions, I've witnessed rich couples fly in from New York and Los Angeles to have Lani read their *tuh-ROH* cards under our Gazebo, before they immediately cabbed it back to the airport — I guessed these tougher times forced him onto Jackson Square.

Except for moaning feral cats, The Square was quiet enough that even Lani's bad ears heard me yell his name. He looked up and waved, not a fingers-open, side-to-side scrubbing-motion, but a cupped-hand, twisting at the wrist: Lani calls this his Parade Wave, the same one debutants brandish from the tops of Mardi Gras floats. Lani puts a lot of emphasis on Mardi Gras, it means more to him than most; he claims the first NO person he met upon stepping off the bus on Mardi Gras day 25-years ago was the woman who's now his wife. I don't think even he knows anymore whether that is true or not.

I pedaled toward Lani, wanting to interrogate him about the future: *What will become of MY first Mardi Gras?* And also about the past: *Weren't the vibrations strong enough for you to pick up on all this BEFORE it happened?* But he interrupted, "Your wish came true!" I stopped silent against his card table. He motioned around us, smiling, "The donkeys are all at home sleepin now!"

I hadn't noticed, but yes, the streets were void of donkey-and-buggy rides. When the occasion arises, Lani sets his table up next to the mules' cement water troughs on The River side of The Square. That's his spot. The first time I visited him there during some festival, we spent the day whimpering, watching the donkeys suffer during the hottest part of the year, with those little hats on and the steel rods in their mouths, and we made a pact that if either of us ever came into enough money where Laws ceased to matter, we would liberate all The Quarter's donkeys vigilante-style, unbridle them, slap their asses and watch them run down the bank of the Mississippi. Unfortunately, on the day we decided this we were still poor, so in the meantime whenever a wooden buggy would creak up beside Lani's table, we'd hiss loud enough for the tourists' attentions, but quiet enough so the driver wouldn't hear us over the sound of his own lying tour-guide voice. "Y'all got cars, right?" we'd then hiss at the tourists. "So why the hell you need a donkey pullin you around? Animals ain't decoration! Slavery ain't *quaint*!" Sick fun until one black lady barked back at Lani, "Oh, give me a break! They used to it by now."

"What the? What kind of cockamamie logic is that," Lani rebutted. "If human slavery hadn't been abolished, y'all'd be used to it by now too."

But today it did feel good to see the donkeys gone. "Except I can't find a job," I admitted to Lani.

"No shit," he laughed. "What'd you think?"

"Why are *you* out here then?"

"You'd be surprised, man," he said, "man" sounding like *Maine*. "Today's been busy as shit. With all This Shit going on, you don't think people want to *know* somethin?"

In my seven months here, Lani's done much for me, but he hasn't read my tarot cards. When we first met, he often promised me a free reading — a $50 value — but always, coincidentally, when his cards were nowhere around. Then recently he stopped mentioning it altogether, maybe because he knows I write mysticism off a healthy 25% of the time. I myself don't bring the free reading up anymore simply because Lani and I are good friends now, so I'm sure he'd just predict something benign and hopeful for me; once you're friends with a mystic, I'm sure they're worthless to you in a psychic capacity.

"Well, that's two bright spots then," I cheered. "The mules aren't being tortured and you're making some money. Though I have no idea what the fuck *I'm* gonna to do about money. I don't have rent yet and my six-month lease is up...I might have to move into the house next door; rent's cheaper there because of the pigeon infestation..."

"I'm not charging people," Lani corrected me, shuffling his cards. "When it's something people *want*, I charge 'em. But right now it's a need, so it's free. I'll tell you what though, if I was chargin I'd be makin a killin." His eyes then lit up behind his bifocals as he announced, "Ah know what! Ah could teach you to read the tuh-ROH, then you'd *always* have a job! I mean, just cause *Ah'm* not chargin don't mean *you* can't. Then you could cut me in on it and Ah could make some money, and still feel like a altruistic person."

We laughed. Then he prescribed more relatable advice: "Fy was you man, I'd go back and sit in The Gazebo in this nice weather and not think about jobs or war or nothin. And you know how normally there's no way you'd *ever* just mosey your bike home *reeeeeeeal* slow down Esplanade?"

I nodded, smiling.

"Well, today you can! So do it!" he rallied. "Get you a beer and ride home with it, ride with no hands, as slow as you need to..."

Still nodding, I promised Lani I'd see him back at Our Mansion, then parade-waved goodbye, and proceeded to follow his instruction.

ch 3: he wanted out

The broken streets of NO are slathered in the run-over bodies of kittens. So concerned animal lovers (lonely old women) trap feral neighborhood cats and bring them to The Hospital, which removes their Reproductive Equipment free-of-charge before releasing them back into their colonies.

Also, I needed a job.

So, after answering a No Experience Necessary ad, my New Boss handed me a net, a hypodermic needle and a bottle of Ketamine tranquilizer, then pushed me into a walk-in-closet-sized room full of hissing, pissing cat carriers.

My New Boss is a good one though, better than most, a mountain of a woman with a big padded face mounted between apple cheeks. She's not a doctor, she just owns The Hospital, and so spends most days at work just playing with the animals and laughing. At night she's actually a struggling standup comedienne, and at any given time during the day she'll break into her routine in The Waiting Room, her face coming out at you when she reaches her punchlines. She hired me, bless her misled heart, because she liked my own sense of humor — which I must utilize each time I open a carrier door so that a cat that's never been touched by human hands can fly out in a desperate panic, spring to the ceiling screaming at me and releasing a slick of urine as I chase its blur up walls and between glass jars full of stethoscopes and fecal lubes, the net smacking loudly against every surface until finally I net the fucker, sit on its back, and shoot it with an ass full of Ketamine.

My co-worker Deb only glancingly showed me the techniques for proper capture and how to anesthetize a cat for Surgery. During that anomalous demonstration, Deb was, as always, dramatically serious. She's younger than me, but as hard as I won't be for another ten years or two heartbreaks. She serves as a complete foil to our boss, with her body the thinness of her own eyeglass frames, and eternally-pursed lips pierced by a small ball of the same silver metal as the kennels. Only once did Deb kneel before me with a freedom-possessed cat trapped between her knees, pointing out, "This nerve right here that looks like a vein, if you stick that nerve you will paralyze the animal." And though nodding, I was distracted down her hospital scrubs, reading the black tattoos drawn from her small, braless breasts to her holocaust ribs: something about "Kill the…" I lost the rest in her armpit's shadow…

I would have paid better attention to her words had I known there'd be no repeat; Deb doesn't teach me because she doesn't want me to learn. Like many animal lovers, Deb treasures animals because they give her control in a world where we have none. Animals are here for her to lord over, to quarantine or set free, to let live or put-out-of-their-misery. And I am an intrusion upon this higher calling. Despite Deb's three-year seniority and extra $1.50-an-hour, the doctor tells us we are equals, but as far as Deb's concerned, I'm only around to free her from sanitation duties. I exist only long enough to mop piss or blood.

But left alone overnight, the animals generate too much piss and blood for just one person. So Deb concedes to clean The Dog Runs every morning. Fifteen dogs. I do the cat kennels. Forty-eight cats. "Because I'm a dog person," she says, but really it's because she can stand up and casually hose dog poop into the gutters from 10-feet away, while The Cat Cages are cleaned on hands-n-knees.

I don't complain though; I love cats. Though I don't own one right now... I do want one, and it's hard not to adopt one with My Boss pushing the idea on me every day, even after I've explained to her so many times that I'm not in the right situation, not right now. I'd need a fenced-in yard at least. Until then, I just can't stand losing them, and mine *always* die, because mine want outside; they dedicate their lives to begging for freedom, which is all I want as well, so who am I to deny them? But then once they're out there, it's only a matter of time... So I can't get another cat until I live full-time in Costa Rica, on four acres of land that cost me eight-thousand dollars, nowhere near any dangerous highway, right on the water, with a lean-to where the cat and I can hide from the Central American sun after a hard bout of running as fast and as far and as free as we can...

Until then though: no cat. But this deprivation makes cleaning the morning Cat Cages an almost joyous occasion. They flirt with me, rub on me, love me, cry out for me. And besides, the last thing I want at 7:30 a/m is the insane screaming of dogs, big fucking caged dogs that are too old for anyone to love; My Boss is always bickering with the male doctor about the way she takes-in dogs that no one wants. She finds them wherever, brings them in, and tries to adopt them out, but of course everyone wants a puppy, so these poor things end up living out in The Dog Runs forever, prisoners of her altruism. She's accumulated so many that by now, when I go out there first thing in the morning, the sound of them throwing their bodies against the their cages trying to get out at me, love me, combined with their crazed barking, sounds like a distorted PA System blasting the sound of sheet-metal being hammered. If Deb can take that at 7:30, then yeah, she's a dog person.

But today Deb still hadn't arrived by the time I finished the cats, so I decided I'd clean The Dog Runs as well, relishing the chance to later tell her, 'I finished my work so I went ahead and did yours too.' First, I chewed paper towels and crammed the wet wads into my ears, preparing for the screaming sheet metal. But outside, The Runs were swallowed in the striking silence of a hanging question. Each dog sat still in each cage, face on paws, barely looking up at me as I walked along the chain-link, searching for the source of their silence. I found it in the last run…

Two red-wet, wilted German Shepherds — a big baby and her mangy, skeletal mother — wept up at me from a bloody mass of blankets. "Jesus Christ!" my mouth yelled, less for the blood than for fear of what I'd do about it without Deb around to instruct… It was more blood than I've ever seen in one place, beating even last week's record set by that emergency dog who'd accidentally sniffed rat poison: his face boiled red bubbles, but the doctor was already busy with an emergency bone Surgery, so in the meantime I held the dog in a headlock, waiting for hours, whispering to him, apologizing on behalf of humanity, until finally he expired in my arms…

I assumed though that these Shepherds had spent the night ripping each other apart, and that the other dogs out there were simply worn-out from staying up, cheering them on. But before I could panic I noticed, mingled in the blankets of blood, one fist-sized, black blob screaming a muffled mew that echoed off The Runs' orange tile. *A baby!* None of us had known the mother was pregnant. Scanning the cage I spotted two other black lumps. Mother Shepherd's tired eyes followed me as I opened the gate, stepped into the red puddle and loaded the three crying babies into my arms. They looked undercooked, eyes swollen shut, toothless mouths screaming. Placenta ran down my pale green hospital scrubs (which I always think make me look important to the other people on the bus) and again recalled that gumbo I'd spilled. *I am redeeming myself now…*

Unless older dogs bear smaller litters I was sure there had to be more babies somewhere. My stained shoe nudged through the blankets. But nothing — until I leaned over the drainage gutters where the poop is hosed, and four more black fists lay inert in three inches of water. I ran the living inside.

Deb was still nowhere, so I lay the babies down on a heating pad in an empty cage in The Cat Room. Meows leaked from every angle, thin arms and paws reached out to me from between bars. When the babies were safe and warm, I stepped back out of The Cat

Room to the sight of hundreds of bloody footprints, as if an Army of the Undead had marched through, and it angered me to realize that *I'd* be the one mopping it all up later, bathing the Shepherds, washing the red blankets while Deb assisted in Surgery. *I do need to quit this god-damned shit fucking...*

I followed my blood-documented path back out to the gutters, scooped up the dripping dead and placed them into a white, plastic garbage bag — until the last apple-sized body whimpered! A pink membrane had kept water out of its lungs! My heart screamed as I ran the slimy little thing cupped in my hands back into The Hospital, where I immediately smashed into Deb, the puppy almost crushed between us...

My happy hand grabbed her pointy shoulder, and over-excited I yipped, "That old German Shepherd with no hair on her tail had fucking *babies*!"

"Don't touch me," Deb said.

I let go and ran. Deb chased after demanding, "Give it to me!" and "Where are the others?!" I didn't think to answer. Back in The Cat Room, I stopped and gazed in wonder at the tiny monster struggling in my hands, screaming beneath a thin layer of bubble-gum. I opened the kennel door and lay it on its back with its siblings. Deb followed me in: "Tell me where they are! Are they in there? Move out of the way!"

Still staring at the pup I asked Deb, "If I break this membrane, will like, the air pressure change crush its lungs?"

"Yes, it needs to be cut," she scowled. "Get out of the way! Let me do it!"

When she stepped toward me I blocked her with my shoulder. Our hot cheeks touched and she jerked away, her mouth clenched into a hard straight line, her skeleton trembling at my elbow. "Give it to me!" she roared.

"You know what Deb," I barked back. "I know you know this job better than I do! But in *no* other way are you superior to me! I am *easily* as smart as you will *ever* be! So from this Moment on you will *never, ever* talk down to me again!" And with that, my shaking fingernails pinched the membrane. Deb was muzzled. *"I am not an idiot!*" I declared to her and the world, unzipping the membrane from mouth to feet like a wet sleeping bag. Its mewls sharpened, escaping into the air. I closed the cage on the squirming babies then leaned back against the kennel bars, calming. Deb was gone. Small paws reached out to pat my shoulders and the back of my head.

- 2 -

Days later I arrived home from the last hour-and-a-half bus ride I will hopefully ever take. Lani was sitting under our giant, frilly gazebo, which always makes me think of slavery... His sandaled feet up on the iron patio table amidst a spent arrangement of *tub-ROH* cards, Lani leaned back whittling yet another walking staff. Slivers of wood fell from him like dead leaves. The Gazebo's shade proved worthless; we both were sweating, he from recently telling the future, I from having walked home seven blocks from the bus stop. Standing behind his chair I lamented to his silver ponytail, "I'm an idiot."

As much of a "student of the soul" as he claims to be, Lani didn't empathize. His sage advice, without looking up from his whittling: "Fuck that job, man."

Then a big pause with nothing in it but his pocketknife biting off leaves of wood, and the skid of chair feet on cement as I sat down, too. Lani's own knotty walking staff leaned against The Gazebo's rail. He was carving this new one for the same client whose just-read cards were still splayed out across the table. Lani made $50 from the reading, plus tip. He'll receive another $100 for the staff. He makes a fair living it seems, and will never be fired, like I was...

But before I could explain *why* I'd been fired, he let the half-carved staff fall into his crotch so that he could raise his arms above his head, one palm up like catching rain, the other gripping his knife: "You live in a goddamned mansion, man!" he reminded me. "*Act* like it! You're worth more than $7.00-an-hour. Specially ridin that goddamned bus a hour-and-a-half outside a New Orleans at 6 a/m. For what? To clean up cat shit?"

"Dogs too."

He laughed his deep Southern laugh, which sounds sometimes nurturing and wise, and other times too nurturing and wise to be taken seriously. "Shit man, I had better-payin jobs back in the 1700's," he continued in his Jackson Square Mark Twain voice. "Cars weren't even invented yet and I still had a easier time gettin to-and-from work than you did gettin to Kenner on that goddamned bus." We laughed together, but then Lani shook his head: "You're crazier than homemade rabbit shit for takin that job in the first place."

This comment relit the passions that first compelled me to ride the bus so far outside of NO to fill out that application, and so I gave to Lani The Pessimist's Defense: "Well, you know, since This War Shit started, I just haven't wanted to serve humans and all their useless formality."

Silence. Whittling. Lani unmoved.

"The whole time I worked at The Hospital," I continued, "the only contact I ever had with The War was maybe accidentally reading a headline on some clawed-up, urine-soaked newspaper. I liked that. The vacation from humanity alone made up for the couple missing dollars-an-hour."

Still nothing but a dull smile and whittling...

So I gave The Economic Defense: "And at least it was a solid gig. Wars don't stop people from caring for their sick animals."

"Only Mardi Gras does," Lani chuckled, referring to a story I'd told him one night under the gazebo while drinking wine with the citronella candle burning: that day I'd been shaving a kitten's belly for Surgery while the doctor was washing his hands and explaining to me how, "More pets die during Mardi Gras than any other time of the year; emergency cases just can't get through traffic. But also, some people'd rather just let their pets suffer-and-die than miss the parades." And while listening to the doctor's Mardi Gras stats instead of concentrating on the job at hand, I blindly shaved off one of the sleeping cat's nipples. A "nipple-ectomy" the doctor called it, laughing, confiding as the cat bled, "Oh, everyone does that once or twice."

During my two months at the hospital, Lani cried with laughter at stories like these. That's another reason I liked the job, and why I'm sorry I lost it... But rather than admit this to Lani, I continued, utilizing The Middle-Class Defense: "I also just learned so *much* there. Working in Surgery was like grad school. I learned *so* much about biology, medicine, Surgery...I'll bet I could now write a book about the art of surgical sterilization; how to use an autoclave, all the particular tools human hands aren't allowed to touch, and when, and why... Did I ever tell you about how we had to wipe the bottoms of our shoes with rubbing alcohol when traveling in-and-out of certain rooms? *So* many tedious little rituals..."

"Sterilization is like Superstition," Lani nodded. I don't know where he formed that brilliant analogy; he claims to have worked every job there is, which at first I thought was another of his story-telling devices. But after this, my 12th firing (lifetime), I'm thinking I may get my own chance to work everywhere in the next 30+years until I'm Lani's age. "Well, it's all well-and-good to learn things you'll never use," he continued. "But you admitted yourself that you barely helped in Surgery. You told me yrself that Deb bitch has you spendin all your time cleaning up shit."

I looked away, up to the gurgling, humping noises of the pigeons living in the lacy trim of the dirty mansion next door to our clean one. In NO people eat pigeons. Except before they put it in their mouths, they re-name it *Squab*. Next door, the Squab' fluffy gray-pink breasts rested in their own whitewash like a picnic blanket beneath them. *No, he's right: I won't miss the shit.*

- 3 -

From that birth scene onward, not the biggest puddle of blood or urine could compel Deb to speak to me. But I couldn't enjoy our calm equality, knowing that rather than conceding to silence, Deb merely lay wait in it.

She lay wait until this morning when, passing the door of Surgery, I caught her ending a conversation with The Doctor: "You can add that to the list!" And somehow I knew The List was her tally of my fireable offenses. I envisioned The List:

>   1) The nipple-ectomy;
>   2) The time he mis-sexed that male cat, causing the doctor to cut open its belly in search of a uterus;
>   3) The time he used the same mop water for the quarantine room as he did for the rest of the hospital, spreading ringworm and kennel cough to the other animals

"But those are understandable mistakes," Lani chuckled, laying aside his whittling to collect his scattered tarot cards from the table. His silver-and-turquoise knuckles jumped over one another as he shuffled the cards, continuing, "They *had* to expect mistakes hirin some joker with No Experience." He peered up at me through his thick white eyebrows: "What *really* broke the camel's hump?"

>   4) Yesterday, when he let that red-haired cat go.

Deb found The Little Red-Haired Cat a few days ago in the employee parking lot behind The Hospital. He was heart-wrenchingly sweet and we all wanted to own him, but he was fat and smelled of cigarettes, so we knew he belonged to someone in the neighborhood. Still, Deb brought him inside to remove his Reproductive Equipment. It irked me, the satisfaction she obviously gleaned from playing Mother Nature in this Surgical Emasculation. And how would his real owners feel when he came home nutless? But I know that Outside Cats with intact equipment reproduce like guppies, and 99% of them end up dead, so this was best, and the voice of dissent died on its way up my throat, until days later, yesterday morning…

I showed up to clean The Cat Room and found The Little Red-Haired Cat still in his kennel, crying his eunuch head off. So I stepped out to where Deb was hosing The Dog Runs and asked, "Why is he still here?"

Her ten-foot spray rolled a turd into the gutter. Over the screaming metal dogs I barely heard her grudgingly reply, "I took him back to the parking lot and set him down, and he just didn't want to leave." But I heard spider-cracks in her icy voice; she'd grown attached, didn't want to let him go, even if it meant his living in a cage forever.

I walked silent and doubt-filled back to The Cat Room where he cried at me the entire hour-and-a-half it took to finish cleaning and feeding them. Finally I had to witness for myself his denial of freedom, and so carried my red-haired brethren in my arms, out into the misty morning parking lot, where the orange leather pads of his feet didn't even touch the blacktop before he was but a blur disappearing under the fence.

His absence went unnoticed all day until 6 p/m as Deb and I replicated the morning routine in preparation for closing. In the sink I was scrubbing the day's bloody tools when she rushed into Surgery. I shut off the faucet to hear her ask/accuse, "Where'd my cat go?" My face flushed. I shrugged, turned the faucet back on and continued scrubbing. Her bony hand reached over and turned it off: "Where is he?"

"I - don't - know," I over-enunciated, looking down at my hands in the sinkful of shark-attack-red and razor-sharp scalpels. And when I looked back up she'd disappeared.

I continued scrubbing, promising myself that *First thing in the morning I'll admit what I did to The Doctor, or My Boss, but I don't need to tell Deb. Deb's not My Boss.*

But over my whistling (*I - can't - find - my - way - around*) and the sound of running water, I could still hear her stomping frantically from room-to-sterilized-room, interrogating everyone, "Have you guys seen my cat? What happened to my cat?"

Until finally, I panicked and broke down: the next time she passed the door of Surgery I shouted, "Hey Deb, come in here…"

I turned off the faucet again and came clean to her. She didn't even ask me why I did it. She just pursed her lips so hard it looked like it hurt — until suddenly she released, relaxed, smiled. The first natural smile I'd ever seen on her face, less tension than I'd ever read in her; she'd lost her cat, but she'd won.

- 4 -

The first time My Boss ever stopped laughing was to ask me why I'd let the cat go. My inner voice eloquently defended, *Well, Deb said that when she'd tried to get him to leave, he wouldn't leave. So, I thought I'd try again. The way she'd made it sound, I thought she'd be happy that I got the cat to do what she'd tried, and failed...*

But my mouth said only, "He wanted out."

Lani laughed, then coughed so hard a card fell out of the deck in his hand. I wondered if the card was jumping out at me, trying to tell me something. But he picked it up and replaced it before I had a chance to see. Not that I would've known what it meant... "Well then, that right there's why you took that job," Lani claimed. "It was fate: you were *meant* to free that cat." He stood, brushed woodchips from his shirt, then patted me on the back: "I'm proud of you." Then he said goodbye, dragging his walking-staffs off The Gazebo, through the garden and past the fountain.

But pondering his blessing, and alternate job solutions, my eyes fell upon his tarot cards on the table and... "Hey Lani!"

Before he could disappear around the huge white-siding corner, he turned around. I pointed at the deck. I should have picked it up and walked it over to him, but I wouldn't have felt right touching his cards.

"Oh shit! Thanks," he laughed, striding back under the worthless shade.

As he collected them I suggested, "You should read my hand now."

"What?" he asked, slipping the cards in his pocket and stepping away, back into the sun; despite his sharpness of mind and tongue, his eyes and ears are beginning to tune out the world, which I wouldn't think would be all bad...

"Read my hand," I repeated.

"Your hands?" he squinted back over his shoulder, confused, walking away laughing, "I'll bet your hands smell like cat piss."

I sniffed them. He was right. *Mystical...* I admired him as he disappeared.

Then I too stood and, reaching into my pocket for my keys, felt the little bottle of Ketamine I'd forgotten to put back in the medicine cabinet after My Boss asked me to leave.

If times get too rough, at least I have that.

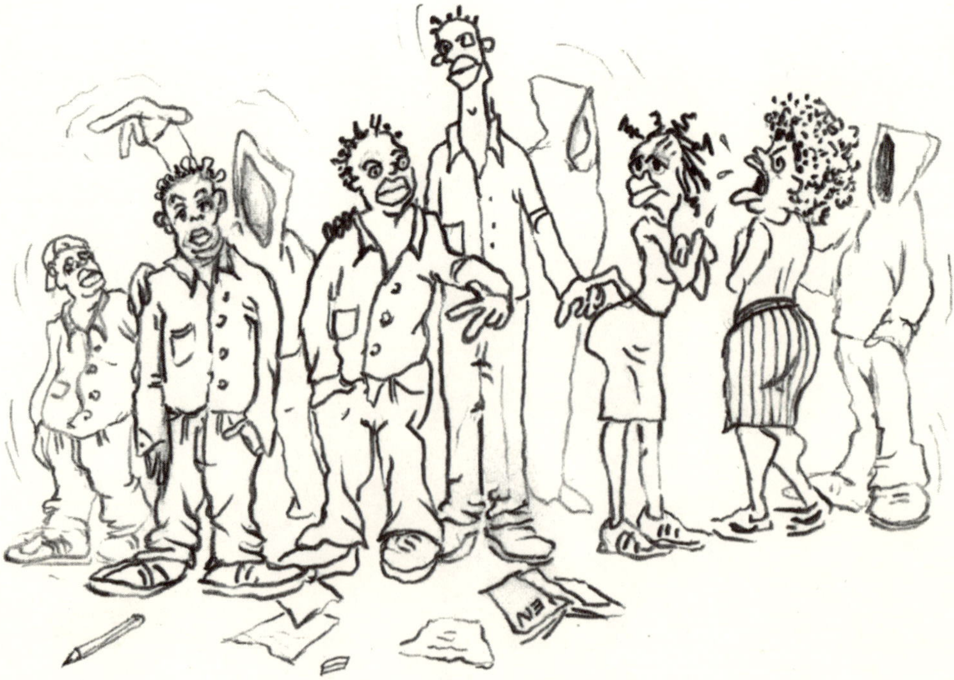

ACT 2: THE STORY (PROPER)

ch 4: schooled

Arranging the interview on the phone, I told the School Board's Human Resources lady that I was strictly a bike-rider, and she was Southern enough to come meet me at The Coffeehouse across the street from My Mansion. She turned out to be a gorgeous perfect, six-foot tall Mulatto woman with a foot-high fern of blonde hair. Her grand mouth took up a fourth of her face and all my attention as we stood shaking hands at an outside patio table.

"That's where I live," I thumbed at the colossus across the street.

But before it could impress her, before we could even sit, we both straightened at the horrifying screech of a truck smashing a motorcycler on Esplanade, just a few feet in front of us. A flake of orange, plastic reflector landed on our table. The rest of the coffee-drinkers ran outside.

In the silence I thought to joke to her, as Lani would've, *'I'll bet one of those two drivers was looking at you instead of the road.'*

I didn't though, and so by the time the tow-truck and ambulance arrived I'd won a temporary, one semester job teaching one, 90-minute Creative Writing class, each Monday, Tuesday and Thursday morning.

As they strapped the oxygen mask on the motorcycler, I asked my beautiful interviewer what had won me the job. "It was what you said about working at the vet after 9/11," she laughed. "How working with animals didn't pan out, so you figured kids were the next best thing."

"I just meant that they're the only other creatures innocent of all This…"

"I know what you meant," she cut me off before, 'War Shit.' "But it was funny how you phrased it. And that ability to laugh in the face of—" She cut herself off, paused, then continued, "It's probably the most important thing you'll need for this job."

- 2 -

Magnolia High School is a bleak building uptown where Black kids in sagging uniforms enter through a metal-detector to wander gray halls in the faint smell of chlorine and pot. There's no Math Teacher at Magnolia, or even a Principal. The Radio holds ultimate authority. I love the same musical bullshit, The Lawn Sprinklers, but Determinism has determined that I digest it objectively, just as it's been determined that these kids never laugh at The Radio, or question its authority. I might memorize The Words — possibly my only in-road to respect at Magnolia — but these kids, I've realized, memorize The Instructions, and The Instructions dictate that 1) guns and jail equal respect and wisdom, 2) it is wrong to love the mother of your child, 3) only money makes you human, and so 4) stealing is ah'ight and 5) the evilest thing you could ever do, would be to rat-out a thief.

In the face of this though, I'm blessed with a good ratio. Five of my fifteen kids don't even show up — Donell, Conterl, Joreeka, Corey and Corey remain faceless names on the roll-sheet. And the ten who do come, even the two assholes, are all smart. If, like me, you believe sense-of-humor is the strongest sign of intelligence, then my class' collective intellect is actually so strong that they often can't manage anything besides making each other laugh, which I relate to unfortunately well; it's surreal hearing myself yell, "Stop laughing!" But again, only two are true assholes: the remaining eight — despite sounding like parrots left sitting by The Radio too long — are good-natured; in their calmer Moments they talk of college, and seem to empathize with their parents' struggles. So I have faith in their distant futures at least.

"But don't trust a one of em," I was warned outside my classroom this morning by Mr. Land, Magnolia's Head-of-Security. The High School I attended in FLA didn't have or need any Security. Ride your bike through the toughest FLA neighborhood and the worst that will happen is someone might shout something at you... But Mr. Land wastes whole days in his stockbroker suit with the fluorescent light reflecting off his brown baldness, chasing cursing kids down the hallways — except this week, he's spent his mornings stationed outside my door, because the lock is broken, and while I was trying to teach over the roar of my own kids, others skipping class in the hall were slamming open my door as they passed. "They'll test you for a while," Mr. Land promised me today, staring out over the kids' creative hair configurations. "Then maybe they'll settle down and like you. But even then, don't trust a got-damn one."

A teenage voice far down the hallway shouted: "*That's cause you a ho an y'mama suck dick, nigga!*"

But Land didn't acknowledge it; cursing isn't against The Rules anymore. Land gets more upset when they bring their CD players to school or wear their uniforms un-tucked. He continued, "I've befriended so many of these damn kids, loved em like they my own. But shit..." he trailed off, rubbing his smooth crown, as in the background: "*Nigga, my mama don't even talk to me like that! You betta respect me, muthafucka! I'm a muthafuckin thug! Y'heard?*"

"Y'CLASS IS THE OTHER WAY, SON!" Mr. Land bellowed over my shoulder, then immediately downshifted back to me: "I was real good friends with some of these kids when they were Freshman, but after they been here a while... Magnolia'll turn a kid bad."

"*The fuck you is, muthafucka!*"

- 3 -

"*I'll* got-damn curse you, boy! And shit, what you gonna do y'little punk?"

Mr. Land's yelling was heating up the 4' x 6' copy room next to the empty Principle's Office. But when he said 'punk' De'von and I winced and Land brought his tone down; punk means something different to the kids. 'Punk' doesn't mean a guy with a Mohawk haircut, or a slow-burning stick you use to light fireworks: to the kids a punk is someone who takes it in the ass in jail, then continues his enjoyment of the practice after he's back on the outside. Mr. Land didn't mean it that way, but it still felt like the official, first-and-only time I've heard anyone mention homosexuality around De'von. De'von is one of my two assholes. But it's not really his fault…

Yesterday when I assigned the kids to write about their idols, De'von stood on his desk and in a loud, proud flourish sang to the class his essay entitled, "I Wanna Be Jennifer Lopez." Right there in print he said, "I don't know why I want to be her. I just do." Given these kids' general homophobia (De'von himself denounces gays), his essay should have made him a magnet of ridicule. But his peers, always ruthless with comedic insults, ignored the subtext of the essay — like they think that saying the words out loud will bring the dreaded concept to life. But until something or someone does, De'von is wound with anger, frustration and fear. When he's happy, he'll stand on his chair and sing his opinions, but when The Invisible Frustration Of Yet-Unknown Origin grips him, he and I share terrible discourse that bring Mr. Land running.

Land attended Magnolia himself, back when the football coach was sanctioned to hit boys. So I can tell he's frustrated by today's limitations on his job. I believe he's a good man who does what he thinks is right for the kids, but he seems to enjoy it too much. As he exerted his power over De'von, I wondered how many times he's raised his hand to students alone in that copy room. But even Land is more delicate with De'von than he is with the others; Land continued his reprimand in an Inside Voice: "You got to be crazy son, comin in here telling me, 'Mr. Patrick cursin me.' Got-dammit,

50

Mr. Patrick can say whatever he got-damn want to you, boy. Mr. Patrick went to college to *earn* that privilege."

I winced again at that one.

"I know you a good kid, D.," Land continued, calming further. "And you the Vice President of the student body, so we know you smart. But you ain't as smart as Mr. Patrick here, and I tell you what, if you do live to be as smart as him, you gonna wish you ain't give him as much shit as you did." De'von nodded sincerely. Mr. Land lightly grabbed and shook his shoulder, patted his back to let him know it was over, then commanded, "Now apologize to this man for sayin you was gonna cut him."

- 4 -

NO is the only place in North America where band-kids are revered by their classmates, rather than considered dorks. When school lets out, every bus stop down Esplanade to The French Quarter is an awkward, shrieking, brass jam session. So De'von is also spared peer harassment because he plays trumpet.

But because Cedar Walnutt leads The Drum Line, he gets more pussy than The Captain of the Football Team — then he took over that title as well… Cedar is my other asshole. His Star Status keeps his other teachers from intervening when during class they see him pass by their windows, his sweatshirt hood covering his face except for that cocky smile. Only I attempt to make him attend: standing out in the hall with Mr. Land today before class, I pointed Cedar out at the end of the hallway walking in the opposite direction. Land corralled him back to my class and sat him at a front-row desk facing mine. Cedar sat there, the only kid in my room, staring at me, into me for ten minutes in the silent stillness, before De'von and five other kids finally arrived.

Both Cedar and De'von were held back last year, so both have already learned all I'm teaching their classmates. De'von uses his foreknowledge to collect easy A's, but Cedar uses his to lord over me, finishing my sentences, making my teaching and me look inadequate. Within another 15 minutes three others sat down, and I finally addressed them with what I considered an acute cultural observation, since most of them claim they've never been outside Louisiana:

Me: Did you guys know that New Orleans is the only place in America where band-kids are not considered...

Cedar: *(in a hushed but assured baritone)* You ain't need to tell us about New Orleans. I was born here, baby. How long you lived here?

M: ...

C: You told us you moved here less than a year ago. You ain't even been to Mardi Gras yet, n'*you* tellin *us*?

M: I'm not saying I know everything about this place. I'm just pointing out one thing, maybe the only thing I know. *(Turning back to the class, changing the subject)* Now, we're going to start a new project this week; I want you all to write a letter to the Mayor of New Orleans. This Mardi Gras, the City of New Orleans has rented out...

C: Who's the Mayor Mr. Patrick?

M: ... *(and suddenly I worry, realizing that the governmental information I'm about to pass on to them came not from the newspaper, but from Lani...)*

De'von: *(interrupting, addressing the class)* He ain't even know who the Mayor is! The teachuh don't even know!

Cedar: *(to me)* Elections ain't till later this year, so The Mayor's still Marc Morial. But since he ain't gonna be around too much longer, writin to him'd be stupid.

Me: *(head filling with blood, still, continuing to the class)* This coming Mardi Gras, The City of New Orleans has rented Jackson Square to MTV so that MTV can film some concerts there. But the thing is, Jackson Square is public property. Those of you that have jobs, you pay for the upkeep of The Square, it comes out of your paychecks. But while MTV's here, you're not allowed to step foot on that property that you pay for. During that time, they're even kicking all the tarot card readers and street musicians off The Square; people who make their living there. MTV rented The Square from The City for like 12-million dollars, and you're not getting any of it! After all that money you've spent for the upkeep of The Square, you get none of the profit.

The Class: ...

M: So anyway, what I want you to do is to write to the Mayor — leaving the heading blank so we can fill in the name after the election — and ask him where those millions from MTV are going. But first, before you start, on a separate paper I want you to list all the shitty things about Magnolia High that...

De'von: Quit cursin!

Cedar: Man, I done did this exact assignment before. Every white teacher in this school *(of 50 teachers, 6 are white)* want us to write how shitty Magnolia is, but what if I don't think it's shitty? No one ask me if I think it's shitty.

M:*(addressing the class)* I didn't mean it that way. I just didn't say it right. I meant list all the ways Magnolia could use that 12-million. Think about what you see when you're walking the halls. In your opinion, what does...

I stuttered watching Cedar lean across his desk and conspire into De'von's ear in a disruptive, high-velocity whisper. Before the trend could spread through the class, I pointed to a chair in front of a computer cubicle and commanded, "Cedar, I'm sorry man, but you gotta move over there, away from De'von."

Cedar groaned and flopped himself across the room into the cubicle. He made his eyes dead and stared into the computer's monitor.

I continued, "So, before writing the letter, make a list of things you'd like Magnolia to have. Like, for instance, I think we need a bike rack; I have to park my bike in The Library..." Until Cedar began tapping his fingers on the cubicle wall: competently, tight beats and fancy fills he's mastered leading parades. Impossible to ignore: "You been practicing your paradiddles, eh?" I asked him, trying to relate to him as a musician. "Sounds good, man. I like it. We should play together some time since we listen to the same music and all. But for now, seriously, just don't. Just stop."

He tapped out one last loud measure then stopped — for only two more paragraphs from my mouth before continuing his paradiddles. I tried to ignore him, but the other kids were now paying attention to him too. Finally I had to stop again and point to yet another desk in a no-man's-land corner of the room.

"Cedar! Move farther away!" I yelled.

He didn't change seats, but he stopped drumming, leaned forward and put his lips to his desk so that his hood buried his head. I felt lost, the way I always do after I yell, like I've succumbed to something I believed I wouldn't. I half-heartedly gave the class a few more instructions before noticing De'von's watch on his skinny wrist on his desk and, "Hey man, what time is it?"

Silence. De'von smirked, shook his head 'no'.

"Damn man, is that how much you dislike me?" I pleaded. "You can't even tell me what time it is?"

"It's not you. I just do not like helping white people Mista Patrick. I am sorry, but I just can't."

I stepped closer to read his watch myself as, behind me, Cedar commenced his rudiments, this time on the clacky computer keyboard, louder, more percussive. He's a damn good drummer and most of me wanted to give up and listen to him. The kids loved it too. One boy shouted, "Go! Go!" like a street-corner jazzbo. Soon there was so much hooting and clapping I thought a Second-Line might break out. A good teacher could have found some way to redirect all this energy, make it part of the lesson. But I could only point across the room and scream like a woman, "Cedar! Now! Move!"

Again he ceased, leaned forward, and hid inside his hood. He didn't relocate, but was dormant long enough that the kids calmed and began their assignment. I wanted to go home, but instead walked around the class reading their lists over their shoulders…

```
1) Magnolia needs new teachers
2) Big screen Television
3) 32-inch televisions
4) a Teacher who don't curse
5) we need new rules
6) to much of Trash on the Floor
```

```
 7) holds in the roof
 8) the hall is too crowdy
 9) too many bad kids
10)  we need better hallways
```

Cedar allowed me a suspicious amount of silence, and I looked up to find him leaning back in his chair at a dangerous angle, his face aiming upward, staring into the giant Computer monitor he held high in the air.

By the time he saw me notice him, I was still too astounded to bark. He silently set the computer down on the desk and in that same Moment I unfroze, stepped toward him screaming, "Move!" and grabbed and jerked his chair, meaning to drag him across the room. Instead only the chair wrenched away and he landed on his tailbone.

"Oooh, Cedar!" De'von cackled, slamming fists on his desk. "Mista Patrick played you, baby!"

The room filled with shrieking laughter like bats and crows. Suddenly I could see nothing but Cedar's eyeballs. "I'm gonna break your jaw," he said calmly into my mouth.

I knew he was too smart to hit a teacher, especially when he's already on parole... So we just stood, both of us smart and unscared, spending a long Moment there with each other's eyeballs, until finally the bell rang and the white eclipse passed, leaving me in an empty room.

I turned the lights off and walked out, sticking the key in the door behind me, despite knowing the lock is broken.

- 5 -

I haven't really described the good kids, the eight out of ten. But that's the best way to describe them: the majority pushed so far into the background that they're barely part of the story.

ch 5: the donkey show

He rallied The Class Pitch higher and higher until in a calm rage I puked the insult: "I'll see you at the Popeye's Chicken drive-thru in 20 years, De'von."

I said this. To a child. De'von's peers laughed, reminding him he'd been played. My anger died, replaced by red splotches on my neck. My eyes explored the room on their own without me, searching for *I-don't-know-what option: an instruction manual? > > > A real authority figure? > > > An apology — for De'von, or me? > > > A claw hammer or mace? > > >* Or just my bicycle, which I'd pump miles across town to puff the pipe, fall into bed, and sleep off inadequacy.

"You ain't even got a fuckin car to DRIVE-THRU!" De'von squealed, his fingers blurring in the air around his bushy head."And it ain't no RIDE-THRU neithuh! So you know they ain't lettin you bring that piece-a-shit bah-sickle through, *y'white bitch*!"

White bitch. Somehow I approved of it, even liked the sound: *a biting, forceful name, White Bitch, a superhero name, at least a stage-name, White Bitch, singing the hit, I - can't - find - my...*

Emotionally depleted, The White Bitch barely responded, "Whatever man, I've told y'all before, I *choose* not to have a car because..."

"You ain't got a car cause you a fuckin teachuh at Magnolia High!" he announced over top of me. The others shrieked laughter, breaking off into their own conversations and slap-fights. I didn't stop them. De'von's insult made little sense, but whatever he meant, I deserved it. Deflating down into my chair, drowning in their din, I decided that for the rest of the morning I'd strain only to keep my head up and eyes open. Nothing more. Fuck struggle... At most I'd silently grade their letters to The Mayor — until on my hand's way to my book bag I realized how to redeem my discouraging insult: I stood and faced them all:

"Well, it's not Popeye's, but I just started a new restaurant job too," I admitted. "And I'm not even a waiter. I'm a busboy. 27-years-old and a busboy. Fucking 27."

Deafening apathy, except for De'von's command to, "Quit fucking cursing!"

I've every day campaigned for the kids' approval and respect by 1) talking to them exactly as I do my adult acquaintances 2) demonstrating encyclopedic knowledge of what they still consider Black People Music and 3) illustrating my own poverty. The poverty angle almost worked until recently, when I admitted to them that I'd been forced out of My Mansion, because I couldn't make rent this month. "I don't get paid until the very end of the Semester, "I bemoaned. "Then I get paid all at once. But until then, I had to move into a cheaper, one-room efficiency."

This is true, though I left out that I'm still in the only safe, clean neighborhood in NO, and that I'm still in a mansion — albeit the dingy, moldy one directly beside my gleaming white Former Mansion. The exterior of this house is gray, shit-painted by the squadrons of Squab that huddle under the window awnings, not cooing but grunting, dry-humping noises that inject my afternoon naps with sexual nightmares. I also left the Squab out of my sob story, but still my kids nodded their silent heads with... *Empathy? Respect?* From the back of the classroom a solemn, "Damn, Mr. Patrick..." *Redemption!*

Then Anthony — the only mulatto in my class, the only quiet kid (besides Cedar, who's quiet more for effect), and the only one I can't get to do *any* work *at all* (though I don't bother him about it because he's so nice and quiet) — he asked me, "How much it cost?"

"My new room?"

He nodded.

"$300."

At least four kids, including Anthony who's never raised his voice, all shouted in disbelieving unison: "A-month?!"

My nod sulked, but inside I smiled: *They finally realize that we are all the same... The White Bitch has shown them that we...*

"Damn, you a *chump*!" Anthony laughed.

"Huh?" I asked.

"That's fuckin expensive, man!"

And since then, not even my drawn-out descriptions of scraping half-eaten food off tourists plates will change their image of me as a rich old eccentric who, aside from his expensive apartment, squeezes his money so tight he's forced to ride a bike and dress in second-hand clothes.

"All white people have money," Anthony reminds me.

- 2 -

But my other reason for undertaking this restaurant night job is bourgeois as fuck; I want no part of another NO Summer, so when this school year is out-of-its misery in June, I'll use that one big School Board check to run and hide somewhere more temperate for those months: Central America. For $4 you can cross the entire country of Costa Rica by bus and see only tangled vast jungle and rocks and miles of water out the dirty windows; people are rare, as are buildings. That's why I'm living in a cell right now, to later afford that Freedom. This plan also ensures that until then, when confronted with Cedar's angry nose against mine, I can gaze far back into his tearing teenage eyes and see not anger, but the wet reflections of Caribbean waters. And while I wait for the unfaithful NO Postal System to deliver that one big check, tips from that Fine

Dining place on Canal will more than pay my rent…

I re-visited the scene of my desperate Margarita thievery last Friday: that Spanish lady who on September 13th promised she'd hire me, "if Mardi Gras isn't cancelled," wasn't around. This time a pack of bloated ex-Louisiana State football meatheads in big-and-tall suits interviewed me during lunchtime rush; the flocking tourists don't care that there's a War, no one cares. I didn't ask giant, crewcut Management if that Spanish lady was maybe fired for stealing that pile of money. I stood still and quiet as they waddled around me, sniffing for flaws and grunting, then hiring me as a Backwaiter.

Three waiters serve each table: the Headwaiter, in a white tuxedo jacket, socializes with guests and takes entree orders; the B-Waiter sprints about in the same jacket, dispensing only coffee, wine, cocktails and light conversation; we Backwaiters sport black vests, bring ice water and French bread, and jettison dirty plates to The Dish Pit, where The Radio shouts Black People Music, always. Everyone on The Floor begins as a Backwaiter, but I will also finish as one. Not because they'll fire me before I'm promoted, but because, though it's messier and pays less, Backwaiting is almost peaceful; while the Head- and B-waiters field tourists' questions, concentrate and memorize, I'm left alone with my serving tray and my thoughts, gazing out that towering Picture Window onto a panoramic view of historic Canal while my body mechanically executes My Job.

After a month spent trying to teach, The Service Industry now seems a multigon of bright-sides: in the weeks leading up to Mardi Gras, every single parade will float *right* past the restaurant's Picture Window, a front row view of my first Carnival ever! All year on my bike, beads dangling from the trees have teased me, reminding me what I missed. They gleam from everywhere, always, even in neighborhoods where there's never been a parade… I first assumed they were all from last year's Mardi Gras, until the first time I stood on my pedals and yanked a strand down to find it was actually a relic from many years past, as dull and dingy as my new mansion. But now, at this new job, I'll not only receive my own beads and my own Mardi Gras experience, I'll actually play a part in *The Making of…*!

The Service Industry also means a whole new social environment and cast of characters — the kind of characters, especially in The Dish Pit, who are more than happy to help me procure pot, so that I'm not haunted by the temptation to try and score from my students, or drink that little half-bottle of Ketamine for a buzz.

Plus, the restaurant pays more than Magnolia High; every night I earn a solid $12-per-hour (relative in NO to about $25 in NY), and Management promises our figures will double during Mardi Gras — which hasn't even come close to being cancelled; out The Picture Window there is no War, just tourism. Maybe our Downtown's lack of skyscrapers helps them forget... Or maybe The War's over by now? I haven't checked recently. Whatever it is, Management's already tensing up for the impeding celebration, Jude tells me.

- 3 -

Jude is the shape of a Q-Tip, with minimal shoulders and a long skinny head. Something mysterious bulges under his Backwaiter vest, and his teeth are like a can-opener in his always-smiling mouth. From certain angles he resembles a greyhound, sans that breed's spookiness — Jude is all good vibes. Long before Management assigned him to train me, I'd noticed Jude out-and-around The City. Of course lonely people notice everyone (and ten months here with no friends but Lani has sometimes induced tears), but everyone notices Jude. We all stare at him on Decatur, and at Dixie Tavern punk shows, and at The Coffeehouse across from My Former Mansion. And despite his odd look, he's always in the company of the prettiest girls who kiss his cheeks with Southern affection, drumming up more stares. Since moving into this loneliness, I've studied Jude's smooth social flow at The Shim-Sham Club, The Mermaid Lounge, Pal's, and feared that my own looks aren't my problem, the way I always assume.

So I'd sort of always wanted to meet Jude, hear what type of voice someone who looks like that has... And I was happy to find out he would train me; he'll serve as another strong reason for me to stay at this job; I cannot walk out on this one; I've learned my lesson on that, grown up finally, hopefully…

Anyway, Jude began by leading me behind a wine rack into The Point of Sale (POS) enclave: a small, wooden half-room, a dark cave lit by just the tiniest bare white X-mas light bulb, and the faint green glow of two computers perched atop a counter beside a war-formation of wine glasses. Jude peeled a cloth napkin off the stacks of fresh linen at his knees and began in a wet, gummy voice, "Yeah. Welcome to The Donkey Show."

"What's that mean?" I asked, worrying, "Oh man, please don't tell me the owners of this place have something to do with that Donkey Slavery ring on Jackson Square; I don't want to have to quit already."

"No, no, no," Jude assured, scrunching his face like something smelled bad, which didn't take much rearranging of his features to accomplish. "I wouldn't work here either if they were part of that. But yeah, not The Donkey Slavery, The Donkey Show."

"What's The Donkey Show?"

"It is where you work. Welcome," he laughed little snorts. His long, bony hand like a wing without feathers patted my shoulder, while his other unsheathed silver knives from a pitcher of steaming water. Polishing the knives, Jude's dress-shirt cuffs sagged back almost to his elbows, exposing forearms like hairy hotdogs.

"Seriously," I joked, watching his hands bend around the knives at unnatural angles. "Why is this The Donkey Show?"

But no. Jude veered off: "Yeah. You know, you and me are a rare breed here…"

"Don't change the subject," I laughed, my stomach tickling with suppressed celebration at finally talking-to and getting-along-with someone. I grabbed my own napkin, and spoons from the pitcher, acutely aware of my first act of labor at My New Job…

Still Jude wouldn't explain "The Donkey Show," instead continuing his new thread: "Yeah, we're a rare breed: the only straight, white dudes on The Floor, except Management." Maybe I'm a bad person, but it always feels nice to be presumed straight; at least on the outside I seem like a man…

Then, as Jude added, "Everyone else on The Floor is either gay or black," a white-jacketed B-Waiter rounded the corner into The POS, a light-skinned black guy some years younger than me, with the kind of close-cut, wavy hair my students attribute exclusively to "pretty boys." The lenses of The B-Waiter's gold-framed eyeglasses glowed green, reflecting the computerized Time Clock. He tapped its monitor and without looking up asked me, "Jude talking trash about black folks again?"

"Oh shut up," Jude frowned at him. It was the first time I'd seen him drained of positivity.

The waiter turned to me, smiling a tightly manicured goatee. I shook his hand thinking, *Another black waiter.... Man I'm glad to be out of FLA...*

"Sup bruh?" he asked, then, "Good to meet you. We gonna make That Money tonight baby, y'heard me? You can make That Money here, specially if you workin with me. You just gotta work, work hard, y'gotta roll, y'feel me?"

"That's not true," Jude repeated.

"It ain't true for you cause you ain't know how to roll, Jude," the waiter smirked away from me, while tapping my chest with his chunky gold pinky ring: "But I still always make you That Money, don't I Jude? Even though you slower than a motherfuhhuhuh..." he trailed off, playing the gentleman avoiding curses. He displayed great Comic Timing. I liked him immediately.

But Jude's lips pursed over his bulky teeth. Staring down at his silverware he sighed, "No, I mean it's not true that I'm a racist. And it's not cool that you go around telling The Black Team that I am."

"The Black Team?" I laughed.

Neither stopped to explain. "Naw, Jude, you know I'm just playing whichu, bruh," the waiter continued, then back to me: "Jude here is actually a real nice fellow, a real friendly guy. Jude like everybody. Specially them Fun Boys..."

"Now why would that offend me?" Jude frowned lower. "*You're* the bigot, not me." And as the waiter chuckled his way out of The POS, Jude muttered the phrase I've held hostage in my mouth all semester...

"Fuck you, De'von…"

"De'von?!" My spoon dropped and clanged.

"Yeah, he's a dick hole," Jude said, bringing his lumpy smile back.

"Man, that's weird; I teach at Magnolia High," I explained, to which Jude puckered his face. I continued, "And there's this kid in my class named De'von who's also a dick hole — I mean, I know that's wrong to say about a kid, especially since this kid's just confused… He'll be much calmer once he comes out of The Closet."

"Yeah. He's a Fun Boy you mean," Jude nodded.

"I guess. I've never heard that term. It's stupid sounding…"

"I didn't make it up," Jude said. "They call themselves that."

"And 'The Black Team' made their name up too?"

"No, The Fun Boys did, but the Black dudes like it."

"So then what are we?"

"'Crackers.'"

I told Jude I've always hated that label: "Do you know what it means?" I quizzed.

"Yeah. Pale? Like Saltines?"

"No. That's what everyone thinks. But it really means 'whip *cracker*,' fucking 'slave owner'."

"No."

"Yes. And idiot Floridians are proud to call themselves that. If you've lived there all your life, you're a Cracker. My parents refer to themselves as Florida Crackers."

"That's where you're from? Florida?"

"Yeah."

"Ooh. Yeah. Sorry."

- 4 -

We polished on, as Jude explained, "Yeah, it's weird how much The Black Team hates The Fun Boys. It's like they're superstitious about them. Like, De'von'll pick on me, but he's scared to even *rag* on fags…"

At that, an older white Headwaiter entered The POS: "I heard that, Jude!"

I recognized this guy too. A few times riding around The Quarter, I'd seen him in this same Monkey Suit, walking fast but calmly down Royal, chin up, not sweating, brown hair slicked back and fading into handsome gray, all pride and professionalism like a waiter in a movie about New Orleans. "I should put you over my knee, Jude!" he said now with the same lilt I hear in Little De'von's voice when Little De'von isn't roaring. The waiter then faced me, quick-changing from critical to Welcoming Committee: "I'm Michael by the way; it's nice to meet you," he said, not asking my name before turning back to Jude. *Big De'von didn't ask my name either...*

"Whatever Michael," Jude smirked. "You *love* that word."

"*Fag*? Yeah, and *they* love The N-Word," Michael cocked his eyebrow. "But I'll bet you tonight's tips that your balls are way too little-and-tiny to ever say it around them, even '*affectionately*.' Or '*ironically*.'"

"Yeah, well The N-Word's a lot heavier than Fag," Jude defended. "They're not kissing each other on the cheek when *they* say it. Plus, no offense, but I could go suck some dicks and be gay myself. Then it'd be fine for me to say Fag. But I'll never be black so..."

"Right, right," Michael mock-yawned, then turned back to me, grabbed my hand and held it. This was the first physical affection I'd received in almost a year. "We're not always like this, bickering little bitches," Michael said. "I PROMISE. Actually, we all love Jude very much...I mean, except for Management, they don't like him...and neither does The Black Team, actually, so I guess it's just us Fun Boys who put up with this little fucker. But any-old-way: welcome."

Then he released me and walked out of The POS, still without asking my name.

- 5 -

"This is the best part of the job," Jude said.

His body creaked as it bent to dredge up another large stack of cloth napkins and an empty plastic lexan from below The POS. He carried them, leading me through the empty Dining Room, past the bar's whirring Margarita machine (*I need to tell Jude that story some time...*), past glass tables where crystal dinner candles burned in wait. I wondered if it weren't bad luck to pass beneath the shiny, imposing staircase; *yeah it's huge and gold and spiral, but isn't it still just a fancy ladder?*

At the front of the restaurant Jude and I finally sat, napkins flat across our laps, each at our own table against the 20-square-foot Picture Window. A kingly view, as Jude demonstrated the folding of Dinner Fans and explained, "Yeah, each Backwaiter has to fold fifty of these at the beginning of every shift." His strange hands worked independently of his eyes, which followed the checkered skirt of a fat High School girl (not a Magnolia uniform) intently as watching a manta ray glide inside a giant aquarium.

"This is the best part of the job," Jude reiterated, "getting to sit here, relaxing at the best tables, watching girls. And women."

Then we both jerked to attention at the NO war cry exploding behind us: "Yeah ladies! *Show us your tits*!" It echoed around the tall, empty palace, followed by female laughter, and a chair sliding on tile as a White Jacketed white-girl pulled in between Jude and me. "Give me some," she demanded, stealing half the flat napkins off his lap.

Jude leaned back to smile those teeth at me over her square, white shoulder: "Yeah, and this is the only time the B-Waiters ever help us," he warbled. "When they want an excuse to sit down."

"Jude, you know why I *really* sit here," she said, with melodic sincerity: "Because I love you, Jude."

I had no real reason to feel so jealous, except that her open-mouthed laughter, awkward and pure, unveiled a gap between her front teeth the width of a penny, and while she faced Jude, my eyes took her in: her hair's sloppy bob, her one blue sock and one brown (when Management mandates we wear only black), her beautiful body...maybe. Maybe a small waist and full breasts, but you can't really tell in those bulky Monkey Suits. I do appreciate the way Uniformed Environments force me to save my uncontrollable, shallow judgments for the Christmas Party. Monkey Suits have allowed me to make strong friends out of people I've later found out were paying hundreds of dollars in sorority or fraternity memberships — something I would have determined from their Street Clothes, and fled accordingly. On The Down Side, uniforms have more than once allowed me to fall for women who couldn't have possibly ever understood me. But this girl at my new job... I could tell enough from her lack of make-up, her never-pierced ear lobes and her appreciation for Jude, to immediately convince me of her capacity for understanding...

"I'm Patrick," I told her.

"I know," she replied, pointing a fan-folded napkin at my name tag.

"Oh, right." I blushed, finally realizing why De'von and Michael hadn't asked... "I've gone so long without one," I explained, staring down at my name etched in gold. "I forgot it was there."

"It's so sad then, that you're going to remember it's there," she smiled softly.

I looked down at the mystery of her chest. Hers read: *Mizzy*.

- 6 -

Tonight, teamed with Headwaiter Michael and B-Waiter Mizzy, I was victimized by the busy restaurant, running sprinting dashing slipping sliding sweating around The Dining Room, my brain screaming to itself *WHY are there so many PEOPLE here spending so much fucking MONEY and throwing away so much goddamned FOOD and laughing so goddamned HARD over so many business deals when...isn't there a WAR on?* And whenever I'd catch Mizzy or Michael descending their earned positions to buss or re-cloth their own tables or bring customers bread and water, I'd worry that I was burdening them, and that Management would notice, deem me inadequate, and let me go before I ever found the rhythm. But then just as Costa Rica seemed to be slipping away, Jude would cross the vast Dining Room from his own section to aid, comfort and instruct me until finally, by the end of the night, I'd become a smoothly operating mechanism.

Between hurried breaths, Mizzy and I would lean against the grand, gold staircase, where I tried to make her like me by telling her, "Y'know, whenever I start a new job I remember all the pet fish I've owned, and how when you bring them home in the plastic bag you have to set the bag in the aquarium for like an hour, to align the water's temperatures, so the fish won't be shocked to death."

"And?" Mizzy giggled as if expecting hilarity, which I like. It gave me sorely-needed confidence.

"Well," I continued. "I've mistimed that procedure so many times, and I know how easy it is to accidentally kill the poor fish. So it seems to me that before they put me out here on The Floor with this bowtie and apron and nametag, I should probably just come in and sit at a table and watch y'all for a few nights. Acclimate."

She slapped my vest and gave me a big stupid laugh and I fantasized that we were acting out a society drama wherein I, the lowly, black-vested grunt, was vying for the attention of one of The White-Coats' women…

I didn't want her laughter to die, so when a Hostess led a man in too-short Bermudas, a baseball hat and flip-flops past us into The Dining Room, I whispered to Mizzy, "Sweet shorts…so much for Fine Dining."

The guy heard me and turned around. Walking backwards to his table, he smiled at us defending, "It's OK. I'm local."

When he was out of hearing range Mizzy continued, "Management lets a lot of things kill the ambiance here; cell phones going off and shit. If you have money, they don't care if you come in wearing a diaper. The only *real* dress requirement is a fat wallet."

We were then interrupted by a Food Runner setting a giant oval tray down on a stand in front of us, stacked with brown catfish filets decorated in wet pecans, whole red crawfish humping giant fried crab cakes, pink shrimp like babies' thumbs streaked with pale green sauce trimmed in fried tomatoes, and shards of other vegetables in colors I'd never before seen on food…

We dispersed the plates to our *ooooooooh-ing* customers, then back at the staircase Mizzy confessed, "That's one thing I can say about this place though, the food isn't that great — they make it sort of bland for the tourists — but it at least *looks* more artistic than my paintings."

"You paint?" I asked, then admitted, "Me too! You're My Dreamgirl."

She ignored that, continuing, "Yeah, when tourists ask me if I'll take their pictures with their cameras I always announce, 'Of course! It's the only time I get to use my Art Degree!'"

"I have an Art Degree too! And an English Degree."

"That's why you're at The Donkey Show."

"Hey! Tell me what that is, what it means..."

"What?"

"The Donkey Show."

"That's what Jude calls this place."

"I know that, but..." I tried to say through laughs so loud that Local Guy across The Dining Room pivoted around on his shorts and smiled at us. Quieter, I asked her, "But what does it *mean*?"

"Oh. Well, Jude says that in Mexico you can go to a show where a woman has sex with a donkey."

"That's horrible...I think?"

"I dunno. If I was a donkey," Mizzy giggled, "I'd rather be doing *that* than pulling fat white people around The Quarter."

My Dreamgirl. If I could just see inside that Monkey Suit I'd know for sure... "But why does he call this place The Donkey Show?" I asked.

"He's never explained it to me either. I just always figured it has something to do with making money," she shrugged, smiling her gap, "and getting fucked."

ch 6: mardi gras

A couple months into my living here, the confounding Summer lightened up and then I cried once-a-day for five days — not for the death of summer; actually, I didn't know why I was crying, and that worried me most.

Unable to make sense, I forced myself to just suck it the fuck in, remaining dry while it built and built-up behind me, over me, until finally I glimpsed The Literal Border of Sanity. That cured me, seeing The Border, a long scratch of pink chalk on blacktop, so clear that crossing it felt like a choice, though I assume if you were truly losing it, it'd come as more of a surprise, like someone running up behind and shoving you over.

Anyway, to dilute this severe melancholia, I finally pinned the blame on my FLA friends not calling to check on me, not caring anymore, while I still had no NO friends — well, Lani, but none my own age.

I knew then and still know, that what I really needed and still need, is a cat; I've had far more cats than women. I'm almost fine without women. But now having neither, I sometimes feel intensely deprived — seeing The Border may have scared me running in a positive direction, but it was my time back at The Animal Hospital that allowed me to finally calm, and quit running altogether.

But then lately, I feel myself picking up speed again…

"Adopt yourself a goddamned cat," Lani replied, sipping Complimentary Water on the leather couch at The Coffeehouse across the street. He won't buy anything from The Coffeehouse anymore, since The Coffee Corporation removed all the local artists' work from their walls, and replaced it with spooky surveillance cameras. Now the closest Lani will come to buying anything from The Coffeehouse is stealing toilet paper from their bathroom, to use back at his place. He also saved the last paper cup he ever bought from them, and kept going back in for refill after illegal refill, until finally the bottom fell out of the cup. Now he just hangs out there, sipping their Complimentary Water, claiming that The Coffee Corporation designs the cups to self-destruct like that.

"If I didn't have good reasons not to own a cat, don't you think I'd have one by now?" I snapped back at him, then gazed out the window at My Former Mansion standing across the street, shoulder-to-shoulder with my new Squab-infested one; another reason I'm picking up steam…

Lani's silent nod of agreement humbled me. Quieter, I continued, "It's just that…a few weeks before I left for Costa Rica, my last cat ate a poisonous frog. So that's it for me; I just can't deal with the death of another one. I know some cats are happy staying inside, but I always end up with the ones who sit by the door, screaming for Freedom. And I can't deny them. And then when I let them out, it's… Did you know that Indoor Cats live an average of thirteen years," I quoted from a poster at The Animal Hospital. "And Outdoor Cats live an average of three? But even despite that, I honestly believe that if they could, cats would tell us 'I'll take my chances. Let me outside.'"

"Oh shit, speaking of *felines*," Lani interrupted with a whisper, "Sweet Mother of God, she's comin in the front door!"

Yes. Her. And all the others I agitate myself staring at — The

Coffeehouse is very depressing for me lately. This one just popped up two weeks ago, her Latin body balancing on the precipice of plumpness: after birthing one child she'll expand like a life raft. Until then, she jogs incessantly around Our Block, circling and circling us, perfectly packed into a black unitard just a shade darker than her skin. The lines of her thin neck open into a wide brown jaw that barely accommodates the giant smile she offered Lani in passing…

"Hola," he hummed back. Then when she'd made it across the room to the barista, Lani's joking brow furrowed at me: "Damn son, you don't even smile back?"

"She was smiling at you. That was y'all."

"She was smiling at both of us," he fake-frowned. "Shit man, and here I was feelin bad for you, complainin that I'm you're only friend, and telling me you'd rather hang out with a cat…"

"I didn't say that. And I didn't know she was smiling at both of us."

"What difference would that make?" His jewelry rattled under his bassy chuckle: "Why wouldn't you just smile at her regardless?"

I know he's right. It's me. Which makes me feel a little better actually; at least This Lonely is my own doing, not the creation of those who don't like me. There's hope?

As we stared at her Lani's squint belied his intent to conjure the funniest, most original verbal representation of his lust; he's in a personal-best competition with himself. Some of his dirty phrasings are amazing, artful. But this time after much thoughtful silence he finally whispered to me, "I'd give that woman $100 if she'd just fart in a change-purse, and then let me keep the purse."

"That one's not so funny," I said, distracted watching her pay for something iced.

"It's not supposed to be funny; with that one, I was goin more for poetry than humor." He fell into his NO Tour Guide voice: "Akchully, it was a reference to something Whitman once wrote, bout how his own gas and body odor were life-affirmin smells."

"I never read that while getting my Literature Degree."

"Y'never read <u>Song a Myself</u>? Hope you didn't pay too much for that degree." She mixed in sugar and milk as Lani reverted back to,

"You know, that sweet, dark thing lives in your old place, two doors down from you. Just moved in."

"Lucky her. Now the busses have something better to photograph."

"So why don't you go over and knock on her door, talk to her, introduce yourself?"

"Because it's not her door, it's My Door," I joked sadly, wondering why his idea sounded so absurd. *I'm rusting up...*

Lani switched subjects again: "Well, side from all that, how is your new place?"

"I have to keep all my books under my bathroom sink."

"Damn. Yeah, I hate livin in places like that. Them kinda rooms make you feel like you lost." Watching her clean away her mess, thoroughly, Lani asked, "Y'quit your restaurant job yet?"

"Hell no. Not until summer."

"Well, if you do, don't walk out of that place. Give two weeks notice…"

"I know. I'm never walking out on a job again."

"…cause that place is real famous; family who owns it are well-connected in New Orleans and…"

"Yeah, they tell us that all the time."

"…if you fuck em over, you'll never work at another restaurant. Least not in The Quarter."

Then we held our breath. *Here she comes...* As she passed again waving I felt Lani watching me, making sure I responded in a healthy way. But by the time I could let go my breath and make myself smile, she was out the door. From the cool side of The Coffeehouse's window we watched her bounce across Esplanade.

"Well, if watching *that* display doesn't convince you to talk to her then," Lani said, still ogling, "she also told me the other day that she has a cat. So maybe you can go over and play with her pussy, and quit cryin."

In silence we watched her open the tall iron gate of My Former Mansion, shut it behind her, jog in past My Former Gazebo, past the Garden, the Fountain, the other Fountain, before she disappeared behind My Former Door.

- 2 -

Hammers pounding outside drowned the Squab' humping groans and drew me to my new window, where the dusty lace curtain hangs crooked, but the rod is too far up for me to reach and straighten. Out there to the left, over the fence, in the pristine courtyard of My Former Mansion, the shadows of three black handymen carved negative space into the white siding, which they were slapping with fresh coats of paint. Bare-kneed on the cement among them, Lani pounded nails into something, some strange, mystic, tall, wooden-dragon-tree-branch-mad-sculpture-thing... He and the men all breathed silent white clouds into NO's brand new cold.

Turning my head to the right I faced my new back yard, much more...rustic than my former: in the 8 o'clock position, a dying peach tree casts shade over two dead bicycles slumped against a sickly-leaning basketball hoop beside a gallows-like tetherball pole, its deflated yellow ball hanging like a severed head at the end of its rope. At 3 o'clock rots a clothesline, at 5 a dying lime tree, then directly beneath my window, where the arch comes full circle, rusts a large crab trap.

But redeeming all this is the nucleus of my new dilapidated Eden: a trampoline! A vast nylon radius for bouncing and giggling, much better than any new white paint, or gardens or fountains or gazebos, or extra 500-square-feet of living space... I haven't jumped on it yet though; that would be too obvious a way for me to die. I figure I'll eventually drink enough to just find myself out on it some night, head-butting slimy peaches to the ground. Until then, just seeing it out the window eases some of the anxiety born in this One Small Room, I tell myself.

But lately dampening this bright sight has been a sick Persian cat living under the trampoline's perfect circle of shade. I spotted the cat yesterday morning at the end of my long, frozen bike-ride home from Magnolia. Even from down the street I could see his eyes closed in a look of peace that worried me. Closer, I saw a string of beads around his neck > > > closer I saw a crawfish charm on the necklace > > > closer, I noticed his thinning fur > > > closer, I noticed, beneath the deteriorating Persian fluff, a skeleton skinnier than Jude's > > > closer, I tried to remember some of the health tests I learned at The Animal Hospital > > > but then closer, the sight of my hulking cruiser scared him, and he jogged drunk across the yard to hide under bushes.

    I climbed the stairs to My Room to wait until he'd disassociated me from my scary vehicle. Cats have small enough brains that five minutes later I again stood five-feet from him, watching him pant and squint peacefully under the bushes. But when I extended my hand, he jumped up again and faltered under the gate into My Former Courtyard, coming to a wobbly rest next to dishes of food and water set out beneath My Former Bedroom Window, where her drapes are every day parted slightly so that when I come home late from The Donkey Show my heart beats fast and my pedaling slows and I can't help peaking into her slit…

    That's probably why I couldn't bring myself to knock on her door and demand to know what action she was taking on behalf of her cat. Upon realizing he was hers, my altruism evaporated, shifting from concern to *Well, she'll take care of him, none of my business…*

- 3 -

    Days later, unlocking my bike and rolling off to class, I spotted the cat again, this time lolling in a pile of rotten mulch, closer now to my new front door than My Former Front Door. Twenty-feet after deciding I would not, I slammed my kick breaks to a loud-skidding stop that should have scared him away, but didn't. Over my shoulder his face read more peaceful than yesterday. *Closer to death…* But rolling backwards < < < I finally saw the cause of his problems: He was a She. *And nursing kittens!* < < < rolling back I assumed *Oh THAT's why she's listless, THAT's why my black-haired thoroughbred neighbor leaves her outside* < < < closer I noticed the kittens weren't squirming much < < < closer though, the babies looked fat and healthy enough but < < < finally, jumping off and

76

squatting for the closest look, I saw that they weren't in fact kittens, but matted dreadlocks of fur suckling the cat's heaving ribs.

"Oh no you neglectful cunt…" I mumbled, then bit my jaw shut watching My Former Door, hoping she didn't hear.

I thought to call The Animal Hospital and tell them to make room for a new tenant. My Former Boss wouldn't shy from stealing an abused cat. My first week working there an old, white woman brought in a cloud of intense pet odor and a similarly neglected Pomeranian. An hour after she dropped the dog off, My Former Boss called the stinky lady and claimed, "He's in really bad shape. We strongly suggest you have him Put Down." When the old woman declined, my boss listed all the fictional surgeries, X-rays, medicines and muscle massages the dog would need in the upcoming final month of his life. When the impending cost equaled more than the worth of the dog's love, the woman finally told us to pull the plug. My Boss then de-wormed and shaved the dog, and adopted him off to another old women who smelled like lilacs and leaked tears at the sight of him.

But then I remembered that Ketamine tucked away in my medicine cabinet, above my book collection: *My Former Boss probably never noticed one tiny missing half-bottle, but calling her could mean questions, confrontation…* Then, *Wish I could get rid of the shit, sell it; $100 would finance weeks in Costa Rica, or the removal of this skin cancer on my temple… But $100 is probably a high guess. I wonder how much it's worth… Need to ask The Dish Washers. Or my kids.* Then finally back to the cat: *I don't even have a carrier to transport her in, and even if I did, I can't bring her onto the city bus, especially with that disgusting tumor-of-fur. And she'd scratch the fuck out of my lap if I tried to bike it all the way to Kenner… Lani doesn't have a car. Jude doesn't have a car and I don't know his number anyway… Mizzy? No. Hunting her number down would be too weird, though I'm sure she'd participate in the kidnapping, like me more for it, but…* Option-less, I stared at the sick cat's red beads: *Man, making friends is fucking hard…*

This time, the cat didn't flee or even swipe at the hand reaching down from my bike to squeeze up a fistful of her loose scruff skin. When I let go, the skin slid back down onto her skeleton, meaning that she at least wasn't dehydrated — *Yeah, it could be the heavy fur-tumor weighing the skin down but...*

I needed to get to class...

My foot nudged her water dish closer to her peaceful mouth, and I rode off to teach things to other human beings.

- 4 -

The air in winter is as humid as summer, only now it's frozen water instead of warm water coating my face as I pump toward Magnolia. Like everyday on the ride to school, I tried to decide what I'd teach the kids. I wished I could just have them write rap songs again. I wish I could do that every day; that's the only time they really get into it. Actually, technically I could do that; the Chemistry teacher next door, who's also a part-time NOPD officer, neglects academics entirely, instead spending class periods asking his kids questions that might lead him to drug busts. So who'd stop me from teaching Rap 101?

But by the time I hit Lee Circle where the street cars turn around, I decided I'd have them free-write on the topic, *The Best Pet I've Ever Had*. The rest of the ride I found myself thinking about Mizzy again until...

"I ain't never had no pet, man," Cedar scoffed from inside his hood, followed by a deep, soul-singer laugh.

Anthony the Quiet lifted his head from his desk to add, "Pets is gay, bruh."

I looked to De'von for his reaction..."Don't look at me Mr. Whatevuh-yo-name-is," he commanded. "I never had no pets neither. Pets is nasty. Nasty white folks keep pets. My uncle got a Pit, but that's for protection."

"OK, OK. Then... I guess... Today we'll...write a rap song..."

Over the screams of my kids hammering out their rhymes, the sick Persian haunted me, rubbing against the inside walls of my head *prrrrrrrrrrrrrrrr...* Needing, really needing distraction, I again tried deciphering their writing, grading some old assignments — a task like untangling 15 extension chords — and in the process realized that all of their fiction and autobiography involves yelling, fighting, drugs, guns, up-to-the-minute-slang and dark sexual encounters. So I stood and announced to the class, "You know, I'm grading your stuff here, and I have to tell you: your work has everything middle-class white people love from their authors. Y'all could sell a lot of books if you just learned how to..."

They didn't hear me, wouldn't hear me.

As an inside joke with myself, I shouted, "Do any of y'all know how much Ketamine goes for?"

- 5 -

Back at home, she stood outside My Former Door, the wide jaw of her concerned face hovering five-and-a-half feet over her sick cat. Frayed white denim mouthed her thick thighs — I'd never seen her in anything besides that unitard — still a thin line of sweat worked its way down the neck of her white T-shirt. As I rolled up she pouted and volunteered, "Yes, it is mine." She didn't own the exotic accent I'd expected, but hearing her refer to her cat as "it," I assumed English to be her second language.

"What's her name?" I asked.

"It's a boy. Its name is Marty."

"What's your name?"

"Alana."

"Marty's really sick, Alana."

"Marty?" she asked.

Confused, blushing I said, "You just said his name was Marty."

"No, not Marty," she frowned. "Marty. Marty Gras."

"Oh. Well, Mardi's very sick."

"I know," she whined without parting her lips.

"If you don't take him to the vet, he's gonna die."

Another thin moan escaped her. Distracted by it, I mentioned, "You know, I just moved out of that apartment recently."

"Mine?"

"Yeah."

Her eyes lit up and she grabbed and squeezed my arm. Her nails dug in. "You have to see what I did with the bedroom!"

I took a last look at the cat as I followed my neighbor up My Former Steps...

Inside, My Former Bedroom smelled of freshly cooked, spicy food, but I couldn't see anything; my eyes remained outside in the white sun. *It always was too dark in this trampoline-less cave...* I felt discomfort stepping too far in and so limited my feet to the white rectangles of light My Former Door projected onto My Former Floor, and consciously left the door open wide to let her know we wouldn't be in there together long — whatever sense that makes.

"I painted all of that part," Alana said. I assumed she was pointing to something, but I couldn't see what. "And I took down that ugly thing that was up over there," she snickered. "You didn't put that up did you?"

"No," I answered, my shoulder-blades hugging the doorway, until suddenly in my white blindness I felt her body against mine, her breasts against my chest, her sweet-smelling sweat...

But before the blood could drain back out into the rest of my body, she had passed. Her voice outside on the sidewalk behind me bragged, "They took $100 off the rent because I did that."

"Looks great," I said, following her outside, regaining my eyes. The front of my shirt smelled of her sweat and whatever she'd just cooked on My Former Stove. Hands shaking, I thought of Mizzy again. *I don't feel this oppressed around Mizzy...* Still I managed to inform my new neighbor that I'd been a Veterinarian's Assistant, impressing her with a few physical tests on the cat before reiterating, "If you don't take him to a vet now, he's definitely going to die."

In my professional opinion, unless he has heartworms or Feline Leukemia, shaving off those giant knots and keeping him inside would bring him back to life. I only told her he might die to lend credence when My Former Boss suggested she have Mardi Gras "put down."

But though I hoped they'd confiscate her cat, I had a hard time showing it. I should have loathed Alana, but instead found myself daydreaming how once her cat was dead she'd need company, perhaps from the compassionate soul who'd helped ease *its* misery... *It* stretched its tongue toward its hindquarters to lick its one-pound fur-knot, but its mouth made it only half way down before it gave up, and lay its cheek in the mulch.

"I've been meaning to take it to the vet," Alana whimpered. "But it keeps getting out and running away."

That comment was too moronic for even the soft skin on her body to dissuade me from sternly commanding, "Alana, he's not running away now, so pick him up. Take him to the vet. Do it, or he will die."

She should have worn gloves to lift the cat up; the side he was laying on was black and wet like the underside of a rock. I locked up my bike, she took Mardi Gras into My Former Mansion. Soon we regrouped outside My Former Front Door where the carrier mewed at her feet. I gave her directions to My Former Job. When she thanked me I stepped back, hoping she wouldn't hug me. I was disappointed when she didn't try. She merely turned from me, unlocked the door of her black Chevy Celebrity, loaded the carrier onto the passenger's seat, sealed herself inside the car and started the engine. Then I remembered the Ketamine...

I knocked on her window. She rolled it down.

"Hey, don't tell them I sent you. Don't mention my name."

"I won't," she nodded, not asking why, just smiling that wide mouth. "Thanks again," she said, then drove off.

But standing there, watching the ants dance in Mardi Gras' food bowl, I realized Alana couldn't mention my name; she didn't know it; she hadn't asked...

I surveyed my sweet-smelling shirt, making sure I wasn't wearing my nametag, before deciding I couldn't possibly be neighborly with her again.

ch 7: coming true, coming true

I don't know if I'm a good person, but on paper I am at least always attendant. I never missed one class all through college, even the time Mononucleosis attacked me. So though easily won, this morning's absence from Magnolia can't be enjoyed; it stinks of rotting morals, abandoning troubled kids when once I wouldn't have abandoned even a flimsy Humanities lecture. On the other hand, when *I* was in high school, whenever *I* fell severely ill, *I* spent my Day Off (if I dared take one) hoping-to-god one of my classmates liked me enough to bring my homework to me after school. But from the first time I hesitantly passed through Magnolia's Metal Detector, there's been no way even *one* of my kids would consider even the concept Homework. They'll moan through In-Class assignments, sometimes. But they regard Creative Writing the way I do The Service Industry: *no work off The Clock, you get nothing for free.* They simply ignore my Homework assignments as they would a suggestion to switch from ballpoint to feather-and-inkwell — until finally my choice becomes: either fail all of them, even those who

83

work during class, or else give up on Homework entirely, and take what I can get from them on The Clock, in the meantime wondering, *Are they smarter than me? Braver?* They've definitely learned to control their world in ways I still haven't...

Like today I lost control and crapped-out under the weight of just the thought of them: the grunting Squab woke me at 7a/m and when I sprang up to slap the glass I saw, outside, over the chest-high gate, My Former Front Door white-as-hell. Mardi Gras' food and water dishes were gone. *He must be inside now*, I smiled, but then *Fuck, I wish I still lived there; I could definitely afford it now, and still save enough money to escape this Summer...* The Squab flew back at me eye-level, but I smacked the glass before they could land in their dry shit-blanket. Then, *I wonder what Mizzy's apartment is like...* And *I could never bring her here...* I collapsed back into my mattress and rolled onto my side, facing the small refrigerator against my pillow. Staring at its SANYO logo beneath my alarm clock, which threatened to scream awake in two hours, I dwelled on their Homework Boycott, and every Moment of High Drama they've sucked me into, and my failure to grade their last four assignments because I *can't*, technically *cannot* fucking *read* them, and when I asked Mr. Land if I should maybe throw-in some Grammar lessons, he declared, "They supposed to be learning that down the hall. You teach Creative Writing, not Grammar."

"But they can't even write *un*creatively yet," I informed him. "They need basic Grammar."

"But that ain't what they payin you to teach..." he insisted — over and again inside my head, accompanied by the erotic groans of Squab, until finally I sat up and dialed Magnolia...

My School Board contract allows me nine paid Sick Days, and though utilizing one means breaking the feeble flow of My Lesson Plan, I'll surely use all nine; aside from the guilt, this Sick Day was the easiest. Restaurants have fired me for calling in, even during times when I suffered like a Victorian T.B. victim, expectorating a liquid resembling yellow sperm. Even the most humane restaurants demand a doctor's note before you're allowed back to work, and in the face of losing a night's tips plus $50 to the doctor who'll write you a pass back into The Dining Room, most of us just submit to our Job, and dragging our 24-hour Oak-Pollen Colds out for months. But Magnolia's VP lavished upon me the kind of understanding and affection I've pined for since relocating to this lonely little cave with its cocksucking Squab…

"Yeah, hi," I coughed, "can I speak with the Principal, *(dramatic throat-clearing)* please?"

"Oh, this is the *Vice* Principal, baby." Then, "Aw you OK? Baby, you sound *terrible*."

Black people here call everyone 'baby,' even man-to-man, with an extra, invisible 'e' after the first 'b' swooping the entire word upward before setting it down in an asphyxiated 'y': *Byaybuh*. It's pleasant but (I've finally gathered) as meaningless as *dude*. But since I'm not used to it, when Magnolia girls say, "I'm sorry, I wasn't listenin Mista Patrick, could you tell me again, *byaybuh*?" I smile, repeating myself for them and justifiably or not, feel appreciated or at least enjoyed. But this pretty colloquialism alone doesn't harness the healing power to arrest the rot of my morals…

"Yeah, I am terrible," I admitted to the VP, coughing again to cover the sound of my feet hitting the floor; I wanted her to envision me lying down, but I *have* to pace when talking on the phone. The length of my apartment — three silent steps one way, three back — I coughed, "I have a shitty cold," because using swear-words with superiors denotes that you are truly *not yourself today*. I continued, "Yes ma'am, sorry. Can I please *(hack hack)* — dammit, I'm sorry…"

"It's OK, baby."

"Thank you *(cough)*. Can I speak with The Principal, please?"

"Now you know we don't have a Principal right now, sugar."

I'd forgotten, because no one's ever explained to me what happened to the last Principal. On separate occasions, both Mr. Land and that Cop/Teacher in the classroom next to mine have both put me off the subject, as did the Vice Principal when I asked, "What happened to him?"

"Him was a Her, baby," she corrected, then eluded, "And you sound bad. So don't worry, baby, we got you covered."

So sweet... I didn't remember having ever even met this woman who treated me so son-like that I considered just biting the rag and riding across town... Walking into my bathroom/Library and examining my well-rested face in the mirror I admitted, "Actually, I feel almost OK now that I'm awake and up and around. I think I can make it in if..."

"Naw baby, if you already got any kind of a headache you don't need to be around these kids, getting you some more a one. We got Substitutes," she said, and I cringed in the mirror, in dedication to, or memoriam of, whoever would be lucky enough to take on my class today.

As I walked out of my bathroom the VP asked, "You got someone to take care of you, baby? A girlfriend or someone?"

"No ma'am," I answered, lying back down beside my refrigerator.

"That's too bad, sweetie," she said. "Feel better, promise?" And I swear she made kissing noises hanging up.

- 2 -

But then I pissed on my Morning Off, wondering what fate befell my class, and their *Poor, poor Substitute Teacher who's probably more experienced than me but still...* As penance, I sentenced myself to bite down for at least two hard hours and at least *try* and grade at least *some* of their papers, whimper along to their cries into the darkness... But not while trapped in my room with those fucking Squab. And The Coffeehouse across the street blasts Brass Band CDs so loud that the Med Students' all wear orange earplugs. So since I have no money for earplugs, I pressed my palms against the same window I slap to scare away the Sex Dove; the glass was warm, so I decided I'd go outside, grade papers next door under My Former Mansion's Gazebo, relive a little of that glory, *Fuck it, let them kick me off the property — I can't take the fucking birds...*

Downstairs and outside and over the fence, Lani and his wife, Madeline, sat in two of The Gazebo's skeletal, iron chairs. I don't see

Madeline much. She's nice and sweet, not gruff and bawdy like her husband. Other than continuous mutual smiles, they share very little in common. She's twenty-five years younger than him, meaning 40, Madeline wears clean clothes, a neat, short haircut, and holds a lucrative position under a Lawyer, who bequeathed her $1000 and a new digital camera for Christmas… "Still she's always wantin to bicker about money though," Lani complains when we're alone.

But they seemed to be getting on well under The Gazebo, both silent, her smiling, him not, his eyes closed as he dealt her *tuh-ROH* cards into piles — they opened when I joked to his wife, "Is he telling you lies about yourself?"

She smiled. They both have a sense of humor about his profession. She'd have to… "Hey, don't laugh, they may actually *be* lies," Lani admitted, interrupting Madeline's oncoming reply. Her silent eyes aimed at me, saying *I love him, but can you imagine, Patrick, what I put up with?* as Lani continued, "I don't know if I really trust this deck right here; this is a replacement deck; I lost The Family Deck a few months back, the one I've used since we got married, the *only* one I've ever used to read for my daughters…"

"I'm sorry," I offered.

"Nuh-uh. Listen," his tone flipped confident. "It ain't no big deal; they'll come back to me."

"Right they will, Lani," Madeline managed to wedge in, smiling wryly.

"They will goddammit," Lani huffed. I'd never heard him huff before. "You of all people, Madeline, know I ain't never lost a deck in my life. I lost two goddamned decks, and both of em came back to me. So why you wanna contradict me every single time, Madeline?"

He was serious, but as always a little joking. Her smile shared that ambiguity: "All right, Lani, calm down."

"No, really Madeline, I want to know why you have to contradict me every goddamned time…"

Instead she asked me, "Is that your laptop?" pointing to my backpack on my shoulder. "It's a beautiful day to sit out here and write."

I admitted it was full of the kids' folders, and a red pen.

"Oh shit man that's right, you ain't come over yet and give us the update on your kids," Lani's body straightened. "They as bad or better than the cats?"

"Much worse. But really, I don't even want to talk about them; I'm about to try and grade their papers, which is about the same as me saying *I'm about to try and filet this skeleton*."

"I couldn't do what you're doing, Patrick" Madeline nodded.

"I can't either," I said.

"Well hey man, let's see some of their writin," Lani blinked both eyes.

I unzipped my bag. "No, Lani..." Madeline interrupted. I didn't understand why. I dumped the folders out onto the iron table. A breeze opened one's white pages — breezes never blow through here, yet it wasn't cold out either: another rare day. The blown-open folder was the fattest, meaning it belonged to, I assumed, one of my more conscientious students. I wanted a positive if not accurate representative to show Lani, and so picked the fat folder up and was correct: *Property of 14th Ward She-La*, the cover read. Classwork doesn't thrill She-La, she's taken many Sick Days, and when she does show, she often "ain't feeling [me]." But if she comes, she does try, she remains civil, and above all her handwriting is *perfect*. I'd almost describe her as 'adult-seeming,' if it weren't for the 'adults' around Magnolia — like that Teacher Lady at The Teacher's Meeting Monday morning, who shouted at the VP, "That's some *bullshit* I gotta keep a child in my classroom if they screamin in my muthafuckin face?" Many nodded. Me too, because the second time Cedar ever calmly threatened me I sent him to The VP's Office, not caring where he really went, until Mr. Land brought him back to me *just* as I'd gained order: my kids exploded as Land explained that I'd have to fill out paperwork first, then *escort* Cedar to The Office, personally. While following this Procedure, the bell rang and I returned from The Office to an empty classroom, and a tiring ambivalence — so I would have empathized with the Teacher Lady at The Meeting, were it not for her delivery: "Why I gotta take all *my* class time to write one little muthafucka up? I mean I'm standin *right there* in Land face, tellin the man that boy threatened me, so why Land can't just take the little muthafucka out my face? Shit..." When the VP expressed dissent, the Teacher Lady finally concluded, "Fuck this bullshit!" stomping out slamming the Library door. All this to say that She-La is tall and slim and calm, but maybe not 'adult-seeming'.

Lani chuckled and shook his head when I relayed this story of the screaming Teacher Lady. Madeline shook her head negative. I thought to search She-La's fat notebook for her highest quality piece, but the title printed neatly on the open page transfixed me: Quaracter story. I remembered it, one of the only assignments I managed to grade, because of her handwriting. At the time I'd been trying to teach them *characterization*, and when they swore they couldn't dream up settings for their characters (there's always a reason why "I can't"), I assigned them The French Quarter, and understood why they groaned but... Lani got a good laugh out of She-La's linguistic mash-up: *characterization* + French *Quarter* = Quaracter story.

"Now Lani, didn't Patrick just say he didn't want to talk about his job?" Madeline frowned. "And you shouldn't be laughing at these poor kids"

"Oh Jesus, Madeline, I'm not. I'm *appreciating* them. I really think that's ingenious: Quaracter," he chuckled. Then silence, too much of it. So I began reading She-La's story aloud:

One night I when in the french Quarter with my Mom, my Dad-Dad and my sister, when we first walk in the french Quarter we got us some beer for us to drink.

I stopped reading and pointed out to Lani where I'd written in She-La's margin:

You were drinking beer? Is that realistic? How did you get beer? And remember: your sister is your character. So CHARACTERIZE your sister.

89

She-La's second draft included only,

My sister old so she got us beer. She is very black.

Lani laughed much louder at that one, and unable to help myself I laughed along… "You guys are awful," Madeline said, gathering up the unread cards Lani had just laid out. I heard her sighing "Oh god" and "Lani" at intervals as I continued She-La's story:

After we got the beer we walk for towards to white. they was put up their cloths for prades, we walk pass them and saw some boy dance, some men acting for money. The french Quarter is like a long long long long long Hall with only night light, that's only at night time, with a lot of people, mosely white. The french is a place where you can get mist up. There is a lot of bar, store and restante. The french Quarter can be funer with out a lot of white people.

Lani howled. I did too. I should have stopped, but Lani and I cocked back, ready for bigger laughs as I continued:

The music in the french Quarter is sad. I don't like the music there. They need to get more music for us blacks. I don't like the music there.

There was no laugh in that for us, and Madeline stood up, "Well I just think it's tragic. Not funny at all."

"Aw hell, that ain't the reason we were laughing Madeline. We're not making *fun*…"

I hate the sound of bickering, any suggestion of it. So did Madeline, obviously; she didn't say goodbye. Lani silently watched her pass around the mansion's corner as I continued flipping through She-La's notebook, landing on another essay I'd forced them to write on the vague theme, *OK Then, What Would You Do Then, If YOU Were The Goddamned Teacher?* She-La had written:

> Teaching is hardest. I can see why it would make a man curse words. Our last teacher Miss king said she had to was quit cause if she can't do a good job teaching then she would rather not be teach us.

Words from beyond the grave, addressed directly at me...
Staring at Madeline's empty chair, Lani finally shot our silence through with a small fake laugh: "She'll come back to me, too," he nodded. "I ain't never lost one of *those* yet neither..."
I closed She-La's folder and stuffed them all back into my bag.

- 3 -

Every day before Dinner Shift, The Donkey Show nourishes us with Help Meal, usually a fried version of whatever the customers aren't ordering, whatever's almost spoiled. Today: fried alligator and, inexplicably, corn dogs. I won't eat alligator. I haven't molested and sucked crawfish yet either, and not just because I have no friends... I know that means I'm not fit to brag 'I live here,' but...
But I *have* eaten corndogs before, so my plate of two led me out of The Kitchen to a long row of marble tables pushed together up the center of The Dining Room all the way to The Picture Window. Help Meal is automatically deducted from our pay, though most employees don't take advantage of the food, or let it take advantage of them. Today only Mizzy and Jude ate off the long, naked table, their chairs closer to each other than I'd have liked as they rammed orange meat in and laughed, impersonating the amphibian's once-chomping jaws — *seems like it'd be hard for them to swallow, laughing so hard, in the tight grip of bowties...*
But when I joined their table, their laughter ceased. His odd

head turned away from my plate. She gawked at it, disbelieving: "You chose corndogs?"

"I don't want to eat an alligator."

"It's not *an* alligator," she laughed. "It's *all*igator." Then, "I'll bet that means you don't suck the yellow stuff out of crawfish heads?"

"No." I didn't elaborate. *I'll eat the damn things the next chance I get...*

"You're *obviously* not from here then," she scoffed

"Yeah. He's from Florida," Jude ratted.

"Oh, that's understandable then," she softened. "You have Alligator Issues." Then pointing to my plate: "That explains why you'd pick...*those*."

"Yeah. Those are left over from Mardi Gras," Jude gurgled. "Last year's...if you're lucky."

You can tell Jude's from here, that NO's shaped him, or misshapen him — whichever it is, it's a new shape. You can't tell anything looking at Mizzy though, so I asked her, "You're a native?"

"No. But I moved here from D.C...when? Oh geez. A *whiiiiiile* ago."

"Two years isn't a while," Jude gulped.

"No, but in those years I've lived several lifetimes," she sighed, mostly joking. "But seriously, you really can do that here, live many lives over a short time," as she chewed her orange meat: "Or else you can just eat corndogs."

"Corndogs or alligator, who cares?" I asked Jude. "It's all Fried Shit. You'd think they'd take better care of The Rare Breed, right? Feed us better, maybe a special diet to keep our bones strong and our hair healthy?"

"Yeah. Where is our maintenance?" Jude asked.

Mizzy, irritated: "Y'know Jude you're always bragging about being the only non-gay, non-black guy here but ..."

"I'm not bragging..." he defended, no smile for a second.

"...but *he's* not gay or black either," she continued, motioning toward The Kitchen, and another Backwaiter carrying out another plate of corndogs. He is African-American, but his skin is Spanish roofing tile. He took even, mid-tempo steps like a 30-year-old toward us. I discerned '*Red*' pinned to his vest.

As he passed behind me I asked, "What's up, Red?"

"Chillin.'" He continued on, and on, and on, his steps sounding off the cathedral's dome until he sat finally, against The Window.

I shouted down, "People call me Red sometimes too! Cause of my hair!"

"Hey that's right," Mizzy tapped my arm with her greasy fork. "You're part of an even *smaller* minority."

Man, she does understand...

"True," Red concurred, his deep voice carrying clear, from so far away I couldn't identify the sauce he dipped his corndog in.

My own voice squeaked, "At the high school where I teach, every kid with your color skin is nicknamed *Red*. You yell 'Hey Red!' in the hallway and about a tenth of the kids'll turn around."

"Damn. You a teacher, bruh?" he stopped feeding himself and before I could confirm or deny he intoned, "Teachers, bruh, are down from God."

Nodding agreement felt wrong, so I did not respond — until Mizzy aimed her attention at me: "You teach *here*? Wow. Brave. What do you teach?" She'd remained pothead mellow until that Moment when her interest in me bloomed startling. Beyond her, Jude smirked at me like *Do it man, do it,* so...

"Uh, I teach Sit Down, as well as Be Quiet and advanced Shut Up. Today actually, we concentrated on Stop Swinging That Mouse Around By Its Cord."

The orange specs of alligator she laughed-up were my reward. Behind her, Jude's knotty teeth assured me. When she was finally able: "No, really," Mizzy hiccupped, "What do you teach?"

"I *try* to teach Creative Writing. At Magnolia High..."

"Get the fuck man!" Red's voice uncorked down the table and flew out, booming against the vast glass. "*I* went to Magnolia too, son! Me and De'von both. Mizzy talkin truth, bruh: you a special person to be teachin at Magnolia. That's The Worst School in the City, bruh. Them kids a *coupla* handfuls, yeah."

I pushed "Jesus," through my teeth, nodding.

Touching my starched cuff with her bare hand now, Mizzy

93

cooed, "Anyone who even *tries* to teach in This City is worthy of admiration. So many problems here, and you're one of The Few actually doing something good at the root of the problem." Her fingers on my shoulder now: "You're doing more for this city than most people who live here — even if you won't eat alligator."

Jude and Red nodded again. Her hand went back to her fork. I said nothing. *I am a fraud.*

- 4 -

We punched in before scraping our Help Meals into The Dish Pit — where for some reason the crew doesn't laugh with me anymore, and when I ask them about pot now they don't answer... But outside The Dish Pit, Mizzy swung her backpack around front, unzipped it, removed a big camera and said to me, "Hey, check this out, Professor; I wanted to show you this Project I'm working on."

Professor?

Camera around her neck, she slid an eight-by-ten photo out of her bag and handed it to me. It was of a fried chicken wing, shiny with grease and intense orange BBQ sauce, photographed ultra-close up enough to exclude any background. A bite taken from the wing created a massive crater of meat, pink like an old man's skin around a cloud-gray bone lined with dull-purple veins.

"This is fucked up," I said. "It's good though. Dark, funny. Catchy too; people would buy it." I gushed, honestly, "Damn man, you know, when someone tells me they're an artist, I never assume they'll actually turn out to be A Good One."

"True dat," she mellowed. "Like, *I* don't just assume that *you're* a good artist..."

"Then why assume I'm a good teacher?" I asked, by way of confession.

"Well, I can tell *that* just from interacting with you," she defended me against me, hissing the photo back into her bag, then adjusting her lens and leaning in close on the accumulated Help Meal food-scraps dripping in The Dish Pit. Clicking she explained, "I took that *(click)* chicken picture at home and I thought it turned out good, so *(click – click)* one night at work I got this idea *(click-click-click)*..." Changing angles on the little slop-pile she enthused, "The leftovers here are so amazing! So much more amazing than at home: I mean, chewed-up alligator and corndogs? *(click - click)* So I'm doing Another Series that same way, *(click)* close up, with really heavy *(click – click – click)* color saturation *(click – click – click)*. I'll come back later tonight and take more when we're busy, when The Ware Washers are really backed up and *(click)* there's like fuckin *(click - click - click)* white-chocolate bread-pudding and chewed up steaks and softshell crabs and flounder skeletons in like, a pool of milk and wine *(click – click - click)*... Around 9:30 is when the landscape's at its richest." Then with one last click, she let her camera fall against the mystery of her chest and declared, "I think I'm fuckin *on* to something."

"You definitely are. Definitely. Do it."

She unzipped her bag and I awkwardly lingered in The Dish Pit for minutes as she packed up her gear. *Should I be waiting?* Until finally she turned back to me and in an *I-Expected-You-to-Still-Be-Here* tone sang, "See, you under*stand* things; I'm sure you're a fine teacher." And before I could object, she'd lifted her leg up onto the metal bread counter, giving her leverage to stretch upward like a tree branch and snatch the Dry Erase Marker from the board of Daily Specials. "There's also *this* art Project I have going," she grunted, stretching, wiping away The Specials with her fist.

Then, next to Soup-of-the-Day she re-wrote: `Cream of Deer`
Next to Crepe-of-the-Day: `Manatee`
Next to Sorbet-of-the-Day: `Menthol`

My Dream Girl: beautiful, conceptual, fucking happy. Most people who go out of their way to induce laughter seem so desperate but... She climbed down from the bread counter giggling, "Most times the waiters don't even question it; so much weird meat comes out of this kitchen. A few weeks ago I overheard Michael telling one of his tables, 'Yes, I believe it's made with Deer Stock...'"

Which caused me to remember, "Oh and by the way, I didn't get a chance to defend why I don't eat alligator..." She sighed. I explained, "A few years ago I decided I wasn't going to ever again try any new drugs or new meats. I still do a lot of what I've already done — Weed. Shrooms. Cow. But I've decided I don't need any new drugs or meats in my life."

"That's stupid," she said, and I followed her out of The Kitchen onto The Floor.

"What's stupid?"

"Just, I dunno, deciding what you're going to do like that, what you're going to experience. It's just wrong, in principal, I think." Leading me through The Dining Room toward The Picture Window, she lazily lectured, "I mean, especially the drug thing; drugs are good, man. It's not the poison, it's the dose."

We sat at the best seats and watched Canal in silence together, until finally she added, "Though I dunno. I guess I can understand why you wouldn't want to eat new animals, mammals at least; I don't like the idea of veal. When customers ask me, 'How's the veal today?' I always tell them, 'oh, *very* innocent'."

My Dream Girl…

- 5 -

Later, a song I temporarily love played on The Dish Pit's radio for the fifth time that night: a gaudy electronic R&B tune with a mandatory rap bridge. I don't know how I got this way or where my good taste went, but I hid in The Dish Pit singing along in my clearest falsetto.

On the second chorus, Mizzy ran in behind me, her tone-deaf singing broken by hiccups of laughter. She fucking killed that bridge though, the rap, every word perfect.

Then, at the very last chorus, De'von stepped between us, wrapping his arms around Mizzy and me so that we were a trio, *up in* The Dish Pit, singing like a happy ending from a play.

The song ended.

"Damn, Patrick, you sound good, *dude*," De'von nodded tapping his ring to my vest, one eyebrow lifted outside his gold frames. I hadn't heard that word *dude* since FLA, and even there, black guys never say it... De'von's *dude* wore an upsweeping 'y' before its 'u', as in, "Kick that again for me, *d(y)ude*. Gimmee another verse!"

I did as he said, singing again sans The Radio's accompaniment, just as loud and girly and clear, until his smile uncovered symmetrical gold caps on his canines. The Kitchen Crew grimaced at my voice. The Ware-Washers shushed me. Mizzy laughed nervously as De'von insisted, "Go Patrick! Go man! Hell yeah, *d(y)ude*." And when I finished he complimented, "Man Pat, that was *great*! You should go out on Jackson Square with that act."

"Me and you, dude," came out in my excitement. I'd been cured of *dude* for almost a year but... "Let's me and you go down to The Square after we get off work," I beamed, "and sing Prince songs for money. I even have an original song too."

"You do?" he asked, suddenly serious. "Well, *kick* that shit then!"

I heard Mizzy mutter, "De'von, c'mon" the way Madeline had said, "Lani, don't."

Still I sang for him, "I - can't - find - my -way - arooooound."

De'von snorted laughter because, I figured, he didn't *realize* a white guy could *sound* like that... "Yeah! Yeah!" he laughed, backing out of The Dish Pit, smiling gold fangs, "That is *it* right there, y'heard!" wiping his jacket cuff at tears behind his frames.

When he was gone Mizzy asked me, "Do you not realize he's making fun of you?"

"He wasn't," I insisted, believing it; I like De'von. Even after working under him all night. He was a little...*aggressive* with me, but in a humorous way I couldn't help but appreciate.; he's just a kid, so I forgive his roughness the way I try to with the Magnolia kids. That's just how kids interact, men too, actually: competitiveness with that edge of antagonism, like when Cedar punched Little De'von in the chest Monday morning. After that they still laughed together, once he caught his breath...

Or like tonight, we weren't very busy and I handled my business, but whenever Big De'von wasn't polishing his ring, talking shit or hitting on Mizzy, he was running up behind me barking, "Say bruh, light a fire! Let's go! We gotta roll if we wanna make That Money, baby!" — just to see me rattle. During our only real rush of the night,

I was carrying a shuddering armful of dirty dishes to The Kitchen when suddenly I heard him behind me struggling with his own rattling tower of plates: "Holy Shit, Pat! Coming true! Coming true, *d(y)ude*!" My load threatening to concede to gravity, I ran faster and clumsier to The Dish Pit, clearing an emergency path for him.

But when I finally set mine down, let out my hard-held breath and turned, he chilled there, smiling his Golds, one hand on his hip, the other calmly jostling a stack of exactly two coffee saucers.

Now what kind of person would I be if I couldn't laugh at that?

- 6 -

Outside The Donkey Show, the smell of a burning car engine passed across my face. And because I was in motion on the road, participating in traffic, my nose instinctively told me that the smell was mine, and that *my* car was messed up. But in that same second that my wallet began to ache, I remembered reality, felt the cold humidity on my skin and a relief all-over; *My thick, black Beach Cruiser is Freedom!*

So the beginning of work tonight was landmark when Jude admitted he's also *bike-ridden*. Realizing our shared state, we shook hands again and he pointed out The Picture Window at both of our bikes chained to the same skinny sidewalk-tree. Jude's resembles a woman: purple frame, wire basket bulging like hips on either side of the back tire, its gooseneck choked in purple and white Mardi Gras necklaces. Together, our bikes look like interracial boyfriend and girlfriend...

But after marveling at them for while — keeping my other eye over my shoulder for De'von's incoming Comic Timing — Jude disappointed me with, "Yeah. But I used to own this rad, big, dirty Camaro with BIG tires, and I loved that *so much* more than my bike." He ceased radiating to relate the sad story of the night he and his friends stayed out drinking and playing a game, the rules of which were: punch the other guy, hard. After being evicted from one Mid City bar, they followed each other Uptown in separate cars. It was late, no one else on the road, so at a red light on illuminated

Canal Street almost directly in front of The Donkey Show, Jude's friend stepped out of his car, walked to The Camaro's window and slugged Jude in the head. Gulping laughter I'm sure, Jude leapt from his idling car to wrestle on The Neutral Ground's trolley tracks, their puppy-rolling pausing only for the screeching of tires, and the ass of Jude's Camaro fading down Canal.

But he was back to smiling by the end of tonight, riding home beside me through The Quarter, both of us one-handed carrying after-work cups of beer. Human Traffic bled from the sidewalks onto the streets: obvious Yankees dressed in khaki shorts and polo shirts in icy December, drinking frozen daiquiris. In order to *really* talk about work, music, girls and women, Jude and I *needed* to ride side-by-side, taking-up the width of one car. But all the damned tourists, more than I'd ever seen, eventually forced Jude's bike in front of mine. *News of The War must not have made it up north...* Many of their swimming eyes followed after Jude, staring at him so hard they'd bump into each other, spilling drinks, laughing, "D'you see that kid?" "What's *wrong* with him?" "Those types just *flock* here to The French Quarter!"

I wanted to stop and make that person explain to me what *type* he is... Instead I kept following. And to Jude's credit, anytime he caught someone squinting, trying to figure him out, he raised his cup to them and cheered, "Hey!"

"I just don't understand how you can be so fucking *nice* to these people," I yelled ahead, through the humans. "I can't stand this..."

"Yeah. I don't mind them actually," he yodeled back. "I've lived with them all my life." Before I could ask him why that hasn't had the opposite effect, he added, "Plus, I'm just in a fucking good mood! Mardi Gras's coming!" A stumbling group outside Bubba-Gump Shrimp Factory heard Jude sing Those Magic Words and all screamed at him. When Jude bawled back "Hey!" raising his cup, a little of his beer caught wind and flew back onto my cheek — warmer than the air, the droplets trickled toward my smile as I remembered one night last summer, before I knew Jude, I'd seen him running down this same street, leading a laughing pack of skinny guys in costumes, despite any sanctioned occasion. At the time I hadn't been able to decipher Jude's getup — he looked like a sock puppet with a twig stuck up him instead of a fist — but I do remember wishing that I was with him and his friends, as happy as they looked. So this after-work bike-ride was not lost on me…

Then beer drips snuck far enough down where I could lick them off, and Jude continued, "Yeah. Plus, only one week left for me at The Donkey Show!"

"Huh? No!"

Then Stop — we stamped our emergency brakes on behalf of a man and woman standing in the middle of the road, staring up at nothing in the sky. Their combination is a French Quarter Staple: the thick-necked old man wearing a tight, *tight* T-shirt, and his young blonde girlfriend in a dress of equal tightness: another "Business Trip" the woman wouldn't have attended if he hadn't offered to pay for everything. I always wonder what these couples do once they get back to their lives Up North… For now their 3-for-$10 French Market sunglasses loafed atop their heads, and each held two shopping bags as they stared up at the empty sky, not noticing the accident we'd just spared them. And though half of Jude's beer slopped out in our harrowing stop, *he* apologized to *them* before rolling on.

"See, now how the fuck can you apologize? That was their fault. I've almost died like that so many times… They're supposed to use the fucking crosswalks."

"Yeah," he shrugged.

At Jackson Square I slowed us down, peeking around for Lani: "You have to meet this guy; he's amazing, too." 'Too' accidentally slipped out… The nasty Mississippi wafted in, hitting the donkeys broadside and pushing up a cloud of Animal Smell. No Lani though, only tourists, a few Service Industry people just clocked-out, and fucking donkeys — it's the steel rods in their mouths that bother me the most really; I always catch them working up mouthfuls of foam trying to spit those fucking rods out. "Me and this guy Lani are going to liberate them someday!" I confided in Jude.

"Yeah? Good."

"Actually we just *talk* about it a lot," I admitted, rolling past the asses chewing their rods. "I don't think I'll ever do it really. Not with him at least."

"Yeah."

"Hey!" I lit up, "Since you hate this shit too, maybe *you* could help me carry out The Liberation?"

"Yeah."

"You'd actually do it?"

"Yeah."

But before we could begin plotting, the air-raid sirens exploded. *They're on to us!* No. Merely three white men in tight shirts bellowing, "*Wooooooooooooooo!*" into our passing ears. This same thing happens to me too many times in The Quarter: The International Party Yell attacking me, meant to spill me off my bike, fraternity heroes having so much fun they just want to *fucking KILL SOMEBODY!!!!!!!! WOOOOOOOOO!*

20-feet past these meatheads, we stopped to eye them crossing the street toward Du Monde. They returned the eye. One yelled over the slow-passing cars and carriages in a voice obviously lower than his natural one, "Hey! Give me that bike, freak!" Another agreed, "Yeah, motherfucker." Then all three of them laughed, red-faced and drooly, their sound exciting them, bringing more laughter and confidence. "You guys want to fight for them bikes," one cackled, then they all cackled, working themselves up until finally they switched trajectories, coming back at us. Or rather, back at Jude; they were interested only in him, not me at all, and I suffered an ambivalent jealousy. *To MOVE people like that...*

Jude balanced on his pedals, hovering still like an angelfish, waiting until The Tight Shirts were close enough to hear him make this perfect announcement:

"Man Patrick, the homosexuals in this town sure are *aggressive*!"

Our beers dropped. They had to. Wordless like stuntplanes, we turned and flew through Jackson Square, the sound of their shoes slapping the slick brick behind us. I followed Jude between tarot card tables and banjo pickers, past that artist who dissed me in September, and that clown who sells LSD... Tourists applauded our

101

chase. Feral cats scattered. We pumped harder. On the street, blocks away the applause kept on, letting us know the meatheads were still back there. Finally Jude laughed out, "Take a right! A right! They won't follow!"

They did follow, only for a bit though; their clomping slowed, slower, slower, until it sounded exactly like hooves on black-top. Then finally: "Fuck you faggots!" And we turned to watch their backs fade back into the crowd.

I assumed the Tight Shirts had lost steam due to Circulation Issues, but then I looked up to find we'd landed at the dark, gay end of Bourbon. "Yeah. They won't come down here," Jude panted, leaning over his handlebars, looking like he might die — more so than usual. I often wonder if it's not some disease that makes him look like that, and if it's not impending death that has him so ballsy, so ready, so *happy to be here*...

Jude nodded breathless greetings to the sweating men in the doorways of the Nightclubs on all four corners. Those wearing shirts wore tight ones, same as the meatheads back there... They all have the same tight physiques too. Michael at work told me gay men build their muscles so they can be on top — they earn their positions. I assume Michael would be on the bottom, since he's my size... Two beefcakes kissing outside congratulated our escape.

"Thanks, man," I flipped. Jude laughed at my fake, deep voice. Both winded, we hopped off our bikes, and walking toward Esplanade I resumed, "So what the fuck? You're quitting?"

"I don't want to work during Mardi Gras!" He smiled a smile fueled by a higher octane than simple *impending unemployment*: "I want to have fun!"

"I thought you've lived here all you life. Aren't you sick of Mardi Gras yet? Don't fucking quit. If you work through Mardi Gras you'll make enough money to take all summer off."

"Yeah. Sorry." He added, still smiling, "Mizzy's quitting too." My bike stopped. Against its will I pushed it onward... "Yeah. You know Mizzy was a biker too, until a month ago," Jude continued. "We used to ride home together after work. But then she bought that giant old truck. When she parallel parks, it moans like a whale."

My first thought: *I'll quit too.* My second: *I can't. I must press on, earn my Freedom…*

Besides, my quitting having *anything* to do with her would be ridiculous — she shot me down tonight: after peaking in Management's Big Red Scheduling Log to find out when she'd be off, I'd crossed The Floor and asked her, "Want to hang out some time? Outside of work…perhaps *Tuesday* night?"

"In what context?" she'd asked, surveying her seven tables so she wouldn't have to look at me, when usually she holds my eyes. I should have stopped there. Instead I joked, "Artists are always so concerned with context…"

"I can't speak for the rest of them," she answered, straight-faced. "But it does concern me." Then she walked off to handle her business.

I thought to tell Jude this walking our bikes in the dark, but didn't want to hear it out loud. So instead I asked him, "Does she have a boyfriend or something?"

"Yeah. She doesn't," he answered. "She hasn't had one since I've known her, actually. Almost a year."

"That's amazing."

"Yeah."

"Most pretty girls *always* have boyfriends no matter what," I pointed out. "Even when they don't want one, they can't seem to *not* have one."

"Yeah."

"I wish she hadn't bought that truck."

"Yeah."

"Why's she quitting?"

"Yeah. I don't know. Just sick of it."

"Damn. This sucks. I'm gonna be alone at work."

"Yeah."

"Man, you're so fucking affirmative."

"My parents listened to a lot of gospel music when I was little."

"Call and response…"

"Yeah."

We shook hands again then rode off in separate directions.

ch 8: white bitch

My cruiser beats any NO bus to anywhere by at least 15-minutes, so biking to Magnolia mornings means I get to sleep in. But today, January's air feels like God's hot breath, and pumping my legs would drown my shirt, so this morning I rose early to utilize air-conditioned Public Transportation.

After showering, I dressed in nicer-than-normal clothes, since these wouldn't be ruined with sweat. I also hoped they might command more classroom respect... Then I plucked a book from the cabinet under my sink and moseyed across Esplanade to buy a chicory coffee and wait for the bus. The coffee in my mouth burned the same temperature as the sun on my skin, reminding me that I'd forgotten to apply sunscreen. The little cancer on my temple throbbed pink with lust for the rays. The last time the FLA doctor froze it off he warned, "If it comes back again we'll have to *cut* it out." Without Health Insurance, Surgery will cost the equivalent of one month's upper-middle-class Costa Rican living. This cancer threatens to eat my vacation. But there wasn't time to run back to My Room for SPF 55, so I held my hand over the pink spot until the bus arrived.

Before I'd finished even a chapter of my book, the Esplanade bus had me at the end-of-the-line in the Central Business District. The tourists all still sleeping off last night's Bourbon Street in their hotel beds, I walked beside only businessmen and women, across The Neutral Ground, down to where the mossy St. Charles streetcar would take me the rest of the way Uptown. The streetcar is another example of NO suffering for its quaintness; two miles on the car from Canal to Magnolia High can burn up three chapters of most books. The upside is you'll never wait more than ten minutes for one to show up — while the fucking bus, who knows? That's why after waiting twenty minutes this morning, I knew the streetcar must be dead again…

Onward toward Magazine — where the bus rolls Uptown quicker, but stops farther away from the actual school — fresh morning-air battled The Quarter's hot beer and vomit smell. Work-mornings, when everyone downtown is heading slowly toward somewhere they'd rather not be going, all Canal is gray: the buildings, the sidewalks, the Ignatius J. Reiley statue that isn't nearly fat enough, the gray sky, gray moods, and all of it reflected and duplicated by miles of storefront picture windows.

Approaching the two-block stretch where every window holds captive thousands of pairs of overpriced tennis shoes — each pair as unique in color and architecture as the houses on Esplanade — I spotted De'von far ahead. Not Big De'von from The Donkey Show, the little closeted one from my class. I hung back, watching him dance, pointing at shoes in the windows and screaming about them to a darker boy twice his height. De'von's new braids and the tall boy's terrycloth headband were the only signs of individuality juxtaposed against their tan-and-white Magnolia uniforms. Today they even conceded to the plain black shoes the school demands; many days they walk to school in their expensive, socially-mandatory G-Nikes, carrying their plain black shoes in their book bags, and changing into uniform just outside the metal detector. Then once inside their classrooms, they slip their blacks off, and their G-Nikes back on, until the bell buzzes and they trade back, to step out into the hall where Mr. Land would suspend them for breaking dress code.

With De'von and his tall friend gazing in Shoe Wonder, I was forced to walk extra slow and stop many times to avoid catching up. During one pause twenty-feet away, I thought of Big De'von at The Donkey Show last night, pissed because his table of 12, "Poor-ass, redneck, white trash motherfuhuhuhs…" weren't ordering four courses and $200 bottles of wine, then throwing half of it away like our other customers. His table seemed to be having a great time, but against the gold-trimmed staircase Big De'von complained of their poverty until finally I had to ask him, "What's wrong with being poor, man?"

"Ain't nothing wrong with being poor. Just don't come up in here wasting my time with it, y'heard me?"

"They have every right to save up for one big night out."

"But look how they dressed! They dressed so…" he squinted disgusted behind his gold rims. "At least if a nigga poor, he's still dipped in hundreds a dollars a gear."

Aside from his occasional, "I'm a gangsta!" flare-ups, I still like Big De'von; his Comic Timing is impeccable. But after months in a high school with no Principal or Math Teacher but hundreds of backpacks full of not books but $100 tennis shoes, I had to challenge him: "I dunno man, I think that's fuckin horrible that poor people would spend all their money on shoes and shit that just does not matter."

"Well…" he went serious. "If life don't matter…" he shrugged his square white shoulders and brisked away, back out to The Dining Room to handle his business.

Because of the weight of the topic, I didn't broach it with big De'von again. But watching little De'von leer into Canal's Shoe Windows, part of me wanted to re-open the case. Part of me wanted to ask Little De'von, '*Who told y'all that life doesn't matter?*'

But, the rest of me did not — as much for him as for me; he

wouldn't be happy to see me, and who knows what he thinks he could get away with outside the classroom?

So, far away I waited as they crept along the windows slowly like studying constellations — until finally I began feeling silly, and worrying I'd miss the bus. I inhaled deep lungs-full of smelly NO, then proceeded to pepper-step, toward-then-past De'von and his friend, staring straight down Canal, focusing on that tired group of bus-riders up there, aiming right for them and then...

"Hey, Mista Patrick!"

Except now he sounded like he liked me, for some reason... "Why you ain't got your bike today?" De'von asked with the same sweet concern I heard in the voice of that old women at the dead trolley stop who advised, "Oh please get y'self a hat, baby; you know Redheads don't need no nasty sun on they face."

"I just didn't feel like sweating today," I answered little De'von, slowing next to him. "What are y'all up to?"

"Same as you," he answered. The kids ride the public bus to school, not the yellow kind. I've never seen a yellow bus here. And I've never asked why.

Over his head I nodded *hello* to his tall friend, who didn't respond, just projected loud distrust. Silent, we three walked parallel to each other and our gray reflections in the windows until I interrupted, "So your braids look cool man. Who did em?"

"One of my bitches," De'von giggled down the morning streets.

"Don't call girls 'bitches', man," I reprimanded, then thought of Michael and the other gay waiters and their affectionate, "Bitch," "Girl," "Baby." More silent walking... Then I asked him, "So, what should I do in class today? What should I teach? The bike-ride to school is usually when I decide what to teach y'all — I usually have it figured it out by around Lee Circle."

"Not to tell you your job, Mista Patrick," De'von said, resting long skinny fingers in the crook of my arm, "but you should use more preparation than that." Removing his hand he added, "And you need to quit sayin 'Y'all'. Why you all the time tryna talk black?"

Up there, his silent friend nodded agreement and lit a cigarette. As he puffed I remembered him: last week I was standing outside my classroom rounding up stragglers when he passed, his empty fingers in a V at his lips as he'd asked me, "I can get a smoke?" Kids don't hide that from us anymore either.

"'Y'all' is not a black-owned word," I defended.

"'Y'all' ain't a word, period," De'von claimed. "So you shouldn't be usin it since you suppose to be our writin teachuh."

"I don't agree, man, Did you know that of all the languages in the world, only our shitty King's English…"

"Quit cursin," he warned.

"…doesn't have a word to address an entire group," I continued, repeating a mini linguistics lecture Lani had once given me. "In English, the only thing we have is, 'You guys,' which sounds much worse than, 'Y'all.' 'Y'all' sounds nice, homey. I grew up in The South. I'm used to "Y'all." As far as I'm concerned 'Y'all' is a fuckin word."

"*QUIT FUCKING CURSIN*!" De'von screeched, the way I do in class when I have to repeat myself. Then he returned to smiling and biting his lip.

I wish I could get over it like that, I thought, claiming, "I didn't curse nearly as much until I started teaching y'all," as we paused at the bus stop. "And besides, you guys curse *way* more than I do."

"So. We *kids*," he justified, his thin hands shoving me toward a pile of garbage on the curb.

We laughed together and I pointed out, "Hey! We get along pretty well outside of class."

Picking at the end of his braids and nodding agreement, his head looked like a bell being rung. "We could *always* get along if you didn't be acting so stupid in class," he said, then cackled like a dolphin, and I hoped that someday he'll be comfortable enough to make that sound all the time — until he interrupted my idealism…

"Ooooh, by-the-way Mista Patrick, the class is fuckin mad at you; you didn't go on that Field Trip with us Thursday!"

The VP only told me about the damn trip three days before, at that Meeting where that Teacher Lady ran out cursing. The VP had expected me to be ready to take the children out in public in just three days? *Very* unfair I thought, but then realized, looking around me at The Meeting, that all the other teachers had already known about the trip before then, before me. At that I assumed I'd failed to pay attention at some key point, and so concealed my ignorance by taking silent notes:

```
- Bus leaves Magnolia @ 10 a.m.
- Kids go to McDonough 35 to see a play (that
  some other Creative Writing Teacher's kids
  wrote? How the fuck did that teacher make
  THAT happen?)
- Bus returns to Magnolia @ 1 p.m.
- Tell the kids to bring lunches.
- NEED parental permission & insurance forms
  (or they cannot go)
- VP says: "Invite them all. But if they're
  behavior problems, don't pull they teeth."
```

But then near the end of The Meeting, just before that Teacher Lady ran out in her storm of spit and anger, I discerned from their discussion that I've been missing out on some kind of teacher-wide email newsletter thing, for months. *So that's how they all seem to know what to do, and why...* No one's ever asked for my email address, and The Vice Principal won't answer any of my questions until I'm asking them into her real live ear, and even then... *I'm being left out...*

But rather than anger, this hard evidence of the darkness I've been kept in lifted pounds from my soul, and I jotted down:

```
- It ain't my fault...
```

After The Meeting, each of the many times I solicited my class regarding The Field Trip, they derailed me, crying, slapping, laughing, rapping. I couldn't imagine *any* of them asking their parents, "Mother, could you please pack me a lunch this Thursday, and give me two dollars please, so that I may participate in a Creative Writing Field Trip?" One of my kids who actually heard my announcement even admitted that he didn't have money to buy stamps to mail his Permission Slip to Orleans Parish Prison, so… I didn't pull they teeth.

"But you ain't even show up for class!" De'von continued, leaning against the metal signs reading *N.O. Transit Authority* on top, and underneath: *Parade Route: 3 p.m. to midnight*. "Someone from The School Board had to come down and got us."

"Who?"

"A lady."

"Black lady with big blonde curly hair? A big *fine* girl?"

"That's her, but she ain't fine."

"The hell she ain't."

"She too *light-skinded*."

"How'd she take you without parental permission?"

"What that mean?"

"Your parents didn't sign permission slips?"

"No, that blonde lady let us sign em ourselves." He pointed a limp finger in my face: "And she said you was the only teacher that didn't show up."

My face flushed as The Tchoupitoulas Bus rolled up and De'von and his stoic friend ascended its metal stairs without saying goodbye. "Hey wait, why are you taking this one?" I shouted after them. "The Magazine bus goes straight down to the…"

"You wanna wait, keep waitin, baby," he batted his eyelashes.

"Does this one go to the school?"

But he disappeared inside the bus. I paid $1.25 to follow him to the back and immediately realized that, sitting among his similarly uniformed friends, I'd taken excess liberty; they didn't want me there. De'von would no longer acknowledge me. I removed my book from my backpack and read, looking even more out-of-place among the kids.

- 2 -

Bike-ridden, there are plenty chunks of the city, separate personalities, that I haven't even glimpsed; I learn my safe bus and bike routes, then never deviate. I knew that the Magazine bus would have dropped us close to Magnolia High, so every time I felt the meandering Tchoupitoulas take another turn I glanced up from my book to find us rolling through another section of town I've never visited. Eventually I tried to ignore the turns and not look up at all because I didn't want to think about it and get pissed at De'von for leading me astray. I just kept my nose down, assuming we'd arrive eventually, and knowing that no matter how engrossed I got in reading I'd eventually sense the kids standing up, and follow them off.

But I finished my whole book before that could happen... To avoid eye contact with the kids I looked up, reading the ads tacked over the bus' windows. One for our restaurant read, "[The Donkey Show], where the locals go to eat." *As if that wouldn't scare away locals...* Reading similar sentiments in every other ad, I knew I was late for school. *And this after already missing that Field Trip, fuck...* I needed to know what time it was, but not as much as I needed to avoid asking De'von to see his watch... So I did end up hating him and myself again by the time the bus driver shouted, "End of the line!" *nowhere* near the school.

In some warehouse district under the blessed gray shade of oaks, I followed De'von and his three tall, skinny friends off the bus. They walked 20-feet ahead of me down the broken street, punching each other. My nerves ticked with the late clock and if I'd have known where we were exactly, I would've fucking run to the school. But I was forced to follow slowly behind, trying to let go of my anxiety by thinking about *How crazy is it to worry about being late for Magnolia, of all godforsaken jobs?*

To his credit, once-a-block De'von glanced back — to make sure I was still following them, it seemed, rather than because he hoped I wouldn't be. When they finally stopped I stopped too, and we all waited under an anonymous tree until another bus pulled up. Climbing aboard, I noticed the kids all handing the driver Transfers they'd bought back on the Tchoupitoulas bus: proof that they'd known *exactly* where we were(n't) going from the beginning.

I paid a fresh $1.25 and sat seats and seats and rows away from them. But now De'von wanted to talk to me. If only for the benefit of his friends, he yelled through the empty bus, "That Field Trip was fun though, Mista Patrick! Me and Cedar broke off!"

"Where'd you go?" I asked, using my Inside Voice.

He didn't answer. But whether he didn't *want* to answer or he just didn't hear me over the engine, I wasn't going to repeat myself. I concentrated on the new bus' ads until one of his friends asked him, "So what'd y'all do when you broke off, woadie?" Woadie meaning *Wardie,* meaning, person from one of the 19-or-so *Wards* NO's divided into. Before leaving FLA I heard black kids in a convenience store calling each other Wardie, though FLA isn't chopped into wards at all. Again, The Radio…

"We talked to bitches, baby," De'von smiled, and as he proceeded to detail his and Cedar's female conquests, I studied him as acutely as I've ever studied Mizzy or anyone else, and I caught no trace of self-doubt in his bravado. Then finally he turned back to me: "We even left the *school*, Mista Patrick!"

"What! No." *Man, I'm fucking fired...* The kids laughed at my reaction. I ignored them: "Where'd y'all go, De'von?"

"None of your fuckin business," he smiled. "Y'white bitch."

- 3 -

De'von and I made it to class 40-minutes late. All but one of today's six kids sat silently downloading and printing song lyrics from the Internet. As the printouts were born, She-La, maroon ropes piled atop her head, read loudly to the other kids, the words to *Hey! That song Mizzy and I sing to each other in The Dish Pit!*

Still I commanded, "All right, computers off."

I walked to my desk, but didn't sit down. The kids continued staring into their monitors, pounding it out, keyboards clacking along and the loud printer *rat-tat-tat-tat-tat* like the sound of some War Room. She-La continued her lyrical instruction.

"Please, turn the computers off. I'm here now," I demanded, pleaded. The printer rattled so much louder than it used to; the computers were installed brand new my first day. Magnolia has so many other needs, I don't know how New Computers got on the list before New Principal and New Math Teacher. But by now, the plates of the plastic mice are cracked loose like road-killed turtles, and in whiteout on the sides of the monitors, tribal markings warn, `10th W/D keep da fuckout`. I snatched the pages from She-La's hand...

"You fuckin trippin man!" she yelled and glared.

I continued past her to each computer, reaching over each student's shoulders to kill their machines. Each child yelled up into my Adam's Apple when their monitor blackened. I was ensuring a rough rest-of-the-class, I knew it, but it's the littlest Power Rushes that can drag you the furthest without your permission — sometimes I understand Mr. Land's questionable smile.

Oddly though, the kids remained calm for the next hour, calm like they'd just had sex — which I'm sure most of them have had more recently than I... Some of them were almost friendly, showing interest in things I said. A couple even took *notes*, and none argued when I handed back their Letters to the Mayor (which I still haven't read) and asked them to correct grammar, spelling and punctuation, then re-write another draft — though I'm conflicted as to whether their illiterate first-drafts might not deliver a more powerful statement to The Mayor, whoever that will soon be.

Walking between their desks, answering their smiling questions and feeling like a real teacher, I eventually had to ask the room, "So what, did they give you guys freakin Ritalin for breakfast or something?"

"What's that?" quiet Anthony asked. No one else noticed my question; they were busy working. *I guess all they needed was a Field Trip...*

"What's what?"

"Ritalins."

"Rita-*lin*," I corrected "is a drug to help you concentrate."

"You know what help me concentrate?" he asked. "Weed. They say weed suppose to make you lazy but when I smoke it man, I want to play drums, write stories, draw, just create shit man — I'll smoke the *piss* out some weed." And all I could do was nod; pot does the exact same thing for my ADD: slows my too-fast brain down so that

114

I can concentrate like a normal person. "That's why I should be allowed to smoke for school," Anthony added, smiling. "I don't smoke for school cause I don't wanna get in trouble. But if I did, I'd come in here payin *mad* attention." Then he asked, "You take it?"

Panic fluttered in my mouth. I stalled: "Weed?"

"Ritalins," he corrected.

"No, I try not to take drugs made by white guys in laboratories," I admitted.

"True. I only take shit from God too," he smiled again, before going plaintive: "But if it's gonna get me expelled or arrested, then maybe I should get a subscription to Ritalin."

"'*Pre*scription,'" I corrected. "And you don't need Ritalin, Anthony. You're fine." Then, since I hadn't received an answer to my initial question I asked him directly, "So why are they all acting like this today? All calm."

"Mardi Gras comin," he answered.

"What, Mardi Gras makes kids act good, like The Spirit of Christmas? Like if they're not good they won't get to see tourists and tits and garbage..."

"No, more like the spirit of: they fuck around and get detentions and shit, no one ain't marchin in no parades, y'heard me?"

My pride waned; I thought I'd gotten through to them. Still I managed to appreciate their anomalous tranquility, until the bell rang at 10:10 and De'von shook my hand goodbye on his way out, causing a chain reaction of kind salutations from every kid behind him:

"Later Mista Patrick!"
"Latuh, Pat Pat."
"Latuh P-Diddy."
"Later, cousin!"
"Late, Woadie."
"Latuh Mr. Patrick!"

- 4 -

The stop for the Esplanade bus at Popeye's on Canal is white-hot-bright until 11:30 a/m, when the sun finally scoots over, and Popeye's begrudges a sliver of shade to protect me from cancer. So I decided to stay and wait at Magnolia till then. My classroom was empty, my kids gone. I sat at one of the dying computers with cigarette ashes on its keys. Second period had begun for all the other teachers 15-minutes prior, but kids still screamed in the hall outside my door. I got up and peeked my head out to find boys and girls leaping back-and-forth, laughing and slam-dancing. The loud echoing hallways were as gray as Canal, smelling clean, but in a bad way, like an indoor swimming pool. Other teachers' heads poked out their doors too, but we deterred nothing, so I walked down to the bathroom, chewed wads of toilet paper and stuck them in my ears.

Back at the computer though, I could still hear their screams, and so walked out and down to Magnolia's Library, where I usually leave my bike during class. The Library seems like the only dry place in the city. It's always empty except during Teacher's Meetings, thus it's the only room in the school that looks the way it should: bright new carpet, handy pens and paper, posters of black celebrities reading classic literature taped to the clean, tan brick, three copies of Franzen's The Corrections occupying a *New Arrivals* shelf…The only signs of Magnolia's real personality are the printouts taped up at the still-healthy computers: *'Students are not allowed to visit rap artists' websites and/or print out lyrics.'*

But before I could make it into my email account, De'von came flailing into the Library through a door connected to the Main Office. Falling straight toward me he looked like he might cry, or faint. then almost in my lap he whispered hard, "Mista Patrick! You gotta help me, you gotta say I'm in y'class right now! Please!"

Over the horizon of his braids, I watched Mr. Land stalk into the Library, pointing an authoritative finger at De'von: "This boy's in your class right now?"

De'von's mouth was close enough to whisper to me, but instead he silently searched far back in my eyes. My heart was beating like I too had been chased. I felt as trapped as he was.

"Mister Patrick, is he in your class right now?" Land repeated.

I couldn't answer and Land smiled at his impending win — a

smile interrupted when De'von's tall friend from the bus sprinted in through the same Office door. Seeing Mr. Land, he jack-knifed right and out the Library door, under a picture of Shaq reading Moby Dick.

Land abandoned us to chase the kid out and down the hall. But I knew he'd return after he'd won, so I whispered fast, "De'von, I can't fucking *believe* you'd do this me, man! You want me to fucking *lie* for you when every day you treat me like *shit*?" Struck by my own pleading voice I wondered where the real conflict was in my admitting to Mr. Land, 'No, he's not in my class right now.'

"I know, I know, I'm *sorry* Mista Patrick," De'von wilted, nodding sadly, which surprisingly didn't tame me.

"You're fucking with my *job* man, my fucking *paycheck*!" I whisper-shouted, noticing the librarian looking up at me from her desk. Still I continued. "*You're* the one who cares so much about money and shit and now *you're* fucking with *my* money De'von, my food, my rent, *my* shoes!" I pointed to the pink bump on my temple, "My fucking *cancer Surgery* money, De'von! I can't believe you'd put me in this position. I can't believe you'd do this to me, man!"

Then the Library's front doors swung open and Mr. Land lumbered back in, panting, but smiling bigger. He wiped his bald head with a paper towel: "OK Mr. Patrick, now is or isn't he in your class right now?" I wished I were bussing tables, whether or not Mizzy and Jude are quitting... Staring at myself in the computer monitor, my eyes watered. *If I'm silent for long enough this will resolve itself without me.* "Don't lie for these kids," Land warned, smirking. But still my silence, until finally Mr. Land scoffed, then back to De'von: "So, Mr. Patrick isn't your teacher right now."

By now De'von understood that I wasn't participating, and he'd discounted me as an alias. A foot away, I felt his body forget I was even there... "No, he ain't our teachuh, we just usin his room," he concocted.

"'*We*' who?" Land taunted.

"Our class."

"With what teacher?"

"I don't member, he a new man."

117

A new man... No use to either of them, I silently remembered all the times De'von has told me, "I wish you'd get the hell out, so we could have us *a new man*."

"You just said this *new man's* name a minute ago De'von," Land continued his inquiry. "What was that name you told me? Started with a P..."

"I can't pronounce it," De'von claimed. "He's Chinese. A Chinese man."

Mr. Land smiled back to me, giving me another chance: "Mr. Patrick?"

This time I spoke truth into Mr. Land's eyes: "I can't believe you'd do this to me, De'von."

Mr. Land led him away. It was 10:45. I walked out through the metal detector and into the mean sun.

ch 9: i don't like you

The Picture Window is a giant aquarium. *Am I inside, or outside?* Folding napkins alone today, I watch and I am watched: wobbly tourists draped in premature beads make eye contact and tap the glass in passing; uniformed ghetto schoolchildren point and laugh at *my* uniform; that fat black man in the umbrella hat across the street smiles up at the sky as always, reading the Bible to the sun through his megaphone — I see his breath, but can't hear him at all; a gargantuan rust-and-blue pick-up truck swims by like a great Jewfish, and just before it migrates on I notice Mizzy behind its steering wheel! My elbow pins the stack of napkins to my lap so I can stand up and try to glimpse her Civilian Clothing. But she swims on too fast. *This is what my first ever Mardi Gras will be like...*

And before I could regain my seat, up swims Jude on his bike. The short, greasy vines of hair blown back off his thin neck wilted as he skidded to a stop, hovering there, staring at me. The rest of his hair, what was left of it, made me drop my napkins to the tile and say to the glass: "I can't believe you did that to yourself."

Jude nodded, his silent smirk mouthing, "Yeah" as he locked his beaded bike next to mine, tumbled in through the revolving gold door and walked straight to me, his new haircut so horrible that I forgot to shake his hand. He also wore Civilian Clothes, his Human Costume: tight white jeans, dingy gray tennis shoes, his bony chest like a stingray smuggled beneath his gray Led Zeppelin T-shirt, and *That hair, my god...*

Through his mouthful of teeth he explained, "Management's been telling me to get it cut."

"But it wasn't even long."

"Yeah. I know. Just barely over my ears," he said, pointing to the sides of his head where three parallel lines were now shaved. *My god...* His new cut is common in FLA: short on the top and sides, with a grotesque flap in back to protect the neck from sun; a cut for field-workers, and others in danger of a red neck. Jude's version, with the lines shaved in, is more retro, harkening back to the jock kids who tried to beat me up in Middle School. "When Management first told me to cut it," he continued. "I was like, 'What standards do y'all use to judge hair-length, The Ed Sullivan Show?' Then the second time they asked me to, I..."

"The *second* time?" I interrupted. "Most restaurants would just fire you before any *second* time."

"Yeah. But I was like, 'Well Mizzy's hair is a lot longer than mine.'"

"And Management said, 'But they're women,'" I guessed.

"Yeah. And I was like, 'Oh, you mean *sex*ism.' But that didn't spook them at all. Then the third time they told me to cut it, they gave me a $10 gift certificate for SuperCuts..."

"Man, that's magnanimous," I said. "Most restaurants would fire you before they'd *ever* give you money... and you took it and went down and did *that* to yourself?"

"Yeah," he admitted, looking like an 8th grade soccer goalie with bone cancer. And though I was proud of his bravery — I mean I couldn't do that, couldn't shave myself down to Uncool just for a laugh — I wondered again where his *I-don't-give-a-fuck* comes from. Given the shape of his head, the lumps under his shirt, the way his friends celebrate him and girls cling to him, my first thought has often been *He's got terminal something*: I've suspected it many times, long before the hair.

Before I could depress myself I asked him, "So what now?"

"I'm going to get fired. For my hair."

"I thought you already put in your two weeks notice."

"Yeah. But I want to be able to tell people I got fired because of my hair."

"If you get fired from here, you'll never work at another restaurant in this city again."

"Yeah."

Jealous, I reminded him, "You know, if they see you right now, they'll fire you for coming into the building without your tie on..."

"I'm off tonight. I just came to pick up my check..."

Which didn't make sense, since we make only $2.13 an hour, and our cash tips are deducted from that, so our paychecks usually read: $0.00. But before I could wonder aloud, in the distance behind Jude, beyond the gold staircase, the elevator doors opened and a fat flock of Management stepped out. My pulse jumped, the melancholy lifted: *Uh oh, here we go! This is gonna be good...* I held my breath listening to the echo of Jude's shoes squeaking across The Dining Room and I wished nothing more than that Mizzy were there to watch Jude marching straight up to Management with that True Flag of Human Mockery flapping from the back of his head as he approached them...

But when he finally made it into the center of their circle, Management didn't gasp, didn't frown, did not react. *They don't notice? No. How? No. Are they just too tall, so much bigger than the rest of us that maybe, looking down on Jude, they see only the neatly trimmed crown of his head?* When from where I stood it was like he'd brought them a dead cat cradled in his arms and they just *weren't fucking seeing it.* But no, they could see it, even as they patted Jude's pointy shoulder, then lumbered back into the elevator

121

going up, to retrieve Jude's $0.00.

He loped back to me, his face as perplexed as mine. Swooping in from our right like a Malachi Crunch, De'von carried his stack of napkins to a chair against the window where he sat down, sighed a breath of relaxation then casually glanced up at us, laughing but not smiling: "I betcha boyfriend love that cut, Jude."

Without pause Jude shot back, "Actually *women* love this haircut De'von; they see it and know that I do what I want, that I'm my own person, not a *slave* like you."

Oh fuck. My breath held: *No, Jude's not afraid of dying...*

But De'von responded merely, "There you go then," dismissive, staring into, or out of, our aquarium.

When the elevator returned and Jude left us again to go collect his blank paycheck from Management — *How the fuck do they not notice?* — I turned back to De'von adding, "You know actually man, Jude does get way more girls than any guy I know. You wouldn't think it looking at him, but seriously..."

"Hell no he don't," De'von huffed. "Jude gay as the day is long."

"You don't believe that," I challenged. "If you did, you wouldn't even talk to him."

'There you go then," De'von repeated.

Jude returned: "*Weird.*"

"It is. Amazing. They don't even fucking *notice*?"

"Yeah."

"Like in a dream…"

"Yeah."

"What's your theory?"

"Theory of Relativity?" Jude shrugged. "They probably had this same haircut in college or something, so they don't see it for what it is."

"One man's mullet…" I called.

"Beauty's in the eye…" Then Jude responded.

"It's ugly nough for me," De'von added.

"So what are you going to do then?" I asked Jude.

"Try harder," he smiled. And I wondered how much longer he has to live.

- 2 -

Before riding his last Donkey Show paycheck down to the bank (somehow $1.89), Jude informed me that Mizzy was off tonight too; she had an art opening Uptown. Jude couldn't attend; his dance card was full with, "This girl I went to high school with's birthday. One time she gave me a blowjob cause I helped her find cocaine..." He then blushed and apologized for saying that.

I silently wondered why she hadn't told *me* about her show, and why Jude had to give me directions...

Attempting to follow said directions after work, I again found myself lost, riding slow through towering, wealthy neighborhoods, in silence but for the far-off clomping of hooves > > > past houses so big they'd eaten their entire yards and driveways right up to their fences > > > down streets gorged with mansions attached to mansions engulfed by other mansions, all of it built to make someone feel lesser > > > on-and-on, my cold nose in the air as my eyes took-in awe-inspiring rooftops — until looking back down, it had suddenly all turned to ghetto >>>>>>>>>> my legs pumped at a Need Pace through so much trash it looked like a parade had just come through >>>>>>>>>> fast past Project patios wrapped in twisted iron cages >>>>>>>>>> past signs posted on orange bricks: "No animal fighting permitted " >>>>>>>>>> past stares so heavy in their silence I wished they'd *just fucking shout something at me!* >>>>>>>>>> "I - can't - find - my - way - a - rooooound..." believing that if not tonight, someday I'd die singing it...

But then from somewhere came Esplanade, sweet sweet Esplanade that I was never so happy to see. And that Nightclub where Lani's been attacked so many times. *But at least I know where I am...* My body relaxed deeply — until a man who looked like Mr. Land but much older ran out into the road at me, whipping at my air with long, skinny hands. In the dark I noticed yellow stains on his white tank top, and in his crazy eyes. But lifting a foot from my pedal to kick him in the chest if he came any nearer, I realized he wasn't swatting at me, but waving me past...

"Look out! Get on now! This ain't no place you need to be right now!"

Between his warnings the man glanced excitedly back over his shoulder as if expecting a Tyrannosaur to rise up on the skyline beyond the Nightclub…

"Go! Get on! Fast as you can! Hurry yourself on!"

Figuring some fight was about to boil out the Nightclub's door onto Esplanade, I resumed my Need Pace, yelling back, "Thank you!"

Three blocks away I could still hear him still shouting, "Go! Go!" And a mile down Esplanade, chaining my bike beneath my snoring Squab, I swear I could still hear him, but laughing.

- 3 -

Working at a restaurant, another stupid thing you might do with all the cash you have on hand, is you might splurge $12 on a taxi all the way Uptown at midnight, to view the art of a girl who didn't invite you.

But upon arrival I didn't see Mizzy's food photos on any of the gallery's four walls. Two walls were littered with yawn-inducing oil paintings of The French Quarter — even talented artists with taste can't keep themselves from trying to re-create The Quarter's wild color and textural dynamic. It seems to beg recreation, but in most cases these artists come nowhere near justifying *yet another* painting of The Quarter. The small quirky landscape paintings set in colorful imaginary worlds decorating the gallery's other two walls were much more original, if not moving, interesting enough, but *Where the hell's Mizzy?*

Really though, despite the $12 spent getting there, and the $12 I'd spend returning home, I only wanted to see her art, not her. No, I did want to see her, but I didn't want to talk to her… No, I did want to talk to her, but when I spotted her sprawled across a long wooden table in a corner with some handsome swarthy guy, both of them laughing drunk and leaning into each other, I panicked, sidestepped into a small side room and let myself fall onto an empty couch, coincidentally next to a beer keg. No, I did not want to see her... I needed to leave. I needed to leave, but didn't want to pass back through that small room. Trapped and cowardly, the F-Word running on a loop inside me, I patted my pockets to make sure I had cab fare; my only choice would be to run back out the front door and down the street to the payphone. *Maybe if I get the same driver who brought me here he'll cut me a deal if I explain...* All that trouble to get out there and I didn't even think to pour a beer. I simply took out my money, breathed, stood, *ready...*

And then she came around the corner.

"I *thought* I saw you come in. What are you doing? Get a beer."

She pushed me back down onto the couch then sat — directly in my lap, red-cheeked drunk, a little of her beer falling cold onto my crotch.

"Ooh! Sorry..." All I'd projected onto the inside of her B-waitress coat was realized: indeed big perfect breasts, loudly presented in the Opening-Night Dress stretched across my knees and chest. "How did you find out about this?" she asked.

Aw Jesus fuck man... Not only does she forget to invite me, she admits to forgetting on purpose while her full weight's on me when she has to know how I feel.... Fuck is anyone fair? If I were a Man I'd have said, 'Get the fuck off me,' like Little De'von does when I touch his arm to emphasize even harmless points. But the most resistance I could muster was making sure my hand dangled limp behind the couch, taking no part in her, not even harmlessly, the same way I avert my eyes at strip clubs because I can't respect being assigned a time and place wherein I am *allowed*, what normally I am not.

"Actually, I was just taking off," I said.

"No! Don't!" She nestled so far into my armpit, so close against my body I couldn't see her face. There was just the invisible weight of her and her wine breath wafting up into my face. Always before I've drunk anything myself, I loathe the exaggerated kindness of the intoxicated...

"So why the fuck didn't you invite me then?" came out on its own. And I was glad it did; I didn't deserve any of this from her.

"I'm sorry," she whined, pushing her face farther into my neck her fingers pulling at the orange hairs on my wrist and *Fuck this man fuck this... Alcohol doesn't make people act differently, it's just that they know they can use it as an excuse later. I hate fucking alcohol. I hate New Orleans.*

"So why the fuck?" I asked again.

"Cause these paintings are crappy and...they're old work. I did them right before Mardi Gras last year and I just..." *I need to get the fuck out of this city before I start using Mardi Gras as a reference point on the timeline of MY life...* as she continued, "I'm sorry Patrick. I really just didn't want you to see this stuff."

I couldn't tell if it was a lie. Sometimes everything good seems to be... If it wasn't a lie, it was too flattering. I said nothing — until eventually: "Your paintings need more paint," I admitted, assuming hers weren't the touristy ones. "They look like you didn't work on them for very long."

"I didn't," she giggled.

My ice began melting, down to the truth. "The composition is real good though," I said, my hand creeping up onto the couch's arm. "The composition and the originality are there... They just need more depth. More paint. These little worlds you've created are very convincing and fun, but they just..."

"See!" she sang, bringing her face out and around in front of mine. Gently choking my throat with small, cold hands: "See, at least you're honest! All night everyone's only been telling me how *greeeeeat* they are when I *know* it's not true. But I knew you were better than that!"

"Then why won't you go out with me?" I said, because I knew I could get away with it when she was drunk.

"I will. When?"

"Huh?"

"You'll cook me dinner like you said you would?"

"Yeah. Definitely."

"It better be good."

"It will be. I'm awesome."

"I know."

- 4 -

The next night I experienced The Thrill of Creation in my kitchen, throwing haphazard spices and bits of crabmeat around like some Cajun Jackson Pollack, and also drinking as much as he, not just to quell my fear of being alone with her in Civilian Clothing, but also to ready myself to crack open boiled crawfish bodies and suck out their mustard-colored brains. On the phone she'd promised to pick up a sack — "I don't really want any but since you've never tried them…" — though she didn't sound as enthusiastic as at her art show. She didn't sound enthusiastic. And this was *before* I could warn her about the lacks of My Room…

She rang my door-buzzer late, sober and distant in a billowy t-shirt that hid her even better than her Monkey Suit does. She didn't light up My Room the way I'd fantasized. She'd also forgotten the crawfish. That's what she said at least; my dumb inner voice swore she just didn't want to have that experience with me…

But The Thrill of Creation wouldn't let any of it kill my Momentum. As she sat on my couch silent and nervous, I scrambled across my bed sheets toward the back of her head, to hand her very own wine bottle over her shoulder, and because of where we live, there was no subtext to this gesture. We each drank from our own bottle as I sang solo to my sizzling catfish filets.

Eating later, I sat cross-legged in the dust and crumbs and toenail clippings on my blue hardwood floor while she remained up on the couch. "You shouldn't have done this," she said across the coffee table.

"No no no," I smiled. "I want to make sure you're eating right. Make sure you're satisfied."

She laughed a little, but not much; sometimes she's there with me, sometimes not, and when she's not, it feels like it's her conscious decision. *How are she and Jude so past all this? How does he…* The wine made me throw in, "You know the other night Jude told me some girl gave him a blowjob for cocaine."

She didn't respond.

"That doesn't seem his style," I added.

"No," she said. "That was in high school. He's calmed down a lot since then. He'd never do anything like that now. He's actually very close to that girl now. He's helped her through a lot."

"He used to act crazier?"

"A different kind of crazy, like getting really, really fucked up and crashing cars. Not just bad haircuts…"

For silent minutes I could tell she was still thinking of Jude. *I deserve it though, bringing that shit up...* So I didn't interrupt, just silently waited until finally she stood: "This is really good Patrick, but I've had enough."

She carried her half-full bottle of wine over to my second-hand stereo. She hadn't eaten most of her food, but I was feeling especially resilient; even the leftovers on her plate were still really beautiful, something to be proud of — these Acts of Creation alone provide more comfort to The Lonely than having others over to partake in them… So, nothing bothered me, and when she dialed up the radio station that always blasts from The Dish Pit, I sang along with a full mouth.

Another few gulps of wine and she sang too, and rapped. And by the time I'd finished both our plates she'd polished off her bottle, commandeered the last of mine as well, and was finally becoming my friend again. Finally. She even squeezed in beside me at my kitchen sink and we sang and laughed washing dishes together. Throwing water everywhere she thanked me for the other night at work, when I made her laugh so hard it shook The Picture Window and tourists walking by on Canal heard her and stopped and peaked in and Management hissed at her, "Mizzy shhhhhhhhh!" and at me, "Patrick get away from her!"

"What kind of world am I stuck in that I'm not allowed to laugh?" she asked me, drying china then tucking it into my one-and-only cupboard.

"It breaks my heart that anyone would make you stop laughing," I poeticized, then admitted, "Yeah, I feel like a fucking monster when I have to make my kids stop laughing."

"That *is* fucking monstrous," she laughed.

"Yeah, I have to take their headphones away from them and…"

She turned my water off and turned on me, barely smiling: "Really? Patrick, you don't let them listen to music in class? That's terrible. I'm surprised they don't hate you." I looked away, trying to laugh. She continued. "I wouldn't even show up for work if it weren't for The Radio in The Dish Pit. I couldn't fucking handle it."

Which reminded me that she's quitting The Donkey Show. But before I could interrogate her on the subject, she'd looked out my window, and that was it: "Holy shit! You have a fucking *trampoline*!"

She drained my bottle and I followed her out my door.

- 5 -

"Whenever anyone asks me about living in Florida," I explained, standing barefooted beside her in the splotchy grass, both of us staring across the great nylon disk, "I always say that the only time I was truly happy living there was when I'd stand on the beach facing the ocean, with my back to the actual *state*. And if anyone ever asked, I'd express the same relationship about looking at this thing from my apartment."

Mizzy climbed up, and upon first big jump and loud giggle, Mardi Gras came flying out from beneath the trampoline, shaved down to his skeleton (again I thought of Jude), but running strong in a straight line toward the bushes, not like before — not like Mizzy jumping crooked and drunk... Even under her tent-of-a-shirt there was no hiding them when she bounced straight up, stiff arms at her side, coming down bent, her ass splashing in a mess of rotten peaches. From where I stood beside the rusty crab trap, it was all very beautiful: the eccentric backyard, her laughter waking up the neighborhood, peaches bouncing around her and dripping from her clothes. At the same time I worried for her safety, and she could tell...

"Oh c'mon," she panted, rising and falling. "I had one of these when I was a kid. I'm an expert at trampolines."

And on that noun, like a fucking punchline, her 90-degree knees crashed down onto the outside metal rim of the circle with a loud aluminum *SLAM*! Her body fell backwards, her head thudding the hard grass.

As she moaned on her back, my first and only thought was, *If I take care of her well enough, she will...* "Oh Mizzy, I'm sorry," I promised, kneeling down. Holding her skull between her elbows, water leaked from her squinting eyes. I told her I'd do anything. She requested ice for her knees and head. "The refrigerator in My Room doesn't make ice," I admitted. "It's too small. It doesn't have a freezer, or else I would have bought us ice cream for dessert..."

Her pain wouldn't let her answer. I jumped up and ran around knocking on all the different doors inside my ugly house, all the other apartments/compartments, meeting many neighbors I'd never even seen before: a slender shirtless man answered his door in just tight white underwear, but only after yelling "Who is it?" twice, causing me to suspect that he'd stripped down *after* he heard my knock and voice... But he didn't have any ice. Another decrepit man in his hundreds tried luring me in to commiserate about the loud Squab. But none of the shut-ins in kept ice; all of our little cubbyhole rooms are too small for real refrigerators, and confronting all these lonely people, I feared that if I don't get out of here soon, I will run in the same flock with them for the rest of my life, we'll roost together like dirty pigeons. *I don't belong here, I belong next door* — where I ran to bang on My Former Front Door. But Mardi Gras' owner didn't answer. I peaked in her drapes: all the lights off. I could hear Mizzy groaning over the fence, but none of My Former Mansion's tenants answered their doors. Until Lani...

"Man shit, you know my damn refrigerator only comes up to my damn knees." All he could give me for her was a cigarette. "But don't tell my wife I been smoking. Man, she'll bitch me out," he continued. "By the way, how come you ain't been around? You ain't stopped by in..." Without thinking I slammed his door on his words.

Mizzy liked the cigarette well enough but still couldn't stand up. "You know, I'm very clumsy too," I said, hovering above her, her smoke rising up and stinging my eyes. "We're meant for each other."

She ignored that, wrapping her arms around her throbbing knees. When the cigarette was gone she made me go back for another. Lani was very nice about my previous lapse in manners; he understands what we're all at the mercy of... When her second cigarette degenerated into ash, Mizzy finally stood and leaned on me to limp past the trampoline, up the stairs and into My Room. Her truck died earlier in the week, so she'd rode her bike over. We'd planned to pedal through City Park after dinner, but now she couldn't even ride back home, all the way Uptown, not with her fucked knees. She agreed to sleep on my couch.

- 6 -

We laughed like at a Slumber Party as I tried talking her into staying on at The Donkey Show. But she insisted that Management become Nazis during Mardi Gras, so she wants out by then.

As she explained, "I already have a new job lined up at this real slack Cajun restaurant on St. Charles," I felt very close to her in the dark. Actually I was close, a mere foot away, lying in my bed, parallel to her on the couch as she whispered, "It's a dive and I won't make as much money, but I get to wear jeans and a T-shirt." *Whispering is so pretty, listening to a woman whisper...* "And they have live Cajun bands and Cajun dancing every night, so that might be fun. Or else it'll drive me crazy."

I cannot blame the bottle of wine for lifting me out of bed as she continued, "But at least it's not 'Fine Dining' anymore." And though yes I was drunk, it was 100% me leaning over the back of the couch, my face inches above hers, my very own voice instructing her to kiss me.

"No." She tried to laugh but couldn't.

"C'mon," I nudged, my whisper sounding ugly.

"Why?" she asked, stalling, waiting for me to realize that I was making her uncomfortable.

I don't know why I didn't stop: "Just try it, one time."

Surprisingly she pecked my lips, like ripping off a band-aid, then turned and buried her face in the pillow I'd given her.

"No?" I asked. "No more?"

She said nothing into the pillow.

"Why not?" I prodded.

"I don't like you," she finally muffled.

I climbed back into bed, holding in apologies…

That could have hurt a lot. But I know what she really meant; we're real friends, or we were. It's not that she doesn't like me it's just… When single people get along like her and me, one person's physical appearance is the only thing that ever keeps them apart. And she's gorgeous so… *So it's me, it's definitely me,* I believed, waking the next morning to the sight of her head turned away, her open eyes studying my acoustic guitar across the room. I crawled off the opposite side of my bed and slipped into the shower, washed up, dressed for school. At the sound of my re-entering the room I caught her eyes snap close, and as I gathered my school supplies she played opossum, like a previously molested child hoping the monster will *please* pass without…

Given the pain of last night's wine and rejection, if she hadn't been there in My Room I would have called in sick again, retreated back into bed. But as things were, I dropped a spare key on the coffee table for her, then pedaled Uptown to Magnolia.

ch 10: last night/first parade

It begins tonight and I can't say I'm not excited, even if it will occur on the silent side of the glass. These next three weekends, my first Mardi Gras will careen down Canal: giant fucking parades, plus all the little unsanctioned parades wriggling through the city's veins. Like the Second-Line that made me late for The Donkey Show today — not late because I jumped in; I stopped, waiting for it to pass, like you have to for trains. I did join in a Second-Line one time, the first one I ever accidentally ran into my first Sunday afternoon in NO: some 9th Ward brass band needed fresh air, but didn't want to stop practicing. Soon a dozen neighbors straggled out into the abrasive sunshine behind the band and the convoy marched, howling for more neighbors to join, until by the time the noise penetrated our quiet, safe neighborhood, I peaked my head out my door to the smiling teeth of 100 dancers. And I followed, the only white guy but *Hey everybody's smiling! All these teeth!* > > > rolling and rolling, humans together, more pouring off their porches to follow us, become us > > > following behind young women dragging little kids and old ladies > > > and alongside young men dragging deep plastic garbage cans full of Heinekens for $1, or if you already have a beer in your hand then "I got dimes bruh…" By the time that parade finally paused in the Garden District, thousands of bodies bounced in unison, far far far off in both directions, all of us happy as hell, one of the very few truly amazing things I've ever seen. But since then, many restaurant co-workers, as well as the kids and faculty of Magnolia High, have all sworn that I'm blessed to have survived; they warn that Second-Lines often end in gun-spray. Little De'von even nonchalantly bears a scar from a misguided Second-Line bullet in his hairless calf, a story his classmates are bored with… So now I always just wait for them to pass, like you have to for trains.

    I feel like this same Outsider when I'm at Help Meal, leaning as far as I'm allowed into their conversations, decoding and memorizing The New Words — everything else in NO is old, but there are always New Words. And today, since it was only Red and De'von at Help Meal, talking in code so intense they couldn't notice me, for the first time ever I just went ahead, and sat directly at The Black Table…

    "I ain't gonna kill nothing, bruh," Red was saying.

    "Naw naw, I ain't gonna kill nothing neither," De'von replied. "But I also ain't gonna let nothing die."

    "Bruh, you *been* knowin me since I made *eight*, bruh" Red strained. "So you *know* why back in kindergarten I failed Recess…"

    "Cause you don't play…"

    "And that's real, bruh."

    De'von shrugged, "I still think you scared though, bruh."

    "Bruh, I *ain't* scared. If I'm scared I go to *church*, y'heard me? I am a grown-motherfuckin-man, and I handle a man's business. You talking to a *thug*, bruh…"

    Thug made me laugh, and they turned on me, frowned, then back to each other.

    Poking a spork into my Popeye's red beans (oyster pasta for

Help Meal; I've never eaten an oyster…) I laughed again to myself, remembering Cedar this morning, outside my door before class, wooing some girl with, "Baby, I'm a thug," which The Radio will tell you means Cedar was promising her he'd hit and shoot people, traffic drugs, and impregnate her without regard. *Fucking little kid,* I chuckled to my beans. *Thug.* But then here at The Donkey Show, even the most basic *adult* male interaction is laced with the moral: If We Fought, *I* Would Win. In a good mood it's, "Quit playing pussy-ass *(ha ha ha)* else I'ma kick y'ass." In a bad mood it's, "Quit playing pussy-ass, or I'ma kick y'ass." In the interim, there's talk of who's fought, who wants to fight, what kind of gun who has, and who's locked-up. And in the midst of this fog, Red usually shines as The Donkey Show's wise presence. *So why Thug now? Guess my decoder's busted...*

"She juss want herself a *young* pepper-grinder," De'von continued. "Juss let it go."

"You my nigga De'von, bruh," Red's elegant baritone downshifted. "But you really tryin me. You really are, cousin."

"You guys are cousins?" I asked, not thinking, then thankful they were too caught up…

"I'm just trying to help you getcha mind right, partner," De'von spoke, pensively twisting his pinky ring — the other night I think he tried to make me kiss that ring; when I was weeded and red-faced busy, he whizzed all the way through the crowded Dining Room for the sole purpose of shoving his fist under my nose and straight-faced asking, "This ring look shiny enough to you? Should I maybe polish it again?" Pretty funny I thought, though Mizzy swears he's making fun of me. She obviously hasn't stopped and listened to how everyone here interacts; in comparison, De'von just has a rough sense of humor. At least he knows humor at all. I value that — so much so, that I fear I've let De'von's bullshit become as compelling a question as *What's really under Mizzy's tuxedo jacket?* — which I studied again when Mizzy sat down beside me at The Black Table…

I'd witnessed her sit here before; pretty women get away with everything. I'd never seen her eat pigeon though, but there it was on her plate, as on Jude's: *Squab*. Despite my hatred of that particular animal, I didn't think any less of her for eating it. Go ahead let her criticize me for *not* eating crawfish and their brains; if after Our Trampoline Night she can still sit directly beside me at Help Meal and show me her teeth because she knows I like to see them, then I'll respect her no matter what she eats. Her natural lack of discomfort after the other night is another of the few amazing things I've ever seen; other women aren't like that. Other people aren't like that. *She should take over my job at Magnolia. She'd be the teacher she assumes I am...*

Following our silent but un-awkward greeting, her and I looked up to find Red and De'von staring at us purposefully from across the table. Mizzy deepened her voice and broke the heavy silence: "What the fuck y'all lookin at?"

"Naw, naw, Mizzy. Ain't nothing like that," De'von deadpanned. "It's OK Y'all can sit here. Course. Sure. We don't mind you sittin with us."

Mizzy ignored his mixed message. Or maybe she didn't catch it. Or maybe there wasn't one... That's the beauty; The New Words are partially designed to *elude*, *alienate*, and I don't mind that. Somehow, existing as an appendage to a dominant culture for once in my life registers with me as another of the comforts NO awards — though it does bring me discomfort, not knowing why something like that would bring me comfort in the first place...

"You guys looked worked up just now," Mizzy parted the drama. "What were you talking about?"

Red mumbled, "Uh, my girl left me."

De'von: "Oh, your *girl* now?"

Red: "My daughter's mother."

Mizzy laughed again, big and goofy. Red smiled at her; pretty women get away with everything. Red continued smiling even when Jude sat down at The Black Table, and not just because of Jude's hair, but because, as Red announced to all of us right there, "Jude a smooth character, yeah. He deserve *respect* for his originality. That's my *boy* right there: Jude." Red seemed very sincere, even as he turned back to Mizzy and followed up, "So yeah, De'von here tryna tell me she left cause I won't eat her pussy."

"Hey Red, easy!" came out of me. I turned to-then-immediately-away-from Mizzy, and spoke again to my red beans: "We don't need that while we're eating."

I sounded like a teacher. *A wannabe teacher...a dontwannaabe...* Then looking back up I met De'von's squint: "You gonna sit at our table and tell us what *we* can't talk about?" he demanded, letting my head and neck flush before he turned away, leaving his thumb aimed back at me while confiding quietly to Red, "Anyway, if *that's* what your girl want, then let her go get herself a white boy, y'heard me?" He tapped his pinky-ring to Red's black-vested heart. "These new school niggas ain't got our kyna class, eatin that..."

"*That's not why she left man,*" Red asserted, slamming his fork down next to his plate, toppling the small pile of oysters I assumed he'd picked out of his pasta because they *resembled* sloppy gray vaginas. "I'm telling you bruh," he continued. "She don't care about getting her pussy et bruh; she is a one-hundred-percent *Black* woman. A - *Black* – *woman* - cousin."

Three fat Caucasian chefs in tall, ribbed hats joined The Black Table and I regretted the colonization I'd begun... But Red and De'von were too busy to notice. "Then what's The Real, bruh?" De'von asked.

"It's just funny niggas, man," Red lamented. "I just do not like funny niggas."

"What about Richard Pryor?" Jude interrupted.

I didn't know what to think of that — other than that it was good to finally hear Jude's voice; I'd forgotten he was there, oddly quiet, glum almost, *Maybe self-conscious about his hair? Or just bummed that no one flipped about it...* Regardless, he should have been happy, tonight being his last night. Mizzy's last night too. *Then what, for me?*

"Well, no matter what," De'von ignored Jude. "I gotcha back."

"*That's* real," Red agreed.

"Let them dirty white boys eat that shit..."

"*Cousin, get off it!*" Red snapped. "That's a wrap! Y'heard me? No more."

"Ah'ight. I'm out." De'von showed us his white palms. "I ain't mean to agitate you, bruh." He squinted out the Picture Window at his forest-green SUV parked directly across the street — I don't know how he won that impossible parking spot. De'von mumbled like a cartoon, something about his rims, while opening a Styrofoam take-out container and stabbing in with one of The Donkey Show's real silver forks. *No oysters for him either*, I appreciated, until he lifted what looked like a piece of raw squid, and folded it into his mouth.

"What the *fuck*?" I asked anyone.

"You ain't know nothin about this white boy," De'von answered, chewing with a sound like wet rubber. *White Bitch*, I thought to correct…

"*Clearly* he does not know anything about it, De'von" Jude squeaked in a mock White-Guy Voice. "Or else he would not be requesting that information from you."

"Pig lips, bruh," De'von finally answered, opening his mouth, showing me his progress.

"You'll eat *that*, but you won't eat…a…" Mizzy stuttered, "a girl?"

Red and the chefs and Jude and everyone but De'von roared. De'von continued chewing, chewing, chewing, until everyone was quiet. Then he swallowed and answered, "Yeah Mizzy, and you'll eat a damned *pigeon* but y'boyfriend right here won't," he pointed at me with his fork. "But then I'll bet he eats your pussy all day and night…" Without a pause for our reaction he concluded, "So y'see, there's things *you* won't eat, and things *he* won't eat, and maybe nothing Jude won't eat, but in the end it's all relative. Ain't no good or bad, so let's all just not worry who eats what, and y'all just let me live, y'heard me?"

- 2 -

Again I followed Jude to The Picture Window to fold napkins into triangle tents with Red and De'von. When we were all seated Jude blurted out, "Yeah. *I'm* never going out with another black girl again."

All eyes fell on Jude, who seemed serious — though he and I are both aware that simply refusing to acknowledge the humor kicks the joke up a notch... Either way he's eerily brave or stupid. And either way, I wished he'd stop.

"Jude, you ain't never had a girl in your life much less a black girl," De'von rebuked, not yet mad, but open to it.

"Yeah. Actually, I've gone out with lots of black girls. The last one I went out with was *huge.*" Jude paused to let us picture a huge black girl and then, "We only went out for like a month and she was already like, saying she wanted to have my baby and all this crap. And they all do that. So yeah, I'm never going out with a black girl again." And as I looked around reading reactions — no one as stunned as me — behind me Jude concluded, "Black girls are just too *easy.*"

My head whipped around and hissed only, "Jude!" Amid blank faces, he wore a candy-corn smile of so difficult a proportion that I finally decided *Yes, he does in fact look like Mardi Gras the Cat because yes, he is in fact going to die — the same reason he just announced that black girls are easy; he's not scared of leaving now, because he knows he'll be leaving later...*

But De'von simply plucked up and unfolded one of Jude's napkin tents and polished his ring as Red ogled checkered skirts out the window. I let go my breath, wondering if Jude had known they'd spare him, *Or was he hoping they wouldn't? Is he, in more than one way, hoping to be fired before he can quit*? He even continued pushing them; gesturing toward Mizzy far away laughing into the phone at The Hostess Stand (I wondered *Who with?),* Jude added, "And by the way De'von, you're never gonna hook up with girls like *her* if you keep *announcing* that you won't go down."

"Who? Mizzy?" De'von smirked, glancing back over his big white shoulder to The Hostess Stand. He shared eye contact with her, and then she fucking waved to him... Returning her wave he quietly promised us, "Man, I had That the first week she was here, cousin."

"No..." My heart landed on my stomach. Jude shook his strange, disbelieving head. De'von turned his smiling Golds back at us, and like a fisherman diagramming the size of his catch — 12 inches, in this case — he spread his flat hands apart, palm to palm, and boasted, "I gave Mizzy bout this much."

"No!"

Jude heard it in my voice, and tried to veer us away: "So yeah. How is teaching going, Patrick?"

Before I could even think to answer, De'von interrupted, "Pat, you teach? Not at Public School?"

"Yeah, Magnolia," I offered, enthusiastically hoping he might lay off me. "Where you and Red went."

Red nodded affirmation and De'von laughed: "Damn Pat, them black boys are gonna whoop y'ass, dude." Then he laughed more.

Pretending his prediction didn't scare me, I repeated my blank mantra: "No, my kids are rambunctious, but they're not like *that*."

"Sure sure. You watch, they gonna jump you after class some day. You watch."

"No, I swear, my kids aren't the...jumping type."

De'von laughed so hard that I knew it had to be 15% fake. Laughter filled him like helium, lifting him from his seat. His napkins fell to the tile and his eyes watered behind thin gold frames as his laughter carried him away, across The Floor, into The Kitchen where we all heard him retelling The Food Runners and The Dish Pit, "That boy teach at Magnolia bruh! Shit! I told that boy they gonna whip his ass bruh, y'heard me! And you *know* they will too. But you know what that white boy said bruh? That boy said *his* kids ain't *The Jumpin Type*!"

Red stood up beside me chuckling, "That boy Hollywood stupid."

'*Stupid*,' I've ascertained, means clever, resourceful, though Red also sounded like he might be applying a little of the traditional definition... *Hollywood* though? I'd never heard that nickname for De'von before. Red followed Hollywood into the kitchen.

Then Jude repeated, resilient, "So yeah. Really, how's teaching going?"

"Do you think he really fucked Mizzy?" I interrupted his good intentions, fast to beat her walking back to us…

"Yeah, no he didn't. No way," Jude assured me as she sat down at The Picture Window. Trusting Jude's insight, I breathed again. They watched the silent street, the lawn chairs unfolding, the stands mounting, the blockades growing as Mizzy's hands built napkin tents, and I daydreamed a strange choice: *Either Jude and Mizzy continue working at Donkey Show after tonight, or else De'von didn't fuck Mizzy.* My choice. *OK, pick one.* I could not, not even hypothetically. *Glad it's not my choice to make…*

"Did you know he's got a kid in his class named De'von?" Jude asked Mizzy, bringing me back to them. "And he treats Pat worse than De'von here does."

"De'von here doesn't treat me bad," I defended, watching her gap as she laughed at me. Still I continued, "And the one in my class finally came around this morning — maybe only for one class period but… It was monumental, like one of those horrible, inspiring Lean On Me movies: I brought in this Slick Rick song 'Children's Story,' which is this rap about a thug kid who's killed by the cops after he lets…"

"Yeah, uh huh, of course," they nodded in unison, then shook their heads negative: "Yeah we know the song, go on…"

"Right. Anyway. Since it's a linear narrative type rap — whereas most shit nowadays is more just stream-of-bragging — I had the kids analyze the structure of 'Children's Story' for its beginning, middle, end, conflict, setting, dialogue, blah blah blah…"

"Oh good idea!" Mizzy smiled proud.

Proud? "Uh…yeah, then I had them use that song's same structure to create their own raps."

"I'll bet they loved that!"

"Yeah, they went nuts, I mean *more* nuts; I had four dollars in my pocket and put it up as prize money. They cared about That Money way more than That Art, but regardless man, they were *so* fucking into it. Their raps had all this stuff I hadn't taught them yet: point of view, characterization…"

"See!" she beamed, patting me on the back, literally, again amazing me with how well adjusted she is, how forgiving of my indiscretion around the trampoline...

"But oh man the songs are dirty," I continued. "De'von's was about a girl who had to go to the Magnolia High Clinic for her VD — called, 'That Ho Got a Dusty Hole.'"

"Oh Patrick, no..." Mizzy deflated, no longer proud.

"No, but it was good though."

"Yeah but...you don't discourage that type of..." she fumbled somewhere between sarcasm and pure lack of understanding. "I mean not that I'm a prude or anything...but shouldn't you say something to them about...?"

"Well, yeah, but, it's just *really* creative though," I promised. "And that's all I want, is for them to be creative. So, I dunno if that justifies letting them, uh..." I too fumbled, finally offering, "You just have to read it for yourself: sometimes I accidentally bring their folders to work in my book bag, so I'll let you flip through them some day, the writing is fucking crazy..."

"You let *strangers* read your kids stuff?" she asked. That hurt, "strangers," as did, "Isn't that a little unethical?"

I longed to finally admit *'Yes. Right. Unethical. Fucking oblivious. No objectivity, little integrity — I do hate being late, but... But this is why I won't teach at Magnolia again after this semester: I won't let my human deficiencies harm others. If I can't help these kids, at least I can protect them (from me), which is more than most people do, so at least give me that...'*

But in reality I offered only: "I was just kidding."

Mizzy stood, smiled a forced one, straightened her un-divulging white jacket, then walked away until she disappeared.

- 3 -

Stepping into the elevator, Red's jaw churned tortoise-like, masticating pink, plastic squares: Now-n-Later candy. I hadn't seen Now-n-Laters since Middle School. "And that's how long I been addicted to 'em," Red laughed, cheek full. Management had us fetching extra chairs from the fifth floor warehouse for an unexpected 25-top reservation, one of three big parties tonight.

Pressing the gold 5 button, Red admitted that he and his friends were the Middle School kids who'd buy big quantities of Now-n-Laters, and sell to classmates to support their own habits: "Readyin our-little-selves for The Game, later on in life."

I daydreamt vaguely of money, I think, while watching the antique elevator's gold doors close slower than most people could stand to wait for these days. As we rose, Red's deep voice brought me around: "Say bruh, what's on y'mind, Red?" He's the first human to call me Red since…back when I ate Now-n-Laters. "Y'all scowly and shit," he prodded. "What's up?"

"Not scowling. Just zoning."

"You been scowly since folding napkins, bruh. I notice these things. It's cause Jude and Mizzy leavin?"

"I'm not scowling, seriously. I just have an ugly face."

"Naw, you a good-looking dude, bruh," Red assured. This daring sentiment surprised me. As did, "I bet you get lotsa pussy, Patrick."

"No."

"No?"

"None."

"None?"

"I sort of used to, but not since I moved here. Almost a year."

"Damn. That's why you scowly."

"I'm not scowling," I laughed. "Honestly, when my face is in neutral, my brow furrows like I'm thinking too hard, when really it's just…my brain is blank. My parents look nothing like me — no red hair or anything — but their faces do that same thing. My whole childhood I thought they were mad sitting next to me in the car, when really they were just zoned out driving. I grew up thinking they were these angry people, when really they were just concentrating on The Road"

"That's deep bruh," Red nodded. "It's probably why, psychologically, you ain't aggressive enough now to get y'self some pussy."

Before I could naively explain to him that *No, no it's just so impossible meeting people in a new town where, you know, you didn't go to college, so you don't have a context…*the elevator opened onto a vast gray cave.

The Warehouse's left side was stacked with new and old purple-and-gold Carnival decorations like piles of pirate treasure, causing Red to gyrate his hips and boom, "These next three weeks we gonna make That Money!" He danced out of the elevator, "That Mardi Gras money!" grabbing the first two marble-and-gold chairs from a Noah's Ark march of them stretching 100 yards to the back wall. Dragging his chairs to the elevator he said, "This my first year working here for Mardi Gras. I hear it's gonna be beaucoup parties of like 50, 60, 75 people up in here getting shitty on nothin but $300 wine. We gonna be Made Men, cousin." Then setting his pair of chairs down in the elevator he asked, "You worked here last year?"

"No. This is my first Mardi Gras ever." I grabbed one chair; they're unreasonably heavy...

"Ever?"

"Ever."

"Get the fuck!" he huffed.

I dragged mine to his: "No, really. I've never been to one single Mardi Gras."

"Damn bruh, you gonna love it!" He stepped back out past me adding, "White people really dig Mardi Gras."

"Just white people? You don't?"

"It's OK. I like That Money…" He grabbed the partnerless chair I'd left behind, plus the two behind that. I jumped out of his way as he dragged all three into the elevator. When he had them in, he freed his held breath then came out to shake my hand: "Good looking out, bruh. I can tell you've worked hard in your life." He was serious. I said nothing. He grabbed two more chairs. "You got worker instincts," he said, dragging them toward me. "The way you move out my way instinctively when you seen me comin through."

I moved out of his way again. He set more chairs in the elevator. "Actually," I corrected, grabbing another chair, "it's just my instinct to move when I see a black guy coming at me." Red's laugh echoing around The Warehouse, he grabbed three more chairs as I set mine in the elevator, continuing, "Yeah, usually when I see one of y'all coming, there's at least a street I can cross to get away or something. But here at work I'm stuck."

Laughing harder he deposited his chairs, breathed, then, "I'll tell you what bruh. Honestly. When I was a little G comin up, I didn't really like white people. But I been proved wrong." That was great to hear; I always have thought of myself as a better-than-average representative of a questionable race. So Red's declaration, I had always wanted to hear. *Now I can officially pride myself on it...* I stepped out, grabbed another chair and dragged. Three in his grip, Red continued, "I think white people got cooler since all these Brothers got famous making fun of Them." By Them he meant not him or I... "Since Eddie Murphy and Pryor and The Kings of Comedy came up, white people seem like they chilled out a bit, y'feel me?"

I nodded the whole time, feeling friends enough with Red to admit, "I know I told you nothing was bothering me, but your boy De'von is. Today he is. That shit he was talking, about the kids at Magnolia High are gonna jump me? That gets to me. I don't need that shit, y'know? It's hard enough just teaching without someone trying to scare me. Today I had the best morning with the kids and then he has to go and say that shit..."

"De'von a asshole bruh," Red grunted dragging multiple chairs

"Huh?"

"He fake."

"I thought he was your friend?"

Dropping the chairs Red breathed: "He my nigga. I been knowin him a long time. But I don't trust him. That's why sometimes you hear me callin him Hollywood; he fake."

"That's fucked up," I said, meaning I didn't understand why you'd be friends with someone who...

But Red didn't hear me over his own voice continuing, "Hollywood don't know what he talking about; you gonna be fine at Magnolia."

"Yeah, my kids are rambunctious as hell, but they don't seem like they'd jump me," I repeated, not able to remember if I was telling the truth anymore, *Or am I just practicing a Sales Pitch?*

"Oh, if they go to Magnolia they The Jumpin Type," Red laughed to stress that he wasn't joking. "Even back when I was there, boys come in drunk, just got beat up by they mamma and ain't takin no more shit not today not from Mr. Teacher Man."

I nodded.

"And it's worse today," he added. "With all this music."

I nodded harder.

Red re-iterated, "But you gonna be OK; you got a good heart, Pat; ah k'tell; I hear you in The Kitchen singin and shit all the time. You a *stupid* dude, bruh, and them kids gotta respect you for that. They got to. Even I woulda, back when I was at Magnolia."

Red scanned the warehouse, deciding, "We got enough chairs. Let's go." And I felt happy and hopeful following him into the elevator. He pressed the gold G button. We sat in two of the heavy chairs and it felt so great to rest that we rode down in silence. I even remained happy and hopeful grunting, dragging the chairs across The Dining Room, locking the tables into formation, draping them in vast white clothes then trimming the fresh table with 25 napkin-tents — knives and spoons on the right of each tent (blade facing in), and two big forks on each left.

- 4 -

"Flaming shots…" Jude would whisper behind my head whenever he'd pass me on The Floor. Meaning we'd drink to his final Donkey Show night when it was over. Usually after work he has an old friend he has to meet, something, so I looked forward to tonight's, "Flaming shots…"

Jude and I both worked perched in the upstairs Dining Room with its even more insane view of the Central Business District, a view that's already drawing second-tier celebrities. Before the parade shoved off, I was given the duty/thrill of bringing bread-and-water to ZZ Top. Celebrities don't regularly impress Jude — many stars claim they live in NO because the natives won't fuss over them — but the sight of ZZ Top winded Jude. Shot Talk halted. He barely stammered, "A-a-ask them to take us with them! We'll step into one side of their big red ZZ Car in our Monkey Suites, and step out the other side *dressed sharp, man.*"

I didn't remind him that Management had threatened to fire us if we addressed anyone's celebrity; he'd have recognized that as *too perfect*: 'I got fired for talking to ZZ Top.' So he remained employed, while Management felt so free to interrupt ZZ Meal at least five times as though 'Of course y'all'd want to meet *us*...fellow *successful people*!'

By the end, only Management and De'von (my Headwaiter for the third night in a row) had actually spoken to the band — De'von doing so in his pretentious Englishman's Voice: he usually runs this skillful Stream-of-Black dialect over one padded shoulder — almost Shakespearean in its license with the language — until he hairpin flips to The King's English for his customers, totally overshooting though, overusing pure-white phrases like, "Certainly," "As you wish," and "Very well." Tonight when I overheard him describing the specials to ZZ Top — "Our appetizer for this evening is going to be a delightful veal and crab crepe. Excellent, excellent," he assured the band, enunciating like Young Werther. "This exceptional dish comes basted heavily with a highly pleasurable Southern Comfort oyster cream sauce." — I swear it sounded like he was making fun of me... So I walked behind him and whispered into his neat waves of hair, "You sound like a fucking butler."

I stopped before 'dude,' assuming he'd find my joke funny in that rough, competitive way he and the other NO guys are used to... But I couldn't tell what he thought, until he finished *Specialing* his customers and spun on me, his hand on my back guiding me into The Kitchen as he explained, "Say bruh, I know you think you learned how black folks talk from your kids at Magnolia and them ten rap tapes you own. Hell, you might get to be a Nigga-ese expert by the time them kids catch you out there..." *Catch you out there?* "But bruh," he continued. "If I talk real with the rest of these white folks, I'm always answerin, 'Scuse me? Huh? Whu?' Ny ain't got time for a lot of stupid questions, y'heard me?"

I heard. And I should have apologized for calling him a butler. Instead for some reason I defended, "But you don't have to talk that way with ZZ Top, man. It's *ZZ Top*; they'd understand you; they're dirty guys from Texas, dude."

He walked away until he disappeared.

The parade was just about to start when the band finally called for their check and I awarded Jude the honor of clearing plates from under their long pointy beards. This Going Away Present was basted heavily with a highly pleasurable melancholia... Jude's wet eyeballs shined, passing me with his precious cargo, on route to The Dish Pit...

"Flaming shots... I'm buying."

"Aw."

De'von overheard and, collecting ZZ Check from their abandoned table ($125 tip on a $300 meal) he remarked, "Y'all gotchaselves a little date tonight, yeah?"

"Not that it would offend me if Jude *was* gay," I rebutted. "But I told you, and I was serious: Jude gets more girls than anyone I know."

"Sure he do."

"He does."

"Sure he do."

"I swear."

"If Jude gets pussy I'll...I'd..." I sensed real frustration. "How much you want to bet that Jude a no-pussy-gettin lil dude? I *know* that boy ain't get no pussy." His face scrunched, disturbed by the idea.

"He does. More than any guy I know," I declared, not knowing the truth, really.

"No he *don't* man!" De'von barked, the surprise pushing me back. "And I'd say it's best you quit talking bout it."

He was serious; he did not want to believe. First I disregarded it: "Whatever man, your denial doesn't change the fact that..."

"Man, shut the fuck up," he finally said, walking away again. And that's where Our Funny War began. Or maybe it began back where I called him a butler...

At any rate, as The Dining Room's small docile crowd readied for the parade to swim by The Picture Window, De'von threw a saddle on my back again and began riding, chasing me between tables, flapping his wings, squawking, "Faster *dude*! We wanna make That Money! We gotta roll white boy! Turn and burn! You need me to buss that f'yuh partner? Re-set that table f'yuh? I can get it, if you too busy…"

I always played music instead of sports because I couldn't manage this same kind of Psyche-Out bullshit. It unravels me immediately. So it was hard not to instinctively obey De'von's commands to rush and fluster. I fought to keep faith that my pace was adequate, much harder than I had to fight to avoid anger; that fight was easy: just like at Magnolia I kept in mind, *He's just a fucking kid…*

- 5 -

The aftermath outdid the attack; Canal now looks like a new Christmas morning, like something amazing has happened, though it has not. The first parade of Carnival season was nothing: old people rigid waving from convertibles and motorcycles decorated with scraps of ribbon and construction paper. No real floats, no color, no blood. A damp, 30-degree atmosphere kept much of the crowd at home with their warm, healthy pets. Definitely no tits out. One drunk pressed his naked butt against The Picture Window, but overall the party on both sides of the glass remained thin —though still totally distracting though. My eyes aimed out over my water pitcher, searching for Magnolia High amid the very few high-school marching bands. Eventually they will pass by here, and as my body heated bread, my head wondered/feared what it will do to my Classroom Respect Level when one of my kids finally spies me up here in this Monkey Suit, looking down — before, I thought the apron-and-bowtie might win them over, but tonight, faced with the reality of it…

Still, I couldn't come away from the glass, doting over the whole boring thing, wanting nothing more than to follow the silent trumpets and tubas, my stomach tightening to crush whatever anxious but innocent creature fluttered inside of it.

None of my upstairs co-workers shared my oppression; most of them are from here, so none felt held back from any *magic*. They were more frustrated and angry that, contrary to all promises,

promises, promises, promises, the restaurant wasn't very busy. We didn't really make That Money. The crowd remained outside, deep-throating cart-vended corndogs. And our few customers finished eating and paying up a half-hour before the parade even began, then lingered for hours at their tables, buying nothing more, just taking advantage of the view.

In our commercial stillness, De'von was even able to disappear from his section for the parade's duration and no one noticed. Though Management did waddle behind me at least twice grunting, "Quit looking out the window!" Still I kept against the glass like a dog yearning to pee. Let Management write me up! I would *never* miss Magnolia High marching by with Little De'von dancing blowing trumpet in purple-and-gold fuck no *never* would I miss that.

But then they never did go by. Not tonight. When it all finally petered out and the barricades came down, the small crowd dissipated back into The Quarter, and I *work-dreamed* an image of Cedar dictating to Magnolia's Band Director, 'This parade too small bruh. Ain't worth my time, or my band's, you dig?'

And as the OPP prisoners began the cleanup, I whined to Jude, "You're abandoning me for *that*?"

"Yeah, no; it'll get bigger and bigger until it explodes. Sicker and sicker until it like, vomits," he promised, staring past me to the fresh beaded aftermath glinting from every corner of Canal: as many abandoned necklaces as were caught and taken home, the streetlights illuminating the layers in a cold, white way that really did feel like Christmas.

Still I dread experiencing the rest of it from what I know now is definitely the *inside* of the aquarium.

- 6 -

De'von didn't emerge again until our section was a wasteland of dead wine bottles and beads and half-eaten flan. He came bounding to the top of the gold staircase, "OK c'mon bruh! Let's hustle! Let's clean this shit up! I want to get the fuck up outta here boy! Can't be here all night! Damn you slow, Pat. I don't know if we should work together again man…" And once hurrying meant leaving, I fell into obeying his commands, frantically polishing silverware between running stacks of heavy ceramic from our tables to The Dish Pit.

When the last too-big load balanced under my chin, I spotted him across The Dining Room, talking heatedly with our B-waiter, Steadman. Steadman has worked at The Donkey Show since it opened, but early tonight he confessed to me his plans to quit and go back to college after this one last Mardi Gras. Steadman is older, mellow, so I wondered why he seemed so engaged in whatever De'von was flailing his hands around his head about, the same way Little De'von often does. I assumed Big De'von was complaining about me — and I knew that he was, when we met eyes from far away, and he waved me over…

"Let me go put these dishes away first," I shouted across The Floor.

"C'mon bruh! Now!" he shouted back.

My arms were so loaded I didn't want to hazard cutting through my co-workers all rushing to clean their sections and go-the-fuck-home; dropping it all would keep everyone there longer, cleaning the floor. So I struggled the long, unobstructed way around, arms trembling under all that china. And when I'd finally made it, De'von faced me and calmly, brow furrowed, hands on my shoulders like it would help me hear him, he asked, "Ah'ight. Pat…" Big pause. "Did you see a nigga's suit at the Christmas party?"

Ceramic rattling below my obviously confused face…

"My suit," De'von clarified. "Did you see it?" He released my shoulders to illustrate 'suit' by touching the lapel of his Headwaiter jacket.

I silently disbelieved.

"You member? A pale blue number," he continued. "Tell this man right here that it was all silk; Steadman don't believe me."

I turned and shuffled fast to not drop the dishes. Far behind me I heard, "Oh, that's right, you ain't work here back then, Pat" and then De'von's laughter — I'm sure of it…

But eventually he did apologize. Helping me re-set our last table for the next day's lunch, he admitted, "Say bruh, I know I been high strung tonight. But I just really ain't got time for waitin behind anyone. I know you're new, but you gotta learn to hustle…"

Pitching every chair's napkin tent I interrupted, honestly though smiling, "Tonight I caught a glimpse of why everyone dislikes you."

"Ain't nobody dislike me bruh." He dropped the big wooden salt-and-pepper shakers loud in the center of the marble table. "Who don't like me? Y'boy Jude? I'll tell you the bottom line on Jude f'me: he lazy, so I don't like working with him. And that's why he don't like me. Maybe we'd get along famously outside of work. But not when I'm relyin on him, y'feel me?" Straightening the cutlery I'd laid down, De'von pouted, "I do wanna like Jude. I do. I want to like everybody. But you gotta understand cousin, I ain't got time for it. I been through it y'heard? And I ain't got time to go through it again."

"Oh, you've been *through* it," I condescended. "Man, I was probably old enough to baby-sit you by the time *Yo! MTV Raps!* came on the air."

"Nigga, I'm 37," he smirked. "I got grandkids, bruh."

I didn't even put it in my mouth much less swallow it: I walked immediately away, across The Floor to The POS where Michael was tapping his tips into the computer touch-screen. "How old is De'von?" I asked him.

"Oh, darlin, he's almost as old as me," Michael flourished, not looking up. "39 I think?"

I walked back admitting, "Damn De'von, you're ten years older than me."

"Now you see why I'm serious about making This Money," he regressed. "You just gotta trust me, and not be questioning…"

"How many kids you got?" I re-routed.

"Two," he answered, loosening his bowtie and pulling his collar down to display names tattooed in elaborate calligraphy on either side of his thick, mocha neck: *Shantell* and *Biansay*. "Them's my girls," he tied back up. "And they got kids a they own now. I'm a granddaddy. That's real."

I nodded surprised and reverent: "I thought you were like 20, man."

"Thanks Pat. The ladies also tell me I look good for a mature man." Chin lifted, lips puckered posing, he made his point finer: "That's what Jude don't understand: I'm a grown man, and this is bidness f'me, and I handle my bidness. That don't mean I ain't different outside of work. After work I'm chillin with my chirren, laid back, maybe smoke me That Fire…"

That Fire = pot. I salivated; I've run out. My first weeks at The Donkey Show everyone offered me drugs, but I buddied up to Jude and they all reconsidered. Now I find myself having to investigate: taking advantage of our Momentary good standing, I asked De'von plainly, "Where can *I* get some?"

He looked at me through his long eyelashes: "I got that good shit right now."

Then a pause. I wanted to ask him to sell me some of his, help me out, but I still wasn't sure if… "You're lucky," I continued. "I've lived here almost year and I still haven't found a reliable connection."

"I got you," he nodded.

Does he mean… "You have trouble finding weed too? I thought you've worked here for years? Seems like you'd be able to…?"

"No, I mean I *got* you," he repeated.

"You mean *covered*?"

"Yeah bruh. I got you."

"With weed?"

"Damn bruh, c'mon," he glanced side-to-side.

"I'm sorry. My voice is loud…"

"Shit, I ain't worried about no one hearin us," he bragged. "I've sold shit to every Manager in here. Why you think they gimmeee that parking spot?"

"Management smokes dope?" I gasped. "You'd think they'd chill the fuck out then."

"No, not smoke…"

I didn't ask, just said, "Well damn, thanks man, that's awesome. If you can get it for me regularly, I'll buy from you all the time. I'm a

153

horrible pot addict and I haven't been able to get it here. I don't have anyone I *trust*."

Trust. How nice of me...

And with that I believed Our War had ended.

- 7 -

Because Jude and De'von and ZZ Top and I were all upstairs tonight, I really didn't think much about Mizzy downstairs. It felt good to forget about her — until waiting for Jude to finish his sidework, I re-discovered her, holding The Main Door open to the cold, causing me to realize that *Fuck I forgot my jacket...* She was somehow buried beneath beads bigger and nicer than any of the thin plastic crap necklaces the OPP Prisoners had just swept off the street. Shivering beside her in the doorway I suggested, "Hey man! Let's all go celebrate y'all's last night at The Donkey Show."

She stared at my bike leaning on Jude's out in the cold against a skinny, tree dripping the last of the beads; Canal was cleaner than it ever is. The prisoners marched back up into their busses. "I already promised De'von I'd go with him," she answered.

So that's where he was during the parade... But I had no right to get upset, no reason. I imagined the two of them getting drunk and going home together, but the cold bothered me more than that disturbing vision. Midnight came frozen and wet and I stood unprepared: I'd forgotten to bring Civilian Clothes, which you *must* change into after work, because to wear your Black-and-Whites pedaling home is to wear a bull's eye; they'll know you have cash on you. So I removed my dress shirt, stripped down to my T-shirt, still technically black-and-white — not to mention my frozen testes huddled up under my intestines, but at least I didn't look so *waiterly*, so vulnerable. Especially not after, "Take this," Mizzy pulled a clump of bright red fur from her book bag, a stuffed-animal's skin, or actually, a hat, a girl's hat that covered my ears and was warm and *hers*. My reflection in The Picture Window looked ridiculous, but I was happy to wear it.

Our co-workers cared less about Jude leaving than they had

about the anemic parade. They cared only about Mizzy as a wash of them came at us — Fun Boys marching in a shoulder-to-shoulder chorus line behind the Black Team's V-formation, which swallowed Mizzy up and dragged her off into The Quarter before they could even chastise my dumb-looking hat, or divulge where they were taking her.

Then from behind: "Flaming shots…"

- 8 -

Jude with the hair and me under the hat got happy by ourselves, riding through the creepiest parts of The Quarter, past bars and bars and bars and bars > > > past begging gutterpunks and street musicians and humans not-moving for money > > > through the taunts and whoops of all the fratboys attracted to Jude > > > through Goth music blasting from this club, Prince shrieking from that one, behind it all a four-on-the-floor gay-techno bass-drum >>> faster, past fishbelly white strippers covered in goosebumps and scars, standing buck naked in low-class doorways (Jude: "I really want to open a strip club down here, called *Cesareans.*") > > > past a young couple arguing drunk in a higher-class doorway, both of them wearing khaki shorts — Yankees for sure. Even beneath Mizzy's hat the air was frozen hell, so we rode faster, reducing The Quarter to a blur of crumbling pathos as we passed our Heineken bottles between our hands to avoid the same fate as those Civil War soldiers who crouched in the snow waiting so long for their enemies that when the time came to shoot, their dead fingers broke off frozen to their triggers — until finally we landed at Molly's on Decatur.

Molly's is open air, but always warm and everyone is happy, dirty, but still young and beautiful — like Jude's sexy childhood friend with the giant black goldfish eyes and matching mouth. Her wavy, bed-head bob shone the same color as her fake fur coat, which parted to reveal a half-shirt underneath when she reached into her jeans for cigarettes. She was drunk and while Jude was leaning over the bar ordering, she showed real interest in me — for three minutes. For three minutes she studied me, her eyes trying to focus, the way mine would if I saw her coming from far up the street; a squint hoping that when she could finally see me, I'd be something good. Until then, she asked, "Who are *you*?"

"I work with Jude," I said, and added, because I know it works, "I also teach at Magnolia High."

"Ooh, brave. I like your hat. Is it your girlfriend's?"

"I don't have a girlfriend."

"Ooh..."

In Our Three Minutes, I answered all her questions perfectly — until finally her eyes had me, she found focus, and then it was over: she turned to her childhood friend who had returned empty handed: "Yeah, they won't serve us flaming shots," Jude grumbled. "Something about a fire code." Which phased us not, since every building on either side of Molly's for the length of the city is another beautiful bar you could spend all night in. Jude cared a little that his friend wouldn't follow us out, but I didn't; she only made me think of...

"Where do you think Mizzy is right now?" I asked Jude, my frigid hands trying to unlock my cruiser from a pole where two other U-Locks, both exactly like mine, lay empty at the base.

"Yeah, that reminds me," Jude snickered. "Tonight The Black Team kept asking me if I get laid a lot."

Wind pierced my T-shirt and my keys missed the lock again. *How can someplace so fucking hot just a few days ago be like THIS now, or ever...* "You do though," I chattered, "Don't you?" not hearing myself.

"Yeah."

I got the key in then asked, "Do you really though?"

"I don't know."

My lock opened and, "Have you ever messed around with Mizzy?" I don't know where that came from. From the insane cold.

"No," his teeth peaked out.

Back on our bikes past three bars, four bars, five all denied us, citing Fire Hazard. By our sixth denial Jude implored the cold, wet air, "Since when is New Orleans scared of a little glass of fire!" But god-bless the seventh bar, where our blonde bartendress' dead eyes belied she'd snorted enough of something that allowed her to wear next-to-nothing in such weather. She split one bottle of Bud into two iced pint glasses, then poured us each a shot of Bacardi, layered with Amaretto which she lit *poof* then handed the shot-glasses to us to be dropped into the pints *splash* beer on our shirts, the flame dead, then all is chugged and followed by a direct, automatic, and very real Euphoria; very *very* nice, especially in the cold — until gazing google-eyed and foamy- mouthed to our lefts and rights, realizing we'd splashed everyone else too: wet elbows and frowns all around, except for the bartendress, remaining impenetrably high.

- 9 -

Outside wasn't so cold after that. Our warm fingers unlocked our U(seless)-Locks easily and I felt freer to bemoan, "Man Jude, I like Mizzy so much, really."
"Yeah?"
"I wish she liked me."
"Yeah."
"She's just so…not full of shit."
"I know."
"I mean, a whole year without a boyfriend? Most girls are already fucking the new one before they let the old one go. Mizzy's so…"
"Yeah."
"So what should I do?"
"Watch my bike," he commanded, kicking down his stand and walking into a Sex Shop. The lights inside were artificial bright so I contented myself outside — until the cold came back at me through my t-shirt and fading buzz. *A month ago it's hotter than Central America and now why the fuck isn't it snowing…* I didn't even warm watching Jude pop out of The Sex Shop with his lips around a clear plastic nipple protruding from the back of a fake woman as he huffed, nodding affirmative, breathing positivity into her…
"How much was that?" I asked when she'd grown as big as him.

"$60," he mumbled around the nipple.

"$60!" I gulped. "$60 is all I made tonight."

"Me too," said Jude, clearly now, plugging her hole.

"Why'd she cost so much?"

"I sprang for the vibrating mouth."

"In Costa Rica you could get four hookers for $60. Seriously."

"It's worth it; it'll be funny."

I wasn't so sure; I found the joke a little too obvious. *Touristy* almost. "I hope that's not the only reason you bought it," I said. "For $60, you better do something with it besides make people laugh."

"Yeah." He looked into the eyes of the fake woman under his arm, like into the eyes of a friend...

"So where do you want to take her?"

"To a Cigar Bar," he smiled jagged.

"Uh..."

"Cigars are funny."

I'd never smoked one unless it was full of pot. Still haven't. But I did like the idea of Jude's greyhound head sucking a gar as thick as his forearm, so I saddled up and pedaled behind him, watching his doll's open mouth catch frozen air. Tourists yelped and hollered at the couple, but Jude was too cold to answer or enjoy the attention, even in his thin jacket with the goat's head screen-printed on back, which I stared at in mobile silence during our whole frustrating search for this Cigar Bar. It shouldn't have been but it was, a truly miserable time.

Jude yelled back over his doll, "Yeah. I think we passed it. Let's just go back to Molly's and..."

"No, let's keep on," I insisted. Q: *Why*? A: I didn't know yet...

The dead-eyed doll stared back at me, her keeper hollering, "There are plenty of other places we can just..."

"No man, let's go where we decided to go," I said. Q: *Why*? A: Prompted by an unseen force I wouldn't understand until minutes later, when we finally found the place: a big room of black wood, half-full of the same humans who eat at The Donkey Show: blandly dressed, white with nice wristwatches, unstoppable talk about their jobs and meetings no matter how much fun they could be having.

Locals, I think, though ours were the only bicycles locked outside. Inside: feather boas, a few stage masks, many cheap beaded necklaces lying limp on beer guts, everyone too wrapped up in their cell-phone lives to even notice Jude and his plastic date cutting through them to the bathroom.

Only my eyes followed him until he disappeared, and then they continued across the room > > > over all these people who sell their days to pay for these unremarkable nights > > > across a group of black waiters shooting pool, still in their Monkey Suits, unafraid of the messages the white tuxedos expressed — until my eyes stopped, in a dull corner just behind the waiters, where I discovered the force that I now know dragged me there...

Mizzy?

Mizzy!

And that was De'von leaning forward over the green felt, taking his shot. His defiant Monkey Suit looked warm; it was the first time I ever wanted one. *Guess The Fun Boys already left...* The Black Team's backs faced Mizzy as she bit her nails, checked her watch, then looked up: her eyes caught me and her face bloomed into the same expression as Jude's fake woman: eyes wide, mouth an O. She sprang up and charged me. Half as a joke and half in confused fright — *Why's she so happy?* — I darted in the other direction, scrambled away, pushing yuppies, grabbing handfuls of khaki and cigar smoke to leverage my escape. She chased me in an arch around the room until, before I could duck into the lavatory, she jumped me — I've never thought her The Jumping Type.

"It's you!" she squealed in my ear, "It's YOU!" hugging my neck from behind, hurting my esophagus a bit, but fuck... I turned around and sniffed her face: no alcohol stench, seeming in direct conflict to her affection. Beaming, I led her back to the beginning of our chase and sat her down at the bar. De'von and them didn't notice me take her away. Or maybe they did notice, but I didn't notice them noticing; I remember nothing, not what Jude or anyone else was doing, just that I was happier than I've been since moving here...

"You must be fucked up," I accused. "But I don't smell booze. Did you take X?"

Her fingers manually counting my fingers, she promised: "I haven't had one drink."

"No one's buying you any?"

"No. Well. I didn't want one before. My stomach hurt. But now that you're here…" She reached her arm around my back like a pal, but with her nose pressed into my neck, just like at The Art Show, except this time it didn't make me mad. Somehow now it was comfortable, every angle of it natural. Even after eight hours on The Floor she smelled clean, not a bit like cigar; like a religious miracle, but somehow believable. I told her that her soft cheek reminded me of cleaning The Cat Kennels, how I'd open the doors and kittens would step out onto my shoulders, nuzzling my ear, tickling rubbing *purrrrrrrrrring*, almost begging… Then she kissed me on the mouth, and asked if she could drive me home.

"Not right now though," she laughed, sipping the Bailey's I'd bought her. "I want to drink a little."

Damn… The deal was set, and my head was now free to come up out of our cold-weather cuddling for a second, and spot Jude. He was fine too, across the bar with a dumb cigar in his face. He was right; it was very funny…On either side of his cigar sat girls he's probably known since before he grew pubic hair. And in his lap, the woman he'd just bought. When our eyes met he pumped his fist in honor of Mizzy and me. "Thank you!" I yelled back, then ordered him and her and me each another drink. When those were guzzled, Mizzy bought another for just her and me because, she swore, "Those girls will buy all Jude's."

But after that it dwindled down to just me buying drinks for me: De'von left without saying goodbye, but neither Mizzy nor I had noticed; she noticed only the friend he'd left behind, a younger guy twice my height with coffee skin, tight braids and big, beautiful lips. Between bouts of laughter with me, she'd run off to him, then back to me for a second to scratch behind my ear, then she's off again… Across the bar Jude's face chastised her shameless bigamy, though somehow, she didn't bother me.

The growing crowd breathed a white shag carpet of smoke out onto the ceiling. The lights dimmed and another button opened all their shirts. Mizzy's trips to De'von's friend grew more frequent and I tried watching them over the crowd's thinning hair and eyeglasses but... She came back and squeezed my arm and sipped my drink and smelled my neck and promised, "I'm almost ready to leave. You look so cute in that hat." *Oh right, the hat...* She assured me again that we were going home together, then ran off again. But like some version of Faith, I still didn't care. Jude's head continued to shake until his girlfriends looked bored with him. I took off the fucking hat and shrugged. Far across the room, we all watched her lightly kiss De'von's friend (lighter than the kisses she'd given me), then follow him out of sight into The Cigar Bar's POS...

Jude let his doll drop to the floor, walking over to me speaking clearly, "Yeah, what's that fucking bullshit?"

Aw, sweet... I'd never seen him like this. I shrugged again.

"Why is she fucking with you like that?"

"I don't feel fucked with."

"Yeah. Right. Come with me..."

He led me outdoors. I put her hat back on. We were somewhere outside The Quarter, I'm not sure where, walking up to a dead rusted playground with a long batting cage like a half-buried orange skeleton. As we approached the cage, dozens of birds, sparrows maybe, came awake inside it, speeding in circles around and around, unable to find a way out of the cage. A big hole gaped in a top corner, but in their panic the birds were unable to find it. We stopped to watch their circles, circles, circles, circles, until the flock began thinning slowly as one bird after another finally discovered that big hole. We tried betting on which bird would leave last, but kept losing track of which was which bird. Finally just three blurry sparrows spun redundant laps, then only two, then just the last one: the one we deemed The Winner.

When The Winner flew off, we opened a door in the cage and sat on a wooden bench inside where Jude scolded: "So that doesn't bother you?"

"Mizzy? Not really. I'm not sure why not, but..."

"Yeah. Well it makes me not wanna talk to her anymore."

"Oh c'mon. Who cares? She's not mine. I quit expecting

anything from her a while ago, and I still don't expect anything now." Improvising my explanation I noticed two sets of eyes across the baseball diamond, peaking around the stucco corner of an abandoned concession stand. Watching the eyes I continued, "It's like, in my dreams I don't try to control the other characters' actions, I just wait and see what kind of insane shit they come up with themselves..." I liked how wise I sounded. I believed in myself. But my strength had come with that little attention she'd given me, I realized sadly, as the eyes peaking around that corner turned into two black boys leaning against the dugout, watching us...

"Then *I'm* going to take her home and fuck her tonight," Jude threatened. "Since you don't care."

That twinge of Real rocked me, and when the boys-with-eyes continued across the baseball diamond toward our batting cage I stood up: "No, no. I'm going to do that myself, if that's what you're worried about... But uh, let's go though. Now."

One of the boys shouted something at us, but we made it back into The Cigar Bar just as Mizzy was slithering out from the POS, releasing that guy's hand. I let her run back to me and stick her lips in my ear: "Let's go now." Jude scowled when she grabbed a handful of his mullet and declared, "Your hair looks so dope, Jude."

Then again to me, "Let's go."

- 10 -

Mizzy's truck — the first motorized vehicle she's owned since moving here almost two years ago — is huge and ugly like a fork chewed by a garbage disposal, the same way it's looked since the day she bought it at Bridge House Thrift Store. Except since she's "been owning it" she says, its bed has begun collecting garbage from the side of the road, garbage she claims "insane people" have tossed out, "Garbage that shouldn't be thrown away; it must be harbored." Harbored garbage: "*Harbage*" she calls it, throwing all *Harbage* into her truck, then leaving it there, never doing anything with it... But it is beautiful back there; currently in the collection: several long shotgun shutters, a green mesh fishing net, a wrapped bundle of bamboo rods, a sort of weather-vain-or-satellite-dish, thin brass pipes, a bar stool, a waist-high fan, a bag of red plastic lips, something wicker, a box of feathered Carnival masks (rained on and ruined), a box of tiny gold bells, and tonight my bike — as well as a five-pound clump of black-and-green sod wedged into her back bumper; she ran into an embankment earlier.

Pulling out of The Cigar Bar her truck did indeed moan like a whale and Mizzy admitted she'd neglected to get it checked by a mechanic before laying down $1200 for it because, "I was afraid of what they'd say." She wanted *It*, not reasons to the contrary… The truck's cab is longer and wider than the couch she played opossum on in My Room, affording her room to lean far back, one knee against her chest, comfortable like Monday Night Football as she explained what a bitch-of-a-time she's been having, adjusting to driving again after so long. "Especially here," she yawned. "Driving here is like driving in fucking Mexico or something. Lawless."

On bikes we'd have been home and naked by now. Instead we were stuck in our clothes for extra minutes in The Quarter, pinned against Jackson Square. Out her window I didn't expect to see Lani or his table this late at night, but when my eyes gave up searching for him I did notice out Mizzy's back window, a carriage-dragging donkey chewing on her truck — we laughed as hard as we ever have together, realizing he was eating the sod from her bumper. I saw this as a sign that we were doing *right*…

Once out of The Quarter, rain began falling like BBs, loud onto her truck. I asked her directly, trying not to giggle, "So you're staying at my house?"

"No."

"Why not?"

"I'm just driving you home." Her leg fell from her chest to the seat. "Just doing you a favor."

"Why's that?"

"I like being around you."

"Aw." I looked away out the window, but couldn't see through the rain. *Why are we on the interstate? My house is right up Esplanade…* My eyes returned to her: "If you like being with me then, why not be with me for ten more hours?"

"No."

"Is it because of your Cigar Bar boyfriend?"

"I'd never met that guy before that. I don't even know his name."

"Really?"

"No." The rain's voice crept in on us like those eyes at the playground.

"How did you meet him?"

"I just said, 'You're beautiful.' And then…"

"Then kissed him?"

She nodded — then shook her head negative.

"You're brave," I told her.

"I don't know about brave," she laughed. "Stupid maybe. I don't know why I did that. I'm acting so crazy tonight. I've never done anything like that before…"

In college, every girl I ever did anything suddenly dirty with gave me that exact same line once she was sober. But Mizzy sounded real, un*emphasized*. I won't idealize her, but I do get the sense she's never trying to affect anything, anyone, ever. And dry in the storm, I did fantasize that she'd kissed that guy tonight simply to get something out of her system, before our long and loyal monogamy…

"Maybe you're acting crazy because of The War," I lightheartedly suggested.

"War?" she scrunched her nose, confounded.

"Yeah, like a full-moon; maybe your body is subconsciously reacting to The…"

"Are you talking about September 11th?" she asked. "That was like nine months ago. I mean, not that it wasn't tragic and…"

"No, I mean This *War*," I rolled my eyes. "The War *now*."

"There's no War going on," she snickered. "The President's been trying to go to War all year but… You read The Paper wrong or something."

"Oh, really?" I deflated, but then still defended, "Well, I wouldn't know because I make a point to never read or watch…" But before

164

I could fully incriminate myself I clamped my jaws around my frightened yell, because no driver needs that when they're hydroplaning, scary-as-hell, spinning like a swamp buggy on lake Okeechobee. But we lived. After three or four or twelve full circles, she pulled us out of it.

We didn't speak again until, "Man that sucks," she tried laughing. "I bought this thing because I *thought* it was big and *safe*..."

"Well there's no weight in the back," I explained. "A million pounds of engine up front, but that junk back there doesn't weigh a thing."

"It's not junk," she scolded. Then we went quiet again.

Off the highway and into my safe, quiet neighborhood, she passed up My Room by two blocks then stopped. The chill of her cab bothered neither of us as we made out. Our rhythm was tight, like playing in a really good band where everyone has their parts down: so surprisingly tight she stopped a couple times, pulled away from me to show me her teeth and hum, "Man. Weird. We feel perfect."

The third time she said this, she reached across my lap to her glove compartment and removed a condom. My heart ran uncomfortable laps in there, but the rest of me was fine. "I thought you weren't coming inside?" I kissed her.

"I'm not."

The pitch and volume of our perfectly played song rose and rose until finally I was inside her and I couldn't help thinking: *Yes!* Nothing like this ever happens to me anymore, where I get exactly what I want — though I wasn't dwelling on that at that point fuck no; I thought of nothing and recognized Failure nowhere, not a facsimile of it, not its reflection, not its evil little shadow like an eclipse through a pinhole, not vague memories of past Failures... In Victory, not even the cold could touch me, because it's mostly just *thinking* that makes you cold, and I had given up thinking, hadn't even noticed our disrobing since the cab gave us as much room as we'd have had on my bed. It was just her and me and blessed Lack of Thought like a spell cast — until my neighbors' faces somehow snuck into my head: faces I only ever see taking out their trash or sweeping their walks now distracted me as I imagined them pressed into their phones, peering out at my bobbing whiteness, the same voices that greet me on mornings when I'm pedaling off to go teach now demanding, 'Yes, please send an officer out here right away…'

"We should go inside," I suggested, watching her open her eyes, fall out of the trance. "I know you said you weren't going to come inside but…my neighbors."

"Jesus," she huffed, trying to sit up beneath me. I'd ruined it. It. The Spontaneous Adventure of It, the only thing that had started It in motion, I had now stopped It. Not smiling, she reached behind her head and unlocked her door and rolled naked into the cold, then stood there, disappointed. Watching me search the floorboards for my workpants, she huffed again, "Oh God, *c'mon*. You've got to put your clothes back on? Let's just go. Don't be so…"

I fished the pocket for my keys: "Easy," then dropped the pants back on the floorboard, slammed the door, and chased her naked up my block as she had chased me through The Cigar Bar, except now with my wooden penis sheathed in a condom, and both of us screaming to scare away the cold.

At my door my frozen fingers fumbled with my keys. She grabbed at my loose stomach squealing, "Oh hurry! Hurry! Hurry!"

There was no ignoring the cold now under my bright porch lights. I couldn't get the key in for my shaking. So I gave up for a second, turned to taunt her, my erection warm against her leg: "Don't tell me to hurry. This is a beautiful Moment, Mizzy. Let's not rush it."

"NO! Hurry! Hurry!" she squealed, grabbing me, hot breasts on my chest melting my heart. I dug fingers into her shoulder blades and ass and wished she could come to Costa Rica…

"What made you change your mind about me?" I asked, immediately wishing I hadn't…

"I don't know," she shivered and shrugged, her face in my neck. "The spirit of Mardi Gras?"

I turned and unlocked the door for us.

ACT 3: LOVE STORY

ch 11: another parade

Under daylight, her truck is harder to romanticize — both as an object of ragged beauty, and as a symbol of some turning point for Us. She woke spacey and distant, hungry, but too listless to eat. So we stayed naked, flipping through a giant art book I haven't opened since college. She didn't cover herself, she let me see it, gave me the right. Still she was spacey and distant, and obviously didn't like me as much now. But *fuck it*; in That Moment everything's fine: The Pipes are clean, pores and corpuscles yawning open, breathing like they haven't all year.

Then finally food Uptown, at some creative breakfast spot with a squiggly name. When she first suggested leaving my bed I fibbed, "I have business Uptown too, then Work. If you gave me a ride, we could have breakfast. My bike's still in the back of your truck if it's not stolen; you wouldn't have to drive me home."

"OK."
"You sure?"
"Whatever."
I stuffed my unwashed Monkey Suit into my backpack, smiling.

My Uptown *business* was actually just a *hope:* I didn't work until tonight, but I wanted to meet De'von outside The Donkey Show before his lunch shift, to buy weed. He said that'd be a good time to catch him. He also gave me his cell-phone number, but I forgot to call before following Mizzy out my door.

I figured that either way he and I would hook up, I was safe, so between the promise of weed and the smooth flow of my new Clean Pipes, I was happy despite her spacey distance...

Until her Fried Green Tomato Po-Boy arrived and took her away from me. That Sandwich had all her attention for the duration of breakfast. No conversation. Just her chewing her bites halfway before shoving in the next bite, leaving her bites standing in line, two-deep on her tongue. I didn't like the way she ate. But I liked the fact that I didn't like it so in the end what's the difference...

Then even after That Sandwich disappeared, we still shared no vocals. Hers wasn't a solemn silence, not like she wanted out and away from me, but... It still made me wonder if maybe I'd taken advantage of her in a weak Moment — though *I swear I didn't think she had those. Or shit maybe her silence is just biological: a full belly plus her own Clean Pipes and her thoughts can attach to nothing*? Mine attached to her easy enough but... Or it may have been as simple as the weed we smoked before leaving my room. Or the reality that I will indeed be discarded quickly, and without thought.

- 2 -

De'von wasn't around The Donkey Show and since I'd forgotten his phone number, instead of waiting for him to materialize I rode all the way back home and called him, then walked across the street to wait for him at The Coffeehouse because it's better than My Room. I'd bought a cup of coffee there last night, but since drinking two cups before bed isn't smart I hadn't exercised, at that time, the One Free Refill Law. Instead I brought my paper cup home, planning to use it again this morning, while waiting to buy drugs. I often buy coffee at night then collect my refill in the AM; I know refills are In-

House Only, but I live right across the street and I buy at least one cup a day and this is a neighborhood in the truest sense, so I shouldn't have a problem.

And it's never been a problem, not even this morning; they poured my owed chicory on command as I chatted with my dark brown neighbor standing behind me in line. I asked her how Mardi is doing, while silently wondering why The Hospital let her keep the poor cat, and hoping she hadn't seen Mizzy and me…

"It is much, much healthier," she claimed of Mardi, as I collected my coffee, and noticed the Manager whispering in the barista's ear — surely, I believed, about me.

The Manager there is new. It was once a tall red-haired guy I trusted, but now it's a woman, young, fat, buried in base makeup, and *into it*. This last part is the saddest to me because her Coffeehouse is part of a huge NO chain that could never care about her the way she proved today that she cares about Them. She cared enough to harass me on the couch where I sat sipping and reading: "I'm sorry to bother you, but when were you in here last?" she asked me.

"You mean the refill?" I pre-emptively admitted. "I was in here last night but didn't get a refill then, so I just…"

"Who was it that served you last night?"

I didn't remember.

"Well, none of my employees remember serving you either," she stated. "In fact none of my employees remember you buying coffee here, ever. Just refills every time…"

Wait… I'm being accused? No. I spend almost $14-a-fucking-week here. And even if I wanted to, I couldn't keep using the same cup over-and-over; y'all design them so that on the third use the bottom disintegrates out and coffee leaks onto your clothes — and what kind of crooked shit is that, by the way? Y'all would rather fill landfills and the streets of New Orleans with bunk paper cups than EVER let anyone make off with four fucking cents worth of your coffee?

I thought to impose all this on her, but instead remained silent on the leather couch, bewildered by her continuing, "Sir, I don't want to make your visiting here an uncomfortable experience, and I understand what it's like to not have money, but sometimes you have to buy…"

"But I do," I finally defended, still too confused yet for anger: *She 'knows what it feels like to' what?*

"Well, from now on I'm going to have to ask you to keep your receipt," she said. "And show it to the barista before we can issue you any more refills."

She turned and walked away. *She has a huge ass. Why am I being singled out? Sure they see me everyday when I first get out of bed, but I didn't think I looked criminally disheveled. This shit is like Cedar claiming: "Why should we listen to someone who wears shoes like that?" But I thought it was just the kids... Do I project poverty? Maybe that's why it sometimes feels good inside my Monkey Suit... But then the rest of the time I look shystie?* Had my Pipes not been flushed-out the night before, her accusation would have gotten to me. Actually it did regardless: *I can't go to The Coffeehouse anymore. I can't give them any more of my money after this. All the employees have noticed? I'll be stuck in My Room… My Coffeehouse is gone.*

I wanted to leave that instant. But more than that I wanted weed. So I reached a compromise, stole a newspaper from the stack labeled, "For Sharing with the Neighborhood!" and walked outside to the patio tables, to wait for De'von.

But out in the perfect weather, the *Picayune's* Front Page told of a new insane Murder, right there in my neighborhood, three blocks from my front door…

- 3 -

Murder.
Murder.
Through the fog that headline inflicted, I noticed that De'von looked good; his Civilian Clothes were more conservative than I'd expected; no big logos littered his puffy beige jacket, or the black turtleneck covering his daughter's names. *Murder.* He also wore a

discreet diamond earring, and shaking hands as he slapped my back, I noticed a thin, white bracelet — yes, he gave me the often insincere Man Shake, but it was nice; he emitted a comforting vibe I hadn't read from him before. I guessed it was *true*; he does chill out beyond The Donkey Show. *Murder.*

We climbed inside his SUV with its bright rims, the same type of car being described by the voice blasting from his nice stereo... *Murder.* But it was comforting to be inside a nice, new truck that smelled clean, high off the ground, started confidently, the radio loud, but creamy. *I can see how a woman would want a man with a nice car. Murder.*

"Wait, wait, Pat, Pat, check this out..." De'von tapped the CD player off to mumble and beatbox, "I-*boom*-can't-*bip*, find-*boom*, my-*bip*, way *boom-bip*, *b'boom-boom-bip*..." He laughed deep, "Kick that shit one time f'me Pat! Kick me a verse of That Original you got, "I-can't-find-my-way-arouuuuuuund-*boom-bip*, *b'boom-boom-bip*."

"You're doin good on your own, man." *Murder.* I didn't feel like singing. We pulled away from The Coffeehouse's patio, which I'd never traverse again, but didn't care; my mind on the Murder and the Murder on my mind: *Should I move away? That kind of shit doesn't happen in Costa Rica...* My Neighborhood is the only place in the city I've felt truly safe, until these killers came at 8:30 am, just after I'd ridden off to go teach, meaning my neighbors were being Murdered as I argued with the mere two kids who showed up to class (the rest had Mardi Gras duties to respect). Driving wherever with De'von, I was even too drained and distracted to leak to him where Mizzy had slept last night. So I definitely didn't feel like fucking singing for him.

But calm down, soon there will be weed... I tried concentrating on that, and the nice stereo, my Clean Pipes, light banter: "We work at the same place, *dude*," I said, giving him that word he likes, the way Mizzy gives me her teeth. "How come you got 20-inch rims and I have 28-inch?"

"28-inch?"

"On my bike."

He laughed then didn't mind admitting, "Cousin, I made forty-one grand at that place last year."

"As a server?"

"Damn straight."

"Wow. I gotta aspire upwards then."

"Yeah, you can't be no Backwaiter if you want That Money. And speaking of…is $25 cool?" He slid me a small but heavy sealed envelope, down low, so surrounding cars couldn't see. U-Turning at the cemetery I thought I spotted a nutria leaping off the seawall into Bayou St John, but it was just a cormorant — I did onetime see two actual nutria, on the day I moved here, when I was walking around the Bayou feeling safer than I should have. I haven't seen any since…

Driving back toward My Former Coffeehouse, I didn't open the paunchy envelope; I wanted to be vulnerable with him, blindly hand him $25, just *trust* he'd hooked me up. In front of my house on *Murder Street* I was so amped to go inside and get high that I jumped out fast, slamming his truck's door on my own last, "Thanks, man!"

But in My Room, the heavy *envelope* contained mostly army-green seeds. After 15-minutes trying to pick the seeds out of the little bit of actual weed, I finally just dumped it all onto a Van Halen vinyl album sleeve, then tapped the underside with my finger causing the seeds to roll off the edges, leaving behind barely enough pot for two joints. $12.50 a joint. It takes me three hours to make $25. *Son-of-a-bitch.* I twisted one up and smoked, hoping they don't pair me with that motherfucker again tonight…

- 4 -

Crossing Rampart into The Quarter I needed a break from the cold air slamming up my nostrils, so I pulled over and walked my bike. Halfway down the first block's sidewalk, my shoulder almost knocked a featherless baby Bluejay off a chain-link fence. I don't know how he got up there; no way could he have flown up; he was too young to even jump that high. *How's he gonna get down*? And if he didn't die stranded there, below him on the sidewalk two cats paced back and forth, waiting for him to fall. The bird had his head sunk down between his downy shoulders, staring forward, nothing else he could do.

Now, maybe it's giving humans too much credit to assume that anyone who came upon this scenario would immediately think of it as A Symbol. But I did, as I do assume most people would. *But a symbol of what? Am I the bird? What does the cat represent? Or wait, maybe The City would be the...*

Then, "Yo Mista Patrick!"

Behind me Cedar and two big friends were coming up fast. A little Fight-or-Flight surged in me. I thought of shark cages as they passed on either side... But just ahead of my bike Cedar turned and walking backwards smiling asked, "Sup *whoadie*? Where you off to?"

"Work," I replied, "The Donkey Show."

Cedar's friends rounded the corner as he paused to ask, "Donkey Show?"

Then suddenly a loud shriek: the cats, eyes squinting mad, ears back, claws out and up, ready to fucking do it. Then just as suddenly their stances relaxed and one cat licked the top of the other's head...

"Uh yeah, the restaurant where I work," I continued. "I told y'all about it."

"That's the name, Donkey Show?"

"No."

"Where it's at?"

I explained and he knew the building: "Actually, that's the buildin that one Ignatius dude went into on the first page of That One Book by That Man Who Kilt Hisself."

Holy shit he's right! Ignatius' lute string! I hadn't even realized... To compliment but not patronize, I gave Cedar just, "Damn, bruh." He smiled then jogged backwards asking, "You can get me a job at The Donkey Restaurant?"

"Of course," I said, not considering the possible consequence.

"I'll talk to you about it in class..." as he passed around the corner, following his friends, leaving me wondering how he can be so nice to me now, so different after... I wondered which one was real. *Though the cats fight and then let it go, never hold grudges, and that's all completely natural... Maybe it's not real anger, just angry sounds*... Reminding me of: *the fucking Bluejay!* I spun, and up the fence, the bird was gone. The cats still tongued each other on the sidewalk, no hint of carnage. I leaned over the fence to search the grass and even the branches higher up, but I just could not figure out what the fuck happened to him...

But I had to get going, so I wouldn't be late.

- 5 -

This one was bigger, but...A few small floats tonight, every one's passengers uniformed in capes and masks reminiscent one of nothing if not The Klan. Still I wanted at it, couldn't peel my nose off the glass. Especially now without Mizzy and Jude, there's nothing left but these parades, self-pity and De'von on my Enemies List — he worked upstairs with Red and Michael tonight, so it was easy for him to avoid me. But just as the parade revved up, he slinked behind me at The Picture Window: "So how is it?"

"It's just starting man." I didn't turn.

"No, I mean that *stuff*," he whispered. I turned to his sincere smile and squinted eyes imitating *high*. "That's That Fire, right? I told you."

"Are you talking about weed?" I turned back to the mild, silent festivities outside. "I didn't buy any weed from you man. I bought a *Grow Your Own Weed Kit*."

"What you mean?"

So many more important things going on in the world right now: if not Murder, than at least parades and Clean Pipes and meeting Mizzy after work at her new job on St. Charles... De'von continued vying for my attention until finally I repeated, serious while yawning, "Leave me alone, dude." I immediately wished I hadn't said it, but at the same time my voice sounded *good*, solid, not angry and irrational, simply, elegantly dismissive. He finally stomped upstairs muttering racial slurs.

Yet somehow I made it through the worknight dwelling only on the sex I'd have later. Despite my wanting out, tonight flowed smooth and mellow — I even somehow easily found the 50 Dessert Spoons we *must* polish every night before Management will release us from captivity, back into the wild; usually after polishing 45, I'm stuck searching The Dining Room an extra hour for *those last five fucking spoons I need to just go-the-fuck-home...* But when Stupid Ass trekked away to find a Manager who would perform the *Checking Out* ritual, he/I left all my silverware carelessly exposed in The POS... Servers expressing end-of-the-night needs already climbed all over Management like piglets at the teat, so to me Management growled, "Not now!" And when I moped back to wait at my silverware, my Dessert Spoons were gone.

I ran out to our tables to make sure someone hadn't accidentally set the spoons out on the tables, though of course no one would do that. So I marched upstairs to De'von, who answered my question with laughter.

"You fucking did it," I accused him. "Give them back, dude," my voice not sounding so good now...

"I don't know what you mean, Pat," he smirked. "Don't go accusing if you ain't know the truth. Only the truth can set you free..."

"Red will get them back for me," I threatened.

"There you go then..."

But Red, in back by the espresso machine just beginning the struggle to gather his own Side Work silverware, claimed ignorance.

Back at Management, I again realized how much they remind me of big fat cops, and I hate cops, and I'd never call cops unless there was a Murder, *but now here I am calling them over fucking spoons? And not even spoons for real food: fucking Dessert Spoons...* Management hovered like banyans as I cried my situation up to them. But at the same time everyone else was loudly explaining *their* situations, thus Management heard none of us.

So I marched off again in search of my spoons as De'von laughed, and I knew I *was* ridiculous searching and searching especially after a gay, white waiter who wished to remain nameless admitted, "I saw De'von take your stuff, darlin." Still despite, I returned to the espresso machine to again ask if Red had heard or seen anything yet. In the silence following my question, I noticed that now, fifteen minutes later, he had a dozen polished forks, a couple knives, some soup spoons and miraculously, a heap of Dessert Spoons, at least enough to meet his quota. Still I couldn't accuse him, for the same reason I haven't been able to see that De'von isn't just *being funny*, but rather, he hates my *fucking* guts…

"Did De'von give you those spoons, man?" I begged Red. "Cause if he did they're mine; he took them from me."

"I dunno bruh. I just polished all these. And ain't nobody taking none of mine, y'feel me?"

"OK" Though I didn't believe him… See, this is what they do to you: strap you into a vest and bowtie then pit you against each other in the most ridiculous, demeaning, worthless situations, when outside and down the street from *your* house, Murders are being committed which you'll forget about for a minute to dwell on the loss of some fucking spoons. I nearly hate Red now — over spoons? And not even spoons for *needed* food…

Trapped beneath layers of injustice, I ran to Management a third time. As Michael stood waiting his turn to speak I asked him, "You're working with De'von man; did he take my spoons?"

"Probably child, I don't know."

"He did," I hypothesized, but received no concurrence or denial. "Michael," I pleaded. "I don't want to stay here an extra hour looking for 50 spoons that I already worked hard to find and polish already. So tell me man: did he take them?"

"Yes," Michael whispered.

"Then please tell Management or else I'm stuck here…."

"Nobody likes a rat, child," Michael turned and trotted off fast before his turn with Management, who then turned on me….

"Now what do you need?" Management asked.

I yelped like a dog hit by a bike, "People have fucking *admitted* to me that De'von took my silverware, but *no one* will stick *up* for me as if it's worse to *tell* on a thief than it is to *be* one! Well, I'm not *look*ing for any more fucking spoons, and I'm not *pol*ishing another one either! I already *did* my work for tonight!"

I was surprised and thrilled when Management deemed that the entire staff would stay until I'd found and polished 50 Dessert Spoons. Management did this — *for* me, not *against* me — hoping someone would turn De'von in. But no one did. De'von and Red even strutted up to me empty-handed as I stood beside Management waiting for my spoons: "Pat, just do you work bruh," Red frowned. "Don't blame it on us. I ain't stayin here late because of you."

"Because of *YOU*!" I pointed and yelled at both of them.

De'von laughed at my high voice. Red didn't. Red unfolded his arms, palms up offering, "Anytime you want bruh…" Management probably thought Red meant, '*Anytime you want* to polish those spoons…' But I knew he meant, '*Anytime you want* to fight.'

Fight. Fight. Fight. Jail. Murder. Fight. See, this is what they do to you…

- 6 -

Mizzy's New Job is much more lax. She's still trapped directly on the main parade route, but now she wears just a black T-shirt and dirty little apron, and aside from tolerating the Cajun bands, her most daunting task is helping the geriatric crowd navigate the temporary, Mardi Gras buffet line.

Both of our restaurants had been closed a while before Michael finally hunted down and polished 50 new Dessert Spoons himself, then walked away without response when I whined, "Thanks man, but I wish you wouldn't have…" And ridiculous as it is, the Guilt stayed with me all the way until I rolled up outside her new, small picture window, and recognized celery peeking out from a Bloody Mary being handed to her by a weasel-face, pony-tailed, goatee'd white guy younger than me. I gauged him a cook. Not a chef; a cook. And I didn't like his white hand on her back, but when she finally noticed me outside, she jumped up away from him to come unlock the door and lead me inside by the arm.

The weasel introduced himself as yes, a cook, also Kitchen Manager, "But really I play drums." He's also donating four rolls of X to Mizzy in exchange for her watching his house and dogs in Algiers over This Holiday Season. He leaves every year during Mardi Gras: "I'm mellow man; it's too much for me." When he disappeared to the bathroom, Mizzy's face beamed close to mine like *We are going to lose our minds together!* We imbibed a couple more free drinks, which helped wash away the last traces of my sour worknight. I didn't relate my stupid spoon struggle to her; if you go around re-living these trivial work traumas with your loved ones, that means they *really* have you… I remained more concerned with the weasel cook's white hand, which I accidentally touched on my own way to her spine — from there on I regarded him as The Enemy. Even after he removed a small, white-plastic bottle from his dirty cook's apron…

"Y'all can split the rest of this," he pronounced, straight from The West Bank. "I've had enough." It was prescription cough syrup, with codeine.

"Arc you *allowed* to take this?" Mizzy teased me. "I mean, you wouldn't want to try any *new drugs*?" But actually, yes I'd previously tried codeine syrup, and thought it great shit; you feel asleep while awake, translucent blue ribbons circling your head. He'd already drunk half the bottle, but the remainder between her and me tasted delicious, and gave us an immediate warm, calm buzz, reminiscent of that flaming shot, only much much *deeper*, like winter by a fireplace. The elixir also seemed to coat my stomach, awakening a craving for much much alcohol…

From the unlocking of our bicycles, our Comic Timing played in odd signatures to the tune of screaming laughter that propelled us down skinny French Quarter streets and though I knew it wasn't, it felt like love. Of course the Bloody Marys and cough syrup helped… And the six shots of sake and two beers at the Shim Sham club — only $5! Leaving Shim Sham we decided on To-Go Beers, but before we could order them, some tourists who'd been watching and enjoying our Joy sent us two beers, along with two Lemon Drop

Shots, which we downed, before carrying the beers outside, where I finally got what I've wanted: a bike ride beside her, balancing one-handed beers, flying past the Jackson Square mules awaiting their burdens, and not even thinking how fucking mad that makes me.

Those beers were gone by Mythique on Decatur, a dark little velvet hole where kids younger than me play very old records and wear happy black lace clothing and sit on the floor reading and writing and drawing and painting and drinking, somehow unpretentious. After two Greyhounds there, our drunk really took flight, and lying on giant pillows we accidentally met the owner of Mythique, who allowed me to convince him that I should host a Reading Night at his club. Impressed, Mizzy squeezed and kissed me like a girlfriend, though no girlfriend I've had…

Two more glasses of wine and I asked if we could go back to her house, sleep in her big clean bed. But, "I like your room a lot actually," she insisted. And riding up Esplanade, under the overpass, I knew I'd give my domicile another look through her eyes… My whole neighborhood was actually *even better* with her laughter echoing through it after I told her about that Coffeehouse incident this morning, that Manager lady's fat ass, and waiting for De'von — which naturally lead to The Murder…

Chaining up on the very street where it happened I detailed, "Yeah, just three blocks away, a couple were coming out to their car to go to work at 8:30 a/m yesterday, and this sedan pulled up asking for directions… Suddenly two guys jumped out of the sedan with shotguns and ordered the man to lay down in the driveway…then they drove the woman to an ATM which took a sweet photo of the guys." Clumping up my stairway under the burned-out bulb I continued, "When they got back to the house with the money, they made the lady lay down next to her husband…then they put the shotgun to his chest, killed him, then to her chest, but the gun jammed so they ran off…"

"They left her alive?" Mizzy asked, stunned on my couch, removing her work shirt so that just a thin tanktop barely held her breasts. "I would have rather died," she claimed, same as I've overheard all my neighbors at The Coffeehouse claiming…

"I know," I replied, cranking on my tiny, dangerous gas Space Heater, though I really wasn't cold. "It's some fucked up shit. I know."

"Three blocks away?" she asked.

"Yeah, it's fucked up."

"In *this* neighborhood?"

"Yep, fucked."

And then we had sex.

ch 12: parade practice

"Every week it says *clearly*, right there on the fucking schedule: you either work *one* shift a day, dinner or lunch, or else *both* shifts, a double. But then I just found out that if this week's schedule says 'one shift', it means one shift that's *all - day - long*. They just sprang that shit on us last minute!"

"Why you complainin? You gonna make That Money," said She-La, the sometimes class-spokeswoman with the long skinny appendages, who for some reason sat at my desk this morning, the side of her face on my book bag.

"Well, it's my first Mardi Gras ever," I talked down to the back of her maroon braids.

"So."

"So, I want to experience *some* of it."

Her bony shoulders shrugged: "I'd rather have That Money."

"But I'm not making any more money than I did before Mardi Gras. Just more anxiety…"

No response from any of them. Normally they don't listen because they're screaming, but today they wouldn't even lift their heads, which is better but… Today it was just two girls, Anthony the

185

Civilized, and Cedar, who somehow disrupted band practice this morning, so they kicked him back to me, creating another point of pride for Cedar: "It means they *know* I can handle my bidness, whether I practice or not."

The rest of them were out again either marching or practicing to march. In all, Mardi Gras means as much time-off school as Christmas. Still I need one day extra, so I continued, "I'm going to this parade on my birthday, so I won't be here this Thursday. Now I'll make *sure* you have a Substitute Teacher this time…" My last Sick Day, the kids were somehow left *alone* — I can only imagine that insanity, flying computer parts…

"Damn!" She-La lifted her head. "We ain't comin back here till Thursday after *that*," her eyes bleary red because who knows where they go and what they do at night? She reminded me, "And you only work but three days a week anyway; if you take off Thursday, that's like 9 days off you gonna get? Shit. We only get five," she challenged. "It ain't fair, you just take off whenever you want."

"Y'all take off whenever *you* want," I argued.

"So, man!" Her scolds disintegrated into laughter. "I only been absent three times since you been our teacher anyway. You been absent what? Five?"

"Four." *Though maybe…* It's a lot of days either way. But this impending Day Off is needed; I've spent every holiday since moving here at home in solitude drinking. And that was in a cool apartment… So I *need* this birthday with her, taking X. And I vow: no more Sick Days after Thursday, especially now that the kids in their dwindled numbers have finally stopped threatening me so often. Plus they *loved* my journalism lesson this week: I recorded mix-tapes then made them write reviews of the music. Though they were unable to grasp the idea of journalistic *objectivity* — I explained repeatedly that I wanted only *descriptions* of the music, not judgments — but the reviews came back,

```
That beat sound so stupid They need somebody
like Mary J to sang off that beat they will make
it sound good
```

I'd correct them, "No, no. Objectivity. *Objectivity*. OK? Try another song…" But the reviews returned:

```
I don't like this song. It sound like he is yell
at everybody and I don't like that
```

But at least they've been writing. Not a good time to leave. Still, "I swear y'all: I will not miss one more day after this parade Wednesday night," I promised. "C'mon, it's my birthday!"

"Oh yeah, Wednesday's a big parade too," Anthony said. "We marchin in that one…"

"Wait a minute," She-La rolled her sleepy smile back around and up at me. "I thought you was taking *Thursday* off?"

"Yeah…but…because Wednesday…my birthday is…that parade…"

"Cause you gonna get toe-up Wednesday night!" Anthony revealed. At the sound of The Truth all four kids' heads lifted smiling as Anthony added, "You gonna take that Ecstasy, boy!"

I scoffed but realized *Jesus amazing*… Unable to refrain from smiling, I tried to twist it into one of condescension to pull off telling them, "You know you can get in a lot of trouble for accusing a teacher of taking illegal drugs."

"Your book bag right here smell like weed," She-La said.

"She-La, give me that please." She lifted her head, and as I ripped my book bag away and stashed it under my desk, the day's assignment came to me: "OK. Now. Uh. Today, I want y'all to write about some experience you've had with drugs." Topical I thought. Provocative. No one moaned: a good sign… "I definitely won't tell on you, or let anyone read it if you want to write about the first time *you* tried drugs."

Mumbles: "Yeah, right," and "Hell naw."

"But your story can also be about a friend of yours who takes drugs," I assigned, "or maybe, just, a time when someone just *offered* you drugs or…" But before I could finish, two of the four kids were already scribbling. *Success!* See, *I can do this!*

But when I laughed out loud, She-La and Cedar's heads rose up off their desks, then sank back down: *Oh, I don't have them all...* Since she was closest (and she wasn't Cedar) I asked, "She-La baby, what's the matter? How come you're not working today?"

She raised her bleary head and I admired her for having the balls to admit, "Man, I can't write this shit today, Mr. Patrick, I am too damn high right *now*." She buried her face in her thin, dark folded arms: "And remember: you just said you wasn't gonna tell if we admitted it, so..."

"I know. I won't," I frowned. "But shit... You still have to do this assignment She-La. I'm not gonna bitch at you for smoking weed — though I do think you should save it till college at least — but you still have to do this assignment."

In back, Cedar stood up with his own, big pink-eyed smile: "Yeah me too, Mr. Pat-Pat. I ain't feelin this today." He strapped on his backpack, hid inside his hood: "See if you can bring me a application for that Donkey restaurant you work at."

"Not if you walk out of class."

"I promise I'm a better Worker than a Writer, Mr. Patrick..." Cedar snickered, opening the door and stepping out, closing it gently behind him, leaving me with... *Objectivity. Objectivity helps you let go of anger and disappointment so you don't take valuable Class Time away from...*

"Anthony," I turned to him and, "Hey man, didn't you once tell me that you *like* to write when you're high?"

He sensed I was looking for help and so said to She-La, "Yeah girl, you come up with the best shit when you lit." I really like Anthony and believe he'll do fine.

I bent down to She-La: "You know, your boy Louis Armstrong smoked a lot of weed because he said it inspired him, just like all those rappers on The Radio; pot's famous for going hand-in-hand with creativity...supposedly..."

"And damn, girl," Anthony interrupted, "next time, come talk to me if you and Cedar gonna smoke before class."

"Now that's not what I mean." I met all eight eyes: "If y'all start comin in high all the time I'll..." *What will I do? Nothing. I could never...* "Just fucking don't," I warned.

"I don't like that topic though," She-La grumbled.
"Drugs? Well what do you want to write about then?"
"Nothing."

I tried to dream up another topic; *they could write about? Mizzy. No, they don't know Mizzy... How about...* I saw written on her notebook: *She-La love Lil'Toot.* "Why don't you write about your boyfriend? Describe him..." I suggested.

It saddened me when a very fat girl I rarely notice announced, "What if we ain't got no boyfriend?"

"I ain't got one either," She-La growled.

"What happened to Lil Toot?" I asked.

"Fuck that nigga..."

"OK then, write about your *ideal* significant other, the perfect one you haven't met yet. Make someone up." And when I looked back down at my desk, She-La was writing. I looked up, and they were all writing! *I did it! I can do this! And Mizzy's back at My Room, waiting in my dirty bed...*

I'd fucking *love* this holiday, if it weren't for The Picture Window...

- 2 -

Back when I was suffering high school, I always considered it extremely unfair that teachers rarely completed In-Class Assignments *with* us. Especially art teachers: I never witnessed any of my art teachers ever draw *one* thing, *ever*, so what grounds did I have to trust those people? Thus, I've decided to take on my own writing assignments. Though today I couldn't decide between *Describe Your Perfect Significant Other,* or else *Drugs*; my mind was gorged with thoughts of this parade Wednesday night, which will involve both topics. But it didn't seem prudent to divulge my elicit plan, so instead I remembered a great *anti*-drug story, about the *last* time I tried X with a Significant Other, on my birthday for that matter... I always set the kids' limit at 500-words, because in <u>The End of the Affair</u>, Graham Greene's narrator mentions that whether he's in the mood or not, he always writes 500 a words a day — even if he's inspired to write more, he stops at 500. But since my class always complain that 500 words is too heavy a load for one class period, I made sure to write three times as much, before standing and reading it to them:

By my 26th birthday I was still very stupid, but my friends threw me a party anyway, a midnight cookout in the courtyard of my house. It was hot as shit outside despite the late hour, per usual for FLA. Mine was a total sausage party: no women, just dudes. My friend Damon got me a nice glass marijuana pipe. My friend Aaron gave me an expensive bottle of rum. Johnny T. bought me a quarter of brown, Mexican dirt weed. Jack gave me a joint. Crispen gave me a joint. Cameron gave me a joint. Sean bought me a six-pack of gourmet, imported beer and Lance gave me a hit of Ecstasy. I did see the pattern, and instead of enjoying the party, I spent it feeling silly about my image at the age of 26.

But my dismay over the telling gifts didn't come close to the despair that marked my birthday proper: the morning after my party, my girlfriend, or, ex-girlfriend, Angela called and said she wanted to take me to lunch. Her offer was a rare show of civility in the three weeks since we broke up. So I couldn't decline, even though I was pissed she'd skipped my party the night before to hang out with that eighteen-year-old boy she's been fucking for five weeks now — you do the math. If I'd declined her offer, it would have been my first birthday we'd spent apart in four years. I knew this day would end in a fight, as it had the past four years, but I guess that not spending my birthday with her was an act of letting go I wasn't yet ready for.

Before she picked me up, I ate Lance's birthday Ecstasy, thinking it would improve the situation. The couple previous times I'd done X, it was weak — I could have pulled off a job interview — I never lost my face all lovey-dovey hyper-idealistic. X never made me love the people of Earth any more than usual; it simply made me feel less guilty for not loving them. On the sub-par X I'd done, everything was just lucid, and my idealism dissipated, which was nice, but...

Anyway, I figured that eating X before lunch with Angela meant I'd calmly smile my way through the inevitable fighting, and see clearly and unsentimentally that we do not belong together. I needed that.

So I welcomed the chemicals rumbling in my twitching extremities as she hugged me at my front door. I noticed that she smelled differently and assumed it was the smell of young boy, but chose to ignore it and wait for the X to choke out my anxieties. I didn't tell her I'd eaten drugs, but I did ask her to drive; I didn't want to swerve off the road and kill us both if I saw God or something...

In her Nissan my body tensed terribly as the chemicals overtook it, but that always happens at first; no matter how good I feel later on in any drug experience, I'm always engorged with nervous energy in the beginning, like I'm not accomplishing something that really *needs* to get done.

Angela's madness began when she asked me where I wanted to eat and I told her I didn't really care; many of our fights revolved around my inability to suppress my opinions, so it always infuriated her when I'd say I didn't have an opinion. And since she flounders in the face of decision-making, she grew more and more angered by my apathy as we wandered for miles in her Nissan through residential neighborhoods where there obviously weren't any restaurants. She rolled along really slow, as if a restaurant might suddenly appear out of nowhere, in the meantime asking me again and again, more and more aggressively each time, "Where do you want to eat?"

I closed my eyes and faced out the window, and in the blackness I pictured the calming effects of the drugs racing against her growing anger like two noisy, silver trains on parallel tracks. I rooted for the drug train, but, surprisingly, the anxiety train was winning: I felt worse and worse as the X welled up in me. I suggested that she drive downtown, where there were restaurants, and I'm sure it seemed to her that I was just being dramatic by staring out the window and not looking at her when I talked. But whenever I opened my eyes, the scenery stuttered like a defective VCR tape, so I hid my eyes from her in case they were doing drug-induced back-flips.

By the time we got downtown, I knew the X was bad; I was sweating, face flushed, my soul felt rotten. The veins in my arms looked darker than normal and I wondered if there wasn't dirt in my blood. My stomach was cramped, the world skipping, I couldn't see, and when she yelled at me for being too quiet, I was too miserable to hide it anymore: "Listen man," I said turning to her, "I know you're gonna be even more mad, but I took some Ecstasy that Lance gave me for my birthday and I don't know what the fuck is going on, it must be dirty or something, cause I'm freaking out."

The word "dirty" reverberated in me as she yelled and pointed in my face, her other hand on the steering wheel: "This is YOUR fault and I'm NOT going to stop. You fucking *deserve* this, you stupid druggie!"

She's taken enough acid to know what kinds of dark shores your mind can run aground on when you're tripping, and she was ready to happily take me there, despite my pleading. Her relentless yelling made me feel like a cartoon character being pounded into the ground like a railroad spike by a giant hammer: "Please please PLEASE, don't yell at me, I'm suffering enough. I feel like I want to die already without you yelling at me!" I was holding onto the car's door handle the way prostitutes do, ready to roll out at any second if their john gets weird or violent. My view was totally pixilated and I was SO disoriented that I must have told her I was sorry a hundred times. But Angela was merciless, growing louder and uglier, until begging for her mercy I claimed, "It's all my fault, everything, just please stop, I'm so sorry, trust me, I'm sorry, you're making me want to die, just please stop. Save it for later; after I come down from this I will stand still and quiet for three days straight and let you yell in my face like a drill sergeant if you promise to just NOT MAKE this any worse *right now*."

"Really?" she stopped, smiling, it seemed, with morbid curiosity. "You will?"

"Yes," I said.

"You will let me yell at you as much as I want

for three days and you won't fight back at all?" she asked, still smiling, calming considerably.

"Yes," I assured her, ready to do anything to make her stop.

"I don't BELIEVE you! I don't TRUST you!" she continued to rail.

At a stoplight, just as I was sure I was about to cry dirty, black tears, I looked over and spotted a policeman a hundred yards away on horseback watching us wig out in her car. I made eye contact with his horse and wished I'd opted for a birthday pony ride rather than an X trip. I thought I saw the cop stretching his arms out to me as if offering to hold me and comfort me. I was drawn to him and my hand moved independent of me like in that "Evil Dead" movie, and suddenly the car door was open and I was stepping out and walking toward the cop, planning to ask him for a ride home on his horse.

But somehow in my delirium I realized that if I ran to him for salvation, I'd have to admit that I took drugs, and he would arrest me. Angela screamed at me to "Get back in the fucking car!" So with the policeman and his horse both watching me, I stepped in, lapsed into a puddle of tears and asked her to drive me home, lunchless.

I stared back out the window at the skipping scenery made more abstract when refracted through my tears, and I fell deeper and deeper into sooty despair as she continued to yell at me all the way home.

When we pulled up out front of my house I opened the passenger door before the car stopped moving and she actually sped up. I ran toward the house and she backed the car up and stopped, screaming at the back of my head, "Get back here and shut the fucking car door!"

I slammed my front door and locked it, ran inside and lay in bed, ready now, to finally let go...

When I finished reading, the kids remained quiet. Then, "Did that really happen, Mr. Patrick?" She-La asked. I didn't answer.

Then Anthony began clapping. I thanked him as the two girls joined in, clapping, nodding, then hooting, then all three of them slapping their desks, pounding fists, shouting until they were screaming so loud they didn't hear the end-of-class bell; I finally had to yell, "OK! OK! Class dismissed! We'll continue this next Thursday!"

"Happy Mardi Gras, Mr. Patrick!!!!!" they roared back over their shoulders...

- 3 -

Instead of bras Mizzy wears thin, tight tank-tops beneath her shirts. At night when we sleep, these tank-tops award a view of her chest, shoulders and neck so softly tactile that to not touch would be agonizing. Thankfully, somehow, I'm allowed. These tank-top views give so much that she tells me she never wears them in public, not even in blazing hot summer, meaning I'm the only other human lucky enough to experience them — until that band passed by My Room this morning, marching back to their high school, two blocks from my house...

I'd just biked home from Magnolia when their awkward clamor reached our resting ears and we ran out to follow. Lani and his pigtailed baby granddaughter were already there, waiting at the high school to take pictures of the band with that digital camera Lani's wife received from her boss for Christmas. With it, Lani obtained actual photographic evidence of Mizzy in her tank-top, her arms smothering my smiling head. In the background of the photo, the marching band is entering their fenced-in basketball court. In the middle-ground, teen girls with maroon ropes like She-La's press their fat faces against said fence, fawning over the band boys wrapped in tubas and weighed down by colossal bass drums while trying to hold their khakis up perfectly between *on* and falling *off*. You can almost see the little hearts and lovebirds swimming around the girls' braids, and you can almost see them over Mizzy, too, in the foreground, her squinting smile aimed at the sun after just having stumbled down my stairs like chasing the ice-cream truck, so fast and sloppy we would have plowed over Lani's baby granddaughter had he not scooped her up and out of our way with the hand not snapping our photo — all before I could even ask why he'd shaved his head…

"My wife likes it better this way," he hinted above the band's drums sloppily burying their accompanying brass, which wasn't yet worth hearing anyway. *But they're just kids, just practicing…*

"Now that you're not flying that white flag from your head you won't get attacked so much," I joked before remembering that attacks aren't funny now that one has occurred just a block from where the marching band now practiced — peering down the street I could see the house, the driveway where she'd lived and he hadn't, still blocked off with yellow police tape in the last neighborhood you'd ever expect… "It looks good though; your hair," I complimented, to avert the on-coming Murder Topic; The Murder killed the mood at a couple social gatherings this week: Mizzy had re-told the bloody story to her laughing friends at an art show Friday night, and after that everyone stopped laughing and wanted to go home. Someone else brought it up this Sunday night at The Krishna House where the scruffy hipsters gather for free Indian food, and after that the curried potatoes tasted mushy and sad. So now I wanted to talk about Lani's hair: "You don't look so crazy anymore," I said.

"Which is ironic…" Lani said, setting his granddaughter down on the sidewalk and she stumbled over the grass to press against the fence with the other girls. "Remind me I got somethin to tell you bout *that* later."

"About what?"

"About crazy," Lani chuckled — *sadly*?

"What about crazy?" Mizzy offhandedly asked. She'd never met Lani before, yet when she motioned for him to give her the digital camera, he obeyed.

"My wife handed me divorce papers," he continued, watching Mizzy experiment with the camera: "Bout 10 days ago."

"Oh Lani, I'm sorry," I chuckled painfully, actually more sorry that he'd brought it up right then — I mean, of course I wanted to know about it, but in private, later. Now was not the Moment to remind us that the Earth can fall out beneath us all at any time, no matter how safe we feel. But then fumbling to avoid this Mortality Discussion, I stepped back into, "Hey by the way Lani, did you hear about the Murder that happened right down there?" Mizzy looked up from the camera to frown at me. *Fuck...* Without realizing, I found myself pointing down the street. We all looked away from the band, to that taped-off driveway down there. Lani's granddaughter kept her eyes on parade practice.

Thankfully though, Mizzy and I do think similarly: she jumped to quick-change my sloppy subject, pointing to her truck between the Murder Scene and us, "That's mine right there!" she announced.

"It's a beaut," Lani said, totally sincere.

But when my eyes fell on her truck I gasped and grabbed her bare arm: "Mizzy!" The truck was burned and gutted and... *Oh wait, that's not...* Her truck hid *behind* that one. The burned truck was actually a van, I think; it looked like a rotted tooth, its center blown out burned black with specks of surviving white enamel around the bottom edges... Behind it Mizzy's truck looked to be waiting in line. My stomach hurt looking at it.

"Yeah, someone was actually *living* in that van," Lani informed us. "The other night they fell asleep smoking."

Two dead on my street in one week? Two dead, one divorce... My stomach pinched tighter. Mizzy walked off to crouch in the grass taking pictures of Lani's granddaughter and the black girls, with the charred van in the background. The marching boys executed their music sloppier, distracted by Mizzy's tanktop. I wanted to go back inside to bed, and so suggested it loudly.

While Mizzy was away shaking goodbye hands with the baby, Lani whispered, "Seriously man, we need to get together n talk soon. I didn't want to tell you bout it in mixed company, but I ended up in The Nuthouse for two weeks…"

"Huh? What? What for?"

"Well shit, when she served me them papers I liked t'bout die — ny figured I'd do it myself…"

"You got Baker Act-ed?"

"Yep. How you know bout The Baker Act?"

"I got Baker Act-ed once…"

"Then we *definitely* need to talk," he nodded. "I'll tell you about it later," he whispered as Mizzy returned to us, then I swear he added, "I want you to put it all in your book..."

Book? What book? He must be on medication… Mizzy didn't care what we were keeping from her; before returning Lani's camera she scrolled through all the images on the viewfinder one more time, looking for the one of her hugging my head with her happy eyes closed. "Ooooh!" Mizzy squealed when she'd found it and wrapped her arms around my eyes, recreating the captured pose while singing, "Everything's so *fun*!"

But looking at the photo, with the van beside us and the police tape down the street and the band sounding like shit in our real-time background, all I could think was *This picture is really going to depress me some day…*

- 4 -

Then Mizzy decided she and I should take A Night Off from each other, since we'd rendezvoused after work every other night this week, plus my birthday together tomorrow — I'd say I don't know how I've tricked her into award me so much of her time, but I do know: by sexing her right. I never *win* like this, so given the window for once, I throw everything into our bedtime. Again, athlete I'm not, but with Mizzy I display a desperate athleticism, and since she doesn't seem to notice the desperate part, she meets me every night after work (except tonight), and every night and morning I drive myself at a sexual pace I won't possibly, *possibly* be able to keep up if she and I are still together, after I'm no longer so amazed she's letting me do this to her.

Anyway, her wanting A Night Off continued my upset stomach at work. I knew it shouldn't though, so I tried concentrating on my recent triumphs with the kids, and the fact that I work in the building where Ignatius bought his lute string and the Freedom my bike provides, especially during this holiday — my co-workers are forced to leave their homes two hours early to accommodate a struggle through traffic that ends in a jacked-up $20 Mardi Gras Parking Rate. Not that I love biking through this shit either though: skidding and starting, swerving around drunken car doors opening, fratboys screaming in your ear plus *Divorce* and *Murder* and *A Night Off*... Then at work my ears must endure the constant grinding of my co-workers — all of them: The Fun Boys, The Black Team, The Kitchen Crew, The Dish Pit, The Salad Line, The Dessert Line, The Expeditor, The Hostess, even Management — hurling whole lexicons of verbal threats at each other, both fake and real, way worse than the Magnolia kids. They're why I requested to work under Michael tonight; he's very sweet, especially with me. He offers me breath mints, asks me questions about myself and Mizzy. In the eyes of The Black Team, my asking specifically to be paired with Michael pretty much makes me an honorary member of The Fun Boys, but at this point *fuck it*.

Michael and I worked together with a new B-waiter, Jason, who ended up quitting before the night was over. Jason was nearly seven-feet-tall, but looked even taller because he's skinny as a drinking straw. Despite his blond crew cut, Jason referred to himself in the third person as "This Nigger Right Here." Though one of the most obtuse people I've ever met, Jason had somehow skipped Backwaiting to be hired directly as a B-waiter; he must have known someone. Helping Jason learn The Floor tonight meant having to listen to him complain and threaten ghosts under his breath: "Man, fuck this shit, bruh. This Nigger Right Here's ain't gotta take that shit from..." He's easily as gangly and odd as Jude, on top of sounding like a bad impersonation of a The Black Team. Yet, The Black Team accepted him? I'm dead to Red now, but he and De'von shared expansive conversations with Jason, allowing him to say nigger as much as he wanted. "D'you hear that bitch talking like that to me?" Jason would ask, and everyone but me would nod waiting for more. "I'll lay that bitch out y'heard? Motherfucker ain't talkin to This Nigger Right Here like that. I'll tell that motherfucker: 'Motherfucker, your Bananas Foster'll be out to you when I'm ready to bring it,' y'heard?"

So appalling and ridiculous was Jason that I ended up missing the parade in lieu of observing him — and also because Management closed the curtains across The Picture Window after a man pressed his penis to the glass. The closed curtains drove our few customers outside, but even in our emptiness Jason stomped around threatening anyone who'd listen, like in the kitchen: "Listen up: one a y'all motherfuckers better show This Nigger Right Here where the fuckin creamer's kept or I'ma..." Until, after five hours of listening to whose ass John was, "fitna kick," it began to really wear on me, and being tired at work is the worst, especially when you already felt like puking before you arrived... So after overhearing Jason half-heartedly threaten to kill this little black waitress, I finally prescribed, "Jason man: easy."

"What'd you say, bitch?"

"I said easy with the fighting shit. Quit talking like a meathead."

"Fuck you bitch. You want some?"

"Some?"

"Yeah bruh. Some."

"Some of what? What's the some of..."

"You know what. Just keep being cute, bitch..."

It's White Bitch... But out loud I asked, "Isn't 'bitch' what gays call each other?"

"Just keep being cute, bruh."

"You think I'm cute?"

"That's cool man. Keep talking and we can meet outside after work."

"For a drink?"

"Just keep fucking talking. I'll see you after work." He walked away.

After that, every time we shared eye contact on the floor he'd refer to my impending ass-beating. It seemed to shorten the night, waiting to see if he really meant it or if, like Cedar, he would in the end find objectivity and leave his threats in the classroom. But then as the time drew nigh and I polished silverware, Jason jumped into The POS, tapping the computer screen and babbling, oblivious to my presence: "I'm out of this fucking hole, bruh; Customers disrespect This Nigger Right Here and then fuckin Jarhead Manager motherfucker gives em free dessert for being assholes? I don't need this shit, bruh; I got two big-titty stripper bitches back at my house waiting for me to get off. So... I'm off now — beyotch!"

I poked my head out of the POS to watch his long arms swing at his side as he marched out the revolving door onto Canal. *So that's what I look like when I walk out...* On the other side of The Picture Window, Jason unclipped his bowtie and tossed it into the prisoners' brooms still sweeping away beads.

Lucky bitch...

- 5 -

Jason had avoided Michael entirely because Michael is, "A fucking homo." But after Jason bolted, Michael was eager to know what I'd been talking to Jason about; Michael considered him "cute".

"Oh no, Michael. You couldn't possibly..."

"Physically, he's my type," Michael defended, raising his eyebrows, his hands out in front of him, clasped together like when he dictates Today's Specials: "Tall, lanky men are always well-endowed. But also, Jason looked sort of naïve and, innocent somehow."

"A dork, you mean."

"Yes. I *loooooooove* dorks. Not that I don't also enjoy men like De'von as well..."

"You have really horrible taste, man."

"I'm not saying I'd fall in love with De'von, but you can't deny he's a gorgeous man. And I *know* he's got some gay in him somewhere." Michael opened his clasped hands and, "Yes, Hollywood's definitely got some sugar on him," then he closed them again...

"You'd fuck anything then."

"Now hold on there, child," Michael rebelled, indicating seriousness by hiding his hands behind his back, like when a customer is complaining: "I am not a slut like the rest of The Fun Boys. Not anymore. I've tempered my concupience..."

"Your what?"

"Concupience: man's natural tendency toward sin. I'm a Catholic, child..."

"Then what do you do during The Southern Decadence Festival?"

"Oh, I hide out... Don't even talk about that horrible, horrible holiday."

"You're not out there on Bourbon circle-jerking with all those hairy old men in their leather underwear and suspenders?" I joked.

"Oh god please," he closed his eyes and held his forehead, very serious. "You're bringing back horrible memories..."

"Aside from Ernie K-Doe's wake, Decadence was my first real New Orleans experience," I recalled. "Those two experiences were the first times I really realized how *different* this place is... I mean, guys blowing each other in the streets? Not at Ernie K-Doe's wake but... I'm from Florida, and Floridians would shoot a bomb straight up into the air and let it fall back onto the state before they'd let thousands of guys suck..."

"Christ, stop child!" He put his hands up: "I don't want to talk about this. Fuck that disgusting holiday and anyone who celebrates it. The *only* thing I miss about that whole scene is the drugs."

"Oh yeah? What kind of drugs make people act like *that*? X?"

"Yeah, but you can't get good X anymore so..."

"So then what do you like to get fucked up on, Michael?"

"Oh if that isn't just The Pickup Line for the New Millennium!" he laughed, like a man, but with one hand patting his padded white heart, the other grabbing the crook of my arm. "Oh, you're funny, baby," he sighed affectionately, and it felt nice. "But to answer your question," he continued, hands clasped in front again. "I've always preferred Special K."

"Ketamine!" I shouted to my long-lost customer...

He looked side-to-side: "Jesus child, calm down."

"You mean Ketamine, like what the raver kids take?" I asked to make sure.

"Yes, but we discovered it *long* before *those* little faggots," he defended, just as Red entered The POS.

Red patted Michael on the back laughing, "Michael, you a fool yeah, talkin bout faggots. You crazy, yeah." He addressed only Michael, never looking at me. After they'd exchanged smiles, Red looked down and began polishing silverware. Goddamned silverware...

But I was too excited about the possibility of making some Drug Money to care about Red. I wasn't, however, ready to admit what I had. First I asked, "So how much is K worth exactly?"

"$60 a bottle, maybe."

"So, thirty dollars for half a bottle?" I asked. "Would half a bottle do anything?"

"It depends; is the bottle half-*full* or half empty?" he touched my hand. "I'm just kidding... But yes, half a bottle would do one person pretty good for $30."

$30 = six nights of beachfront lodging in Costa Rica or two Tica hookers if Mizzy's gone by then... But before I could announce to Michael that this was his lucky day, he'd slipped out of The POS leaving me with Red, and Red's first words to me in days....

"Say bruh," he began, rubbing his jaw. "I look like I need a shave?"

Uncomfortable, I answered, "I dunno."

"You don't know?"

"I mean, I can't tell."

"Damn bruh." He met my eyes. "I'm that fuckin *Black* you can't *tell?*"

"No, no..." I laughed. "I mean I can't see any hair. I guess that means you don't need to shave."

He pretended to laugh a little, then asked, "So you got some

Ketamines huh?"

I didn't correct his pronunciation, just asked, a little anxious, "How do you know?"

"All them questions you was asking: you got half a bottle a Ketamines." If he desired, he could use that information to fuck me up somehow — which is exactly why I admitted myself to him freely, hoping to gain back his confidence by being vulnerable, honest without hope of gain... At first he replied, sarcastic, "Damn bruh, you in The Game. You a gangsta too."

"No. Not at all."

"Sure you is: slangin drugs and shit?"

"I've never sold drugs before this. It's a total fluke that I even have..."

"Don't deny it bruh. You ain't no bettuh," he said, not laughing anymore. Silence. Until he slammed a polished fork down adding, "You just as much of a nigga as you take us for, Pat." Walking past me out to The Dining Room he pointed back at his silverware pile and warned, "And don't be touchin my shit..."

- 6 -

Outside after work: no Jason waiting for me, just my bike in a twisted metal knot... "FUUUUUUUCK!" carried out over artificially lit Canal and its still-sweeping Prison Brooms. "*Fuck* that Jason mother*fuck*er!"

Management had been standing outside all night making sure no one threw anything through The Picture Window, and that the waiters weren't mugged at the end of the night by thugs misled to believe that we had money on us. "It wasn't Jason," Management mumbled, wrapping one huge hand around my bike's neck and the other around the front rim, then pulling in opposite directions.

The metal began to straighten. I noticed the seat was ripped too... Livid I asked, "How do you know it wasn't Jason?"

He laid my bike down on it's side on the pavement, placed a shiny black shoe on the back rim, grabbed a handlebar and *streeeeeeeeetched* its spine, grunting, "I been standing right here the whole time watching; it was just folks standing on it to get a better view."

Jesus, the parade must've been huge to do that to my poor... "Wait, why didn't you fucking stop them?!" I shouted at this person who could kill me with one punch. He didn't get mad though, just kind of smirked like I do at small barking dogs on leashes. The crooked smile made me madder and bold enough to yipe, "And where's all the *money* you guys promised us? I made fucking $40 tonight."

"It's slow," he deduced, still not looking up, busy with the task at hand: *focused*. That's how they make it to Management...

"No shit it's fucking *slow*. But you've only been in this business for *how* many years and you didn't *realize* it would be slow before you fucking *lied* to us?" If I were him, I would have fired me; fifteen people-a-day drag themselves into The Donkey Show dressed in suits-and-ties to fill out applications with their gold Kross pens, hoping to make 40-grand-a-year. Maybe Management didn't fire me right there because he heard the helpless weakness in my voice and understood that it traumatized me to see my bike like that. Or maybe he was distracted, having too much fun contorting my cruiser. Whichever, I was able to shout again at the back of his crewcut, "Why are we now making *less* money? Why! I don't even have money to fix my bike! *WHY*!"

He stood straight, tire between the knees of his slacks, and looked at me just for a second. *My god they're all so big...* "Why?" he asked himself while bending and squinting one eye, peering down my bike's spine as if down a rifle site, checking the alignment before finally answering, "I dunno. Sept 11th?"

"Sept 11th! What the..." I grabbed my untangled handlebars from him. "You can't even tell that ever fucking *happened*! Look around; it affected nothing! It didn't stop *anybody* from..." Fuck, man... I rode off without thanking him.

ch 13: our parade

On the 28th anniversary of my birth, I'm drinking wine and waiting for her. Before leaving my bed this morning she surprised me with a skinny joint, which she told me to save until she returned from her Lunch Shift, but... She'll need it after work; her new restaurant foisted another new duty on her: teaching the old people Cajun line dancing. She definitely has it rougher than I do. Especially today, I have it damn good: not shit to do but breathe and wait for her to punch out. Maybe I'll brave The Trampoline! Or take Lani up on that free reading — or just supply him with friendship, talk to him. Not about Divorce though. I'm sure he's past needing to talk about that by now; he seemed fine watching the band with us the other day, composed, relaxed. "I'm not mad," he'd said. "She's a nice lady," meaning his ex. But he also mentioned being medicated, "marinated," as Little De'von calls it in his writing. And I'm a little too marinated right now (11:43a/m), so I'll talk with Lani some other time. For now I'll just wait here for her.

- 2 -

It's funny, or it's not, that just days ago, escorting her out to her truck I cooed, "Thank you for your sweet affection," and in response she huffed, "Oh Jesus," barely kissing me before rolling up her window. But she's very different in the days since… There are times now when we're lying together after I've pulled it off *again*, and she's staring into me with what seems like 'I love you' trapped in her mouth. And now that we've had crawfish together, that's it: *Consummation*. Crawfish have allowed her to fall into me… Not fresh-boiled, but whole boiled: two, sitting as garnishes atop our French Market Take-Out jambalaya rice littered with thawed-out, re-boiled, rubbery tails. I carried our Styrofoam containers through the icy gray wind, following the direction of the grass blades all blown flat, pointing at the Mississippi's bank, where Mizzy seized the bag from me, holding the white boxes under her chin for warmth.

On the big cold rocks we smoked what was left of the joint I hadn't really saved for her and watched the giant ferry out there, coming and going from Algiers. *Fucking god, amazing*… Still I was wishing we had a sack of fresh-boiled; it felt for some reason *important* that she and I participate, together, in this shell-breaking, guts-sucking raccoon ritual. Then a sudden dramatic excitement when we opened our Styrofoam containers to find whole-but-not-fresh, one each atop our take-out.

"I'm not eating that thing though," she laughed. I could barely hear her over the wind.

"What? No c'mon, we have to, together…"

"Nuh uh."

She was serious when she warned that they were just garnish, that they'd burned in some freezer for years and weren't fit for consumption. But this was important to me… "They're rancid," she protested the entire way through demonstrating *How to Crack the Body Cleanly from the Head*, then the *Meat-Removal Ceremony*.

For separate reasons, neither of us drank the yellow brains, but she wouldn't even eat the tail. "C'mon…" I beseeched. When mine tasted fine, distrust flared in me: *She's just making excuses*… So

THIS will be the ONE thing she will not give me? Why? It doesn't seem in her nature, but I swear she regarded Whole Boiled Crawfish like The Last Step before she'd have to care about me for real — like a prom night fingering, crawfish equaled obligation...

But then, as I was about to suggest we find warmth, she popped it into her mouth, grimaced, then validated my distrust; after that she really fell into me...

- 3 -

After our fall closer, it began raining ice. We dashed to our bikes and pumped through it, back to her centrally heated Uptown apartment where her mattress is bigger and cleaner than mine. There we stripped off wet layers, dropped to our knees and rummaged through her footlocker full of costume supplies — she actually has one of these; she is ready... The sky out her window wasn't so dark yet that we'd need to turn on the lights; it was just dim enough where I could comfortably stare at her hair hanging wet on her bare smooth jaw: *the only thing better than a trunkful of...* "Costumes are the whole reason I moved here," she claimed, then recited the trunk's inventory: "My dentist's X-ray vest, the white plastic mold of my head from that MRI, my ankle bells — fake knives — fake blood — a bald head, and... karate jacket — a toy chainsaw — a baseball, probably — my David Hasslehoff face — graduation hat — I swear there's more; probably in storage at my parents' house in DC."

"Jude would love this," I told her, hinting for corroboration of the innocence Jude claims. "This trunk, I mean."

"He's seen it," she confronted.

"Oh," and a cold pinch in my stomach...

"He's really into costumes."

"I know," I said, imagining so many bad things, the two of them in costumes... The crawfish said, *Don't let it bother you, bruh. Be cool.* So coolly I asked, "Did you ever go out with Jude?"

"No."

"Why not?"

She leaned in and quick kissed me to change the subject, then brought forth a plush elephant mask...

But I continued, "Because he's ugly?"

"Don't be a jerk."

"Oh whatever! He doesn't care. You know the other day I told him I wanted to write a book with him in it and he told me somebody already *was*... Yeah. Another person's featuring him in a movie. He gets as much positive attention as...as *you*. He'll be famous without ever even doing anything — I mean, unless he can actually act; then he could be our generation's Marty Feldman. But what I'm trying to say is: he doesn't care if I say he's ugly."

"What *I'm* trying to say is that he's *not* ugly."

"You don't ever wonder if he's got some terminal illness?"

"Don't say that."

"Why not? He seems like he's OK with that, too..."

"I know," she said. *Man*... I dropped it there. Back to the trunk...

- 4 -

Mizzy's roommate didn't laugh when Mizzy leapt out into their living room in a hospital gown, big gray football shoulder pads, long black rubber gloves and that elephant mask. To me this getup served as further proof that she towers over her peers, over people like her roommate who couldn't even laugh when Mizzy proclaimed her costume: "Bellaphante goes to The Hospital," or something. The roommate is a pretty but plain white girl with very long, healthy hair. When Mizzy retreated to go change costumes I asked the roommate, "You don't think that's funny huh?"

"Mizzy? Yeah she's weird alright," she evaded. But I read complaint into her describing, "Sometimes I come home and there'll be like, a weird little sculpture in the middle of the floor that just like, popped up out of nowhere, right where people walk. And they're just balanced there, not with glue or anything, so you can't move them out of the way; if you touch them they fall apart everywhere."

My Dream Girl... But her roommate wasn't amused. "You don't find that funny," I fawned. "At least interesting?"

"They fall apart everywhere," she repeated.

Theirs was a roommating of necessity because the rent's $1000. But it's worth it for the entire third floor of an Uptown mansion: three long shotgun rooms of vast hardwood with smaller nook-rooms cut into the walls plus an additional loft, a separate art studio out back by the washer-n-dryer (she wouldn't let me survey it), and most importantly (my hands shake with such excitement I can barely type the words) she has a fucking Pool! The only thing I miss about FLA is swimming. Before moving here, I hadn't gone one whole week without swimming since I was 11, almost 17-years. This past NO year has been totally without swimming as well as love. See, that was the problem. But now there's a girl and her pool. *I - have - found - my - way around?*

But exactly 28 years from the day of my birth, her pool was too cold for swimming. "If we turn the heater on now, it will be ready by the time we come home from the parade..." Until then, the iced glass of her bedroom window radiated cold above the trunk, out of which I culled a costume that kind-of looked like Prince: a purple satin jacket over a frilly white blouse, frilly silk scarf, frilly lace gloves, and a wig of loose black curls leaning over one eye. She *has* all this on hand; she is ready... Then, gratuitously accessorizing, I wrapped her giant plush boa-constrictor doll around my neck, down around my waist, tucking its pointy tail inside my open fly: *The Little* Prince, maybe...

Pedaling back to The Quarter was easier; the sky had stopped crying and my lopsided wig protected at least one of my ears from the amazing cold — though it also made me think of my only real girlfriend ever: in college, this Polynesian girl, the girl from my bad X trip. She'd harvested ass-length black hair, which of course she always pinned up during FLA summers. But in the winter, given the occasion, she'd unpin it, and when she did this she always sang her own little invented tune: "Let your hair down - if it's - cold outsi-yide." And almost always when it's cold I still remember that, her and her little tune, and even here, states away from FLA, I still always feel sad.

But *fuck no* today!

- 5 -

Our happiness had nothing to do with the Ketamine. Her drug dealer cook guy failed on the X, so we split and drank my half-bottle of yellow K (*Sorry, Michael*) hoping it would anesthetize us to shaved-ice from the sky. But nothing: my wig and snake were damp and the cold kept us from getting drunk. Lee Circle where the Streetcars turn around is supposedly The Place to camp out and riot. But my birthday found us practically alone in the shit weather. The statue in The Circle's center stood lit up, surrounded by ropes and cops on horses, and definitely an air of expectancy, but not another civilian on either side of us for 100-feet.

"Last year here it was just disgusting heat and naked steamy flesh and vomit and *ahhhhhhhhhhhhhh*!" Mizzy shouted through chattering teeth. Her description warmed me; that's the festival I *expected*. Our real-time lack of crowds and a good drunk were disappointing and no X, but *you know what? Fuck it.* It was just as easy to see it as *We have Mardi Gras all to ourselves! The Rich always talk of wanting Exclusivity…* We paid for it in icy rain, but this was truly exclusive: each float hulking by and all 10-sets of Ku-Klux eyes aimed down at only us with no choice but to heave onto only our wet heads *all* their beads and cups and beads and trinkets and beads and dolls and beads and panties and spears and mini-slot machines and inflatable crayons and beads and all the crap tourists usually kill each other for. With no one else around to catch it, That Rain of Toys was ours alone, more intoxicating than the six beers we drank, each. Rolling up and seeing how much shit we had already, some floats merely waved rather than throw us more — we decided this must be a first in Carnival history… So many necklaces tossed out, just to hit the ground, so many pretty, dirty beads smothering The Circle's wet pavement in the parade's wake that I wondered how the floats were able to avoid sliding off into The Circle Bar…

The Circle Bar: another place I'd never been. It's warm inside, dark and orange. We used The Circle Bar for its shelter, and for buying more useless beers, and I'm sure now I'll go back — it's scary and great, all the new things and places that arrive with each new person into your life. Like I've obsessed over sharks and aquariums all my life, yet never even considered visiting The NO Aquarium until today when Mizzy told me she's, "really into fish." Alone this whole time, I really haven't experienced NO. Now I will, at least for a while.

The cops were distracted trying to stay warm, so when we needed more beer, Mizzy just went ahead and cut right through the parade to The Circle Bar — after removing her mask and pads, she slipped through the Marching Band in just her thin, wet hospital gown, open in back showing green panties — until halfway in, she decided to drape beads around each marching kid's neck. The hot little, unenthusiastic baton girls in wet hot pants warned Mizzy, "Don't put yo hands on me, bitch." But the boys remained stoic in their lines, unbreakable Gamefaces, no recognition for the rain, nor for Mizzy, their eyes focused forward like that baby Bluejay.

Even when the parade paused for a tractor stalled ahead, the boys remained dead-eyed, the sky again pissing on their shiny black faces. Mizzy took this pause to bejewel each boy, and kiss his cheek. This finally broke them; each boy couldn't help smiling or grimacing, but still no movement anywhere but the faces. *Strong*. No way I could hold so still in such weather, or keep such quiet. I would've whined to the silent boy beside me who was playing the exact same instrument as me: 'This is fucking inhumane, isn't it? *Inhumane*...'

But these young men: marble — until Mizzy made it all the way to The Drum Line. There, as she was about to kiss his cheek I yelled, "Damn! Cedar! *Dude!*" happy to see him. Of course he wouldn't turn around, not in that Moment. *So why yell, especially when he's only five feet away...*

Then before Mizzy's kiss could land on Cedar, she stopped and asked me, "You know this kid?"

"Yeah this is my school!" I stepped back, elated, "Magnolia!" I rallied, taking in the green and gold Mardi Gras colors they wear all year round. "De'von!" I recognized him and a couple others all trying not to look at me.

"So you're *Cedar*?" Mizzy growled close to his face, recognizing him from my whiney descriptions. "You're a *prick* to Patrick," she accused,

Whoa! "Hey, wait, Mizzy, don't…"

Cedar stared straight, unsmiling, drumsticks poised. Over his tall white hat she cried out, "All right, who else is mean to Patrick!?" De'von smiled, tried not to laugh, trumpet against his side, frost in his braids. "All of you who are pricks to Patrick," she continued. "Admit it *right* now so I can kick your black asses!"

"Oh, hey! Mizzy! Whoa! Easy." *Maybe those beers weren't wasted on her…* Then red-and-blue lights exploded, bouncing off buildings and The Circle's phallic statue as cop-cars began trying to press through our minus-mild party. Voices from their CB amplifiers demanded we step aside. Another adult voice called out bare from behind the thick of the band, "Ah'ight kids, relax. Po-Lease tryna get through. We gonna be here a while."

The boys all slouched, letting their curses escape into-and-for The Cold as Little De'von screeched at me, "Now. What did your bitch just fucking say to us? Mr. *White Bitch* better get *his* bitch to shut her *bitch*-ass up!"

We all laughed, together. "Oh she's just kidding," I assured him. "Chill out De—" But I stopped before his name, not wanting to set Mizzy off; De'von's the one I've most often described to her via complaint. So Mizzy just laughed, still eye-contacting Cedar, who leaned his arms in the puddles on his drumheads while shyly surveying Mizzy's wet hospital gown. They both knew she was just fucking with him; he's smart. But then she grabbed his face…

"Is Patrick a good teacher?" she demanded, mocking but hopeful.

"Mizzy! Hey. Seriously, you're gonna get me in trouble…"

She let go of his jaw only to allow it to admit, "Mr. Patrick ah'ight. He do the best he can given his situation."

He what… Understands? Chains snapped, almost all of them, the ones pulling on my shoulders at least. *He understands! And on my BIRTHDAY!* The cops' blinking lights stirred everything, making

The World seem more festive, alive. They were almost out the other side of the parade when Mizzy threatened Cedar, "Well, then be fucking cool to him!" Her hand on his sequined chestplate shoved him back. Then leaning over his drums she kissed his cheek, before running on into The Circle Bar...

When she was gone Cedar asked me, "Damn Whoadie, thatcha girl?"

"Yeah. Pretty much."

"I ain't know you roll like *that*; I like *her*."

"But if she disrespect us like that again," De'von squealed rows down, "I'ma knock her the fuck out!" Then when the laughter in his honor quieted he asked, "And who the fuck you think you supposed to be? Prince?"

"Hey! Good guess De'von. Yeah, Prince."

"Motherfuckuh always tryna to be black," he declared to the band. We all laughed again, together. *Yes, we are blessed...*

The band's adult voice then bellowed again and the boys snapped back to attention, ready to make their noise. When the parade started back up Magnolia sounded like drunk robots falling down stairs. *But how does that Band Director get them to obey like that? I suppose it's The City they obey, its traditions...*

Mizzy returned to me and the cold and the rain, carrying our last cups of beer, just as Rebirth Brass Band danced out the tail end of the parade, drenched as usual, though this time only with rain... When the thing was definitely dead, we lugged our literal buckets of trinkets (on our bicycles, somehow) back to her house, skipping her now-hot swimming pool in favor of her bigger, cleaner, warmer bed.

And now I am 28.

ch 14: fucking parades

I worked my lunch shift buzzed off Mizzy. I worked hard and well, projecting an aura of strength. At the beginning, Management paired me with De'von, but I was so lit from the previous night that I stood up for myself: though De'von couldn't have gotten to me like usual, I still told Management, "Sorry, I don't work with De'von. Personal rule. Trade me out with someone else." And they obeyed. Control was mine, almost — there was one point when I ended up in the bathroom at the same time as Red, and feeling strong I went ahead and asked him, "So what did I do man? Why don't you like me now? Not cause of the silverware…" And he replied only, "I just ain't feelin you no more bruh…" then walked out. But the rest of the night was under my control, and I admit, I have Mizzy to thank; as the owner of her attention, I'm now able to choke down a 12-hour workday taunted by huge silent parades, and still somehow pedal home feeling as if I also own myself…

Back in My Room I would shower, change costumes, then huff back down to The Quarter to chase Fun with her, I thought. But before stripping off the Monkey Suit beneath my army jacket, I indulged in my couch; frost lined the walls of my lungs from the ride home, plus I was sweating. I poured myself a wine and tried scraping the resin from Mizzy's glass pipe while dialing my answering service — I gleaned no resin, and only one message, from Magnolia's Vice Principal: "Yes, Patrick, I regret to inform you that the students in your first period class got into a physical altercation with the Substitute you left them with this morning." She stressed the *you left them* part. As did I. With no 'baby' or sweet concern she continued, "You neglected to leave the Sub a lesson plan, or warn him about the behavioral situation in your class... Two of your kids pushed him out into the hallway yelling, "You are not our teacher!" When he tried to re-enter the classroom, the one named De'von screamed in his face, "Get the *F* out, bitch."

My teeth tightened. *Oh De'von you little fucking idiot...* Their "You're not our teacher" line did feed me a strange pride but... *I'd rather bus tables; that's what people like me are meant for...* I no longer owned myself; darkness had me from the inside, as the phone sucked the outside of my skull — the same phone I bought the day I moved here, $3.99 at Thrift City, I brought it home and immediately stepped on the antennae so that ever since, people sound like they're calling me from underwater. But The Vice Principle's voice came to me full and clear and so heavy it took me down onto my mattress, laid me out, still in my Backwaiters vest, her voice rolling over me: "When Mr. Land arrived at your room, the substitute teacher had De'von pinned to the ground under the lockers outside your door. The sub says it was self-defense and I do believe him, but now the parents are involved, and honestly Patrick, I'm questioning the way you govern your class... How did you let it escalate to this level without involving us? I'll definitely need to meet with you when school recommences next Thursday.

"Happy Mardi Gras," she added.

The phone released its grip on my skull, allowing me to reach over and plop it back down in its cradle, then close my eyes. *Busted-ass phone...* It seemed to ring at intervals through the night, either in my dreams or in real-time. Whichever, I couldn't answer.

- 2 -

Ha! I begged and won escape from another night of watching the world happen on the other side of glass! I harbored no ambition but to run alongside the floats with her and the rest of the idiots. But not until tonight; first, a Brunch Shift.

Weekends we serve — or rather *they* serve, and then I clean up — a big fat NO brunch of crawfish omelets and crabmeat over poached eggs and champagne, with a three-piece ragtime band wing-tipping around The Dining Room satisfying tourists' requests. This band is more annoying than you'd ever expect. You'd think it'd be fun, a live band at work, but aurally ingest "It's a Wonderful World" seven times *in a row* over tourists' squawking cell-phone conversations *while bussing fucking tables*, and we'll see *then*... Or worse is, "God Bless The Child That's Got His Own." I mean, gorgeous song, but in the context of The Donkey Show the lyrics remind me that I do not, in fact, have My Own. *If I did, This Nigger Right Here would walk the fuck out this bitch*... And when I did, would Management follow me to the gold-and-glass revolving door singing, 'God *bless* you child! You got your *own*!'? *Hell motherfuckin no.* I do reserve oceans of empathy for musicians' need to eat, even if it means their playing over-done cover-tunes, but all oceans evaporate when I'm trapped behind their giant wooden bass tub smack in the skinny aisle, balancing armloads of ceramic, wearing the same uniform I slept in last night until they're done playing "God Bless the Child," again...

The Brunch Band is one reason why — after they'd packed up their banjo and shit at the end of Brunch and I'd finished polishing my allotted silverware — I *performed* for Management: inspired by Magnolia's VP, I told them, "I have to attend a very important meeting at Magnolia..." not yet lying.

"When?" Management grunted.

"Soon," I said, still not lying...

"Well, you *have to* be here tonight," the neck-less oaf ill-phrased: "You don't have a choice."

My mind's eye replayed the scene of his bare fists wrenching my bike back into shape. Still I dramatized, "Oh. Sure, making sure fat tourists get fatter and your restaurant mogul boss gets richer are more important than the educational welfare of inner city kids?" Yes, I actually said this, in real life. I almost stopped and apologized. But remembering my ripped bicycle seat, I kept on, finally breaking into a lie: "I have to be at Magnolia at 5p/m today and there's nothing I can do about it."

"Having a meeting tonight," Management scoffed, "is like meeting on Christmas Eve."

"Yeah? Then this shit you pulled with This Week's Schedule is like *tricking* us all into working *doubles* on X-mas Eve!"

"Wait a minute," Management paused, Paleozoic brow furrowed. So I waited — in silence but for the slow-grinding gears in his brain, and the faintly clanking silverware — waiting — waiting — wiping my sweating hands on my vest until finally — *no, wait* — *now* he continued, "I got kids myself, so I happen to know that school's out till next Thursday."

"Yes, well that's why we…this is the only time we can meet," I fumbled, "When we're not…busy…teaching."

In his stupefaction I assumed victory and unclipped my bow tie until, "How long you gonna be?" Management challenged. "Your meetin's not all night?" He had me. My own silence admitted it. Management smiled, "Be back here by eight…"

I wanted the night off, but was offered a mere three-hour break? *Good enough!* And so grateful was I not to be missing my "important meeting" that I pumped home at a Need Pace, planning to shave and shower for a good enough impression to hopefully save my job, for some reason — until a block before the Claiborne overpass, I remembered that I'd lied, and slowed my pedaling. And that's when I noticed the signs…

A fresh-bloomed garden of cardboard signs mounted on wooden sticks ran up and down Esplanade's median forever in both directions; there's some Election Day in Louisiana soon. But the sheer glut of this *Vote For Me* propaganda, *so* many, too many, millions of the same messages over-and-over glowing abnormal electric pink lime green orange lemon yellow — more like celebration than political manipulation. At a red light I planted my feet, chuckling at the signs: *Right, a funeral is a party, a political campaign an accidental art installation...* NO's jovial methods of attacking important events brightened me — until the red light wore out it's welcome, giving me time to remember my kids' still-ungraded Letters to The Mayor... Cars pulled beside me farting black clouds, their music rattling my chrome fenders and *It's not my fault I COULDN'T READ their fucking letters; the grammar and spelling and handwriting were just...* By the time the light finally ripened, I'd come around to suspecting that *If even the losing candidate had taken the money they spent on these fucking signs and donated it to Magnolia, that would have done more good for Public Education than whatever the winning candidate will ever do once elected...*

The cars' loud farts and music grew in the reverb of the overpass as I vented my disappointments into the first hard pumps of my legs. But before I could really get going, the *loudest* fucking music swallowed The World, and I turned to find a giant Camaro like an old black shark swimming alongside me. "I got it back!" Jude screamed from inside, his chicken-claw fist pumping out the window as he pulled over into a gutterful of rainwater and beer and piss and beads.

Giant round sunglasses made Jude's head and shoulders seem extra skinny, his teeth extra big, the hair in back extra stringy: a rock-n-roll chemo patient. It all comes together with the car. I'm sure he knows that. Over The Lawnsprinklers hissing from his Radio, his shouting voice explained, "I've been keeping a set of the keys in my pocket this whole time! Just in case! Then I spotted it yesterday on Rampart! Outside Louis Armstrong Park! I just unlocked it, threw my bike in the trunk and stole it back!" Again his bony fist pumped, his happiness as genuine as everything else about him. "And best of all..." his non-pumping hand cranked The Radio until it represented the aural equivalent of a flashlight in the eyes. I squinted, rolling backwards, instinctively escaping. Jude somehow screamed over it, "The fuckers put in a new stereo!" I was 10-feet away when he finally turned it off, but The Lawnsprinklers kept on sputtering in my head, faintly under Jude's shouting, "I win! I win!!! I *wiiiiiin*!!!!!!"

"Yes you did," I agreed, gesturing toward the thick of political signs. "And you didn't even have to campaign like these fuckers…"

"Yeah."

When I asked his plans for Fat Tuesday, he turned The Radio back on and answered, "I don't know! But we'll *definitely* see each other! No matter what!"

Cryptic… But I hoped he was right, since watching his car fart away I realized I'd again forgotten to get his phone number… *Oh shit, and I also forgot to tell him about my kids beating up that Substitute; he'd have got a kick out of that…*

- 3 -

My small, warm room soothed and I felt *sooooooo* much better that I didn't want to jeopardize it by checking my messages again… But had I not, I wouldn't have heard Management's recorded voice burp, "Patrick, you just left here. If you get this message before you ride back, just stay home tonight; we got someone to fill in for you. Everyone's calling up wanting to work. Everyone wants to make money but you. So have a good night off. And call us if you want Brunch off tomorrow too."

I freshened my wine with the phone against my ear, then again laid down on my bed, which smelled like Mizzy, even as her voice barely escaped the receiver — she's aware my phone is unintelligible, so normally she annunciates loudly. But now on the other side of the static-blanket she gave just the tiniest, "I'm hurt…" Then a huge pause. I plugged my open ear with my finger to concentrate on her squeak: "I wish you were here (*sniffle*). Please call…" *Click.*

My answering service's robot voice told me her message had arrived at 3am, last night when I was passed out in my vest. I called her cell-phone immediately. She answered, safe on her end, stretched across gray plastic chairs in Charity's Hospital's waiting room. Whimpering, she explained how last night she was riding her bike home and the next thing she remembers is waking up in the middle of the street, on her belly, on those beautiful breasts, with a bloody hole in the back of her head. "I think I got hit by a car," she said.

"You '*think*'?"

"I'm not sure."

"How can you not be sure?"

"I don't know."

Right off, I held theories I hoped were wrong as she retraced her event last night: she drank a lot at work, then rode her bike to Snake-and-Jakes to meet co-workers. There they all ate pills, drank, drank more, and drank. In the parking lot they crushed more pills on the hood of a car and snorted them before Mizzy hopped back on her bike, hung a left down Magazine, then woke up with a head-hole. She locked her bike at the scene of the accident or crime or whatever it was, and walked the rest of the way to her apartment, where she called me. When I didn't respond, her roommate assured her she looked fine then laid Mizzy down. From bed she called me a few more times before passing out. In the morning she woke on bloody pillows and in the daylight decided her wound was worse than the amateur had diagnosed. On her way to work, Mizzy's roommate dropped her off at The Hospital, where Mizzy lay on orange vinyl for five hours before a doctor finally cleaned and stitched her, wrapped a bandage around her skull, then ordered her back out to wait for further instruction.

"The doctor didn't find any clues how it happened?" I interrogated. "Like, flecks of bumper in your skull?"

"No."

"How fucked up is your bike?"

"Not at all."

"How could a car hit you and not fuck your bike?"

"I don't know," she sighed then laughed, "Ugh; they had to shave a big chunk of hair out of the back of my head..."

My first accidental thought: *Oh no. Great. I finally get a cute girlfriend and...* Shallow, yes. But I suffered no guilt; she sounded fine, so happy to hear my voice that I couldn't help feeling more curious than sympathetic. Instead of condolence I aimed question after question at her: "Did you maybe just hit a pothole, or maybe..."

To no avail. Finally I gave her the hypothesis I'd assumed since first hearing her pathetic whisper on my answering service: "Maybe you were attacked…"

"No, I had $200 in tips in my purse and it's all still there." Then tired-sounding but abrupt she added, "Now please Patrick, don't make me answer any more questions. Not right now. Please."

Blunt yes, but perfectly non-dramatic. She's a good influence. I ended my inquiry, and appreciating that she'd called me of all people, I gave her, "Poor baby."

"Thanks," she cooed, sounding more than fine, sounding better than me, though she did admit, "They gave me a bunch of Vicodin, so I'm a little *marinated*. My head doesn't hurt at all now — more than the pain it's just been so lonely here, waiting all by myself. I want you here more than anything."

Those pills must be strong to conjure such affection from her: she purring sadly, confiding all the ways her injury has her re-evaluating her lifestyle and her Need to get fucked up — I could feel how detailing her disappointment in herself was simultaneously convincing her that she needed me. And I feasted on it.

"Oh! And I finally got X!" she squealed loud enough to block out the sick groans in her background. "We're gonna have so much fun on Lundi Gras!"

Regardless of whether her affection was just a side effect of the pills, I offered to pass up the parades tonight, jump on my bike *right now*, and mow down every tourist dawdling between My Room and Charity Hospital…

"No, I'll be home in a couple hours," she said. "Just meet me at my apartment. I can't wait! I wish you were here now!" Then she added, "I wish you would've answered your phone last night; if you'd answered you would've made me go to the hospital right then. I know it." Her soft voice soured, "I can't fucking believe my roommate let me go to *sleep*. With a concussion? Fuckin-A. I could have never woke up. Stupid bitch…" she laughed, calming and reiterating, "I wish you would have answered last night."

"I do too," I told her, at the same time fully realizing that I was glad I *hadn't* answered, because *What could I have done for her?*

Especially after the VP's message, and the deflation that followed... I would have only somehow wrecked the cool I'm sure she kept even as her brain leaked down the back of her downy neck. No, it's better that I know about her accident only now, when everything's fine...

- 4 -

The tall barbed-wire gate of her courtyard opened and her smiling head emerged, wrapped in a thick hat of wounded-soldier bandages. Seemed like I'd seen her in that state before; Post-Trauma looked comfortable on her. She was healthy though, strong, her hugs hard and deep, deeper than before — she didn't let go of me from the front gate, past her fountain > > > past the swimming pool > > > between her junk-sculptures in her stairwell > > > up into her room, where she seemed to really need me — though again, I've never eaten Vicodin... In the meantime I assumed hers to be 100% non-pharmaceutical sincerity, and I stopped thinking — until in her bed, her bandages against my bare shoulder, she continued feeling like a failure, a drunk: "I'm so fucking stupid," she moaned twice in a row.

Poking my nose into her ear: "Oh, you're not stupid."

"I work in a *res*taurant," she evidenced.

"You're only 23," I reminded her, yearning to tell her about the time during my 23rd year when in the heat of young battle with my ex-girlfriend, I locked myself in a bathroom and threatened to kill myself (as Lani must have...) and so ended up pinched in the backseat of a squad car on my way to a Mental Health Agency where a half-assed grad student would ask me the 1000 nervous questions his teachers had taught him, or were in the process of teaching him. That's where I learned the term Baker Act... Mizzy might have felt less stupid hearing about how I'd wanted to just admit to that psychology student, 'I bluffed man, I'm sorry,' but that I couldn't manage through my stupid choking tears. I wanted to assure Mizzy she's never been *that* stupid and never will be, but I didn't know what that would all do for my cause... So I said only, "Getting drunk and falling off a bike doesn't sound that stupid to me."

"No, I'm stupid," she assured, rolling over, giving me her back, and when she groaned inward, at herself, I knew she was about to admit… "I kissed someone else."

That sentence... I recognized that sentence; that same week as my visit to the Mental Health Agency that same ex-girlfriend spoke That Same Sentence to me, which I found out later translated into: *I fucked someone else.*

"No, I only kissed him," Mizzy promised, then repeated, "I'm so fucking stupid."

For the same reason I didn't inform her of my long-ago Baker Act, I didn't get mad at her either, didn't bark. I held my cards, said only "Shit…" as she continued apologizing. Then finally I asked, "Who was it?"

"That cook at work…"

"Shit…" though who-it-was actually made it easier; she *had* to have been fucked-up to touch *that* guy; his ponytail and goatee alone muted my anger and drama. I even laughed a bit to let her know that I can't be upset, that I don't lose myself, that there'll never be reason to call The Authorities… But I gave no real opinions, made no statement; at 28 I know that anything I'd say after first being handed infidelity news, I'd surely disagree with not too long after. So I let her stew silently, believing that this more economical method would also be more apt to cure her, if a cure exists — I fucking hope it does.

In her bed she lay heavy atop me and over my mature silence declared, "I will never do it again. I promise. I'm sorry. I was stupid. I want to be with you. It was stupid to put it at risk… I don't need anything else, I PROMISE."

Staring into her ceiling fan: *Shit man. Shit. Why not believe her? She's different in so many other ways, maybe she's honest too. Though I'VE never gotten fucked up enough to cheat on anyone… But I've also never snorted pills… Maybe I should tell her she's just not allowed to snort anything when I'm not around…Tell her if she does it again…*

But I said nothing. At Mizzy's age I'd have screamed furious; a true redhead I was. But at 28-years-old — after she'd rolled halfway off of me in her asleep — I calmly snuck out from underneath her, off her nice bed, rolled my bike out the gate of her mansion, and pedaled back across The City.

- 5 -

Biking home was cold, but I sweated feeling stupid having ridden all the way out there to comfort her. *Where's my comfort?* I rode miles out there so she could take my comfort from me. *I might never go back...*

Locking my bike up at home, I noticed Lani's short hair standing beneath the moldy awning of the apartment on the other side of mine, outside the door of my other neighbor's room, not My Former Front Door. *Yes! Empathy!* I'd assumed I'd have no one to talk to about her, no one to help me regain *my* comfort... But even from far away I sensed Lani's own dark mood, and jogging up I realized *Maybe right now isn't the best time to discuss female betrayal and forgiveness...* Especially so close to Mardi Gras Day, what Lani claims would have been his 25th wedding anniversary.

He didn't turn to me. He stood smoking, staring over the fence at The Gazebo where he usually gives his readings. I sat down behind him on my unknown neighbor's cement steps and leaned against the door. Down the sidewalk to our right My Spanish Neighbor waved to us stepping into her car. Lani didn't wave back. At my feet, I noticed a deck of his *tuh-ROH* cards on the sidewalk. I assumed he'd been giving a reading, and the thought flashed that he should finally read *my* cards. *But I don't deserve it...*

Instead, attempting to reclaim him from whatever had him by the soul, I told him at least part of Mizzy's story — her First Version, about the pill-snorting and Charity Hospital, and her not-knowing how that hole got in her skull. When I finished, Lani spoke what I'd also thought, at first: "She's a perfect target..."

But I withheld The Truth of her accident, which Mizzy had finally admitted to me before falling asleep... I continued misleading Lani with her First Version: "No, she had $200 in her purse and..."

Removing his glasses to massage his eyes Lani informed me, "Well, there is some New Orleans gang whose initiation is they have to attack a white person. Not necessarily mug em, just kick their ass."

My memory scanned the black faces in The Dish Pit, on The Floor, the inflated faces of the kids blowing horns on the basketball court, the screaming faces of my first period class... "No, I don't think she was attacked," I maintained — still not admitting to Lani that she'd simply run into a fucking lamppost because she was fucked up... Maybe for the same reason she'd lied to me at first, I continued lying to Lani, "I think she got hit by a car."

"Let's hope that's what happened," he said, his back still facing me. Fixating on that spot where his ponytail used to live, I heard him say, "But other than that, you two sure *sound* like you get along well..."

"Huh?" I asked, also wondering whose apartment we were at, and when they'd come outside. "What do you mean?" *Maybe he's just sarcastically pointing out that I haven't talked to him since Mizzy...*

But before I could hand him the excuse that *I just...well...I didn't think you needed anyone bragging to you about their lovelife, not in the place you're at right now...* he continued, "Yeah, I hear y'all banging against the wall..."

"The wall?" I asked the back of his gray shorn head.

"The wall. My wall. Our wall. I guess you *wouldn't* know," he turned his scowl around on me finally, and pointed a silver-ringed finger toward his cards at my feet. As I handed the cards up to him he continued, "I had to move into this here room."

No, I hadn't noticed, not at all; I've been busy banging against the wall... Lani's mouth lay straight and tense as he explained, "Since my wife got the house, yer landlord's been lettin me stay here in return for I do some repair work. I been here for four days so far. You're right about how small these rooms are..." Shuffling his cards he added, "On the bright side I found my family's *tuh-ROH* deck! This weird-lookin motherfucker brought em to me after I put up a sign…"

"Lani, I'm sorry," I interrupted, so sad at the thought of his finding The Family Deck just as he's losing his family, and now having to live in that cubbyhole because he has no other choice, rather than because he longs for Costa Rica…

"No, you ain't gotta be sorry; I don't mind the sound a y'all. It's better than them damn pigeons. Listenin to y'all makes me less depressed…until you're finished and then…"

"No no, I mean I'm sorry I haven't come to visit and talk," I said.

"Aw hell naw, I understand man," he insisted, his necklaces rattling as he shook off the rest of his scowl. "I ain't mean to snap at you. You got a good girl for once, and I totally understand you'd rather do that…" *What a sad thing to say… He's just making it worse…* He rubbed his temples: "Naw, it's just that I quit taking that Heartbreak Medicine they gimmee, so I'm in a foul mood. M'nerves are bad. I had to get outta that tiny little box for a while, get me some air. You smoke a cigarette in there and you can't see your hand in frunna yer face for the next half-hour…"

"I know," I said, "I know," because I do.

"But who the hell is that I hear you yelling at in there?" he asked. "I know she ain't letting you yell at her like that…"

I had no idea. She and I have never fought — today was as close as it's come, which makes this extra hard… *But I have no idea… Yelling?* "Oh wait! You mean like a short little *AH*!" I demonstrated

He flinched, then, "Yeah. That's it."

"Oh. That's what I do to scare the fucking pigeons away when I'm too lazy to get up and slap the window."

"Man I hate those fucking bastards. They sound so goddamned…"

"Sexual. I know. How are there no pigeons on Our Former Mansion?" I asked, pointing next door, and feeling it hurt us both, my use of past-tense…

"The Old Man puts bleach in the fountains where the birds drink," Lani answered, then suggested, "We need to buy a fuckin pellet gun."

"I'll *definitely* chip in…"

Then he turned his back to me again to pine for The Gazebo and a life without pigeons. I could still hear them humping against the windows above us. Since now I knew that he was all right, I asked his back, "So, you're all right?"

He nodded. I returned to silence. Neither of us talked as the sun set.

When NO was finally dark Lani turned to me one last time to shake my hand. Then before stepping inside his new room he added, "And whatever *really* happened..." His eyebrows hiked up, letting me know that he *knew* without my telling him. "Whatever it was, it'll be fine," he promised. "She's a real sweet gal. Just don't worry about it."

When he'd disappeared I rose, walked to My Room, and slept through another night of parades.

ch 15: lundi gras

By early afternoon, Space begins shrinking. This is how it begins. Out The Picture Window, people consume all available Space with their bodies and cars and lawn-chairs and tall, crazy structures they've built to stand above each other. By darkness' decent, Space has been reduced to just that waiting swath cut through the bodies — until the towering floats come, eating up the rest of the street and the sky humans couldn't get to. Then an hour-and-a-half later it all dies, Space opens back up, the prisoners and their brooms come out, and I am none the richer.

Still, despite Management's offer to let me go home, I decided that after Brunch Shift I'd just stay at work, put my head down and keep going, accept my much-less-$-pr/hr and feel even more justified in my bitterness. One good thing about restaurant work: it can sometimes anesthetize, like checking oneself into a Mental Hospital for a *rest*. Plus Mizzy gave me a few Vicodin. Actually she didn't give them to me, I grabbed them off her dresser on the way out of her room. She'd offered them earlier, but I'd reiterated that I didn't want to try any new drugs. But changing my mind at the last second made work more tolerable; one second I would long for Freedom, for that shrinking space out there — until I'd get caught-up staring drugged into the fiery pan of some A-Waiter's Bananas Foster — until I'd remember what Mizzy did, and scribble on seven different napkins before saying it to her like this:

Damn Mizzy,

Why, yo? Now I don't know how to feel about you. I think I feel like: if you can't avoid doing That Shit the DAY AFTER Our Parade, then how can I ever make you happy enough to never do That Shit again? I mean: these past weeks we've been as happy as we're EVER going to be, so if you can do That Shit the DAY AFTER crawfish then… Shit. And that guy isn't even attractive, Mizzy! He has a ponytail and a goatee. So I can't imagine what chance I'd stand against say, that beautiful mulatto friend of De'von's you jumped across The Cigar Bar for. I think I feel like: I'd rather just cry for a few days RIGHT NOW over having to let go when I like you so damn much, rather than cry for MONTHS later, when I've begun counting on your loyalty — the same way that whenever a doctor asks, I always choose the quick needle over drawn-out weeks of pills…
Since this is your first offense, I wouldn't be any less of a man for letting this go and simply giving you an ultimatum in regards to Next Time. But True Thugs don't forgive — I don't think they do; I'll check on the Internet when I get home… But regardless, I'm positive that ultimatums won't stop whatever's bound to happen when I'm not at parties with you, and you're partying, and the ponytails and goatees are trying so hard to tempt you away... No,

ultimatums would only keep you from telling me
your secrets, and then what's the point? So I
think I think that we shouldn't go out anymore,
or spend Mardi Gras together, I think.

    Damn bruh…
    White Bitch

Then, in the middle of concocting some strained P.S., The Donkey Show awarded me an event I will never forget as long as I live: A Life Moment addressed directly to my present dissatisfaction with Mizzy…

Jimmy fucking Swaggart came in.

Most people only know Swaggart as that awful crying face begging for TV forgiveness, that Media Moment that made so many of us feel better ourselves because *At least we aren't him…* But when I was little, a group of my less sophisticated relatives got sucked into PTL, and any other television ministry they could give their money away to, while abandoning any type of *fun* — I remember my Dad on the phone once pleading with my uncle: "But The Lord doesn't want you to stop *fishing* for Christsake!" Debates and fights and arguments within our extended family were eventually followed by years of silence and cousins I was no longer allowed to talk to. Which made pouring Swaggart's ice-water and warming his bread *so* much more poignant for me — his wasn't even my table, but I just had to do at least *that*, before walking away and staring at him from behind the gold staircase, forgetting all about What's-Her-Name.

Swaggart sat chuckling with two other Southern-looking, gray-haired men in gray suits. His wife wore a yellowish-silver beehive hairdo and pearls. I'd already known that, long before his tearful Media Moment, Swaggart was famous for his singing. Still it amazed me when our annoying Mobile Ragtime Brunch Trio came by his table, and he sang a song with them. *At my job?* Beyond them, out The Picture Window, my bicycle provided background as Swaggart sang low, to his friends only, earning my respect by choosing a song

I didn't know, rather than "Wonderful World," or "God Bless the Child." None of our other customers paid attention to the scene — the same people who would stare whenever Jude crossed The Floor. A-waiter Michael didn't give a fuck either, distracted playing with a light-up Harrah's Casino pen someone had given him as a tip. Not looking up from his new purple-glowing toy Michael informed me, "Oh God, Swaggart always does that when he's in here."

"And that doesn't phase you?" I asked Michael.

"Does what phase me, baby?" he asked, clicking his pen On. Off. On.

"Uh, that *Jimmy fucking Swaggart* is singing *at your job*?"

Then before Michael could answer, my entire thought machine focused on Swaggart's second song; usually the band plays only one per table, but I suppose at least *they* appreciated the uniqueness of the situation, and so continued, playing the only slow song I've ever heard them do: "Amazing Grace." Swaggart sang this one louder, not for the other customers, just louder for himself, eyes closed, Jimmy Swaggart, *at my job?* The Picture Window's sun shot through his now gray, wispy hair, illuminating his skin, which sags in a way that makes him look as if he's still crying, a permanent allusion to what he's famous for. *At my job?* But as I gawked at him, my co-workers stared only at me, as if my not working for *one moment* was more incomprehensible than Jimmy fucking Swaggart booming: *"To-o-o saaave a wreeetch like meeeeee. I wuuuuuunce wa-a-as lost bu-ut now I'm fouuund…"* a minor re-enactment of his Media Moment, a private plea for forgiveness, at *our fucking job*!

When it was over, the Brunch Band members each shook his hand, and Swaggart's wife waited until they'd walked off before leaning in and kissing her husband, sincere, sweet, proud, causing me to finally remember Mizzy. *If SHE can forgive HIM* then…

I held my breath, shook my head, felt crazy, ate another of her Vicodin, worked another huge parade I don't remember at all, made $50 then rode home with that napkin in my pocket.

- 2 -

Since I've spent all my other NO holidays alone, *I'll give her that napkin on Ash Wednesday*... Until then, that goateed bastard finally came through with two rolls of X, which we've planned to eat tonight: her payment for watching his house, feeding his dogs, eating his food, sleeping in his bed...

But during Lundi Gras' morning hours, a little wine, weed and more of her Vicodin are helping me to forget all of that, and just be thankful That Fucker is out-of-town, not dangling out his Service Window trying to tempt her into his Kitchen. Brain deadened, it's infinitely easier to sit here calmly waiting for the end of her Lunch Shift, or the end of whatever else.

- 3 -

No dreams. I came-to at 9p/m, three hours from Mardi Gras. Foregoing any costume, I sprang up and out and panicked pedaling back to The Quarter, still marinated and wrapped in sleep, the ride slow and difficult — and this was *before* my buzz wore off and I noticed I'd forgotten my jacket *again*; at first I noticed nothing, until finally my legs took a break from pumping hard and fast and I leaned heavy on my handlebars, and in the darkness, head lowered, breathing heavy white steam, eyes closed, relaxing, not nodding off, just relaxing, my brain warned *Hey! Look up! Jesus! Dumbass! Closing your eyes out here is fucking Murder*... But I couldn't bring myself to worry. I mean, I definitely lifted my head, but The City I saw around me did not provoke fear. Maybe it was the pills but *I'm barely scared of this place at all anymore*... Not that I still don't believe *It's just a matter of time,* but *Who the hell cares?* Like how I suspect Jude feels. I don't know what it will do for my cause but...

That ride took years and halfway there, fuck I was cold, wearing only a 'funny' silk shirt and her fucking red fur hat that didn't even cover my ears. Iced-air whipped through my silk, as cold and wet as snow and yet *No snow? How the FUCK is it not SNOWING?* — until finally, Decatur.

Except for my teeth, I remained silent, waiting for her inside Restaurant Angeli. *Of course she's fucking late...* I stared out the foggy window of the too-hot restaurant, not thawing until I watched her roll up and U-Lock her bike: she'd taken my advice and dressed as a Civil War soldier with red food coloring dripped onto her head bandages, and medals pinned to the layers of military jackets suppressing her boobs and keeping her warm.

Stepping smiling into Angeli's heat she read my face and immediately proclaimed, "Aw Patrick, I'm sorry..."

"Don't remind me..."

"Please don't think about it," she hugged me deeply, her medals poking my heart. "I'm sorry. Seriously. I swear I am." I didn't hug her back. I wasn't mad, just... "You look so cute in my hat," she added.

"Right. Thanks."

"It's my favorite hat. You better treat it right."

"Right. Treat the *hat* right..."

"Patrick c'mon..." she rolled her eyes. Then silence. Then, "Here, this will put you in a better mood." She opened a tin of mints and removed two that looked *different* from the others....

"If you're in a shit mood, does X fucking attack you?" I asked, "turn you in on yourself, the way acid does?"

"Patrick, c'mon; I said I'm sorry."

"Stop apologizing. Let's just take the shit..."

"Dude," she backed off. "Either abandon me, or let it go, one or the other. But don't pout; it's gross."

You can't argue with Truth. "Sorry," I admitted. We were both sorry. She kissed me (I still couldn't kiss back) before scanning for witnesses, then poking the pill between my lips and pushing it back in there with her thumb. She then popped and swallowed hers, following it immediately with, "Patrick, I love you, Patrick."

"Wow yours kicked in fast. I don't feel shit..."

She laughed. I was serious; I'd heard her words but... Too much drugs already and my brain was *white-chocolate bread pudding, crabmeat cheesecake, menthol sorbet...* "I just wanted to say that before it *does* kick in," she continued. "Because I know that I'll definitely say it *after* it kicks in — because it's true, I do love you — but I knew that if the first time I said it was when we were rolling, you'd just brush it off — the way I wish you'd brush off that other thing I did when I was fucked up…But I do love you."

Not without feeling but without thinking I said, "I love you too," stopping before 'I guess…'

She blazed her gap and with hardly any sarcasm sang, triumphant, "Awe! How romantic: falling in love in *The French Quarter!* It's like being *famous*!"

And though I'd downed enough sedatives that my face couldn't register it, my Inner Face sobbed like Swaggart's.

- 4 -

The strong part lasted only a half-hour, and even that was weak; the most this X *could have* been was merely pleasant, had we not spent that half-hour struggling our bikes through the costumed pukers and the unreal depth and breadth of spent, plastic cups. Not until the X died in us did The Soldier and The Cold Person finally give up and lock their bikes to poles and drag each other by the hand through the party, chased by archaic music and others' laughter — *others'*, not our own; we were bland. I kept silent, busy mentally dissecting how the drug felt in relation to how I've been told it feels, or how it felt in relation to sobriety, or *how in the world is she now allowed to claim she fucking LOVES me, and how are we going to get out of THAT one, because eventually we ARE going to have to figure our way out of it and…* Whenever she'd kiss me with the pinkest little out-turned lips, I was so distracted thinking *This is it, I'm kissing on Ecstasy, now what does it FEEL LIKE?* that I never could let myself just fall into her. And then buzzing in the eternal background: The Cold. The furry red hat was impotent. None of her military jackets would have fit me, so I wasn't offended that she didn't offer one. X is supposed to cast a spell that makes you more accepting, and yes, it did allow me to unselfconsciously accept that I was freezing and wanted to be at home, with or without her.

Then as an encore, it wore off and I was frozen sober. We felt cheated. *Cheated. Cheating. Forgiveness. I need a fucking jacket...* My only consolation, small as it was, came in knowing that the goatee who'd given her the X had proven himself unreliable, or as I put it to her, "impotent."

"Yeah, what an asshole," she agreed. "He's lucky he didn't sell this to me for $25 a roll, like he's been trying to for weeks."

"We can still make tonight fun though," I smirked, just to be contrary — but hearing myself say it, I realized it was true, or that it should be true; this Lundi Gras had all the makings, even without drugs or *Wait, I'm on tons of other drugs already... And this is EXACTLY what I want, have wanted, need, have needed, exactly: to be* cold but *loved during the main attraction at a Major Tourist Destination...* I did indeed want to just let go, let myself appreciate Mizzy's long, real kisses on dark, bead-strewn streets wet with filth but... Breaking free of my negativity seemed a very realistic goal, at least for one night but... *If it just weren't so fucking COLD....*

But it was. So cold that we paid no attention to Bukowski's HANK WAS HERE carved in the cement — we ran thoughtlessly over the signature into The R-Bar, where the clientele was unfortunately happier and more fun than I was able to be, but because she is well adjusted, gets along with people, doesn't overthink life, owns deep, full curves and that gap, Mizzy was instantly surrounded by best friends, ex-roommates, pals from former jobs, all happy as hell to see her. Plus tonight, all of them were on X. The right kind of X: real, strong, sweaty X that rolled their eyes back white. Mizzy gleaned a contact buzz from their attentions, abandoning me in favor of sitting in the laps of all the rolling girls and boys, smearing her hands sensually over their faces as they all moaned and giggled and I suppressed anger — until, one of the red-cheeked males announced, "Man I am so fucking hot! This jacket is a fucking drag, bruh! I wish I wouldn't have brought it!"

Mizzy heard him, and on my behalf ran to his lap next, where she talked him into loaning us his jacket for the night: a thick, beautiful, goose-feather ski jacket worth hundreds of dollars. Had his mind not been fucked, he wouldn't have done that, but The Soldier climbed down off his crotch and brought the prize to me. "See! The spirit of Mardi Gras!" she sang, opening the jacket wide, wrapping me in it while whispering, "Let's leave."

"Yeah yeah. Cool. I think Glorybee's playing at the..."

"No. I'm tired. I want to be alone with you."

Warm and happy and amazed she would abandon this night for me, I asked, "Where to?"

"I have to go back to his apartment..."

My heart cracked and the very last of the drugs leaked out... She noticed and hummed, "I know. I'm sorry. But I haven't checked on the dogs all day. And it'll be fun!" Without saying goodbye to anyone she dragged me outside to our bikes, continuing, "We'll get to take the ferry over there! And we'll have his whole place to ourselves with all his food and liquor and his TV and we can screw in his bed."

"Oh. OK. Awesome," as my hand in my pocket searched desperately for my keys...

- 5 -

It wasn't midnight yet as the ferry crossed the Mississippi to Algiers. I don't remember any stars, but it was perfect. Even without the drugs it was perfect. I'd never taken the ferry before; *so many things I've never done in NO. So many places I can go now if I can just forgive her. Aren't all these unseen places and things worth a little blind faith and loss-of-pride...?*

The ferry landed and we pedaled nicer, less broken streets to his big purple shotgun house. The inside was jealousy-inducing: central heat, towering healthy plants reaching toward impossibly high ceilings, track-lights illuminating original paintings and lithographs, matching end-tables and deep velour couches of which he was obviously the first owner, a giant-screen TV that couldn't even fit in my room but left open plenty of *his* unscratched hardwood floor-space, and every mile of it clean...Aside from too many video games, a knee-high hand-blown bong and an oversized Bob Marley poster, the house was unexpectedly tasteful for someone with a ponytail and goatee. I didn't like it.

"I don't *smell* any dogs," I sneered.

From inside the refrigerator (with ice-and-water spouts in its door) Mizzy removed the dozen ingredients it takes to make Bloody Marys, while explaining that the dogs were in the bedroom. She asked me to let the dogs out into the yard, which I took this as an invite to invade his Private Space in search of something unimpressive.

I flinched upon walking in on two big German Shepherds laying 69 in the middle of a waterbed. The dogs lifted their heads out of each other's crotches and stared at me with cowardly eyes. "Should they be up in his bed like this?" I yelled into the kitchen, crossing the bedroom to open the cold glass patio door. The dogs leapt up and dashed out.

"They sleep in his bed with him," she yelled back.

"Jesus. Gross." I shut the patio door. It was the last we'd see of them until morning...

Minus the dogs, the room was equally tasteful: bed neatly made with new matching maroon comforters and pillows, bookshelves lined with the entire lineage of White Guy Lit I wish I had money to own. No pigeons groaned outside the windows. The nightstand contained no porn. The insides of his closets didn't stink of socks. His clean underwear lay folded in his top dresser drawer as if my mother had been there. Goatee or not, he seemed more capable than I, and I contemplated this, worrying about myself and my future — until I found the drugs...

In his second drawer: *Yes!* two big blocks of black hash *Fuck yeah!* A bottle of liquid Vicodin. *Ooh!* A ziplock bag containing a perforated sheet of paper I assumed was acid and *Oh shit!* three orange bottles of pills: Valium, Xanax, Oxycontin, and a third, unlabeled bottle, which I opened to find the same pills we'd taken earlier, along with a few other types. Without much thought — except one: his out-of-date whiskers brushing Mizzy's chin — I ate two of the unfamiliar pills, then carried a third out to where Mizzy was garnishing our drinks with zucchini, spicy green beans and olives.

"Look what I found." I set the pill down on the cutting-board-island, only then realizing that maybe she wouldn't be so excited about my going through his drawers and… But before that doubt could even fully form, the pill disappeared, and Mizzy was gulping Mary.

"Hey, you didn't split it with me," I accused.

"You didn't already take one?" She handed me my Mary. "I'd be surprised if you didn't take one already…"

I sipped, wishing a Nobel Peace Prize upon whoever invented The Bloody Mary. *Wait though, is she supposed to be drinking on her antibiotics? I suppose abstinence is a worthless cause at this time of year. I hope her brain doesn't get infected…* "I took two more actually," I admitted.

"Oh shit."

"What?"

"Let's take a bath."

"OK."

He may own two shower nozzles — one on each end of a bathtub big enough for three — but I had *her*: her wet naked breasts, her loud, goofy laugh echoing off his clean tile. The bathroom was so clean I was sure he must have a maid. And if he has a maid then he could surely afford us filling his tub up with $40-worth of hot water, both showerheads raining from above as we sank in facing each other. She likes the water hotter than me, and I suffered it as if experiencing *her* through this uncomfortable temperature, this heat I wouldn't have chosen for myself — it was really kicking in now. And as The World began to wobble I looked around and noticed, on the shelf above her bandaged head, more bath products than I've ever seen in one place save that store in the mall: sample bottles of blueberry body wash, rose-scented bubble-baths, dozens of little shampoos and conditioners for his fucking ponytail. Like those political signs on Esplanade, the sheer volume of bath products seemed sarcastic. Or else…

"Maybe he's gay?"

"No. He's not."

"But look at all that…"

"Trust me, he's not."

That hurt. Made me wonder if she'd touched his dick *Fuck man why am I here, why am I…* But then I looked down at my own dick, limp and floating, harmless and *Who fucking cares? Who really fucking cares…* The X was welling up, giving me perhaps an artificial level of understanding, but one so innate that I didn't question my *Who cares! It's fine. Everything's fine* — much more the reaction I've always expected from this culture-defining drug: the opposite of self-conscious. She must have been there too; after dipping just the ends of her hair into the water (can't get the bandages wet) then letting out her big breath, she began explaining what I felt I already understood…

"I'm really sorry I did that to you," she said, wiping her eyes. But this apology wasn't distraught like her others, because now *she* understood that *we* understood, that we were now simply rehashing something we'd weathered together, something we'd survived, a struggle that was over now, had passed, meaning and injuring nothing…

"It's OK!" I laughed to prove its nothingness, pointing behind me at his sink: "No problem, I'll just piss on his toothbrush!"

"Yeah, steal his drugs and then piss on his too- too- too…" she couldn't finish through her laughter, which was of an even higher velocity than usual, echoing around the bathroom.

I confided, "You know, when I was little my sister made me mad and I did that to her once." I was feeling confessional.

"Pissed on her toothbrush?" Mizzy asked, shocked into calm. "Patrick, that's terrible."

"I've never told that to anyone," I blubbered. I was beginning to lose it, but I wasn't afraid.

She changed the subject back: "Yeah, uh, anyway… I've been trying to figure out why I did That, and aside from the Jaegermeister, I think I did it because I knew I wouldn't be kissing anyone else again for a long time and like…" she trailed off, ponderous, her smile dripping water down her chin. "At the Cigar bar too: I think seeing you that night is what made me kiss De'von's friend, because I knew that this was It, that you and I were…"

Wait, didn't I guess that? I confused myself wondering *Did I?*

Or am I just fucked up or… No, I had, in reality, guessed. "I thought that was why you did it," I declared, belying no surprise. *I'll sort out the coincidences later…* For now I added, "I thought you were going to do the same thing with Cedar at Our Parade the other night."

"He is cute. But I won't do anything like that again. I promise"

"Yeah," I heard myself say in Jude's optimistic voice, my breath warm and sweet in my mouth as, without verbally co-coordinating it, we both leaned in at the same Moment and kissed. Water ran down our chins. We parted and leaned back amazed. She squeezed my toes underwater. They felt like ten penises. It was kicking in hard: "I really do love you," I said, unafraid, my words broken by sharp breaths and black blurs whizzing before my eyes like limousines by The Picture Window — I could even feel their wind.

"I love you too," she smiled. "I really do."

"I know. I know." My breath sharpened, hurting a little, kind of nice but… I remembered that bad birthday trip I wrote about for my kids, but then blocked it out and *Slow down, slow down… Slower… Slower…* But the limos circled faster… Mizzy emitted a satisfied hum that vibrated through the tub's ceramic, around into my back. "Oh my god Mizzy. This is fucking… Fuck man."

"I know."

"I love you more than I love my parents," I blurted.

Her light, watery, "No, Patrick," oscillated the water and entered my skin. "You love your parents," she claimed.

"I do but…"

"But what?" she smiled.

"But my parents don't make *art*…"

"No. Mine either."

On cue we leaned in.

- 6 -

"You shouldn't have taken so many," spoke a gentle voice from somewhere.

"Oh my god man holy fuck…" The circling limos blurred into

fast black cumulus clouds over a barely audible soundtrack of screeching tires and faint applause. My lungs tickled as if full of orange soda, the little mouths in there trying to breathe but clogged with syrup.

"Oh, poor baby," I heard someone say, and agreed…

"Oh yeah. This is fucking serious man." The drugs carried me up and up and up and up and darker as up and up and "Holy fuck man…" Until finally, I did break the surface, hit a pocket of clean air. The black limos slowed down then drove off, leaving me eye-level with his bath products collection — I didn't remember standing up; a second before I'd thought the little bottles had fallen down onto me in the tub… Now Space opened everywhere in the bathroom, bringing with it light that painted the tiles white again. "Fuck man, *whoa* that was fucking close." Pressing my knuckles into eyeballs I breathed: "Oh Jesus, thank *God* that passed." And not only did it pass, it left me feeling better than I ever have! Ever! A state so divine it brought forth curses: "Thank fucking *God!*" I joyously wiggled my ten penises down there between Mizzy's submerged ankles descending my testicles back into our hot water.

When I was finally sitting wet and warm and comfortable again I suggested, "Hey let's get out."

"OK."

Watching her stand up above me dripping was *Holy fuck…* It played out before my eyes like the first porn video in history with a great plot — the tape a bit warped, maybe left under the seat in her truck for too long but… Her two hands as if stretching down from heaven offered themselves, lifted me out of the tub, dried me off, chest, hair, ass, crotch, "Holy fuck Mizzy. This is just fucking…Mizzy."

"I know," someone laughed, somewhere.

Then my taste-buds violently remembered, "Our Bloody Marys!"

I left Mizzy there and, dripping testicles swinging, I somehow hunted down that little cutting-board-island in the center of the kitchen. *There you are!* Before anything else, I relished two or three huge gulps of mine and then just stood there, eyes watering. *Holy fuck…* The flavor so intense I closed my eyes, cutting the tears loose to roll down. Peaceful sharks swam on the insides of my eyelids. *I love sharks*...and so watched them for a while before opening my eyes again to the site of all the Mary fixins strewn about the cutting-board island. I counted the fixins then gazed down into my glass: even from behind my blur I could discern each little floating grain of pepper and white horseradish. I looked back to the island: *Damn there are so many...so many fucking THINGS in here. And this guy has them all? At his house? He'll use them to take her from me...*

But *Nah*, I couldn't resent him anymore. *Who cares; this is a nice fucking place...* After inspecting his walk-in pantry (*Tupperware containers full of whole-grain pastas...organic dog biscuits? And he's not gay?*) I walked out to the violent glow of his yellow walls, a glow that seemed to come from *inside* the plaster: electric walls gorged with lightening. But when I flipped a switch to turn the walls off, they exploded *even brighter!* "Holy fuck! *Beautiful*!" I ran from room to room turning on all the walls, dripping water and Bloody Mary onto the polished hardwood *Weeeeeeeeeeee!* (except in cursive: write *weeeeeeeeeeee* down on a piece of paper in cursive — it felt exactly like that)

But then I couldn't find my way back to her. I'd gone too far into the shotgun and now I was lost. *Lost*! I yelled, "Mizzy!"

"Baby what! What's the matter?"

"Where are you?"

"In here."

I followed her voice to a carpeted back room containing another computer, another TV, more good books, an exercise bicycle and best of all, a brand-new sweet mother-of-pearl Slingerland drum kit. "Holy shit!" God I fucking love drums kits: the most cathartic contraptions. It'd be a hard choice between a drum kit and a cat. But I've never had Space for a kit — most of the music equipment I do have remains wrapped in dirty towels under my bed; my Space and my wallet are too small for a kit. But fuck I do love them. And this Slingerland was so nice that at first I didn't notice her lying naked on the carpet in front of its bass drum, on her side, hugging her knees, fetal. She turned her head to look up at me, "Hey."

"Damn, a fucking *drum kit!*" I handed down her drink.

She reached up took the glass. "Play something for me," she commanded.

"No, no, no I can't play his kit."

"You want to?"

"Yeah."

"Then kick that shit!"

"That's wrong."

"You stole his drugs."

"Yeah, but playing someone's kit without asking is wrong."

"Wow. That's beautiful," she said, sincere, then attempted to sip her drink without sitting up, trickling red down her cheek.

"How the hell does a cook afford all this?" I asked.

"Uh. Sells drugs."

"Oh, right." I watched her in her cramped pose, cocking her head at different angles, trying to drink. "What are you doing down there?" I asked.

"Waiting for you to lay down so I can rub on you." She unfurled her legs, sat erect, pushed her fake-bloody bandages up her forehead, took a full, hearty drink and admitted, "Damn, you're right: holy fuck."

Then taking another gulp myself, I noticed her eyes watering. Actually, not just her eyes, her entire body watered, as if standing behind a Costa Rican waterfall…

"Honey why are you crying?" she asked.

"Oh. It's me?" My whole body heaved with my breaths.

"Huh?"

"I thought it was you…"

"You should lay down," she suggested with a concerned face and a trail of hands suggestively patting the empty Space beside her on the carpet.

She stood. I lay. The carpet was damp from her and I wallowed in that dampness, her dampness, squirmed around in it as she towered over me laughing — until I kicked my Mary over on his carpeting. "Shit! Shit! Fuck!" Screaming laughter we scrambled for towels. After dabbing at the tomato juice a while she asked, "That looks OK right?"

The stain throbbed pink.

"Yeah. Sure," I shrugged, almost adding, 'Fuck him…' before closing my eyes and rolling onto my stomach. Soon there was a cold slime feeling on my back — not bad though; nothing could have felt bad; I would've drooled in sensual rapture during a root canal. My eyes fluttered as her hands dug into me: "Oh Mizzy, *holy* fuck." The cold slime was some kind of body cream...

"I know," a female voice giggled.

She squirted another line of cream down my spine, rubbed it in slick, poured on more, rubbed it in and poured more until my back was a lake, her hands one of those planes that lands on lakes… She added and added cream until a cold trail of excess ran down into my crack, and only then did I remember Sex; I'd actually forgotten about it, since everything else in The World seemed *easily* as important and fascinating and fulfilling — until I remembered Sex and prioritized it, causing my hips to begin rising off the carpet. She poured more cream at the base of my spine. It ran down and under, along the sides of my balls… "Oh holy fuck. Mizzy… More."

She poured out more. It was like electric shock, if shocks were good. My hips rose higher for her. She poured and rubbed my back and ass and poured and poured and my hips kept rising until I was up on my knees, with the side of my face pushed down into the tomato juice stain.

"Oh fuck man *more*…"

It dripped down and around underneath, defying gravity across my stomach. I opened my eyes a second to the sight of four little sample bottles sitting empty by her knee. I saw the clock: 12:20. *So this is Mardi Gras…* Peering down my chest and past my stomach I watched body wash dripping down off the end of my penis onto the carpet. When I laughed, she noticed the drip too, and to stop it she finally grabbed me there…

"Oh, holy fuck!" My laughter stopped. This was serious. My eyes welled: "*Oh Holy fuck, Mizzy. Oh my fucking…*" I almost demanded she let go, before she laughed and squeezed tighter. I almost passed out.

I can only liken this experience to a My Bloody Valentine concert I once attended; loudest band ever, so loud you could barely hear the music for the sound of your eardrums freaking out, and on top of that, the stage was surrounded by walls of airport lights aimed right into the audiences eyes, so that as the band played you couldn't hear *or* see. And that's what Mizzy's genital massage was like: too, too much. I remained mute as she slid the cream up and down. I couldn't even moan. For the past two days, or actually since we first met, I've been so fucking self-conscious with and about her that *man* it was *so* fucking good to be there with her, like that, my hips high in the air, being milked until I cried, ridiculous, as vulnerable as I've ever been and unafraid. "I love you," I coughed.

"I love you too," she laughed, milking.

When she'd emptied that bottle she let go of me and I heard her rise and walk back into the bathroom, leaving me like that, in that position, feeling much stupider alone than with her there witnessing it. I yelled for her to come back and her laughter reverberated from next door before she ran back in, found me the same, immediately knelt and emptied a whole small bottle onto the backs of my testicles. When she began rubbing it I passed out. I will forever regret that remembering nothing after that — until finally someone somewhere said, "OK. My turn."

I came-to, moaning. We switched positions. Mizzy grumbled about the puddle of conditioner on the carpeting but *Ha ha! Fuck that guy!* I poured another half bottle onto the small of Mizzy's back and spread it around. Her hips rose as mine had; one of the drug's ingredients makes you want to be overtaken, makes your body desire positions in which it could more easily be killed. I poured and rubbed and her hips rose up to my face. I slid in fingers and she cried a little, made little choking sounds.

We laughed like retarded children. But the cream was disappearing too quickly into her skin — even this guy's gay collection would not sustain us. *Oil would work better...* "Hang on." I stood up, almost fell down; I could barely see, but on the way out of the room I paused in the doorway for a good minute, gazing at her hips shining, bent up in the air like that and *Holy fuck man*...

But then no oil in the bathroom? *All this shit and no oil?* I don't know what that says about the guy but... Then I remembered the walk-in pantry. In the kitchen the X welled up so strong I had to stop walking and slump my head and breath deep. Exhale: "*Hoooooooooooly fuuuuuuuuck.*" It just kept growing stronger, better, but before it would get better, it always got worse: first The World would darken threatening thoughts of death in failure and then just as Zeus would cock back the bolt that would be my snuff-out, the X set me down someplace *AWESOME* — a fluffy place where just holding that bottle of Wesson Oil in my hand and rubbing the greasy label, was a fucking beautiful tactile Moment.

Back in the drumkit room I sunk my knees in the creamy carpet before the shrine of her ass and, overzealous, poured the fast Wesson out onto the small of her back, used to the slow cream, bottle tilted at 90-degrees and waaaaaaay too much gurgled out. She yelped as half the golden bottle ran from her peak, down her vagina <<< down around her stomach >>> as well as down her spine >>> between her shoulders >>> up her neck >>> into her bandages as well as off her blades and onto the carpeting — lots on the carpeting, in the shape of a shiny snow angel... Mizzy didn't notice.

"Oh, fuck," we both repeated, for different reasons.

And before I could rub it in she turned and jumped me and we splashed down and slid, two raw nerve endings leaving a slick across his carpeting...

ch 16: the war seems over

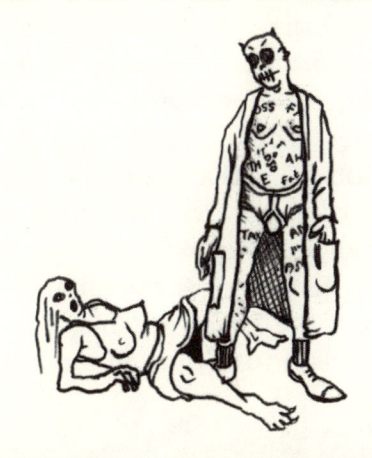

She swore she'd feel better than OK working the morning after That: "I'll be in the *mooooood* to dance with the old people today." She sprang out of bed, his bed, her blood still thin with drugs: "That Zydeco crap might actually sound good...." She wouldn't release my forearm, kneading and kneading it even as she dressed, strapped on her gumbo-stained apron, kissed and promised me, "We'll both feel great all day..." And yes, the blankets and cool sheets and clean pillows and her kneading and kneading: *otherfuckingworldly*. Before even parting the drapes, I was sure that the air and sun would behave perfectly today because *this is my will*! *What choice does the day have?* Today would wait on me hand-and-foot and at the end of it there'd still be some paycheck, somehow.

"Yeah, the Brain Demons won't come around looking for all that Seratonin we wasted, until tomorrow," Mizzy warned. "That's when we'll start bickering…"

She dropped my forearm and ran out and still *Holy fuck* my soul felt light — less perfect than last night, but still wrapped in a thin protective veil of Perfection and a believable sensation of Power. My powerful hearing was able to hold onto the far away squeak of Mizzy's bike's chain grinding toward the Algiers ferry. My insides glowed as temperate as I knew it *had to be* outdoors: a perfect day for cycling: I lay there listening to the mild wind kissing her hair and light sun warming her teeth as she pedaled onto the ferry, over the river, onto Canal Street, her bike chain squeaking...

I possessed Mizzy's same drugged-up energy, and wanted out into all that Perfection, *needed* to pump my legs and ogle Mardi Gras, free in this weather to finally just *enjoy* a fucking parade. But I was sure the parades would roll all day, so saw no reason to interrupt the Perfection of just laying there in her lingering smell. Since I wasn't being forced to work I remained in bed, his bed: with his dogs humming sadly at the back door as they had since last night, I'd fall into light sleep, then wake, then sleep, then wake and masturbate a bit more of the X out onto his sheets, into her invisible smell, before sleeping again to the sad humming of his dogs...

- 2 -

See I knew it! The air and sun were indeed like music well-mixed through an expensive P.A. system: cool with a fleeting warmth at the edges, a little too bright, perfectly so... Biking to the ferry, I would have shivered without the perfect costume Mizzy'd laid out for me: a billowing, long brown gown of coarse, thick fabric, old-smelling and comforting, sort of a monk's robe except with elaborate, quilted wings sewn under the arms from the wrists to the knees. Modeling the gown before his full-length mirror, my foot slipped on the slick carpet in front of his drum kit — *Shit we'll have to rent a shampooer or...* — but upon my bike I stood graceful, releasing my grip of the handlebars to let my wings fill with *Jesus this AIR!* The sun and lingering X rolled me through Algiers' creaky deserted neighborhoods of wood planks and lacy ironwork, along dead streets where I could spread my wings and just *listen* to them flapping in this silence, The Last Silence of This Day. *Cause once I'm over the river man...*

It was about 2p/m when the ferry captain yelled down at me

from his crow's-nest, "Get off and walk!" because you can bring your bike on the boat, but you can't *ride* it up the ramp. The ferry was under-populated today though, so it was hard to respect that rule. I stayed coasting long after he yelled, until he opened his mouth to yell again; then and only then did I jump off my bike to enjoy watching the captain's silent, wide mouth contract. I'd assumed we'd all stand, pinched shoulder-to-shoulder in a mad scramble to get over to NO, but I could have ridden laps around the empty lower deck nearly unimpeded — I *would* have but…

Instead I leaned my bike on the brown metal bow railing and sat cross-legged against my back tire on the warm metal deck. *Shit, I forgot sunscreen…* My hand shaded my cancer as I counted exactly twelve other people on-board, all white, homeless drunks — or maybe rich people who'd spent too many hours partying. Balloons tied to many of their wrists barely swayed from ninety-degree angles as the ferry drifted toward NO. *My God this FUCKING AIR!* Carnival hadn't impressed me at all until today — today so amazing it didn't seem strange that an old woman dressed like a gypsy, or perhaps a real gypsy, would come kneel on the deck, her ribs against my knees, her witchy fingers squeezing my bike tire, her eyes searching my face, and then the water, then my face, then NO in the distance… Squinting and counting the ferry's same dozen passengers one more time I asked her, "So where are the rest of the people?"

"Oh, zey're already over een ze city, sveetheart. Veer late for ze party…"

Sveetheart nodded, squinting, humming *I - can't - find - my way arouuuuuuuund…* until the boat rammed the dock. Balloons bobbed and everyone laughed sloppily. The gypsy woman released my tire, gathered up her purple skirts, stood and ran. I climbed onto my ripped seat and pedaled off the ferry, wings billowing, the captain yelling at my back, this time over the intercom. Everyone laughed at everything.

At the ramp's end I had to slow down to roll through all the humans squealing and hugging their Algiers friends as if after a long overseas voyage: *"Oh finally you're here you dirty fucking people!*

Yeeeeeeeeeeeeeee! Happy fucking MARDI GRAS!" Emerging onto NO soil, the atmosphere remained so graceful that *grossly* cliché thoughts flourished, thoughts regarding this invisible yet absolutely tangible *Feeling* my bike was cutting through: in that Moment I thought, believed even, that this *Feeling* was indeed *in the air*. A *Feeling in the air*. I know; a bad rock lyric, but… Blame last night's X, but NO's air felt gorged with Freedom, like X-mas, except today instead of the hateful pressure of gift-giving and receiving, all of us humans (save the NOPD, whose humanity I've heard debated many times) would concentrate, simply, on fucking ourselves up. Freedom's sucked out of our Holidays at the age when we begin working overtime to pay for them, but This Day, with This Air, gives it back. And if the idea of reclaiming that Freedom brings the rest of The City to as teary-eyed a state of Happiness as it does me, then with all of us glowing, vibrating in our Freedom all at the same time, of course this would vibrate *the air,* where we would indeed *feel it,* as well as breathe it in, until we can't possibly care if what we're feeling is cliché.

    Up on my pedals again like an Angelfish on Decatur, my first sight was Lani — or really, Jackson Square: the black iron gate behind Lani's card table, the hat-tipping statue, the steeple piercing the ubiquitous gray sky, twice as many street-performers doing weak tricks for pocket change, twice as many white tourists — not as many as I'd expected, but enough to light fear in the wet eyes of twice as many donkeys pulling twice as many carriages. A gross scene, especially after having forced my bike through it so many times. *But the boat docks where the boat docks…And there's Lani! Sooooo good to see ol Lani*! Almost artificially so… Next to Lani stood that Giant Wooden Thing he built, or has been in the constant process of building since 1978, he claims. Lani calls this mass of twisted branches, round wooden pegs and melted candles an *Apopkykno*, silencing the second K — I always assume he's pronouncing it wrong. By now Lani's Apopkykno stands five-feet tall, having sprouted new gold bells and carved-in words every time I've seen it, which hasn't been often; he only unveils it on special occasions. I wanted to ask him who drove that giant thing down to

The Square for him, or where the hell he stores it in his new little room next to mine, but The Apopkykno has developed into a work of such disturbing complexity that a large, inquisitive group of drunks kept Lani from noticing me.

Pronunciation clear and fake, Lani stood atop his chair, spitting the bio of The Apopkykno over the crowd's heads something about, "Two stems" and "Forks at the bottom" and "A big cuuuuuuuurve in it" that "creates a vortex" something, something, "Divination!" Then, "The Apopkykno altar has twenty-one candles in different positions..." And I chuckled at his 'altar has' instead of 'altar's got'...

But Lani looked in better shape than he has the very few times I've seen him recently: eyes brighter behind his big lenses, his constant chuckle returned with the hair sprouting back in a thousand directions from his head, jaw and lip — or maybe not *better* necessarily, just more vivid, more alive, maybe just drunk.

Regardless Lani engaged his crowd so directly that a cursive missive dangling from clear tape off the edge of his card-table had been placed in charge of making sure the drunks lined up to take photos with The Apopkykno knew they'd be charged $2. And as Lani loudly explained what each candle and peg symbolized, I noticed he had someone else working his Collection Plate: a skinny-as-death, withered old man who counted 1's with long, wormlike fingers. Silver and turquoise dripped from his diseased skeleton as if he'd raided Lani's Jewelry Box and layered everything on at once. I was sure he was bald under his gray wig — chemotherapy perhaps — and he overcompensated with a fake ponytail. *Death in Venice...* He might have scared the tourists away had aviator sunglasses not covered most of his long face, as well as a beard, a gray... *Fake beard? Wait... Jude?*

"Jude?"

"Yeah."

My joyous eyes watered: "Hey man! What the fuck!" I pushed through the layer of gawkers to stand beside him, eclipsed from Decatur by *The Apopkykno*. A steady stream of tourists snapped photos, handing Jude bills, keeping him too busy to look at me while reaching around and rubbing my back: "Yeah. Happy Mardi

Gras!"

"Uh, you too." But I was confused… "How do you know Lani?"

"From an ad at The Coffeehouse." Cramming handfuls of bills into the pocket of his adventurer-style beige vest, Jude almost toppled over: drunk too. I was the only one not drunk yet. But my X hangover was good enough…

Hands emptied, Jude started over collecting money as behind my back Lani barked, "When building an *Apopkykno*, the mystic adds new limbs over the years as he *learns how,* meaning that *It* grows as I grow. Also, along with its mystical properties, the *Apopkykno* is great fun when you are on acid," Lani chuckled, slipping into his real voice: "You kin just stare at the sun-a-bitch and have *visions*!" The majority of the crowd laughed, because they like a little spice, just a little, they expect it, but not too much, not too much please… A few people moved on, a few more stopped to listen.

"From an ad?" I asked Jude.

"Yeah. He lost his tarot cards, some real important ones I guess, the ones he uses for his family or something…"

"Yeah, he told me he just got them back."

"Yeah. They were in my Camaro."

"Huh?"

"When I stole it back…"

"No."

"Yeah."

"Holy fuck."

"Yeah. It was crazy: the backseat was like, full of purses too, and I've been trying to return them all, but then I'm like, 'Tarot cards?' Then the other day I saw an ad at that Coffeehouse that someone had lost their tarot cards. It showed a picture of the little bag the cards were in and everything so…"

"Man. Damn. Fucking weird."

"Yeah. But so the day I brought his cards over to his house he…"

"Hey I live right next door there!" I interrupted, eager for anyone to stop by, anytime. "That's where I live! Next time…"

"Yeah," Jude continued, "Anyway, within like five minutes of knocking on his door he asked me if I'd help him do this on Mardi Gras Day…" Jude finally turned his hidden face to me beaming the lumpiest smile underneath my giant reflection in his sunglasses: "Because he said he *sensed* that I was special."

"Lots of people sense that," the X and I complimented.

"Yeah," he repeated, not necessarily agreeing, before turning back to his job.

I asked his costumed profile, "What are you supposed to be dressed as?"

"What do you think?"

"Lani?"

"Yeah."

"You didn't know Lani when he had a ponytail," I pointed out, just then realizing that *Shit, that's right, Lani had one too, just like that fucker…*

"He gave me a picture to go by," Jude explained out the side of his mouth. "He suggested this look, this era; he says he looked better before he got divorced."

At that I felt guilty again, and admitted, out-of-context, "Yeah, we used to be like best friends. But I've kind of neglected him since Mizzy and I started going out."

Jude looked up again but past me. I turned around and together we watched Lani continue, "The *Apopkykno* helps guard against the *Tehota*. The Tehota is the imaginary mist that keeps one from seeing reality. It is in this way that the Apopkykno is most important, because it is of *the utmost importance* that we never *ever* lose track of Reality…" he quipped, subtly deprecating himself, and This Day, then pausing for their laughter, but no one got the joke.

"I'm sure he understands though," Jude assured me, and my soul sighed relief. My affectionate hand reached out and squeezed his pointy shoulder. Tourists taking pictures dripped clumsy beer on the Apopkykno and Jude returned to taking their money, while trying to continue informing me that Lani's now set on winning his wife back, ever since his cards returned to him: "He thinks it's a — *Two dollars sir! Thank you* — he thinks it's a sign," Jude said. "And ever since I met him all he's been talking about is meeting his wife tonight at some parade — *Yeah. Two-dollars* — at some parade tonight on Bourbon Street. Today's their anniversary and…"

"Oh shit, that's right." *Fuck. Poor Lani…*

"Yeah. He says they've gone to this parade at midnight on Bourbon Street every year for the past 25-years. He says he knows she'll be there tonight. But the parades are over…"

"Over? Huh?"

"Yeah. They ended at like, two. No more."

"Fuck." *All that fucking struggle and I never even got to…* Defeat settled inside me, along with the kind of conflicted Loss women must feel after giving birth. "Damn. So what do I do until six o'clock then?"

"Get out of The Quarter," Jude nodded emphatically, shaking his big glasses down the bridge of his thin nose. He pushed them back up with a fist full of bills: "Go ride around The Marigny; it's awesome down on Frenchman." Then he asked, "What's at six?"

"Mizzy gets off…"

"Yeah." And then the explosion.

A gigantic BOOM shook the perfect air causing the crowd and the donkeys to all flinch in unison. *A bomb! That's right, there's a WAR going on people REMEMBER? Your celebration has angered The Gods of War and NOW…* But *no.* It was actually just a loud kick-drum, followed by a stream of rapping…

"MTV!" Jude screamed to me over the beat throbbing from the cathedral side of The Square where that little jazz band usually sets up.

"Oh shit that's right!" I remembered, "Wait! I thought MTV was kicking all the tarot readers and shit off Jackson Square!"

"I don't know anything about that!" Jude shrugged, not looking at me but at the money in his hand.

I studied his grotesque wig for a Moment and hollered, "So, this is the big costume you been talking about!"

"No! That costume's for later!" he shouted back, stuffing more 1s into his pocket, emptying his hands to refill them again. He turned his glasses on me one last time: "So come with us tonight!

You'll see it then! I'm gonna follow Lani down to Bourbon, make sure he's OK!"

Lani finally turned at the sound of his name, pointed a bejeweled a finger at me, slipped into his real voice to acknowledge, "Patrick, goddammit!" before re-engaging his flock, his dramatic hands trembling above their heads. *At least Jude's got his back...* One more time I squeezed Jude's shoulder good-bye, promising to follow him to Lani's mythic Last Parade. We agreed to meet on Bourbon and Esplanade, 10:30p/m.

- 3 -

Jude was wrong! A parade! On his advice, I'd cut straight over to Rampart to avoid The Quarter's lengthwise mess on my trek to The Marigny. Aside from not many partied-out drag queens leaning laughing in drowsy Nightclub doorways, Rampart lay dead, a bright but tranquil openness forever in both directions — until coasting past Armstrong Park, I glanced back over my burlap shoulder to see float after float turning slowly off Canal, onto Rampart, sneaking up behind me in the opposite trajectory of every other parade so far, but *HELL MOTHERFUCKIN YES!*

My beach cruiser drew a long black skid on the broken sidewalk. *Here it comes!* The air warmed as the parade neared, eating up Rampart's blankness *But wait... The floats are...empty?* A baseball hat, Oakley Blades, flannel shirt and a moustache shielded the white man piloting the first tractor, towing the first float. I waved at him, but he didn't acknowledge me as he passed dragging a vast, pink wall that smothered every corner of my vision. I held my breath while my world was pink. But no revelers rained crap down upon me; the pink one was barren, and then it was gone. I didn't bother waving to the next tractor driver, but *Holy fuck!* High above, a woman's giant paper-mache head smiling lips like fat red seals in a missionary position cast its car-sized shadow over me, only me > > > then a world of yellow inches from my nose > > > then another tractor driver wearing headphones > > > towing a giant blue crab bigger than that woman's head, mounted atop an all-consuming wall of baby-blue *beautiful, tranquil, celestial, so fucking...MINE!* it had me sweating, near crying.

Wiping my eyes I looked around hoping to share a laugh with someone. But the drag queens remained more impressed with themselves; again, no one cared. Again, just me.

- 4 -

Jude was right! The Marigny provided a local scene, Frenchman Street clogged with costumes and music and half-naked hippy girls selling nitrous balloons and shirtless men breathing fire — people I see everyday in tamer situations, employees at other restaurants.

But the first human out there I actually *knew* was that mulatto School Board woman who hired me. I almost rolled over her legs where they hung off a curb, bare mocha knees bouncing a dark black baby. But before she could recognize me I veered off, fearing I was still visibly high: teeth grinding, eyelids fluttering, plus carrying a beer — most of which spilled when I jerked left into some quiet, soulful residential neighborhood.

From there I allowed myself to get lost, the way Travel Agents advise people to do in Venice, Italy — though no one would *ever* advise you to get lost in NO, today the city seemed weightless. *We'll see how that's reflected in tomorrow's obits, but...* For now, I felt safe and warm rolling through new worlds of expression down every street > > > through mobs of gay men in asphyxiating shorts and wife-beaters > > > past more gays and yuppies and yuppie gays > > > around a group of elderly white men who'd somehow dragged their Jacuzzi into the middle of the street; they all howled and splashed water at me, but in a nice way as I passed, pumping my fist, onward > > > past a violin/accordion/clarinet trio sitting on a blanket in a driveway, conjuring tinkling gypsy music and selling big sunhats they'd woven from palms > > > between crazy houses now prouder and happier and drunker with humans hanging out their windows > > > past many compliments on my quilted wings > > > around huge stacks of LOUD amplifiers powered by a heavy-metal band performing buck-naked in the street, screaming aggro, though no one watched them > > > past a tall, ornate doorway where a national television star pissed with his back turned, despite his old-man hat pulled down low, pedestrians still recognized the star, and when they yelled his TV name he shouted back, "Fuck you!" > > > down a few more blocks to where a wife and kids' father had just been *caught* pissing in public; from atop a tall steed the cop gave the tourist an ultimatum: either clean up your mess with your own polo shirt, or go to jail > > > through a massive barbecue in a beautiful old 9th Ward neighborhood that I usually avoid, but today was free to roam — until someone hummed an egg at my head. The egg missed, but still I turned back, racing alongside a gang of straight-laced middle-aged white men in easy chairs they'd equipped with wheels and motors. When the Army of 15-mph Chairs had faded far back over my shoulder and I stretched my wings to slow my bike, I noticed a pair of woman's legs protruding out from under someone's tour bus and *Oh shit, I'm back in The Quarter...*

 I paused to watch the masses of uncostumed tourists quarantined way down Bourbon, joyfully drowning in a sea of spilled drinks and shimmering beads, not knowing where else to go. The sun hinted that it would set in an hour or so. *Time to go meet her...*

 But before cutting left toward silent Rampart, I noticed another sign, lying face-up in the street, this one hand-lettered, thus qualifying as *Harbage:* something one might pick up and carry, maybe only until one accidentally leaves it behind when distracted by a man in assless chaps offering one a riding whip, begging one to take it and a swing at his cheeks, which already shine Corvette-red... But I'd try to harbor this garbage to show to Mizzy, this posterboard sign reading, in red marker: *NOTHING FAILS LIKE*, then in black: *PRAYER. Nothing Fails Like Prayer.* Sounds like a bumper sticker, so maybe it's not that clever, but as I'd never heard it before, it was allowed to affect me, make me laugh, even spook me a little... Whether I believed the sign or not, I respectfully rolled it up and tucked it beneath my wings, before moving on...

- 5 -

Outside her Cajun Restaurant Hell Buffet I bent, locking my bike to her bike while watching her through her Picture Window, her chin atop the withered white head of a happy old man as they danced. She'd already discarded her bandages and it turns out the doctor really hadn't shaved too much hair off; she still looked good. An elaborate blue bird mask had been painted across her face, making her eyes small and wild. Her new uniform showed her off more, her breasts bouncing as she laughed against the old man. Watching her, I felt in perfect love.

Turning, I surveyed the hundreds of drunks swarming St. Charles, stumbling between empty parade bleachers trampling the layers of baubles and beads that hid any hint of pavement. The sun was setting, but the beaded world twinkled like a cat's view from inside an X-mas tree. *You can't help but feel FREE in all this trash...*

Then to make it better, as I slipped my keys back into my pocket she was on me, biting my neck, squealing in my ear, dripping Bloody Mary down the back of my winged gown, her winged gown. Handing me the Mary she pointed out the area between the bleachers where the cops had let her stand with them during the parades, in their Space, an empty car-length blocked off by barricades. While the dense crowd had been clawing each other's eyeballs for trinkets, Mizzy caught what she wished, free of competition. "There's no way I'll even be able to carry it all home on my bike!" she trilled, kissing me again, then offering me another Vicodin.

As I sipped, washing the pill down, she stared at me. I swallowed. She stared, stared until, "What?" I finally asked, wanting to hear her say it again...

"Nothing." She smiled so hard her eyes almost closed, but through happy slits she kept on staring, staring...

"Why are you staring?"

"Because I love you." She grabbed me and squeezed until my eyes leaked into her ear. Hearing my blissful sniffle she asked softly,

"Oh, baby, you're still feelin That Stuff, huh?"

"Yeah. But that's not it…"

- 6 -

They charge the old people $150 apiece, but Mizzy's restaurant gave me The Wristband for free: an all access food and alcohol pass. "We just love Mizzy so much!" raved her female Manager. "Any friend of hers…" I drained two more Bloody Marys waiting for Mizzy to finish her Sidework, and ate so much fried chicken and jambalaya and etouffe and boudin balls and bread pudding with whiskey sauce — everything but the fried alligator, in an attempt to clean out the buffet trays so Mizzy wouldn't have to stay all night scraping them out.

"You did a good job," she finally said, waking me up after I'd passed out on the table she was wiping. I wasn't so energetic anymore after eating all that, plus the painkiller, plus last night's athleticism…When she announced that she was almost ready, I rose and walked outside to restart my circulation. The sunset was bringing in a more official kind of cold, which the Vicodin kept from bothering me. Muddled minutes later she joined me, carrying out a large purple bag with yellow '*MARDI GRAS!*' splashed across the side. She set it at her feet then removed her shirts down to her murderous tank top. *She must be numbed by pills too*…Still she asked, unlocking her bike, "You got any papers?"

"No, but if you have a pipe I have some hash."

"No way!" The eyes inside her blue facepaint swelled. "Where'd you get hash?"

"Your co-worker's underwear drawer."

"Oh no!" she slapped my winged arm laughing, then conceded, "We can use the roaches in my truck." She suggested we go get them and roll them with the hash into an extra powerful cigarette that, on top of every other buzz, I really, really didn't need but…

"So we're heading back to your apartment?" I asked.

"No. My truck is only three blocks away, under that overpass on Calliope."

Calliope: a year ago just that mispronounced name wrongly gave me jitters. Now it conjures up images of underpopulated indy-rock shows at The Mermaid Lounge — not too far from where it turns out Mizzy's truck died just before her accident/infidelity, which was only three or four nights ago, but now felt far *far* away. Luckily (or I guess, unluckily) she'd gotten into the habit of keeping her bike in the bed, awaiting the truck's imminent death. "It konked-out by The Bridge House Thrift Store, where I bought it" she continued, pointing down St. Charles. "And you know, I was thinking I might just..." There she stopped. Silence. She bent and turned the key in her U-Lock.

"You might just what?"

"Nothing." She threw the lock in her basket then picked up her purple bag.

"What?" But she straddled her bike and pedaled away across the dead bead sea, toward *Cal-ee-ope*. I followed. When we arrived at her truck I asked again, "You might just what?"

"I think I'm gonna just leave it here, donate it to The Thrift Store."

"No!" I whined, sad and offended; *Our First Time was in that truck*...

But she'd obviously pondered this for a while, having previously removed her entire *Harbage* collection from the truck's bed, which was now clean for the first time since she bought the beast. Now she was picking the last of her valuables out of the cab: cassette tapes, screwdrivers, wrenches, jumper cables, a set of oil pastels, a small rusted metal shark, a rubber mask, letters from her grandmother, a pipe, at least seven half-joints, "And this!" she cried, holding up our used condom-wrapper. She smiled.

I didn't: "How can you just get rid of it? It's...special..." I stopped before 'to us.'

She stuffed it all into her Mardi Gras bag, explaining, "I just don't need the inconvenience, or the expense. I mean, with all the money I've spent in the past four months towing it and fucking with it, I could have been leasing a brand new Lexus."

I sucked air through my closed teeth and shook my head; my

parents have a Lexus.

"I know, I know. It's just an example, whatever…" But she'd decided: "I'm donating it." Then batting her eyes, same as I was, only purposefully: "Will you push while I steer?"

I saw this perfect opening for a power play: *'No Mizzy, I can't push the entire truck out of this lot, up an incline and into that lot across the street ALL BY MYSELF…' Then maybe by the time she finds some other sap to do her bidding, she'll have changed her mind about getting rid of it…* But one of the few things I've really held onto from my college Lit classes is the belief that one shouldn't have to *relate* to an idea in order to *appreciate* it, so… *Plus then she'll then return to a Bike Life…*

Still I couldn't push the damn thing by myself. So before agreeing to the task out-loud, I glanced around for someone to help me. It was pretty deserted around there though, with everyone still in The Quarter. "Please," she pressed, her hand sliding up under my robe until it found skin. She kissed my neck then rested her mouth there. But before we could say *that* kind of goodbye to the truck, over her shoulder, just down Magazine, a bright flash of pink distracted my eye, a shirt of some sort hanging on a wooden fence at a sort-of sale or something, a rummage sale in an empty lot. No one was buying anything, or even looking; the only person anywhere near the sale was a light-skinned black boy with… *No way!*

"Anthony!"

I watched him push his glasses up his nose and squint, trying to figure us out. As we crossed Calliope to Magazine, my wings blowing back Anthony began laughing: "Hey Mr. Patrick! Where you at?"

"Hey! The only good kid in my class!" I turned to Mizzy as we approached him. "Anthony's my only good kid!"

"Oh this is *Anthony*?" she mock glared at him, stopping close to his face. "You mean the one who won't do *any work*?"

He blushed, smiling, looking away. His civilian clothes consisted of a simple t-shirt and jeans, no logos, and the same plain black shoes he wears to school. He's a good kid.

I asked him, seriously, "Yeah Anthony, how *are* you ever going to graduate?"

"I dunno," he smiled, still blushing. "Guess I ain't."

"Then what are you going to do after high school?"

"Computers, man. Ima go to a Technical School."

Nodding agreement, Mizzy skipped past Anthony to inspect his wares. "I wish I would have done that instead of going to college," she declared, sifting through the junk, and it was junk; he certainly hadn't *stolen* that three-legged barstool, that bladeless ceiling-fan... Anthony's eyes followed her, squinting at the little bald spot on the back of her head as she added, "I got so little out of college," inspecting a rusty role of chicken wire, "I want to go to technical school and become a welder!"

Anthony turned to me: "A welder?" he whispered. "Damn whoa…"

"I told y'all: I don't fuck around…"

"You ain't lyin,'" he agreed. Then he reached out and smiling, touched my cheek: "Y'all been makin-out in that truck?" He pulled his hand back, showing me his fingertips smudged with Mizzy's blue bird makeup.

I just smiled back proud, evading, "So, you out here alone?"

"Naw man," his forehead wrinkled. "My boys was here before, but they left to go get a *cold* drink…bout two hours ago."

"What are you doing out here?"

"What it look like?"

"Well yeah…but I mean…is this where you live?" I looked around the empty lot to a realtor's For Sale sign. "No," I answered my own question. "You just dragged the stuff out here and set up." He nodded. I nodded back: *Damn: ingenuity, gumption. He'll be fine…* "The cops haven't bothered you?" I asked.

"Naw man. The Po-Po all in The Quarter and The Projects today, and getting drunk theyselves. But I ain't makin no money anyway so…" He shrugged again, then stopped, squinting, studying my eyes: "Damn, you been smoking weed Mr. Patrick?" Which was funny because I'd *just* considered telling him that if he helped me push her truck, he could come smoke hash with us — he'd think me the coolest after that, especially since most of my black friends have never tried hash, or Ecstasy either — but that thought passed quick and *Hell no* I didn't offer. Instead, like a joke I leered, "It's Mardi Gras, bruh; we been doin all kyna shit."

"Man, you sound stupid sayin *'bruh...'*" Anthony shook his head smirking. Then he offered his Native's insight, "Aw! You just moved here, so you prolly ain't seen The Mardi Gras Indians yet! They down on Washington right now! You should run go see them! Them boys is *fools*, yeah!"

"Uh, I didn't just move here, Anthony," I corrected. "Tomorrow's my one year anniversary." Unimpressed, he turned away to watch Mizzy slip his intense pink sweatshirt over her tank-top and model it for us: it too advertised, 'Mardi Gras!' above a cartoon cat's smiling face; *Mardi Gras the Cat!* We all agreed that the sweatshirt suited her, before I continued to Anthony, "No, I've never seen the Indians, and I'd like to, but right now we're busy donating her truck to the Thrift Store."

"Donating?" His face screwed up.

"Liberating," Mizzy interjected.

"Yeah, I know," I said to Anthony, "fucked up."

"Y'all could donate and liberate it to me," he suggested, quietly for me only.

"Talk to her," I pointed over his shoulder.

"No, that's OK," he blushed again, turning away, both of us watching Mizzy glow in that sweatshirt.

"I'm definitely buying this," she told him. "But the rest of this stuff..." she waved it away.

"What?" Anthony frowned, re-evaluating his lot. "I got good shit."

"So do I," she said. Anthony and I nodded agreement. Then she fucking said it: "Hey Anthony, we'll let you smoke hash with us if you help Patrick push..."

I spun on her. Her bird makeup was smudged above her drunk smile. The X helped me laugh: "Mizzy you're gonna get me fucking fired!"

"Oh, shit..." she realized.

"What, you think *I'm* tell on you?" Anthony shook his head again. "Naw man. But actually, I quit smoking for a while. I ain't smoked for two weeks." *Two weeks? I can't go that long... See, let him be, he'll be fine...* "But how bout this," he continued. "I'll help y'all push, if y'all help me pack up all this shit and throw it away."

"What about this sweatshirt?" Mizzy asked, hopefully. "It comes with the deal?"

"Two dollars," Anthony hard-nosed.

We walked together back under the overpass where he and I grabbed handfuls of the grassy bumper and pushed the truck up into the Bridge House lot next to the already For Sale cars. When we'd accomplished our goal he slapped me on the back, which made me even happier. Mizzy wrote an explanation note to pin under the broken wiper, then kissed and patted the hood, just as Anthony's friends finally showed up, three of them, all at least five years younger than him. Anthony denied they were his little brothers, or his sons, as they walked a straight hard line right to me and one of them asked "You could give us each a Quarter?"

"A Quarter each? That's 75 cents," I tallied. "Man, I don't have money to just give away. I need it to live. Sorry, man."

"Don't apologize to this little nigga," Anthony ordered me, then barked at them, "Back off man! This my teacher, bruh."

The littlest one asked me, "You teach at Magnolia?"

"Yeah."

"No wonder you ain't got senny-fy cent."

"Man shut the fuck up," Anthony laughed. Then to me: "Y'all ain't gotta help me pack this shit up. They gonna do it; they done left me out here by myself for bout three hours." He frowned down at the kids: "Mobilize, niggas; get this shit cleaned up!"

And they did. Anthony, at least, will be fine.

- 7 -

The river rested quiet and dark and lonely, perfect. The drugs and the chill forced our hands up each other's festive clothes as we climbed down to our favorite wide, flat rock and sat facing each other, creating a little windless cave between us, where we could twist one up. Inside the dark safety of my wings we blew smoke into each other's mouths a mere seven rocks away from the water that took Jeff Buckley's life — his is the only death that's ever made me sad, meaning, my life has been too easy but... After five or so heavy hash hits I swear he was singing, his feminine howl across the water, or maybe a tugboat's whistle. Whichever, when Mizzy sang along I did too, the three of us harmonizing...

Then suddenly: "Let's go. Let's go ride around..." I heard it before I knew it was my voice. Smoking had relit the remaining X like sparklers inside my chest and brain, and I had to stand slowly and *Breathe now...breathe...breathe...* "Let's go. C'mon," I insisted, my hand helping her up, still *breathing...breathing...*I needed to stretch and run and pump, jump back in and see more, more *MORE NOW!* Yes: *need.* So she rode grumpily back with me to Decatur, where the scene had mellowed, the streets had cleared. *Already?* Bike travel was easy and disappointing. *Already?* Music still floated from many doorways, the same old bland jazz onto streets paved with refuse, but it was over: an orgasm followed by vague regret.

Mizzy read me and raised a smiling eyebrow: "We could go home, jump back into bed."

How could she possibly want more sex? I don't ever want to see my cock again for at least... "No, we're meeting Jude and Lani for some parade at midnight."

"There's another parade!?"

"No, but..."

We locked to the rickshaw outside The Dragon's Den, slithered sideways down the skinny alley, up the winding red staircase that's surely killed a few drunks, and into the blackness of the tiny music room upstairs. The Dragon's Den is an opium den sans opium, and sans chairs, just pillows as big as sea turtles sleeping across the floor under nothing but tiny red X-mas lights: the perfect place to come down.

100 other local humans agreed, leaning forward onto their Indian-style knees, or passing in-and-out in lovers' laps, smiles barely visible in the red dark. The club charged no cover to hear Michael Ray from Sun Ra's Arkstra and Kool-and-the-Gang screech and wheeze and circular breathe, knocking up the excitement level of

some mediocre jazz band. After ordering glasses of red wine, we somehow found space on the ground against the wall beside another couple. My head plundered Mizzy's lap, my eyes fluttering their last as her hands combed my hair and the band sounded amazing. On the insides of my eyelids peaceful sharks swam laps in time to the drums, up and over a vast coral reef, scattering millions of small colorful fish, me down there with them, the music way up there on the dry side of miles of water — until a loud female voice dragged me up and out: "Oh my god did you *see* that?" the girl laying to our left asked her boyfriend. "How tacky!" The couple dressed like they'd only recently punched-out at their office jobs. Catching my eyes the girl repeated, "Did you see that guy?"

She pointed to pillows against the far wall, where a white man in a trenchcoat stood with his back to us, looming over a short-haired girl on the ground, leaning back on her elbows. Past the bottom hem of the man's coat, his calves stood out bare except for some words written in black marker, which I couldn't read in the dark. "He just chased her over there and threw her down!" the office girl beside us announced, through a half-smile now. "He's like, trying to like rape her!"

The accused-rapist turned to us like he'd heard her, but he was only surveying the scene, glancing around at us all packed against the walls, his shining eyes admitting that he wasn't really *seeing* any of us; the same shiny eyes I wore last night: *Good Drugs*. His hair was short, and wild like his eyes. Beneath his coat, he wore only small white underwear, and more indiscernible black-marker words written over every inch of middleclass-flabby skin. The woman below him laughing hiked her skirt. Michael Ray blew an intense shriek, instigating the trenchcoat to guy aim his face skyward and primal-scream in that same key. I sat up from Mizzy's lap. Turning his profile to us, the man pushed the front of his white underwear aside, letting it dangle above her.

Beside me: "Oh my god! What is he *doing*!"

The girl below him laughed harder, hiked it higher, then reached out and rolled his penis between her thumb and first finger. He howled again, madly as his penis grew. When it was full-sized (though still not as big as mine, Mizzy assured me in a whisper, while never taking her eyes off his...) the guy fell on top of the laughing woman and as far as I could tell from my angle — she ceased laughing, her eyes closed over his shoulder — he slid inside her. Humans began migrating from the stage to gather around the couple writhing and biting each other's shoulders as if alone. The woman's face grew tense and serious. I turned to the office couple beside me: that girl didn't seem offended anymore, watching silently with the rest of us, her lips moving slightly without her knowing.

The band's song ended and Michael Ray peeked over the crowd to find out what we were all engrossed in. Beholding the couple, Ray's trumpet screamed an animal noise and everyone laughed, except the couple, and the office girl next to me who'd removed her officemate's eyeglasses and was now attempting to unbutton his shirt as he laughed nervous, trying to hold her hands still. She swatted his grip away: "Oh, c'mon."

"C'mon what?" he chuckled, nervous. But she didn't relent... I flinched at Mizzy's cold hand up my gown, her eyes aimed across the room to the trenchcoat man, now down on his knees, with his girl's knees tucked under his armpits. As the band discussed what to play, in their musical silence I could hear her over there, her pigeon-like grunt building and building *hmm, hmmm, hmmmm, hmmmmm, hmmmmmm, hmmmmmmm, hmmmmmmmm, hmmmmmmmmm, hmmmmmmmmmm, hmmmmmmmmmmm, hmmmmmmmmmmmm...*

"Not here!" the office guy beside us blurted, and I turned to see him removing her hand from his crotch.

"It's Mardi Gras! We can do whatever we want," she hissed into his neck.

"Yeah, and we can also do whatever we want at home, in private..."

Across the room, the hum of the girl from the floor grew into a slow, quiet, "Oh...my...Oh, my...fucking...God..." as the band finally broke into something that sounded too familiar. Torso up on a pillow, head back, throat white, she was near to being finished off. *Good job man, good for you...* Another man, dressed as a pirate, walked quickly behind the moaning woman, removed his own penis, rested it on top of her head, looked up to pose smiling as a flash bulb exploded, before he ran back into the thick of partiers against the stage. The couple noticed none of it, never opened their eyes.

"You're such a *pansy*!" the office girl beside me stood up yelling, knocking their drinks onto the pillows. Mizzy and I watched her barge through the audience, her officemate stumbling after her buttoning his shirt: "Wait! C'mon! Please! C'mon, there's *people* around baby, what do you want me to *do*?"

When they'd disappeared Mizzy said, "He deserved that…" I got scared…

The couple sexing across the room screamed once together louder than the band before finally collapsing. Michael Ray looked confused when we all clapped in the middle of his solo.

- 8 -

So much, too much movement occurring simultaneously at 360 degrees, on every level, in three or four or five different dimensions, especially when you're high. Though the world had indeed mellowed by 10:30, even then the amount of movement occurring around us as we waited for Jude and Lani on Bourbon and Esplanade would be impossible to accurately catalog, document. Of course, way down there, Bourbon's many-colored neon signs combined to paint the air orange over its ubiquitous, indiscernible human mass. But even leaning on Esplanade against an old brick building sipping wine was as visually frantic as biking the wrong way down a 4-lane highway — an over-stimulation of detail distracting us from the fact that it was past 11 by the time a clean-cut young man stopped and addressed me as "Sir?"

His grandfather beside him called Mizzy "Ma'am?"

Then the young guy's open-mouthed laugh exposed Jude's teeth… All his abnormal hair butchery had grown-in, the mullet excavated down to just a simple, side-parted Dad-cut, gelled into symmetry: exaggerated *normalcy*. For the first time in the year I've known him, Lani wore no beard or moustache or jewelry, just a baby blue polo shirt tucked into tan shorts, Docksiders with tube socks, several strands of beads, Jude and Lani both. *Horrible*...

"You'll *never* guess what we're supposed to be," Lani baited.

"Assholes?" Mizzy answered.

"Oh it's much more complex than that," Lani promised.

"Yeah. It's real good," Jude added. "High concept. I thought of it."

"What are you?" I inquired directly.

"What time is it?" Lani ignored me.

"No," I persisted, "what're you supposed to be?"

"You'll see once we get into The Quarter. What time it is?"

"11:20," Mizzy read from her cell phone.

"The Last Parade's in forty minutes!" Lani announced, his intense face hinting sick worry between the clean clothes and neat hair. We followed behind him, briskly down Bourbon, glancing at each other from the corners of doubtful eyes. Lani's naked legs ran ahead toward the thickest part of the crowd, allowing Jude private room to reiterate to Mizzy and me: "Yeah, I've lived here all my life and I *know* there are no more parades..."

To keep it light, Mizzy babbled drunk giggles, recalling her day to Jude: the giant swath of Space the cops had shared with her, all the plastic crap she caught so easily, the liberation of her truck — as I watched Lani up ahead, his gray head turning sharp angles, obviously, desperately searching... I thought to use Mizzy's cell to call his ex-wife and get her down here because *How much disappointment can one man fucking take?* But I don't know her number now that she's moved in with her lawyer boss... The best I could do was run catch up to Lani: "So hey man, I thought MTV was kicking y'all off The Square today," I asked.

"Yeah, my best day of the year and those motherfuckers want to shut me down," he mumbled, to himself, as if my question had come from inside his head.

"So then how'd you end up working out there today?"

"Huh?" he turned to me, waking up. "Oh. All the readers pay a little monthly fee to keep a lawyer on retainer. Our lawyer made them give us that one side of The Square."

Damn. I could have been following that story this whole time with my kids. That would have been so good for them, but... I shook it off, vowing to work harder, be a stronger, better teacher when school kicks back in Thursday. *After all of this, I think I'm ready now...*

Lani said something I couldn't hear over my optimism. Then when I asked him to repeat it he was no longer with me; his searching eyes were leading him away toward the heart of Bourbon's orange glow. Wanting to pull him out of his sadly hopeful head I tagged behind asking again, "So if you're not dressed as tourists, then what the fuck are y'all?"

But on the precipice of the crowd he paused, smiling at me with disturbing hopefulness. *Poor Lani...* I felt incredibly guilty; the drugs were wearing off, and this was *my fault; if I'd been there for him...* Stray partiers detached from the human mass to straggle past us into the quiet, looking happy, if drained. When Mizzy and Jude were caught up, Lani finally answered me with a question: "Alright, now...what do *you* think of my costume?"

"I don't understand it."

"But aside from that...How do I look?"

"You look fucking crazy." Maybe not the best choice of words to someone fresh off a *rest* but... Lani laughed. I turned to Jude: "*You* look especially insane."

"Alright. Then I'll give you a clue: watch *this*..." Lani said, stepping out into the path of a stranger, a white man barely younger than him with no gray hair, but in every other way visually similar to Lani, as Lani was on this day. Lani asked his almost-twin, "Do you like my costume?"

"No!" the tourist laughed. His group of two females and one other male paused behind him. We all shook hands, laughed together, wished each other Happy Holiday.

"No?" Lani kidded the man. "Well, what about *his* costume?" He motioned to Jude, who hid his teeth, looking frighteningly straight-laced.

"Costumes?" The man studied Jude, then back to Lani then back to Jude, his smile fading. "I don't know what you're trying to pull," he said finally, losing his humor. "But I don't get the joke." He turned to his group: "C'mon…"

"When they'd left: "OK. Now," Lani spun on me, "what are we?"

"I have no idea."

Mizzy shrugged: "The Theory of Relativity?"

Jude stopped smiling: "Whoa."

Lani squinted wet eyes at her: "How the hell…"

"What? That's it?" she asked, slightly startled. "I guessed it?"

"Yeah," Jude answered. "Good job, girl…"

"See, I'm smart," she announced, squeezing me, celebratory.

"Wait." I reminded her, "I thought you said you were stupid. I swear I heard you say it a bunch of times…"

"I'm not."

"I know."

- 9 -

From that skinny intersection of gay clubs and the gay hamburger stand onward, The World was suffocation. We inhaled deeply, dunked in and slowly swam the flesh which crushed like fathom-deep water pressure. Up through the orange air we saw mouths full of teeth screaming down at us from balconies. Mizzy and I held desperate hands, dragging each other through, but my distracted eyes often lost Jude and Lani ahead of us, dressed as two needles in a stack of needles. *Relativity?* Layers and layers of happy screams equaled an all-consuming static and the only clear words I could make out came from a vague memory: *'In the end it's all relative…Ain't no good or bad…'* True words but *Who said that?* I couldn't place it. The phrase's melodious inflection told me it was a Black NO voice. *A new song on The Radio?* Maybe a lyric: *'In the end it's all relative…Ain't no good or bad…'* But *No, that doesn't sound like something The Radio would say …* Plus I don't know the new Radio songs; The Radio's not so compelling now that I've seen what it does to these kids… *Or wait; did one of my kids* say *that? Anthony? Seems I would have remembered something so strong and clear coming out of one of their… Wait…* I remembered: De'von at work, eating the pig's feet: *'In the end it's all relative. Ain't no good or bad, so let's all just not worry who eats what, and y'all just let me live, y'heard me?'* At that, it didn't seem so prophetic anymore. *And THAT's Relativity...*

We came up for air, regrouping in a less dense area coincidentally near an open window selling *$1 Tooters*: test-tube shots of Jaegermeister, Mizzy's favorite. We downed three Tooters each as our swimming eyes took in the drunken world. The majority exchanged gentle gestures of love, pretty kisses, intimate, sincere smiles and hugs, but there was also plenty of what the Holiday is famous for: a transvestite having his/her picture taken with a female cop on the hood of her squad car, as against the far bumper a man gave another man a blowjob; in an open window above us, a thin young girl turned her shirtless back to the street, pulled down her jeans and massaged her bare butt with long white hands, her perfect smile facing over her slender shoulder, relishing the roar below — the first random female nudity I'd witnessed this entire Carnival season: "I thought that was a huge Mardi Gras tradition," I queried Lani, "flashing for beads."

"Used to be, till *that* sorta killed it," he answered, pointing above the heads of the woman's screaming male minions, to their dozens of hairy arms stretching up toward the woman like flowers toward sunshine, every hand holding a digital video camera. "Most girls quit showin their stuff cause they don't want to end up on the Internet," Lani added, pausing the hunt for his wife to soak in this gorgeous, bare woman: "That there's just a stripper. She don't give a shit." It was true: far down Bourbon I saw intermittent tangles of arms sprouting up from the crowd like coral reefs, marking every spot where deviance was occurring, pointing it out, focusing in, and by trying to capture it, ruining it.

"I flashed this morning," Mizzy cut in. Our eyes all came down from the ass on the balcony. Lani and Jude smirked at each other and I wished I could halt the gears in their minds. "There were no video cameras on St Charles," she added. "I don't think..."

"Hey, easy," I said. "I don't need to hear that shit."

She rolled her eyes. "Uh, oh. The drugs are wearing off," she said.

"Here it comes…" — just as thousands of tiny lights exploded behind her, spinning red, white and blue through Bourbon's orange glow. The crowd hushed.

"The parade's coming!" Lani cried, his face flushed with angst. "C'mon, c'mon dammit!" He shattered his last Tooter onto the ground and was gone. We rushed off after him, the flashing lights coming closer, Lani's searching head darting like a cartoon bird's, his body hockey-checking tourists, spilling their beers. Even over the throng I could hear him: "Madeline! Madeline!" Out front of Love Acts he demanded of the sky, "Where the *FUCK*!"

The balconies screamed back at him, lights bouncing from face to face, brick to brick, slatboard to iron vine, closer and closer until finally a voice boomed ferocious:

"MARDI GRAS IS OVER! CLEAR THE STREETS! MARDI GRAS IS OVER!"

The crowd unanimously leapt onto the sidewalks, clearing a path for an oncoming line of tall, muscular Police horses > > > followed by another identical line > > > then another > > > *Oh fuck a RIOT!* Watching a few drunks run for the safety of side streets, my heart again demanded Fight-or-Flight. But my friends and most around them held their beer cups in their teeth, freeing their hands to applaud the cops who smiled and waved from atop their steeds — an image in direct conflict with the unfriendly, amplified voice coming nearer:

"MARDI GRAS IS OVER! GO HOME NOW! MARDI GRAS IS…"

Behind the horse-cops marched an army of foot-cops > > > manic lights splattering the helmets of the first row > > > the second row > > > the third row of storm troopers waving to the cheering masses — until the lights were directly upon us and:

"DISPERSE! MARDI GRAS IS OVER!"

The voice detonated from speakers mounted on flashing squad cars rolling just behind the foot-cops. I expected mass revolt, rocks thrown, bones broken, at least flying beers and *BOOOOOOOOOOOOO!* But the crowd continued their non-ironic applause for the cop-cars > > > cranking it up even louder for the OPP cleanup crew > > > then finally calming as the street-sweeping zamboni truck pushed through grinding tons of beads and cups, at the rear of The Last Parade.

- 10 -

With lowered voices the crowd poured back onto the freshened pavement. Some began the exit process. Many continued littering. Those leaving would wake early tomorrow to be blessed with gray stains on their foreheads. The rest of us would sleep through aches. For now I yelped, "Jesus that was fucking *cathartic!*" shaking still, digging happy fingers into Mizzy's arm as she paid for our last beers at the *Tooter* window. Jude nodded.

Lani's hair looked whiter against the cold orange air as he turned off down a less crowded street, shoulders slumped, untucking his polo shirt, his brilliant costume. The polo hung down past his shorts like a nightshirt, making him look naked, vulnerable. *He cleaned himself up for her, to live up to...* I ran behind him: "Lani!"

He stopped, turned on his heels. "So, y'all enjoy that?" he asked me, smiling absent, a brownish lacquer of Jaeger on the eyes behind his glasses.

Ignoring his question I blubbered, "Hey, I'm sorry. I'm sorry she wasn't there man. I'm just sorry..."

"Nah, fuck her," he lied, walking again, back toward Decatur.

"Yes, you're right, fuck her," I declared, looking to make sure Mizzy and Jude followed. "Fuck her in the fucking mouth."

Lani laughed. And like spotting a tiny bit of seashell coming up through the sand, I wanted to dig and dig and dig up more, and drag him up and out. But I was spent, stupid, couldn't think of anything funnier than, "Did I tell you about how this kid in my class calls me White Bitch?"

But he didn't hear; he'd stopped to listen to some Gutterpunks sitting on the road's shoulder, goading a wrinkled but meaty old black man. The old man wore a derby hat and a vest, like a relic. From inside their hooded sweatshirts The Gutterpunks threw lit cigarette butts at the man's shiny shoes. One's first tendency would now be to believe that *the Black man* lived here, and that the punks were migratory; I've heard fables that Gutterpunks all come from good, well-off families, and that sleeping in pissy doorways is merely a rejection of their backgrounds. If so, then NO dirt covers that up real good...The Black man's back faced us, but we clearly heard his rusty throat yelling about the G-punks all needing jobs "Motherfuckin good f'nothins..."

"A job torturing animals?" a shoeless pregnant punk shouted back, "Like you, you sick motherfucker." Her dirty white finger aimed across the street at a carriage strapped to a mule's skin-covered bones: the old man's mule, staring her Master's back as Jude and Mizzy caught up. I laughed support, but then remembered all the times I've seen Gutterpunks kick their dogs or lift them off the ground by their collars, so *fuck them, too*; I also heard they only own dogs because it makes them more inconvenient for lazy NO cops to arrest, and I have no more respect for that than for someone who crams a steel bar into an animal's mouth then pulls back on it until foam gushes forth — *so fuck all y'all...*

Still I watched the old man: "I been out in these motherfuckin Quarters since before there was *cahs* you lil piece a shit," he coughed. Tourists paused their straggling to watch and smile at the argument: just another Mardi Gras one-act...We all crossed the street toward the man's carriage, noticing en route that his mule was male — we stopped ten-feet from the testicles as Lani continued stepping forward to begin plucking the decorative flowers out of the mule's mane. We suppressed our full volume of laughter, but the driver was too angry to notice anyway: "I got the *got-damn* right!" he howled at the G-punks, while right behind his back his mule's flowers were landing around Lani's Docksider shoes, petals clinging to his tube-socks.

When the flowers ran out, Lani's bare hand wiped some foam from the animal's mouth. from 10-feet away we watched the beast's pained jaw churning, trying to spit that fucking rod out, conjuring fresh spit in the process, which Lani again wiped away — causing me to remember: "Oh hey Lani! Check this!"

Anticipating his real strong laughter, I reached beneath my robe and pulled the mangled posterboard from my pants. I laid it out against a brick wall, flattened it with my fist, then stood aside and showed them all.

"*'Nothing Fails Like Prayer'*," Lani read aloud. "Wish I'da known that earlier today…" he chuckled again, mild and fake, turning back to the donkey's dead eyes.

"Wish I'd a known that years ago!" Jude high-pitched, jovial.

Mizzy held her hand out, silently wanting the sign. I handed it to her, then watched her little eyes in her bird mask read the slogan from the first word to the last, before returning to the beginning, and reading through to the end…

"At least I'm out here making a honest fuckin living!" the black driver choked at the punks.

"It is *not* honest!" a dirty, sleepless white boy of 15 raged back.

Fuck you both… And when I looked away, down, and there at the curb lay my sign Nothing Fails…trampled by tourists in a foot-deep gray puddle: "Hey! What the fuck man!"

"That sign offend you, Mizzy?" Lani laughed over his shoulder, "I didn't know you was religious," he stroked the mule's muzzle with the rings on his knuckles.

"I'm not," she said.

"You threw away my *Harbage*!" I accused.

"No, that's garbage," she wrinkled her nose. "Cynicism is garbage."

Jude and I nodded. *My dream girl…* We grabbed each other. Lani looked past us — making sure the mule driver was still embroiled. I knew, even before Lani unlatched the headgear: twitch of Lani's thumb and *pop* the escape artist proves himself again… The donkey closed his eyes as Lani slid the torture rod out of his mouth. The eyes sprung open and the big tongue jumped out, licking the newly-exposed areas of his mouth, digging into the farthest corners. I swallowed my ambivalent screams of celebration and sadness so as not to aware the driver of Lani groping his wrinkled human hands along the animal's long body and *pop* *pop* *pop* five or six locks in five or six seconds, straps and reigns *pop* whatever would come undone *pop* until the two wooden poles along the donkey's sides finally hit the ground SMACK! But the driver was still too righteous to notice, pointing his arthritic thumb, but thankfully not his eyes, back at his carriage: "This is a *tradition* you white freeloada motherfucker! You got no respect for *tradition*!"

A new confidence lifted Lani up by the armpits; he'd actually *done it!* He'd *actualized* The Liberation, when he never really dreamed he would! I knew that in that Moment, his Moment, there existed no reason for suicide, no lost cards, no personal traditions disregarded by former loved ones, no murder in his neighborhood... He was *back*: for our entertainment Lani strolled back around to the donkey's balls and pantomimed a smack on the ass' ass, laughing, knowing full well the hoof-in-the-face that would earn him in Reality. So, instead he just barked, "Go on! Get man!!"

But no. The donkey didn't lumber forward, making a slow break for Esplanade; the animal must have known that no matter how far he got, even if he escaped, he'd eventually be owned again. *So why waste even one step forward?*

Still, "GO motherfucker!" Lani yelled, his wet smile flat-lining, his glare projected onto the beast's wide brown haunches an image or cause that only Lani could see and understand. Jude and Mizzy stopped laughing too, and none of us looked back at the driver any longer, making sure we wouldn't be caught. "GO you STUPID ass!" Lani shouted, near anger between hacking coughs, attracting the attention of the dying party around us. Some who had been watching the Mule Driver vs. The Gutterpunks now watched and pointed and laughed at Lani yelling at the donkey. For me it was scary, seeing him like that, the thin white skin of his face flushing purple, spit bubbling in the corners of his old lips: "YAH motherfucker! YAH! Go god*DAMMIT*!" Until Lani's hands finally did fall upon the animal's flank, pushing the donkey as Anthony and I had Mizzy's truck: "MOVE goddammit! *MOVE GODDAMMIT*!" I was sure Lani's troubled heart would explode, or that the animal would kick Lani's glasses into his already blind eyes. But as usual, worrying was in vain; the animal didn't even look back. He just fucking stood there.

FORCES

- Guilt
- Freedom
- Want
- Need
- MTV
- Depression
- Lawnsprinklers
- Calliope
- Joy
- To-Go Beers
- Help Meal
- Bourbon
- Tank-top Views
- Worknight
- Night Off
- Discussion
- Comic Timing
- My Room
- My Mansion
- My Former Mansion
- Slave Quarters
- The Cat Room
- The Dog Runs
- The Hospital
- The Invisible Frustration of As-Yet-Unknown-Origin
- The Fun Boys
- The Black Team
- The Black Table
- The Words
- The Class Pitch
- The Dish Pit
- The Radio
- The Rain of Toys
- The Meat-Removal Ceremony
- The Cold
- The New Words
- The Jumping Type
- The Game
- The Last Step
- The Radio
- The Floor
- The Dining Room
- That Original Shit
- That Art
- That Fucker
- That Sandwich
- That Money
- This Money
- This War Shit
- This Day
- Sick Day
- Mardi Gras
- Esplanade
- Gazebo
- One-Free-Refill Law
- The Neutral Ground
- Monkey Suit
- Civilian Clothes
- Prison Brooms
- Clean Pipes
- Streetcars
- Gamefaces
- Dessert Spoons
- Bounce Music
- Fight-or-Flight
- FLA
- NO
- Sex
- Whole-Boiled Crawfish
- Them
- Sidework
- Mortality
- Murder
- The Donkey Show

*M*usician/painter Michael Patrick Welch was 29-years-old when The Donkey Show was published. Prior to that, he served three years as a Staff Writer at The St. Petersburg Times in his home state of FLA. MPW was once the up-keeper of the ramshackle, exhaustive and self-destructively honest on-line journal, Commonplace, several entries of which were somehow published at OpenLetters.net, McSweeney's.net, Pindeldyboz.com, Ink19.com, Mezzomint, BIGNews (that newspaper homeless people sell on the NY streets for $1) and few others. In 2000, MPW self-published the Commonplace book and moved to New Orleans.

Along with documenting his own continuing saga, MPW currently writes mostly freelance music articles for local New Orleans rags and women's magazines, as well as performing stories and sketchy electronic R&B music under the name The White Bitch. You can e-mail Michael at **mpw@equatorbooks.com**

*A*rtist Marcus Bjernerup somewhat-recently returned home to Stockholm, Sweden after graduating from the Chicago Art Institute, then living in NY for a couple years. While he and the author both giggle admiringly at the drawings Marcus churned out for this book, we both also agree that these crass little cartoons are not representative of Marcus' usual work, which is of a grander scale, and deeper depth — the author is super glad Marcus lowered himself for this project! Marcus can be reached via **bjernerup@equatorbooks.com.**

But y'all can contact Jude directly: **deadjude@hotmail.com**